The Long Road Home

Rukis

This is a work of fiction. All characters and events portrayed within are ficticous.

The Long Road Home

Published by FurPlanet
Dallas, TX
http://www.FurPlanet.com

ISBN 978-1-61450-239-5
First Printing, July 2015

Cover art by Rukis

Table of Contents

What came before:

The Long Road Home is the direct sequel to *Off the Beaten Path* and *Lost on Dark Trails*. This book completes the trilogy of a bobcat female of the *Katoshen* tribe. After an abusive arranged marriage to *Methoa'nuk* of a neighboring tribe, her cub was killed and she was subjected to a ritual intended to end her life and purge the alleged evil spirits she had brought upon her new tribe. She took the name Shivah after being saved from death by her spirit animal, the vengeful Crow, and rescued from her grave by the hunter-trapper coyote name Ransom, and his companion, the healer Puquanah, or Puck.

Seeking vengeance, she made common cause with the Marshals led by the husky Grant Wickham, who were tracking raiders led by an otter, Rourke, who Methoa'nuk joined. As they sought to unravel any pattern to Rourke's deadly and vicious raids throughout the countryside, they began to see a connection to the disease of Seer's Fever.

Against the backdrop of this danger, Ransom is forced to confront the demons of his past, and how they hurt his relationship with Puck. Shivah also contended with her unexpected feelings toward Grant, and sought to reconcile her growing love for him with her sworn quest to avenge her child and destroy her husband.

This story picks up shortly after *Lost on Dark Trails*, after Shivah completed her vengeance against her husband. Her success was empty, as immediately following the raid, Grant was killed by the mysterious assassin Shadow. In the wake of Grant's death, they discover that Rourke was being directed by a government agency unable to find any other way to control the spread of the deadly disease. Her purpose in life shaken, she now follows Puck to the distant colony of Serwich, across the seas, in the hopes of learning how to cure the Seer's Fever that is becoming an epidemic in her homelands—but also in the vanishing hope to catch Shadow and stop her from inflicting more pain in the world—by any means necessary.

CHAPTER 1

Arbordale

The journey itself was fairly uneventful. Just long, tiring, and far too full of empty time for my thoughts to wander, and nights spent dreaming about the painful memories I was trying desperately to repress. I tried to distract myself learning more Amurescan. I was making remarkably good progress, according to Ransom and Magpie, at least.

Puck had been very quiet and serious throughout the three-week trip, likely deep in thought. I'd never seen the small fox so intense, and I was starting to get a good feel for how frustrating this must have been for him. His hands were tied until we came across the contagion again, and yet despite that, finding another infected settlement was the last thing all of us wanted to see. But it was the only way he could study the disease.

There would doubtless be victims of the Fever, possibly even current victims, at this colony. It was the birthplace of the disease, after all. It made sense to go there, otherwise we'd just be chasing our tails trying to find outbreaks here on the frontier. And Puck was hoping there'd be healers... Physicians, or apothecaries there at the colony, who'd have valuable knowledge for him, and perhaps help him make sense of how it spread. It was even possible someone there might already know. It was hard for specific information like that to make it across the ocean, he'd told me. A lot of valuable medical knowledge got muddled or lost entirely, going from territory to territory, let alone country to country. He wanted to learn something, and then bring what he'd learned back home. It was something that simply had to be done personally.

It was strangely elusive, truth. Simple truths like the fact that constantly drinking water, even while ill, was important, many people just didn't know. According to Puck, some of the tribes had been doing the exact opposite and treating the fever with sweat-lodges, trying to 'purge' the illness from their bodies, which was apparently the worst thing to do.

Puck was on a quest for knowledge. I still wasn't sure what I was looking for. Right now, I was just forging forward. The ashes inside me were simmering, and I felt no strength from them, as I once had. Maybe I'd die in this foreign land. It was odd that that thought alone gave me some peace.

I had kept most of it to myself, until one night while we were camped, and for once, Puck and I were the only ones left awake. I'd had a lot of trouble sleeping of late, so I spent most night staring into the fire long past the point my companions dozed off. Sleep generally came when I was too exhausted to keep my eyes open anymore, and that was the best I could hope for.

"Shivah?" I heard the fox calling my false name from where he sat near a thick, flaking birch. The fox had been sorting through some of the herbs he'd picked that day along the trail, most of which by now I recognized. Nothing special. Mostly seasoning for food, and ingredients for tea.

I glanced over at him. "Hm?" I murmured.

The fox's eyes seemed to be looking at me, even though I knew they weren't. "Why haven't you grieved for Grant?" He asked softly.

I looked away from him, back into the fire. The question had always been there in the fox's eyes, any time the husky's death, or memories of the man, had been brought up. I'd seen all of my companions, even the wolf we'd left behind, visibly distressed by his memory, on more occasions than I could remember. Magpie was full of regret, Ransom was more stoic about it, but he grieved his loss like he would a brother, and Puck... Puck just cared about everyone. I'm fairly certain the fox had even grieved for Xeli.

"What good would it do him?" I said in a dull tone, tossing a stick into the fire. "He's gone."

"Grieving his loss isn't for him," Puck said. "It's for you, Shivah. Grief's like a wound. If you ignore it, it doesn't heal. It just festers."

"I'm handling it," I said, sounding more irritated than I'd wanted to.

"No, you aren't," the fox said, and I knew by his tone he saw right through me. "Shivah, I know you. You're an emotional woman, even if you don't show it all the time. Trust me... I have experience with people like that."

My eyes flicked over to the softly snoring coyote, slumped unceremoniously against a nearby tree, his long legs splayed out, muzzle tipped back with a leather traveling hat half-obscuring his face.

"How does he sleep like that... ?" I wondered aloud.

"I would have thought by now you'd seen what repressing something painful does to a person," Puck said, not allowing me to diverge from the point. "Can't you learn from his mistakes? Look what it did to him."

I leveled a long stare at the fox. "Yes, well," I murmured, "luckily, he had you to pull him out."

"You have me," Puck said, narrowing his eyes. "You have all of us, Shivah. We're your friends. We're here for you. I know you're not going to let the loss of a man in your life be the one thing that breaks you," he said, clearly appealing to my pride.

"It's not just Grant's death, Puck, and you know it," I said softly. "It's so many things. So many things I've lost. My son. My tribe. My feeling of worth in the world. My faith, on some levels. And there's no recompense. No justice. What little I've gotten hasn't fixed anything. It's just reminded me of what I lost."

"Vengeance doesn't bring peace," Puck said, emphatically. "It never does. It never can. You can stop people from doing more harm to the world, but you can never make up for the harm they've already done. And it isn't a good way to honor someone's memory, besides. Do you honestly think your son, if he were alive right now, would want to know you'd killed his father for him?"

I was silent.

"You can't move forward by ignoring the pain in your past," Puck said softly, his pale eyes drifting towards Ransom. "You can only move forward when you recognize it, and accept it."

"I can't accept it!" I snapped, in a low, angry whisper. "I will never accept it! How do you accept that the world's a cruel, uncaring place where innocent, good people die, and wicked people prosper? How do you live with that, Puck?!"

"Actually, Shivah," the fox said softly, despite my angry tone, "it sounds to me like your husband suffered greatly at the hands of the raiders. Evil repays evil in kind, eventually. Even if it doesn't seem like it. People like that are empty inside. They die miserable and without love. And I'm," he paused, then sighed, "I'm worried that you are shaping yourself into one of them. You're a good person, Shivah, but your anger is poisonous. You beat Xeli to within an inch of his life. You're forcing yourself not to care about a man who loved you. The anger's taking over."

"What else do I have?" I asked, flatly.

"Us," the fox replied, simply. "And whatever else lies in your future. You're alive, despite everything. That's practically a miracle, considering what you endured. It is for all of us, honestly," he murmured, flicking his ears at our sleeping companions. "We've all walked difficult roads to be where we are right now. And now we're doing something—together—that's very important."

His voice cracked a bit on the last word, and I could feel his passion as he said it. "Isn't this important to you? Isn't this enough? Aren't we enough?" He asked, quietly.

I should have just given him some kind of confirmation. But my throat was seizing up. This whole conversation was bringing up so much I didn't want brought up. So much I couldn't handle. Puck didn't understand how this felt. I couldn't endure it. I'd break down. I'd be right back to that moment in time, when I'd been holding Grant's body in my arms, remembering my son being taken away, remembering finding my tribe slaughtered, remembering all the abuse I'd suffered under Methoa... It was just too much. It was all too much. I'd hit my breaking point. This was the only way I could cope.

"Alright," the fox said at length, his ears tipping back. He stood slowly, and gathered his herbs. "Alright," he murmured again, and moved off.

I knew I'd hurt him, but I was too engrossed in my own hurt to really fully grasp it. Pain has a way of turning us selfish.

Arbordale was overwhelming. We passed through a full day of towns on the outskirts before we even made it to the city proper. And even throughout the day when we'd been moving through the outlying hamlets, I'd seen many things I'd never known existed. Red stone buildings the color of river clay, which the men had told me were in fact made of something called 'brick'. They were amazingly uniform rocks, apparently. Rocks made by people. I hadn't even known people could make rocks.

There were vendors amidst the streets, even in the hamlets, selling food I'd never seen in my life. Fruits I didn't know existed, including bright-sunset-colored ones Puck insisted we pick up, called 'oranges', appropriately enough. He said we'd need them while we were at sea. I couldn't imagine why, but after my first taste of one, I wasn't arguing.

I was beginning to see different sorts of people as well, the closer we got to the enormous settlement. Peoples I'd never before heard of, or even imagined. More and more varieties of Otherwolves, felines with brightly-colored fur and wild markings, spots and stripes and patchworks of different colors, and some peoples I couldn't even begin to identify.

By the time we reached the city itself, I'd been seeing it in the distance for nearly half the day. The hilly terrain surrounding this 'Arbordale' sloped down onto the flatlands that lead towards the ocean, so we could see the immense, sprawling settlement after we'd crested the last of the rolling mountains along our trek. In fact, it was all I could see for miles.

It was intimidating to think that any civilization could have built something so massive. It wasn't that it was just bigger than a tribal village. It was bigger than even the God's Maw. It was like they'd turned an entire piece of land into a settlement, and there was nothing but houses, roads and walls as far as the eye could see.

As we began making our way through the outskirts, I could already see buildings in the distance that were larger than the fort at Crossroads had been. Spires that reached towards the heavens, impossibly high. Ransom told me those were churches. One of the first ones we passed by had a procession of men heading out who were wearing coarse brown robes, chanting, as something rung through the air overhead. The sound caused me to freeze and look heavenward.

There were so many sounds, so many smells, so many sights here I had never before known. I barely knew where to start.

"Just the bell tollin' noon, sweetheart," Ransom said, soothingly, pulling Molly up beside me. "You alright?"

"I just..." I stammered, letting out a thick breath. "This place is... It's like a world unto itself. I don't even know where to begin, I—I..." I looked desperately to the coyote. "How am I going to find Grant's family here?"

"I know what suburb they were in," Magpie said, hitching one leg over the edge of the saddle and jumping down, landing on the dusty, paved street. Paved! They'd even covered the earth!

Magpie retrieved his rifle and his small pack of belongings, and looked up to me. "I'll find 'em, Shivah. Don't worry. Wickham ain't a common name, and the CO told me enough about his family. I'm pretty sure I can hunt 'm down. Y'all focus on findin' us a boat. I don't wanna be in this shitheap any longer than we gotta."

"I don't think any of us do," Ransom muttered. "But I know where the harbormaster's at. Done business with her family before, when trade up north was slow. Best just to go straight to her, she'll know what boats are goin' where."

He glanced down for a moment, worriedly, at me. "Harbor's a rough place, kitten. Maybe you oughta' go with Gabriel."

"Actually, I think it's probably best if she sticks with you," Magpie said, surprising Ransom. "I was gonna go through Debriss. See some family."

"Yeah, alright," the coyote nodded. "Lesser of two evils. C'mon, then," he hitched up Molly's reins, and we parted ways with the rat. I followed him, glad at least to be atop Helios. The horse made me feel just a bit safer in this unfamiliar place. People on the road made way when you were on horseback, you didn't have to walk through strange, filthy puddles... I could see why Grant had treasured his mount so much, if he'd grown up here.

It took us nearly an hour just to get to the port. I spent the whole while terrified yet transfixed by the city we were passing, and the strange menagerie of people who lived in it. I tried to get a feel for how it would have been to live here, to grow up here, but I couldn't even begin to imagine it. It was too overwhelming, too crowded, too strange.

The smell was indescribable. Ransom told me that the longer you lived here, the more you got used to it, but I was struggling not to cover my face with my cloak the whole while. How could anyone get used to this?

Soon, though... soon, an entirely different, yet overpowering scent began to overtake the reek of the city, and it was a far more welcome one. It smelled more earthy, more like water, and yet nothing like a river. Salty, like fish and reeds, and with a hint of decay, but natural decay, not the terrible odors in the city.

It was more like what I knew, and yet so totally different.

The first time I saw the ocean, I was mesmerized. I had known since I was a child that it existed, of course. The river that passed through our valley flowed out into it, eventually. Here in this city somewhere, apparently, into a massive bay.

The river was life to our people, as much as it was to the Otherwolves. Almost all of the tribes in my nation were along the river, connected to one another, just as the spirits had intended. Water didn't just give us life. It unified us. It gave us connection to one another, connection even to other tribes outside our nation. It was the universal tie that bound us.

But until that moment, I'd never realized the sheer scope of how true that was. The river may have bound the tribes together, but this ocean—this ocean had brought the Otherwolves here. It had, in a very real way, bound our civilizations together, as well. And even if that had brought with it a lot of conflict, it had also brought some truly incredible things into our lands. And, I could only imagine, had allowed the Otherwolves to partake in our wonders, as well.

Freedom was like that. Treated irresponsibly, it was as equal a force for evil as it was for good. But looking out over the endless expanse of blue, breathing in the salty, clean winds and seeing, for the first time, that the world was so much more massive than I'd ever imagined... I wouldn't have traded that for isolation and safety. Not any day.

I was a little girl from a little, closed-off valley. To know there was so much more out there, to really see it, for the first time, was one of the most pivotal moments in my life.

"Beautiful, huh?" Ransom said from beside me.

I pushed back some of my mane, the wind whipping it about. I nodded serenely, watching as a bird circled high overhead and dove down towards the harbor.

"The docks ain't as pretty," Ransom warned me. "Stick close, a'ight? And don't talk to no one, even if they try t' talk to you."

We moved down into the maze of small, squat buildings near the docks, the majority of which seemed to be used for storage, or as makeshift trade areas. The crowds down here grew thicker, and as we finally broke from the last of the tall buildings, I began to see the towering masts of massive ships in the distance, further down the beach. I'd seen a ship with sails before, once or twice. Some of them were able to come down our river. But none were like these. It looked like a forest of leafless trees, with spider webs of rope slung between them, and massive bundles of cloth bunched at the cross-sections.

But my more immediate concern soon became the bustle of the people around us. There were so many pushing through the choked streets here, and so many with beasts of burden and carts, there were times we had to come to a stop entirely just to let people through. The reek had returned, only now it was fishier, and smelled of wet, unwashed fur, as opposed to the smell of dry, unwashed fur from deeper in the city—not an improvement.

For all of Ransom's warnings, though, no one in particular bothered us. The people here seemed too busy to harass us, or even notice us, in most cases, unless they bumped right into us. The horses helped keep us from being overrun, and I was beginning to feel I could handle myself here, at least physically. The smell was honestly the worst part.

At one point I saw a line of men in matching blue uniforms moving down the street, all of which were armed with rifles and were moving with enough precision that I recognized them as being a militarized group of some sort. The other people in the street made way for them, and so did we.

Almost everyone here was armed. The primary weapon of choice seemed to be pistols, or those strange 'crossbows' I'd seen being used amongst the raiders. Ransom had taken the one we'd found in camp. Apparently they were a very expensive, deadly weapon, and one he'd long wanted to own.

He'd yet to figure out how it worked, unfortunately. Or perhaps the one we'd gotten was broken, somehow. We'd tried to figure it out along the trip, but had no luck. The trigger didn't seem to be working.

One large building, made of stone, towered over most of the shacks in the area, and the outskirts of it were densely crowded. There were wooden, shield-shaped signs with Amurescan writing all over them, around the outside of the building, and almost a dozen different flags hanging from the upper windowsills, flapping in the strong winds coming in off the sea. We seemed to be headed for it, so I leaned over to Ransom and asked, "What is this place?"

"Merchant's Guild House," Ransom replied, which didn't really answer my question, as I wasn't sure what that meant. "It's where most of the Captains and big time merchants out here come to post for work, exchange currency, take on fares... y' know. It's also where Malina tends t'be, and she's who we need to talk to."

"This 'harbormaster'?" I asked, curiously.

Ransom nodded. "Yeah, she'll find us a ship, if there are any goin' where we need t'go. Her family's big into trade, all over th' world. I think her father was a big name Don runnin' ships between here and Mataa fer awhile."

"I'm impressed there's a woman in a position of authority in this city," I admitted, surprised.

"The Coros tribe's big enough... and I mean that literally, they're polar bears," Ransom said, clearing his throat, "that no one questions it. Lady ain't no one to mess with. I worked with her a bit in the past, back when I was with a larger outfit of trappers who did business with the Amurescans lookin' to buy here. Good money, but..." he sighed, "Ain't worth having to stay in the city so long, honestly. And it's a long trip. I'd rather sell fer less back home."

He dismounted once we got near the building, and I followed suit. Ransom helped Puck down, and we tied up our animals. Being on the ground for the first time here, I really began to feel closed in by the crowds. But I persevered and followed closely behind Ransom as we shouldered our way slowly inside.

If the outside had been crowded, the inside of the guild hall was stifling. There were several stands around the room where men were selling things, or just calling into the crowd, presumably looking to hire on men, judging by what few things I could catch. There was a counter with heavy bars along the small window, and a man sitting behind it, stacking coin for a waiting canine, and people... so many people... milling around and speaking in a myriad of different dialects, even different languages.

At the very least, I felt like my presence was being lost in the crowd, which was for the best. I had yet to see a single other woman in the room.

Ransom made his way towards an open archway into another room off to the side. Once we made it through, the crowd dissipated some. This room seemed a lot quieter, and looked to serve as a meeting place of sorts. There were tables arranged throughout the space, and a few desks in front of large wooden cabinets, with many small shelves heaped in papers. There was still enough conversation throughout the room, and the busy hum from the room beyond, that I would have considered it loud, but nowhere nearly as bad as where we'd come from.

The polar bear was hard to miss. She was sitting at one of the tables near the far end of the room, speaking with a canine in a blue coat, with a red sash tied across his waist, and a fox dressed in simpler tan clothing, who wore the same red sash. I'd seen a few men with something that looked similar, while we'd been making our way through the streets. I'd thought it an oddity at first, but by now, I was fairly certain it meant something.

When Ransom made his way towards her, the bear looked up, as did the black canine she was talking to. The bear was a very large woman, built like most bears, dense and strong, but definitely female. She was wearing a richly-colored blue tunic with gold trim, and a long, cream-colored wrap skirt beneath. She looked very regal, very impressive. It wasn't often I saw a woman who commanded respect. It was refreshing.

"I know you, don't I?" the bear said with half a smile, pointing a finger at Ransom. "I never forget a scar."

"Aye, ma'am," Ransom said, stepping up to her and putting out his hand. She gave him a hearty shake. "M'name's Ransom. We did some business... lord... must be six years back. I'm glad yer still here, I don't know many folks in this city."

The bear gave a deep chuckle, "I'll be here until they haul me off to lay in the ground. Well met," she smiled, gesturing to the two of us, as well. "All of you. Malina Coros. How can I be of service to ye?"

"We'll let you finish your conversation with these gents first," Ransom said, indicating the two men she had been talking to.

"Oh, these dogs?" The bear snuffed, and waved a large paw at the man. "Don't worry, you're hardly interrupting anything important. Just keeping appraised of the situation down south."

"Actually, that's sort of why we're here," Ransom said, and I saw Puck's ears perk. "We need to get down south. In a hurry."

The bear looked dubious. "I'm hoping you mean the ports in the Southlands."

Ransom sighed. "No. If that was the case, we'd just go by land."

"We need to get to the Dark Continent," Puck spoke up. "Serwich, in particular."

The polar bear went silent, and serious, very quickly. She seemed to be formulating what to say, when one of the men behind her, the black-furred dog in the blue coat, to be specific, spoke up.

"Whatever your business be down in that savage place, you ought to put it out of your mind," the man stated, in Amurescan, but with a far richer, almost elegant accent than I'd ever heard before. "The colonies, and all their surrounding waters, are a no-man's-land these days."

"Especially the northernmost ones," the fox said with a grim nod. "I was with a crew that was nearly dispatched to Serwich last year. The fact that I was transferred is the only reason I'm alive, now."

"Aye, there aren't many who risk those waters anymore," Malina said, shaking her head. "It's been bad for the last decade or so, but of late. Things have gotten a lot worse. Fewer and fewer Captains are willing to risk the trip any longer, no matter the profits."

"I heard the colony's paying quadruple for merchants willing to bring in goods," the fox said. "And there have still only been... what... two merchants who've gone down this year? That ought to tell you something."

"Three, as of last week," Melina sighed. "The Nightingale made for those waters... I believe ten days ago, or somewhere thereabouts. But she's got that frigate escort, so I suppose Captain Langer thought it was worth the risk."

"The Nightingale's a good ship," the man in the blue coat said with a nod. "Amurescan-made, refitted second rate ship-of-the-line, 90 guns, I think."

"Aye, she's a beast," the bear nodded. "And with the frigate escort... I'd put a wager on her, is all I'm saying."

"But this ship already left?" Puck asked, his tail drooping in dismay.

"Ten days back, like I said," the bear nodded. "Not certain if she was headed for Serwich in particular, I think they meant to make several stops along the northern coast. A lot of the colonies there need supplies, badly."

"How the hell'd it get so bad down there?" The coyote asked, sighing. I could see the unwritten look in his eyes, and I was feeling the frustration myself. Of course, when we needed to go, this had to be happening.

"It's always been bad," the canine said, shaking his head. "My crew was stationed in Lidyaburgh for nearly three years. That land was never meant for us. Never. The crown made a mistake, trying to settle it, and now they're pulling away, trying to scrape up what they can before we lose it entirely. They've recalled almost all of the crown's fleets by now. Most of the men left defending those colonies are either citizens, or serving in Pedigree fleets."

"Pedigree fleets?" I had to ask. I'd heard the term before, but I wasn't certain if I was misunderstanding it now.

The bear blinked at me, and then suddenly gave a soft laugh. "Oh, spirits. I'm sorry, lass, but I honestly hadn't realized you were a woman until now."

I blinked, then glanced down at myself. I had my cloak and my leathers on, and as I always did when I was worried I might have to use my bow, I'd bound my chest. Not that much of it could be seen when I wore my leathers, anyway.

I suppose I could see why she might have made that mistake, honestly.

"Pedigree fleets are fleets the crown... the King... doesn't own," the fox explained. "Not part of the country's navy. A lot of the Pedigree families use them as merchant ships to build their fortune, but some of them... seems like less every year," he said, and the black canine nodded in agreement, "... some of them choose to serve the crown in military engagements, or to protect the crown's interests abroad."

"They get paid a military stipend," the black canine continued, "but it's mostly for the honor in Court, or to curry favor."

"Or to puff themselves up," the fox said, rolling his eyes. "Big, important nobles, doing big, important things. Never mind that we do the same damned thing every day, just to feed ourselves."

"Aren't you the same people?" I asked, confused.

"My father couldn't buy me a ship," the black canine said, snorting. "I worked my way up in the ranks the old-fashioned way. Effort and prowess."

"Yeah, well say what you will," Ransom said, sounding none-too-impressed. "Those boys are down there, in this warzone you're talkin' about, and you're here nice'n safe, yappin'."

The two men glanced away at that and looked self-conscious, and I felt the need to break the silence.

"So this ship, it left?" I confirmed, and the polar bear nodded. "Ten days ago?"

"I believe so," the woman said. "I know Captain Langer. He's a good man. Good seaman. No matter how bad it's gotten down there, I think he'll be able to handle it."

"Damnit," Ransom growled. "That don't help us none."

"It does less than help us," I said, bitterly. "Shadow is probably on that ship. She beat us to it."

"That's a good bet," the coyote muttered.

"Could we just take a boat to one of the other colonies?" Puck asked. "If there aren't any ships headed directly for Serwich, we could take a boat to a nearby colony instead. I could do my research at any of them."

I ground my teeth at that. I wanted Shadow. But I couldn't say it. This was supposed to be about curing this disease. That was the key goal.

But I wanted her. Even more now than before. She'd just barely slipped us, again!

The polar bear looked uncertain for a few moments, before clearing her throat. "There's one other ship I know of headed for the colonies. Serwich, actually, in particular."

My eyes snapped up to her at that. "What? Where? When?" I demanded.

The bear put her paws out. "Now, lass, there's a reason I didn't mention it before. It's not a passenger ship, or even a merchant ship. A man might be able to hire on, I suppose, if you're that desperate, but—"

"Hell," Ransom sighed, "it's a warship? Amurescan?"

"No," the bear said, "and it's a fleet, actually, albeit a small one. Three ships. I think he's even hiring, but—"

"We couldn't get Shivah on-board," Puck said softly.

"Why?" I snapped.

"It's a warship, honey," Ransom explained. "They don't let women on warships."

"Why?" I asked again, growing tired of this.

"A lotta' reasons," the coyote sighed. "Superstition, most women ain't cut out for th' work... ."

"If you could handle it, so could I," I growled.

"War is no place for a woman," the canine spoke up again. Before I could argue, he held up a hand, still speaking in that unflappably civil tone, "Besides, it isn't safe for a woman to be amongst an all-male crew. It's for your own decency."

"You wouldn't want to enlist with this crew, in any case..." the bear muttered.

"One of those 'Pedigree fleets'?" I asked, crossing my arms over my chest.

The bear actually gave a rumbling chuckle at that. "Hardly. More... private contractors."

"Privateers," Puck said with a soft, dejected sigh.

"If you really want to look to enlist, I can't stop you," Malina said, shrugging, and went over to her table, sitting back down heavily. "The fleet's been docked for a week. I don't know why they're heading down south, but word's been going throughout town they're looking to hire. I gather they lost a significant amount of men on their last 'venture'. One of their ships was still bailing out when they pulled into port. Thought it was going to sink right there in the bay for a few days."

The two men at the table chuckled at that, as well, clearly remembering the event in question.

The coyote glanced down at Puck. "Sounds promising, Puck," he said, the sarcasm so thick in his voice, you could have choked on it. "What d'you say? Wanna look these blokes up? They come so highly recommended."

"Yes," Puck said without question. "We can't afford to waste time. If there are ships going where we need to go—any ships—it at least bears looking into."

"Their 'hiring man' isn't here right now, I'm sorry to tell you," Malina said.

"Where is he?" Puck asked.

"You could try the Salty Dog," the bear said, smirking. "He's there most of the time when he's in port."

"How exactly are we going to get around the fact that Shivah's a woman, Puck?" The coyote insisted, throwing his head back and sighing as we made our way back towards our mounts.

"Maybe he'll overlook it if we pay him enough," Puck offered. "Privateers are all about coin."

"They're more superstitious than they are greedy," the coyote insisted.

"You can't possibly know that," the fox snapped.

"All mariners are!"

"Puck," I said suddenly. Both of the men turned to look to me. "Do you..." I struggled to remember what it was called for a moment, then snapped my fingers, "that oil that you use on Ransom's furs. The hideous-smelling stuff..."

The fox blinked. "Patchouli?"

The coyote sneered. "Lord, I hate that shit."

"Well if I don't use it they reek like your curing process for weeks," the fox protested. "And they get infested."

"Honestly?" the coyote snuffed, "I'd rather smell piss and scrape bugs off 'em than deal with that reek."

"It's strong," I stated, "and it clearly bothers you, Ransom, so I'm guessing it will bother a lot of people. Enough that they won't detect my natural scent."

"And?" the coyote seemed confused.

Puck got it immediately, though. "You're going to try to pass yourself off as male?"

"The woman there assumed it without even questioning it," I pointed out. "And to be honest, I think a lot of the people in this city have been, as well. Ever since I started wearing hardened leather, I haven't gotten anywhere near as much attention as I used to. I think people just assume."

"They'll know when they hear your voice," the canine pointed out. "She did."

"I could lower it," I said, making a weak attempt.

"Maybe just say you're mute," Puck offered.

"Now you're hoppin' on this wagon?" The coyote said, incredulously.

"It's a good idea!"

"Until someone finds out!" Ransom pointed out. "Then she's stuck on a boat, at sea, with no way off. The ONLY woman on a boat. On a ruttin' pirate boat, at that!"

"I thought you said they were 'Privateers,'" I said, confused.

"They're the same thing," both men replied in unison, except that Ransom said 'same damned thing'.

The Salty Dog, as it turned out, was a tavern—of a sort.

It was more a rotting building right off the docks, near the farthest end of the docks, to be specific, where the reek reached entirely new levels of vile I had never imagined in my wildest dreams. The area this far out was less-crowded, but I didn't take that as a good sign.

The people here were varying shades of drunk, filthy, or frightening. Even the women. And there were a lot more women down here, but not the sorts I ever wanted to get to know.

I'd tried to be open-minded ever since I'd gotten to know the women at the Cock and Barrel better. But these women were not like the ladies who worked there. These reeked of sickness and desperation, they spat and swore, and more than one had cursed Ransom out for not taking her up on her generously-inexpensive services. One of them had had a baby on her hip while she'd propositioned him.

I was again glad I was on my horse.

When we had to tie our mounts up outside, I was glad Helios was such a difficult beast, because I was honestly afraid someone here might steal him. I took all of my valuables... most especially the box of coin... with me when we headed for the half-unhinged doorway into the darkened tavern.

The reek inside the dingy place was only minorly better, and only because the smell of alcohol was so thick inside, it overwhelmed almost everything else.

There weren't many people here, thank the gods, but the few that were didn't seem to want anything to do with us. One or two looked up when we entered, but went right back to staring at their drinks, or in the case of two of the men, playing a game of cards. There was a bit of a ruckus coming from a few tables in the back, and I heard feminine laughter. A group of men were gathered in the back, carousing with several women who looked like some of the ones we'd seen outside, but in far better spirits, likely because of the spirits they were imbibing. I wondered if our man was amongst them, or one of the others in the place who were keeping to themselves.

Malina had told us the ship that was hiring was called the Manoratha, and that we should look for a dark-furred wolf. Other than that, I wasn't certain what sort of man we were looking for.

We headed to the bar, where a middle-aged canine woman with a drooping face was cleaning glasses. She stopped when she noticed us approaching, and leaned with one hand on the counter. I'd never seen a less friendly hostess in all my life.

"What can I do you for?" The woman asked, in a flat, uncaring tone. She clearly enjoyed her line of work.

I was supposed to be mute, so I stayed silent. The Patchouli at least seemed to be doing its trick. One of the women along the road had actually propositioned me.

"We're lookin' for a man," Ransom said, leaning on the counter, "a wolf from some ship named the Manoratha. Ring a bell?"

The woman picked the glass back up, and began rubbing at it with a dirty cloth. "Payin' customers only. You don't like it, there's the door."

Ransom sighed, and dug into his pocket for a coin. He tossed the copper piece on the table. "Whatever swill you're sellin' is fine. D'you know him or not?"

The woman took the copper, then began pouring him a cup of... something. It did in fact smell like swill. Acrid, awful swill.

"You mean Reed? Yeah, he's here. Hasn't left since yesterday, the lout."

Ransom looked out over the bar. "Can you point me to him?"

I looked as well. I actually hadn't seen a wolf yet. Hardly surprising. I couldn't imagine any wolves who'd come to a place like this. Maybe the woman had been wrong. Wolves were a proud, majestic people.

"Back table there, near th' window," the woman said, spitting in the glass she was cleaning.

"I don't—" Ransom began.

"You might want to check the floor," she said dryly.

We slowly made our way over towards the table she'd indicated, not certain what we'd find. As soon as we got close, I could hear someone, though—loudly snoring.

"Fer god's sake," Ransom muttered, pushing a fallen chair aside with his foot, the wood whining as it scraped against the ground. There was a man there, quite literally under the table. Most of his face was obscured beneath a dreaded mane, but he might have been a wolf. One of the 'establishment's chipped glass tankards lay at his side, the likely culprit for his current condition.

And there was also the smell, of course.

Ransom gestured at the unconscious man to Puck. "You want to rouse him, or should I?"

I stepped forward and moved around the chair towards the snoring man, unabashedly shoving him with my foot. It didn't seem to wake him, so I shoved him harder.

Still nothing.

I gave a sigh, and physically kicked the man, hard enough that he rolled over. I also got my first look at him. He was in fact a wolf, and a moderately young one, at least in comparison to Laesom. It was hard to tell when he was horizontal, but he looked to be a tall man, probably built somewhat thicker than Laesom had been, although his build was hard to make out with the layered clothing he was wearing. His tunic seemed fairly similar to others I'd seen men in port wearing, but he had a long, dark coat with many brass buttons along it, a bandolier and several weapon belts strung across his chest and waist, and his mane was threaded with various gold and silver beads, lending him a very bizarre, eclectic look. I wasn't certain if he was a tribesman, an Otherwolf (there were actual wolves that had come over from across the sea, after all), or something else entirely.

The kick had, at last, roused him. But even as he blinked his eyes open, groggily, I saw them slipping closed again just as fast. So I kicked him again.

"Alright, woman..." the man groaned, and I was briefly fearful he'd found me out already, somehow, but then he continued in a groggy mutter, "Give me a moment to gather myself, would you now? It's not like you need the bloody table..."

He blinked up at me, his blue eyes focusing, slowly. They weren't blue like Grant's had been. They were darker, more grey, and bloodshot. "You aren't Tabitha," he noted, at length.

"Astute," Puck murmured, from somewhere behind me. I stepped back to let the boys through, as the wolf thrust a hand up to grip unsteadily at the edge of the table, and tried to pull himself up into the nearest chair. He failed several times before Ransom gave a grumble and reached down to grab the man by the armpits, lifting him with a grunt.

"Who the hell are you? I don' know you. Do I?" The wolf wondered aloud, slurring his speech. I wasn't sure if he was still drunk, or just hung-over, but either way, I didn't see how we were going to get anything out of this man.

The two men seemed to realize that fact as well, and Ransom turned to Puck, switching to Katuk. "This is ridiculous, fox. Come on. This clearly ain't meant to be. We can still go home. Shivah can find the Wickhams, give 'm the money, and—"

"And what?" The fox countered. "We go back to the valley, and just wait for the Fever to tear this country apart around us?"

Ransom sighed. "What d'you want t' do, then? Find the ship? Talk to the Captain direct? I don't think we're gonna get anywhere with this'un."

"Let me handle this," Puck insisted, and before Ransom could argue, he stepped past him towards the wolf, who was half-falling asleep again, his cheek resting against his palm, slumping slowly back onto the table. Puck moved up beside him and gently tapped him on the shoulder. The wolf opened one glassy eye and regarded the fox for a moment, before muttering, "Who're you now?"

"Puquanah, ah..." Puck paused, "You can call me Puck. You're... Reed?"

The wolf blinked his eyes, sleepily. "Grayson... call me Grayson. Who're you?"

Puck sighed, and reached into the pouch at his side, slowly pulling out a few things, and feeling along the small leather pouches until he found the one he was looking for. I'd deduced by now that he left different amounts of twine strands loose on each bag, so he knew what was what. He produced one, and opened it, then gestured to Ransom. "Give me that drink."

The coyote glanced down at it, then shrugged and handed it over to him. "He's pretty far-gone. Your shit gonna work?"

I gave him a questioning glance, and he waved a hand in Puck's direction. The fox was emptying some of the mixture into the drink. "Puck's wakeup mix. I've had t' take it every now'n then."

"If it was only 'every now and then' I wouldn't have a bag of it on-hand at all times," the fox muttered, contradicting the coyote, and placing the glass down on the table beside the slumping wolf. He tapped the wolf again, then indicated the glass. "Drink."

That, the man seemed to understand. He grabbed at the glass handle like it was a lifeline, and slowly downed the awful swill. I don't think he came up for air once.

Roughly five minutes later, the wolf seemed to be coming to his senses. I could see the sharpness returning to his eyes, and he'd begun to correct his posture some. The first thing he did that seemed fully cognizant was look to the empty glass in his hand and ask, "What 'n the hell was that?"

"Fox magic," Ransom replied.

Puck sighed. "An herbal mixture I perfected over the years, out of necessity." He said the last bit pointedly in Ransom's direction.

"Damn," the wolf said with a grunt, "do you sell it?"

"I can do you one better," Puck said, picking up the chair that had fallen over with the wolf, and hopping up into it so he could be level with the man. Ransom and I stood flanking him. In particular, I was watching the wolf warily. He might be of more use to us sober, but he could—likely was—also more dangerous. The man had at least three pistols on him I could see.

"Shoot," the wolf said, clearing his throat and looking back down at the glass, lifting it and giving a frown, as though he were mourning its empty state.

"First off, we'd like to know why the crew you're a part of is heading down to the colonies on the Dark Continent," Puck stated. "You... You are the hiring man for the Manoratha, yes?"

The wolf slowly smiled, like he found that amusing for some reason. "Is that what you were told?"

Puck only nodded.

"Yes," the man said at length, "I'm responsible for hiring."

"Why is the fleet... it is a fleet, yes?" Puck asked.

"Three beautiful ladies," the wolf said with a nod, tipping the glass back and sticking his muzzle into it for a moment to lap up what was left in the bottom.

"I suppose by that you mean ships. Alright," Puck cleared his throat. "What is your purpose down south? Ah..." he paused, looking to Ransom a moment, then just asking, "p-piracy?"

The wolf gave a deep chuckle, reverberating inside the glass, until he pulled his muzzle out and put the mug down on the table with a heavy thud. "Now, now. We're not pirates, lad. Privateers. Get it right. We have a letter of marque, and everything. UCN territories, and all adjoining trade routes." He gestured in a broad circle with his paws at that.

"You ain't said why you're goin' down south," Ransom pointed out. "I don't care if you call it Privateerin' or Piratin'. If you're goin' down there to blow holes in Amurescan ships, we don't want no part of it. We ain't lookin' to get involved in that pissin' match."

The wolf blew out a sigh through his nose. "Only madmen and fools plunder those waters. That's Cathazran territory."

"What?" Puck blinked.

"The natives," the wolf said with a yawn. "Bloody lizards. Last time we tangled they set our fourth boat on fire, she plunged to the depths, and they rammed one of our other girls. I never wanted to go back there. Doesn't matter how fat the convoys are, it's not worth the risk."

"Then why are you going now?" Puck asked, confused.

The wolf got a disgruntled look and stared out the window. "Old debt."

There didn't seem to be more forthcoming, but Puck pressed. "So, what? You're bringing supplies to Serwich?"

"Supplies, and firepower," the wolf said. "We won't be there long. Not enough gold in the world to keep me there any longer than's needed."

"Alright," Puck said a bit uncertainly, then looked to the two of us. After a few moments, he looked back to the wolf, "I'd like to hire on—"

"Done," the wolf muttered, waving a paw.

Puck blinked, clearly shocked at how fast that had been.

"You got any more of that shite?" The wolf asked, tapping his glass.

"Ah... yes, but you really need to take it with alcohol, or tea," Puck murmured, digging into his pack.

"Stick with booze," Ransom muttered. "Hair of the dog."

"Aye," the wolf grinned, flashing his canines. He began to stand, but Ransom had been reaching into his own pack, and at that point, produced a square-edged bottle of his own. I saw the wolf's brows shoot up, his attention immediately diverted. "What've you got there?" He asked.

Ransom poured him some, then took a swig of the bottle himself. "Just drink," he instructed.

The wolf shrugged and waited for Puck to put in more of the mixture, then downed the small amount of alcohol, and twisted his muzzle up. "Whiskey," he muttered, "you mountain folk and your whiskey."

"Hey, this isn't shit whiskey," Ransom said defensively.

"All tastes the same t' me," the wolf shrugged, then chuckled. "But booze is booze. What are you, then? And the little one there," he squinted at me, and I went still, worrying now that he was actually really looking at me that he might discern my gender.

"You a kid, or just wee?" He asked, confused.

"He don't talk, or write," Ransom stated. "We just call him 'cat.'"

"Mnh," the wolf muttered, then looked back to Puck, "and you're... What, a healer?"

Puck nodded. "I can work as—"

"Something wrong with your eyes?"

Puck sighed, softly. "Yes, sir, I'm— I'm blind."

The wolf seemed to consider that for a few moments, then shrugged. "Well we need a medic, and I'm in no mood to be picky. We need to shove off soon. Can you do the work?"

Puck nodded, emphatically.

"Something's better than nothing," the wolf muttered, reaching forward and grabbing the bottle from Ransom, who looked irate, but didn't stop him. We had to work with this man, after all. 'Grayson', as he apparently chose to be called, leaned back in his chair and put his paws up on a nearby stool, swigging from the bottle.

"I'd be the only medic on the boat?" Puck asked a bit nervously.

"In the fleet, actually," Grayson chuckled. "Our last man got eaten."

"'Eaten'?" Ransom repeated, in disbelief.

"I warned you about the lizards, didn't I?" the wolf said, honestly looking like he wasn't certain, now. The man was still barely sober. He looked between us for a few moments, then gestured to Ransom, "You, I'll take. You look like a strong lad. The little one there, though..."

I narrowed my eyes at the man. It was so frustrating to stay silent.

"We travel together," Puck said firmly. "And he's stronger than he looks. And an excellent shot, besides."

"You don't fight Cathazra and win," the wolf said, darkly. "The best you can do is lose a little less every time. I'm hoping we don't see combat this time around. So mostly, you'd be doing labor. Have any of you even worked on a boat before?"

Our silence was telling.

The wolf rolled his eyes, and leaned back in his chair. "Bloody hell..."

Puck looked at the man hopefully, and we all waited with baited breath. "Well?" Puck asked, at length.

The wolf drained what remained in the bottle and let it clatter down onto the table, giving a loose, rumbling chuckle. "Sure. Why the hell not? More kindling for the fire." He spread his paws. "Welcome to the crew."

CHAPTER 2

Difficult Voyages

It was difficult to find a place we could stay that night that was remotely clean or safe near the docks, but since we ended up having to migrate inwards towards the city proper to meet back up with Magpie at the spot at which we'd parted ways, we had a better pick of inns than down at the dock.

Magpie was quiet when he found us and re-joined the group, but the first thing he did say was, "I found them," to me.

My heart skipped a beat, and I swallowed. "Are you sure?" I asked, as he hopped back up into the saddle with me.

"Yeah..." he said, quietly. "I asked around eight different neighborhoods until I found someone who knew 'm. The oldest girl works as a local seamstress."

"I remember him mentioning that," I confirmed.

"Yeah well, fair certain it's them," Magpie murmured. "It's kind of a big thing in a neighborhood in the slums when one 'a the local boys becomes a Marshall. A few folks knew him. Real well."

"You didn't—"

"No, I didn't tell no one," the rat sighed. "Not yet. Figure the family deserves to hear first."

I glanced back at the rat. "How did your own visit with your family go?"

"They're right where I left 'em," the rat said, in an odd tone. I was about to ask what he meant, until he continued, "I put down flowers."

"Hey, you two!" Ransom called to us, as he came sauntering back from the block down the road. "I think I found us a good place to settle in, tonight. The area ain't great," he muttered as he stepped up beside Molly, and Puck atop her, "but it's a fair bit better than most everythin' else we can afford. Food smells good."

"That's enough then," Puck remarked. "We're not going to eat well for a few months. I can't speak for the rest of you, but personally speaking, I'm going to stuff myself until I can't move."

"We shovin' off that soon?" The rat asked.

"According to the 'hiring man,'" I said, sighing at the mere memory of the drunkard, "the Manoratha is leaving in two days."

"I'm not planning to eat much tomorrow night, though, and neither should most of you," Puck commented. "Small meals all day. Unless anyone here knows they don't get seasick."

"What?" I asked, confused.

"Just what it sounds like, sweetheart," Magpie said, sounding uncomfortable. "It's like slugs slitherin' around in your gut. Awful, 'til you get used to it. Took me a week to get over it th' last time I sailed."

"You've sailed before?" I asked, curiously.

"Just for deployment, when I was with the military," the rat said, waving a hand. "Although we were on a real small frigate, and it was nearer to th' winter, so seas were rough." He looked to Puck, "Tell me this's a bigger boat."

"No idea," Puck admitted. "We haven't seen her yet."

The rat crossed his fingers and muttered a silent prayer, and I looked to Ransom. "What's the name of the inn? We'll meet you there."

The slums were a different kind of filthy. A more eroded, degraded, crumbling sort of filth. The very air here seemed stagnant and decaying, and maybe it was just because it was getting later into the day, but I swear, the skies looked grayer and much of the color faded from the tapestry of city life, the further we got into them.

Apparently the neighborhood Grant's family was in now was even in a better district than the one he'd grown up in, and that depressed me, the more we saw of it.

I saw signs of rampant destruction every other block, testaments to what Grant had once tried to tell me about. This part of the city had come under terrible bombardment a long time ago during the war, and the scars still remained. Everywhere there were signs of people struggling to repair impossibly crumbling structures, trying to eke out a living in the ruins no one else wanted. Clotheslines holding disheveled and tattered clothes were strung high overhead between the buildings, and throughout the slanting, dangerous structures, I could hear people going about their everyday lives. Women, men, children.

How anyone could raise a family here, I didn't know. The hardships must have been unimaginable for the Wickhams. I was about to add to them.

The further we got into the neighborhood, the more my apprehension grew. I almost didn't want to reach our destination. What was I going to say? What could I possibly say to these people? How could I make any of this any better?

But eventually, Magpie pointed to one of the buildings, a smaller, two-story house that seemed to be more intact than many of the others. It was painted white and chipping down to the red brick beneath, with a brick stoop and brick windowsills. The lot beside it, in which stood barely the foundation of another demolished building, seemed to have been converted into a garden, fledgling sprouts of what might soon be a vegetable patch just starting to grow. I could hear children inside. Young boys, shouting something on the second floor, likely playing or fighting, or both. They sounded like they might have been teenagers.

I froze in the saddle, unconsciously tugging at the reins. Helios came to a stop, and for a moment, all I could do was stare ahead at that house, too terrified to go any further.

I felt Magpie's hand settle on my shoulder. "Shivah?" He murmured.

I was silent. I'd barely heard him.

"Do you want me to handle this?" The rat asked, gently.

The world seemed to slope towards our destination, blackness flickering at the periphery of my vision. I felt like I couldn't breathe. Like if I moved forward, I would fall. The sensation made no sense, and yet somehow, I knew what was happening.

I couldn't do this. Couldn't talk to Grant's family without reliving what had happened, that day in the field. This would be just like it had been seeing Methoa'nuk, reliving the moment he had taken my child away, all the pain he'd caused me...

I couldn't push it all away if I had to look these people in the face.

I swallowed, my throat hurting as I did. "I owe it to him," I said quietly. "I was with him when..."

Magpie reached forward and gripped my shaking hand on the reins. "You're not alone," he promised.

Slowly, and on quaking legs, I dismounted Helios. Magpie followed suit, and we led the horse as far as the small fence surrounding their little plot, where I looped his reins around a post, and took each aching step up the stairs of the stoop, towards the door.

Every second of it, I was remembering his final words.

I held my fist out, uncertain if I could follow through. But at length, I mustered the courage, remembering everything the man had ever done for me, and I knocked.

It took what felt like an excruciatingly long time for the door to open. When it did, it was only opened a crack, by a canine woman. A husky. The red in her fur was lighter and sparse, but her eyes were exactly like his.

"Hello?" She said uncertainly, looking us over. "Who are you? What do you want?"

She sounded suspicious, and I was doing myself no favors by having such trouble speaking and gathering myself. Luckily, Magpie spoke at that moment, and he was far more well-composed.

"Ma'am," he said, lowering his hood and clearing his throat, softly, "are you Miss Hannah Wickham?"

"I am," the woman said, still sounding uncertain. "What is this about? You're not with the patrols." She eyed Magpie's rifle at that. Even strapped to his back, a gun was a gun.

Magpie reached slowly beneath his cloak, and produced something I hadn't ever known he'd had. But in retrospect, it made sense. Connall had never had a chance to take his away.

His UCN Marshal's Badge.

"I'm with the Marshals, miss," the rat said somberly.

"And you are?" the woman looked to me, opening the door a bit more now that she'd seen the badge.

"I'm..." I stammered. What did I tell her? "I was working with the Marshals," I settled on. "I worked with your brother."

The woman's eyes widened at that, and it took me a moment to realize it wasn't us she was looking at, anymore. She was looking past us, at Grant's horse. She slowly lifted a paw to her muzzle, and I saw the first inklings of realization dawning over her features. It hurt to watch. It hurt so bad.

"Is that Helios?" She asked softly.

"Hannah, is it?" I asked, swallowing.

The woman nodded quickly, her eyes flicking between the horse and the two of us, panic creeping into her features.

"Hannah," I said, somehow, around the lump in my throat, "I'm sorry... I..."

The woman suddenly pushed the door open completely, and gripped me by the shoulders, staring me in the eyes. "Where is my brother?!" She demanded, her voice cracking.

Something inside me cracked, as well.

"He was so excited that he'd made it in, at such a young age..." Hannah said quietly, her fingers kneading at a scarf she'd clearly been in the process of knitting on the small kitchen table in the main—and only—room on the lower level of the place. It was barely larger than most of the rooms I'd had at the inns we'd stayed at in Crossroads. There was a small stone fireplace in the corner of the room, with a chimney that worked its way up along the wall, and widened into what looked to be a well-used stove. The table and chairs we were seated at were missing most of their varnish, but like the rest of the room, it seemed like a valiant effort had been made to keep them clean, despite the poor conditions.

I could hear the two boys upstairs still, and Hannah had already told us the rest of the siblings, save her youngest sister, were not currently at home. We'd only told her so far.

She was making a visible effort not to break down, sweeping away any tears in frantic silence, whenever they rolled down her cheeks. She looked as terrified as I felt, likely for the same reason. She was going to have to tell the rest of her siblings, eventually.

I felt numb. I knew we needed to be here, and I felt it was wrong to turn away and leave so suddenly, after bringing the news. But I was quite literally falling apart, every moment I had to watch this woman, grieving the way I should have been.

"I told him not to rush," she said softly, like she was in a trance. "That he could do the Warden work for a few more years, apply when he had more experience. But then, he got the Command position, and I thought..." she looked down at the scratched, worn surface of the table, "I thought my brother must be a greater man than even I knew."

I'd never felt the true weight of Connall's betrayal, of how cruel the conspiracy had treated Grant, until that moment. It hadn't just been all of his hopes and dreams they'd been mocking, using him as a scapegoat for a mission that was arranged to fail. It was his entire family's. Grant hadn't just been one person. His siblings were a part of him, and the government he'd sworn himself to had betrayed him, in the most terrible way.

Magpie shocked me, when he replied to her. "You need to know, miss, your brother was hired specifically because he was under-qualified."

The woman looked up with tears in her eyes, confused, and I looked to the rat, sharply. I had never intended to tell her about the conspiracy, and I was angry that he had. These people needed to remember Grant in a better light.

"They didn't think anyone had a chance of huntin' down the man your brother was tasked with finding," Magpie continued, "so they hired yer brother to chase his tail for a few years, just to make the people in the Senate happy, so that they could say somethin' was being done."

Hannah's expression became even more pained, and I was about to say something, but Magpie wasn't done.

"The reason your brother died, ma'am, is because he was a hell of a lot more competent, more clever, and stronger-willed than they thought he was," the rat said, in an affirmative tone. "And he actually found the people they tasked us with. He was th' only one amongst us who never gave up. Even when we was all goin' to pieces..." he looked to me, "he kept it together. And he kept his head up, stuck to who he was, and did what was right. Right up 'til the end."

The woman gave a shuddering, soft sob, and looked down at the half-knitted scarf. "Did he..." she asked quietly, "did he help people?'

"More 'n I think we'll ever know," Magpie nodded. "I know he helped me."

"And me," I said quietly. It was the first thing I'd managed to say in nearly half an hour now.

"Hannah?" A quiet, sleepy voice suddenly said from the stairs, and I couldn't help but turn to look towards the child. She was standing timidly at the foot of the chipped, splintering wooden staircase, looking at all of us in a mixture of curiosity and fear. I knew it had to be Anna, the moment I saw her. She actually looked like her picture in the locket. Grant had been right. She was quite the little artist.

She looked between us all, wide-eyed, and her older sister seemed caught in a moment of indecision, before she said in a remarkably calm, soothing tone, despite her condition, "Go back upstairs, sweetheart. I'll come tuck you in soon."

"Are you okay?" The little girl asked, sounding oddly protective for such a small thing.

"Yes," Hannah said, with a nod and a forced smile. "I just need to talk to these people for a bit, and then I'll come talk to you, and the boys. So be a good girl and wait upstairs, alright?"

"Wait," I said quietly, and reached to my neckline, and pulled out the locket that was buried beneath my cloak. I'd not taken it off since Grant had died. As soon as I produced it, Hannah's eyes widened in recognition.

The little girl seemed to recognize it, too. "My brother is supposed to have that," she said.

"I think he would have wanted you to have it," I said, holding it out to the timid little canine.

But she just shook her head. "No. No, he should have it. He should always have it. I gave it to him. It was a present." She looked up at me with wide blue eyes. "Are you going to go see him?"

"Someday," I said at length, not wanting to break this to the child. "I will again someday."

"Then give it back to him," the girl said, as though I were a simpleton. "It's his."

I looked to Hannah, and she just nodded, looking down and very obviously fighting to hold back tears.

"Alright," I said to the little girl. "I... I will. I'll bring it back to him."

She nodded, and took off back up the stairs, in her night gown.

"Thank you," Hannah said quietly, after the girl had left. "Thank you for coming here to tell me about my brother."

"I wanted to tell you all o' this," Magpie said, "because the Marshals ain't gonna. I want you to know he died doing something no one—and I mean no one—thought could be done. And your brother, Grant..." he lifted his muzzle slightly, taking a moment, "he wasn't just good at his job. He was a good man. In fact, he was the best man I've ever known."

He leaned back in his chair slowly, and visibly had to gather himself, for a moment. I had never seen the rat get choked up before. He was the actual sort of man Ransom pretended to be. Unyielding and hard. The rat was amicable and humorous at times, but I'd seen beneath that by now. In reality, he was probably the most steady-minded amongst us. Even Puck was often swayed by emotion. Magpie... Gabriel... was almost entirely unflappable. He probably had to be, to live with the things he'd seen—and done.

His steadiness, his stable presence, gave me some strength. Enough to speak, once more.

"Grant wouldn't," I paused, dragging in a breath, "wouldn't want us to live with regret for what happened. We can regret the loss of the time we might have had together," I swallowed, "but not... not the sacrifice he made. He believed in what he was doing. More than any of us. More than me." My voice grew weak at that, and I felt Magpie take my hand in his again. I was so grateful the rat was there with me.

"He was very inspirational, to me," I admitted, and I felt the tears coming, and I couldn't stop them, and this time, I didn't want to. "He helped me see a lot of good in people... in myself, that I thought wasn't there, anymore. I wish I'd known him longer, but... he..."

I looked up, to his sister. "He wouldn't want us to lose our faith in people, or the world just because he's no longer a part of it. He wouldn't want us to hate, or be bitter, or resent. Even though it seems like there's a lot to be angry over..."

Hannah nodded, silently, and I swear I saw that same resolve I'd always seen in him, in her.

"He restored my faith in people," I said, hoarsely. "We'll see him again someday, and when we do, we ought to show him that the things he did for us... the good he inspired in us... made a difference."

I was on the verge of crying at that point, but then, the woman leaned over, and embraced me. This woman I'd only met half an hour ago, who was all but a stranger to me, embraced me. Just as he had, when we'd been little more than strangers. I couldn't not remember the night on the mountain with him, when he'd first broken down that barrier inside me, and allowed me to feel again. It was no coincidence, I knew, that she would be the one to tear it down once more.

I cried on her shoulder, and she on mine, and in that singular moment, I felt connected to a person again. Not simply a bystander to the woven fabric of the people in my life, but a part of it. Puck had been right. I had to start tackling all of this pain, because it was destroying my connection to people. And everyone I'd ever loved and been loved by, everyone I'd ever lost, was a light in my life that was not being honored by shutting them away in the dark recesses of my mind.

Grant had only ever wanted me to be happy. He'd been patient, and kind, and caring, and he'd given everything, in the end, to ensure I was able to reclaim my life. I was squandering the chance he'd given me that I'd worked so hard myself to claim from the grip of despair, by casting aside the faith in life I'd begun to embrace again.

I didn't know how to beat this sorrow, how to let go of this anger. It seemed nearly impossible. Feeling anger was easy. Letting go of it was so much harder.

I was physically and emotionally exhausted by the time we'd made it back to the inn that night, and all I wanted to do was sleep. But the day was not done with me yet.

We got back late, so I was all but certain the two men would have turned in by the time we returned. So it surprised me greatly when I noticed Puck in the empty dining area, while Magpie and I bought our rooms at the front desk from a sleepy clerk.

The rat put a hand on my shoulder once before he headed upstairs, but he didn't question why I wasn't going up yet when he noticed the fox, as well. Puck was seated at one of the tables in the farthest corner of the darkened dining area, alone. It was obvious something was wrong.

I headed over to him, hesitating as I got near. I knew the fox well enough by now to know when he was just irate, and when his mood was truly black. He looked utterly crestfallen and sad. And he'd been fine when I left. I couldn't imagine what could have transpired in the time I'd been gone, unless it had been...

I gave a soft sigh. "What did he do?" I asked, quietly. I sat down next to him, gingerly moving closer to him. He didn't rebuff me, but he also didn't respond for some time.

"I went out," he said at length, "to get a few more things for the trip. Supplies I thought we might need. He said he was going to rest here. I didn't even," his eyes fell to his lap, "I didn't even question it."

I remained silent, waiting for him to continue.

The fox took a deep breath. "I came back and he... was with a woman. A streetwalker."

My brow shot down at that, and I balled my fist. "What?" I demanded, quietly but angrily.

"I'm not even upset that he did it," the fox said, in a dull tone. "It's not like he hasn't been doing this for all the years I've known him. I'm... I'm upset that he doesn't understand why it hurts me. And I thought maybe... maybe things had changed, since—"

But I was already standing at that point. The fox followed me with his muzzle. "Where are you—" he began.

"Where is he?" I demanded. "What room?"

"Fourteen," the fox replied, at length. "But Shivah, getting angry at him isn't going to—"

"We are about to leave this country," I said, feeling myself come unhinged from the entire day, "we do not have time, and I don't have the emotional strength right now to reason with a man with a brain like a mule! I didn't drag him out of the mountains to watch him hurt you anymore!"

I stormed off towards the staircase at that, Puck following close at my heels. I'd had a hellishly hard day, and my own demons to contend with. This was the last thing I needed, and the last thing Puck needed, and gods-be-damned, that man was getting a piece of my mind!

Puck didn't stop me, and considering he'd only made one weak plea to begin with, I got the feeling, somewhere in the back of my mind and possibly his, he'd sort of counted on my doing this for him. The fox's general method of confrontation just wasn't harsh enough to get through the hard, rocky shell Ransom liked to wrap himself in. Sometimes the only way to break a rock was with a hammer and chisel.

By the time I reached the room, Ransom had opened the door and was leaning out, opening his mouth to say something. He'd probably been waiting behind it the whole while, for Puck. He didn't seem to have expected me, though, or the hard slap across the muzzle I leveled his way.

He stumbled back in stunned surprise and stared at me, shocked. "Wh- I-"

"What the hell is wrong with you?!" I demanded. I heard Puck shut the door behind us.

He looked past me to the fox. "Damnit, Puck, this ain't her business—"

"I pulled you out of a frozen hell, coyote!" I said, stabbing my finger across the room at him. "You owe me your life! Don't you dare tell me what is and isn't my business! Puck is my friend. YOUR friend. Your lover!"

"Keep yer bloody voice down," the coyote hissed.

"You're ashamed to be with him, but not a prostitute?" I said, incredulously.

"Buyin' a whore ain't likely t' get me thrown in a work camp or hanged!"

"I thought you were past this," I said, disgusted. "I thought you cared about him, Ransom. I thought you loved him."

"I do," the coyote insisted, "the women don't mean nothin'—"

"Do not feed me that bullshit!" I yelled, loud enough that the coyote winced back. "I have had a hell of a day, and I don't have the patience for this right now! If you loved him, you wouldn't hurt him," I said, narrowing my eyes. "And this is hurting him."

"It's always been this way!" Ransom said, throwing his arms down at his side. "He knows I like t' spend time with women sometimes. This ain't new!"

"That doesn't make it right!" I snapped. "You're not stupid, Ransom! Look at him!" I stepped aside, so the coyote had little choice. Puck remained silent. "You know this is hurting him!" I continued. "You have to know it. You have to have known it before. Do you just not care?"

"I just don't see what the big fuckin' deal is," the coyote said with a sigh, gesturing at Puck. "They're just whores. They don't mean nothin' to me, I swear."

"I believe you," Puck finally spoke, quietly. "But, it doesn't change how I feel about it, Ransom. I've never liked being cast aside for these women. I'd..." his eyes fell to the floor, "I'd always hoped eventually, if... I was able to help you, to be there for you, I'd be enough. I-I thought we'd gotten closer, lately. After the mountains..."

"I didn't go whorin' 'cause of Dominick," Ransom said, bluntly. "It don't got nothin' to do with inner demons, or whatever. I just like whores." He dropped his arms at that, as if the point were obvious.

"You also like alcohol, and cigarettes, and going months without bathing," Puck said pointedly. "You... clean your gun while you're drunk, and gamble your money away at dice and cards," he sighed, and Ransom looked away, guiltily. "And I never complain," the fox said, beleaguered. "Ransom, I'm not asking you to cast aside all of your guilty pleasures. Just one. One that really hurts me."

"I just don't see why," the coyote insisted.

"Well for one, because those women... especially the ones here in this city," Puck said, tipping his ears back, "can be sick. And you favor canines, which makes it even worse. You could catch something, Ransom. Something bad, something that I can't treat like I did the others. Something worse than fleas and rashes."

"Can we not talk about this?!" The coyote balked. "Or at least talk about it alone?!"

"If you're embarrassed about it, that ought to tell you something," I said pointedly.

"It's not just your problem!" The fox finally worked up the nerve to raise his voice. "Do you know how many times I've gotten them second-hand? Do you know how frustrating that is?"

"I-I'm sorry—" the coyote said, sounding thoroughly humiliated. As he rightly should have been, as far as I was concerned.

"But it's not just that, Ransom," Puck continued. "That's just a small part of it. Most of it is just... how it makes me feel—the doubt. The worry that you'll someday decide you don't want me anymore."

"Puck, we've been through hell together," the coyote insisted, "I... I love you. I ain't leavin' you 'til I die. And if the gods are willin', I'll meet you in whatever's after all of this, too."

The room went silent at his words. Puck still looked hurt and sad, but I could tell he was softening, some. I kept up the pressure.

"If you love him that much," I said, "then you can be loyal."

"I don't like bein' restrained like that," the man said, stubborn to a fault. I was about ready to hit him again. "Look, I'd let him do the same."

"That isn't fair, Ransom, and you know it," the fox snapped. "How many chances have I ever had? I'm blind. I only like men. I have literally never had any other lover but you."

"I wouldn't get on you if you ever wanted to stray," the coyote murmured, "it ain't my fault it's never come up. But I'd let you."

"You're only saying that because it's never happened!" The fox insisted. "You don't know what this feels like, Ransom. And I know you. You're more possessive than you think."

The coyote ran a hand over his face, tiredly. "Look, can we just... Can we just put this t' bed, for now?" He pleaded. "I'm sorry, alright? She smelled clean, but I'll be more careful next time—"

"There shouldn't be a next time, damnit!" I insisted.

"Shivah," the fox said with a soft sigh, "we're not getting anywhere. Just leave it be."

"Aye, we got enough bloody problems right now," Ransom muttered. "You can't blame me for wantin' to have one last huzzah before we ship off to this... hellhole you're so set on. We don't need more drama right now."

"You're the reason for it!" I snarled at the man.

"I didn't know it would cause such a bleedin' issue!" Ransom said, exasperated. "It ain't ever pissed him off this much in th' past!"

"Don't use Puck's passive attitude to justify your right to be a bastard!" I snapped in the man's face.

"I'm sleeping in Shivah's room tonight," Puck suddenly said from behind us, his voice quiet and calm as ever.

Ransom stared over me, and I swear he looked hurt for a moment. "What?! No, y— this is our last full night together... I wanted to spend it with you, fox."

"Then you should have spent it with me," Puck replied, stone-faced. "You made your choice, Ransom." He leaned down and picked up his pack from the room, and made for the door. I gave the coyote, who'd gone silent by now, one last long glare, and followed Puck out.

We made our way to my room, and I used the key I'd been given to unlock the door and step inside. It was a nice, modest room. The mattress was only straw, and there was little furniture other than the chamber pot and a small desk, but it would do. The bed at least looked spacious enough for the fox and I to fit comfortably in, and I never minded sleeping beside him.

Especially of late, it was nice to have someone near me at night. It chased away a lot of painful memories.

I dragged a deep breath in through my nose and put my things down. The visit with the Wickham family had not left my mind, nor had any of the complicated emotions it had brought back inside me. I'd said a lot of things in that house that I needed to start abiding by. I just wasn't sure how.

"I don't know how to make him understand," the fox said softly as he began to lay his things out to prepare to sleep. I meandered over to sit next to him on the bed, leaning on my palms and trying not to get too lost in my thoughts. My friend needed me right now, too. I couldn't get too self-absorbed.

Puck gave a soft sigh. "I suppose a lot of it is my own under-confidence. Honestly, I'm a little intimidated that he's able to be..." he looked down, "intimate with women as well. I guess I worry that if he can be normal, one of these days, he'll realize he doesn't need me. Our being together is so hard."

"Don't make excuses for him," I said, slipping an arm around him. "You're blaming it on yourself. You're allowed to demand his loyalty, Puck. If he can't abide by it, then he's not respecting you. You don't ask a whole lot else from him."

"He makes me feel like I'm being unreasonable," Puck murmured, "sometimes I wonder..." He trailed off, then turned his muzzle towards me, his nose twitching. "Shivah," he said, suddenly, "have you been crying?"

I blinked. I sometimes forgot how perceptive the fox could be, even without his sight.

"Yes," I admitted. "I—I went to see Grant's family..."

"Oh gods, Shivah," Puck said with a long, shuddering sigh, "I'm... I'm so relieved."

I cast my eyes down into my lap, knitting my hands. "I'm not," I said, barely above a whisper. "Puck, I-I don't know how to handle this. It's like everything that's happened is hitting me all at once."

"That's because you never faced it all when it happened," the fox said, looking at me with his soft, pale eyes. "Shivah, you have to grieve the losses in your life. You have to. You can't just throw yourself into anger. We talked about this..."

"Crow wants me to burn," I said softly, in a haunted tone.

Puck narrowed his eyes, then instantly forced away the expression, and sighed. "Shivah, you know how I feel about that. But listen..." He put an arm around my waist and turned me to face him, even though I knew he couldn't see me in the dark room. But he tried. He tried to look me in the eyes.

"Let's say you're right," he said. "Let's say this spirit is real, and it gave you the strength to survive, and accomplish what you wanted most, when you clawed your way out of the earth. I'm not denying it's possible. No one can prove or disprove spirits, or gods so..." he reached to his own cheek, and ran a claw along one of the scarred lines carved into his flesh. A sign of his commitment to his faith, from long ago. "I can't entirely dismiss their existence. A lot of people believe in them. That belief must have a source. But the essence of beings that are so beyond us is that they are unknowable. So, looking for proof, trying to make sense of what lies beyond death. I think it's honestly outside the grasp of our understanding. I accept that there are things in the world we just can't know, one way or the other." He squeezed my hand. "So it's possible. Alright? I'm conceding that."

I smiled softly at the fox.

"But if this spirit came to you in your moment of need, and gave you the power to avenge yourself, it's because that was what you wanted most in the world, at that very moment," Puck rationed. "You were angry. Your spirit was, therefor, angry. But the spirits are like us, Shivah... in fact, this one bound itself to you. Isn't that right?"

I nodded. "He said as much. He gave me some of his fire. His strength. He breathed it into me, and he told me we were forever bound. That when my task was complete, we would burn together."

"You were alone, Shivah," the fox murmured. "Alone, and angry. And so was he. I think you were already bound. Crow is your totem, isn't he?"

I reached down and fingered the small turquoise bead, engraved with a worn, black-etched bird. My totem. Crow had always been my totem.

"I think he's been with you your entire life," the fox offered. "Watching over you. And I think he grew angry and vengeful because you were."

I shook my head. "He was angry because he lost a loved one. Another spirit, whom he was close to. Someone who gave his existence purpose."

Puck wrapped both of his paws around one of mine. "Isn't that what happened to you, Shivah?" He asked, gently.

I fell silent. A lot of what he was saying was making sense, but—

"What would that mean, though?" I asked. "Are you saying I made him the way he is?"

"No, but I think you can affect him to some degree," Puck said, trying to rationalize. I knew all of this must have been hard for him, considering he barely believed it, if at all. "I don't remember you saying anything about him visiting you or seeing him when you were rediscovering yourself, with Grant."

"No" I admitted, dragging a long breath in. "He was quiet, then."

"So maybe you're the one helping him," Puck said. "Maybe you're able to quiet his anger, to show him there is a better way to exist. The spirits are not simply guides for us, you know. We are just as capable of guiding them."

"You think I can heal him?" I asked quietly.

Puck smiled. "Shivah, I believe you can do anything."

I managed the barest hint of a smile back at the small fox. It felt like it was the first time I'd smiled in a very long time.

"You would have been an incredible Shaman," I said, and I meant it.

Puck laughed. "I'll stick to earthly medicine, I think, but by the traditions, you should know... I still am a Shaman."

"No, Puck," I murmured, "you're something else entirely. And I believe in you, too."

Two days later, we made for the Manoratha. Grayson had told us where it was docked, and about what we should be looking for. Although honestly, most of these ships looked the same to me. Some more enormous than others, but...

"Good God," Magpie said, mouth hanging open as we approached one of the boats. "That monster?!"

"Black and gold colors," Ransom squinted upwards into the glare of the morning sun, "Wolf's head with crossed sabers and pistol. Yeah, seems right."

"Well at least it's... big," the rat muttered.

I took in the sight myself, and I had to admit, it was somewhat awe-inspiring. It was easily the biggest boat I'd ever seen. I struggled to grasp how it had ever been built. The sheer amount of manpower, and wood it must have taken...

Well this, I suppose, was why the Otherwolves were cutting down all of our forests.

The ship had three enormous masts, with what looked to be around four sails hung from each, although it was hard to determine the total amount of sails, as they were still mostly tied down. I could barely follow the network of ropes strung across the massive masts, and I wasn't sure how anyone made sense of them, let alone operated them.

I'd be operating them, I realized suddenly. Or at the very least, helping someone who did. The mere thought made me realize how much I was in over my head on this.

The ship looked to have many levels, as well, or at least it seemed to be partitioned that way. There was a flurry of activity surrounding it right now... mostly men loading cargo and moving about inside, and a lot of wagons and merchants offloading crates and barrels to the veritable hive of men readying the ship.

One of the things I noticed that gave me a glimmer of hope was the bustle of men attempting to herd a small flock of goats up one of the planks onto the ship. If they were bringing animals along on this trip, then maybe Helios... .

I still hadn't decided what to do with the horse, and I had literally left it to the last minute. Even with the coin I'd given her, Hannah had said they couldn't manage a horse. They lived in a city, after all, and had nowhere to keep him. And selling him felt wrong.

But my thoughts came to a halt when I saw a familiar figure sauntering through the chaos on the docks, not particularly headed our way, but as soon as he noticed us, he called out over the ruckus, "Is that my healer?!"

The wolf bounded over a few stacked crates and made his way towards us, his gait alone suggesting he was far more sober than when last we'd met. Which meant this was the critical moment. He could still see through my disguise.

Or someone else on this ship could. Gods, this was a risk.

"Ah, yes!" The man chuckled, as he approached, spreading his arms. "My most valuable commodity. I was worried you were just a hallucination. You would have been a real odd one, but..." He glanced at the three of us, then squinted, but not at me, at Magpie. "I don't remember three more of you."

"We tried to explain we had another companion," Puck sighed, "but you started falling asleep again."

"That does sound like me," the man said with a grin, his ivory teeth glinting in the sun. "Well, then. Glad to see you made it. I've got some work for you as soon as we shove off."

"Someone's sick already?" Puck asked, seeming shocked.

"No, but I need you to make them so," the man said, seeming to relish our confusion. "You see, there's a disease in the parts we're going to—"

"Inoculations," Puck said, in sudden realization. "You need me to perform inoculations?"

"Aye," the wolf said with a sigh. "I learned the hard way last time around, and got myself some of the concoction for our surgeon to use on the crew, but then, well, you know..."

"He got eaten," Puck filled in, worriedly.

"So can you do it? I know it's a bit outside a regular surgeon's duties, but..." the wolf looked to him, expectantly.

"I've done them once before," the fox said. "I believe I can manage it again. I will manage it. I can handle it."

The wolf clapped his hands together and laughed outright. "Ah, you are a gift from the gods! You know of the Fever, then?"

"Yes, and I'd love to get started on treating your crew," the fox said, enthusiastically. "I'm actually hoping to study it."

"You're going to the right place, then," Grayson muttered.

"That was my hope," Puck nodded. "When can we get started on the inoculations?"

"Now, now," the wolf held up a hand, "no need to rush. Best we shove off and get to open water. Get out of Amurescan Privateer territory, first. Once we get past the southern current, you can start. Most of my crew's been, so it'll only be a few poor new souls you need to treat. And yourselves."

"I've been inoculated already," Puck stated.

"Better and better," Grayson crowed, clapping a hand down on the fox's shoulder hard enough that I saw the little creature wince. I saw Ransom's hackles go up, and willed the man silently not to make any trouble. Obnoxious or not, we needed to be on this man's good side, at least until we were officially hired.

"But, ah," the fox paused "I should really be discussing this with the Captain, shouldn't I?"

"Admiral," the wolf corrected, then pointed out into the bay. "You see the two lovely gems sparkling out yonder?"

"I'm blind," Puck reminded him, annoyed.

"Right, right," the wolf waved, dismissively, "well they're beautiful, take my word for it."

"Didn't one of them come into port half-sunk?" Magpie asked, dryly. "And on fire?"

"Au contraire," the wolf said with an amusingly triumphant grin, "the flooding put out the fires. It was merely still smoking."

"Oh, well," Magpie crossed his arms over his chest, rolling his eyes, "as long as you had it all under control, then."

"It's a time-honored tradition that at least one of my boats always come into port partially on fire," the wolf explained, as though it were perfectly rational. "Sometimes we just start them ourselves. So the men can tell gallant stories of their heroism to the women in port. With proof still smoking in the bay. Works like a charm, every time."

I arched my eyebrow at the wolf, but not because I found his story ludicrous. It was actually because I honestly wasn't certain he was joking.

"Wait, your boats?" Ransom suddenly asked.

The wolf grinned, and things became clear, all at once. Clear, and mildly terrifying.

"Admiral Grayson Reed," he said, giving a slight bow at the waist, with far too much of a flourish of his arm. "It's a pleasure, once again."

"You this personable with all your muck-and-muck hires?" Magpie asked, suspiciously.

"No, just the ones who bring me healers who make magic sobering powder," the wolf said, unabashedly. "The rest of you, I'll be honest, I don't give a rat's ass about. No offense."

"None... taken?" Magpie replied, uncertainly.

"I still don't know what we're gonna do with the little one," he said, gesturing at me. I stepped back a little bit, self-consciously. "But you say he can work?"

"The cat's plenty tough," Ransom promised. "And none of us know much about boats, but we're fast learners. Gotta be, livin' out in the territories."

"I have relations out west," the wolf said, congenially. "We should talk some time. 'Yotes and wolves keep in touch. May be you know some of them."

"I doubt it," Ransom said, uncertainly. "If you're just tryin' to get at my whiskey again..."

The wolf laughed again. "I'll admit, it grew on me. But I think I'll stick to rum."

"Cliche," Magpie muttered, mostly beneath his breath.

The wolf seemed about to say something more, when his nose twitched, and his eyes fell on me. My heart froze in my chest. The wind had shifted. Had he smelled through my attempts to obfuscate my gender? Or maybe the Patchouli was just bothering him. Either way, it might make him suspicious.

"What reeks?" He asked, confused.

"You," Ransom replied, without missing a beat. I silently thanked him.

Grayson seemed to consider that for a moment, then shrugged. "That's fair."

"So, what're we gonna be doin' here?" Ransom asked, looking around at the chaos on the deck. "I gotta tell you, I ain't never had my feet off the ground before. So just point me at whatever needs doin', and I'll try to catch on."

The wolf pointed, "Get on over to the black rat over there, the one missing his left ear. That's Ewan, my Master Lieutenant. He'll set you to work for now until we can figure out where to fit you in with the rest of the men."

I tugged at Ransom's sleeve, gesturing to Molly and Helios.

"Oh, yeah," Ransom said, clearing his throat. "We'd really like t' bring our beasts, if that's possible. The mule can go if we really need t'be rid of her, but the horse, we'd prefer to keep."

"Once those animals are on my ship, they belong to me," Grayson stated. "If we need to gut one of them at sea to eat, we will. My hold's fit to burst as it is. No dead weight."

Ransom sighed, and dug into his pocket for some of the gold we'd saved. "Look, just... how much to bring him? He's sort of important to my friend here."

The wolf chuckled. "Looks like a good trail horse. The terrain down there's not easy to trespass. I'll tell you what," he said, smirking, "volunteer now for some of the scouting patrols when we get down there, and I'll let you bring him along."

"Sure, fine," Ransom said, confused that it had been so seemingly easy. "We're hunters, so that's where we're at our best, anyway."

"Oh, good... I didn't imagine that, either," the wolf muttered, almost to himself. "Well, your profession might be shite on the boat, but once we make landfall, I'll have more use for you. For now, just get to work."

I tugged at Helios's reins, and looked to the wolf, pointedly, trying to make it clear without speaking what I wanted him to address.

"Right, right... the beasts," the wolf sighed, "fine, then... you and the fox, follow me."

Ransom looked to Puck worriedly, as the wolf led us off. But we'd all known being crewed on this ship was likely to separate us at times, if not most of the time. I'd honestly thought we might still be near enough to one another that it wouldn't matter, but the ship was huge. We could probably go an entire working day on it without seeing one another, if we were positioned at opposite ends.

As we headed towards the gang plank where the men were leading animals on-board, the wolf walking ahead of us reached beneath his coat and pulled something from where it had been tucked into his belt. A thick, tan leather glove with an unusual design. In his other hand, he produced a bizarrely-shaped leather and feathered trinket on a long string.

To fully cap off the bizarre behavior, he began slowly spinning the toy on the string over his head, widening the length of the string as he did, until he was twirling it in a wide circle, above him. He kept his eyes skyward for a while, and I had to continuously fight the urge to ask him what the hell he was doing.

And then rather out of nowhere, a large bird descended from on high, and he put his glove up just in time to intercept it. The raptor looked to be a falcon of some sort, grey with black wingtips, and barred white and black feathers along its chest. He held up a small scrap of meat for it, and it gobbled it down quickly, before regarding us with a sharp-eyed gaze. It made a low chirruping sound that escalated into a louder 'Kak,

Kak!', and I gave the man some distance. The creature did not look terribly friendly.

"Am I hearing a hawk?" Puck asked, confused.

"Harpy is a peregrine falcon," the wolf corrected, scratching at the scruff of the bird's neck, "and she doesn't like to be called a hawk. It's an important distinction."

"Why do you have a hawk, sorry, falcon?" Puck asked, sounding almost exasperated, at this point. It was just one more odd thing about an already extremely odd man. This wolf was... complex. I wasn't sure I'd ever really understand him.

"Because only primping dandies keep parrots," the wolf replied, with a smirk. "And dandies don't get women. Bitches like real men, and bitches like falcons."

I sighed. Scratch that. I think I now knew everything I'd ever need to know about this man.

CHAPTER 3
WINGS

By the first day out at sea, it became apparent whom amongst us could least handle the tossing and slow churning of the boat, and it was Ransom.

He and Magpie, I actually tended to see fairly frequently. We'd all been assigned as the lowest of the low, essentially, what the men here called 'AB's. I wasn't yet entirely certain what it meant, but apparently it translated to a lot of manual labor, and a lot of people screaming at us. The black rat was the most notorious villain in that arena. I was fairly certain he was speaking in Amurescan, but his speech was so marred by a thick, barely legible accent, I hardly ever knew what he was saying. I mostly got the idea of where he needed me based on which way he pointed, or physically kicked us towards.

The first day was all but consumed by the most basic of basic tasks, moving heavy objects, primarily crates and barrels. A lot more barrels than anything else. Most barrels had to be carried by two men, unless the man in question was enormous. There were a few bears, and one massive canine who seemed to be able to handle the barrels all by themselves, and blatantly refused help. I suppose it was a mark of pride.

As expected, I quite literally had trouble pulling my weight. Whatever the barrels had in them, it was heavy. Like they were full of rocks. And I wasn't just slight in figure, I was short, which usually meant the weight tipped my way. I ended up working with several other laborers throughout the course of the day, whereas most men worked in the same team. Ransom and Magpie had managed to work together. But I'd gotten separated when I went to bring Helios to the loading dock, and by the time I'd gotten back, I'd been paired with a man I didn't know. And then another, and so on. No one wanted to work with me.

It was disheartening that I was so outmatched, but sheer strength had simply never been something I possessed. All the same, I worked throughout the entire day, did the best I could, and persisted even past the point that the men were being given leave to take breaks. I figured I could potentially make up for my lack of strength with raw grit and determination.

And apparently, it didn't go beneath the rat Ewan's notice. Despite the fact that he'd been consistently screaming at me all day, when I'd brought in my last barrel for the night, and he was doing his rounds in the hold, I got a pat on the back, and a gruff, "Good work ethic." from the man. It felt good, but I'd have to find something other than simple labor to do on this ship eventually, or I was going to make a lot of enemies. No one wanted to work with me as it was.

I tried to take heart as we set out that first night. It was exhilarating watching as the boat pulled away from the bay, and the land began to disappear. Exhilarating, and frightening, but for the first night at least, the seas were calm, and I got to get my lay of the 'land', or ship, as it were, mostly unhindered. I met back up with Ransom and Magpie, and we joined some of the more senior sailors, who led us around and got us acquainted with the Manoratha. As far as we were privileged, anyway.

The ship had three gun decks, where we'd apparently be spending much of our time during the days. The 'officers', or whatever these men referred to themselves as, kept primarily to the upper decks, although I'd heard the Admiral's quarters was somewhere on the upper gun deck. I'd yet to see it and honestly, had no desire, but Ransom had told me that's where he'd last seen Puck near.

I liked it above-decks, but the upper gun deck was open to the air above in a large section, so it wasn't so bad there. The air was fresher, there was ample sunlight, and I felt less constrained. Below-decks was another matter entirely. We'd been assigned an 'area' in the lower deck, and each given a ratty hammock to hang somewhere. At the very least, we'd been permitted to make our 'home' next to one another, which gave me some security. Having Ransom and Magpie near would be a comfort when sleeping.

The crew with more seniority had posher quarters on the deck immediately above us, the middle gun deck. It reeked less there, and was closer to where they served the food, but I honestly felt a bit out-of-place even wandering through it. The men there were clearly all very seasoned, and very tightly-knit.

Below-decks was a different story. There were a few new men, and a lot of men who apparently just didn't qualify to hold ranks of importance, and while they were a riotous group, they seemed less put-off by strangers penetrating their ranks. Ransom made a few friends just the first day, and Magpie and I didn't seem to cause much of a stir. There was a sizable amount of mockery at my expense from some of the men who had worked with me, but Magpie eased it by explaining to them all that I was just very young, and that seemed to go over well. One of them even told me I had 'pluck', whatever that meant.

Puck eased our fears by making an appearance as darkness fell the first night. He was moving about with the aid of a guide of some sort, a senior officer by the look of the tall feline, who wore an eye patch, and unlike any other lion I'd seen in my own lands, had a dark mane that encompassed his entire face and came down his back. He seemed to be playing the role of bodyguard for Puck, which was probably for the best, considering he didn't know the ship or the men well. I would have thanked the Admiral for being so thoughtful to the fox's needs, but of course I couldn't.

The lion introduced Puck to the men as the ship's new surgeon, which went over with a lot of speculation and hushed murmurs. I'm sure a few of them felt a blind healer might not fare as well at his job. I wanted to defend the fox. I hated that I couldn't speak, but I'd never be able to disguise my voice in any really convincing way.

Puck managed to mingle eventually, he and the lion passing out fresh fruit to the men, which made more than a few men happy. Our dinner tonight actually hadn't been terrible, but I'd been assured the meals would get worse and worse as time went on. Right now we still had fresh food from port. Eventually that would all spoil, so the first few days, we'd be eating extremely well so it didn't go to waste After that, apparently the fare was just shy of awful. I'd already tried a piece of what they called 'hard tack', and some salted fish. Being a cat, of course, I didn't mind the salted fish, but the hard tack was barely edible. And apparently the fish got old fast.

The part I was most worried about was when the men had explained our water would foul as time went on, and we'd be switching almost entirely to rations of watered-down alcohol. I'd never really been able to stomach the Otherwolves' poison water, but the sailors insisted I wouldn't want the normal water, eventually.

Puck hadn't been able to talk to us long when he'd managed to find time to do so, but he'd had a few words for me in particular, spoken in a low whisper.

"Be careful," he said quietly, "don't assume that just because we've made it to sea, you'll be safe if you're discovered. Don't remove your clothes, unless you know for certain you're alone. Try to do so as little as possible, regardless how dirty you feel."

I nodded, my eyes flicking to the rowdy men in the room. The fox was speaking in Katuk, but I still worried someone might hear him.

"Same goes for when you use the chamber pots," the fox said, intently. "I'm working on the Admiral. He's fairly fond of me already, but he might be angry nonetheless, if he finds out we brought a woman on-board. These men are superstitious."

I nodded again.

Puck looked between all of us, and reached into one of the bags he'd brought with him, producing some of the oranges he'd bought a few days before. "Eat these and drink a lot of water now while you can. And try not to overfill yourselves. The Admiral says the seas are going to get rocky soon."

And they did. It started that night, into that morning. I was woken by Ransom getting sick, followed some time later by

Magpie, and many of the other men on-board. By the following day, a lot of the new recruits, and some of the old, were contending with this 'sea-sickness' I'd been told of.

I'd been queasy for a bit, when it had first begun, but I found that so long as I was on my feet, it wasn't so bad. By the time we'd endured the first day of it, I felt remarkably well. Magpie was beginning to recover. Ransom was almost too sick to work.

It would probably be cruel to say it was a small amount of karmic justice, but hell, I suppose I could be cruel sometimes. I felt for the man, of course, but I was still angry at him for what he'd done in the days preceding the trip, and I only felt for him so much.

I received further congratulations from the gruff black rat, for having achieved my 'sea legs' so soon. Again, whatever that meant. The man used a lot of words and terminology I simply didn't understand.

And a few days into the trip, they finally found a job for me I was good at. Apparently it was considered a particularly humiliating task to most of the men, but I was all too happy to accept it, and didn't mind the work in the least.

The hold of the ship, which is where most of the cargo was stacked, was also where many of the animals were kept, including Helios. It was dank, often dark, and reeked of stale seawater and whatever else ended up making its way down here—basically whatever tipped over in the decks above—which could include chamber-pots. But the 'Purser', a thickly-jowled canine who apparently worked for Grayson managing his wares and the payment for his men, liked to keep the place as clean as possible. A never-ending chore, as it turned out.

So I began to spend my days hauling up animal manure and swabbing the lower decks, to ensure the seawater and filth that accumulated didn't rot the wood, and more importantly, the wares they kept down here. There were two other men appointed the task who were far less happy to be there than I was, but I was just glad to be near Helios so much of the time.

And taking care of the few other animals they'd brought on board felt more natural than taking care of cannons, or scrubbing the decks above.

I actually fell into the rhythm of ship life a lot faster and with more ease than I thought I would. It was routine. My chores kept my mind occupied, but also gave me a lot of repetitious tasks during which I could think, and reflect on everything that had transpired in my life of late. And that proved to be time I'd greatly needed.

My life had been moving so fast of late, it was hard to think of any time I'd had to simply slow down and hear my own thoughts. I'd felt lost for a long time now. If I was being honest with myself, probably since I'd first been married to Methoa'nuk. But there had been painful stabs throughout, punctuating new and gradually worsening chapters of my life. Losing my child. My near death. Every terrible thing I'd endured chasing Methoa, and then his un-fulfilling death. Grant's death...

I was still angry. I was angry every day. I had fleeting moments of intense anger, during which I wanted to fall back into that black, all-consuming rage that had been so protective and enveloping, and blinded me from the grief I should have been feeling.

But then I'd remember the promises I'd made to Hannah, and to myself, and I'd go about my duties, and grit my teeth through the pain, and eventually it would pass. And I'd remember the wonderful moments I'd had with the people I'd lost. Sometimes I'd even lose a few tears. We all had our sections of the hold to handle, and no one was ever working near me, so I wasn't afraid to let the feelings overwhelm me sometimes.

One thing became clear, as time passed. Every time I went through that cycle of anger, swelling up into pain, and then sadness. Every time I went through it again, it hurt, but the next time the anger returned, it wasn't as strong. And the moments passed more easily than they had the last time. It was like reopening a wound, every time. But it felt like something was mending.

The question was what really lay beyond here? If we made it to this wild and foreign place, I would help Puck find the source of this contagion, and hopefully, I would do something truly meaningful with my life. But what then? It was odd that I was considering what lay past something so monumental, but I had a lot of time to think about it, and I was.

It felt almost like planning for one's afterlife. I wasn't sure any more if Crow had truly brought me back from the dead, but this life was new, was different than the one I'd had. I'd been forging a new life, even if I'd not realized it. I'd been so caught up trying to avenge the wrongs done to me in my past, I'd never really considered a future. I'd begun to, when Grant had come along, but even then, I'd let my desire for vengeance tarnish the time I'd had with him.

I wasn't certain I wanted any sort of vengeance any more. It felt hollow. I'd been there, I'd experienced it, and it had done nothing for me. The more I let go of my anger now, the more the desire to stoke it anew was beginning to disappear. But what else was there, after all of this?

The real issue, I'd begun to realize, was that in all the time I'd spent turning myself into this new, stronger, more independent woman, I'd never really gotten to know her. All that had really mattered to me was the task at hand, and becoming more adept at carrying it out. But I was a person beneath the avenger, and I'd lost touch with who she was. I'd, in essence, been living for the man who'd once chained me all over again. I'd not been living for myself.

The more I allowed myself to think back on the past, clouded with pain though it was, the more I was remembering who I'd used to be. It was through the eyes of an immature child, because that was all I'd been when I'd been given to Methoa'nuk and the girl I'd once been had been repressed and erased, but some things came through loud and clear. Alongsaa had wanted to be free. She'd wanted to leave the valley, see the world, fly farther away from everything she'd ever known than anyone else in her tribe ever had. She'd known, even then, that there was a larger world beyond the mountains. She'd wanted to chase butterflies. I wanted to find her again.

I didn't know what I wanted beyond becoming the avenging executioner I had been striving to be for the last year. But I knew I didn't want to be that. Not anymore.

I'm not certain how many days into the trip Puck came to find me, with that same lion at his side. He seemed to be a permanent bodyguard for the fox now, or just a guide in general. I was glad Puck's services were so valued on the ship. And I could certainly understand why.

"Hello there," I heard the fox call out to me from across the hold, making his way past the enormous stacks of barrels... I still wasn't sure what was in them, but they seemed to dominate most of the hold. He and the always-silent lion made their way towards me, and Puck smiled at me. I couldn't resist smiling back. The lion, as usual, just appraised me with a firm look, not exactly an unfriendly one, but I got the feeling he was the serious-minded sort. He carried a bow, which I found interesting. Most of the men here chose to carry crossbows or pistols. I think I'd seen a pistol strapped to his hip once or twice, but it was hard to remember. He was clearly someone whose skills ran parallel to mine, though.

"Are you doing well down here?" Puck asked me, as they made it to me. "I've been told it's hard work."

I simply shrugged, and smiled again, so he knew I was happy down here.

"He seems content," the lion told Puck, presumably because he assumed the fox would need to be told. I knew by now that Puck could all but feel my moods, but the lion was clearly trying to do his job, and that was fine.

"I'm sorry. This is Ariel," the fox said, inclining his head up to the tall lion. "The Admiral felt it best he appoint one of his men to guide me about the boat and make sure I was safe while performing my duties. He's been very kind."

The fox inclined his head back towards me. "Well, I'm sorry to interrupt your work, but you're going to have to take time off for a few days. I'm performing inoculations later tonight. You and the few others I need to tend to are going to be quarantined to sickbay for however many days it takes you to get through treatment."

My brows came together in concern. I hadn't been looking forward to this, of course, but I understand why we had to do it. Still, I'd been enjoying the fact that I'd not been sick so far on this trip.

"Ransom and Magpie will be there," the fox told me, "so you won't be alone. And I'll be tending to you. Don't worry. I'm going to take good care of you all, I promise."

That at least made me feel a bit better. Sick or not, this would be a rare opportunity to spend time with all of my friends again. And that was something.

There were almost twenty men in total who needed to be treated, so the sick bay was a little packed, but I didn't mind. I had some time to catch up with Magpie and Ransom... who in particular, seemed to loathe the idea of the inoculation most of all. He'd already been sick on and off for the last two weeks, now. He'd been getting slightly better, of late, but when the seas were especially choppy, he was miserable. He'd taken to eating even less than he normally did, and smoking like a chimney. Sailing was proving to be very detrimental to his health.

I was more worried for him than I was for myself. One of the things Puck had once said was that the body had to be strong to fight this disease off. Ransom was tough, but the two weeks we'd spent at sea had weakened him significantly. I worried he'd have a harder time of it than the rest of us.

The actual process of having the inoculation applied was unpleasant, but minor. Puck cut a small laceration in each of our arms, and applied a paste that smelled awful and burned at my nose, some. Apparently it wasn't just an extract of the disease itself, there were other herbs included with it that were supposed to make sure we had a weak infection. He also had us eat very little the day beforehand, but drink as much water as we could, and eat what was left of the oranges.

And then we simply... waited.

I spent the time listening to Magpie and Ransom speak, for the most part, and Ransom sung some, which kept the other mens' spirits up. But that was of little comfort when the first of us started getting sick.

It mostly resembled sea-sickness at first, and men were going to the chamber-pot fairly often. My own stomach was a bit uneasy, but I'd always been very resistant to getting physically ill, and I was terrified of using the chamber-pot too frequently in such a small room, even though Puck had put up a curtain to give the people using it some privacy.

Ransom actually still seemed to be doing well when the first real symptoms started hitting me. The first night we tried to sleep through the illness, I found myself waking fitfully, what seemed like every few minutes, because I was too hot. I wanted to leave the room and get some air, but we of course couldn't do that. We were under quarantine. I felt myself sweating through my paw-pads, and I drank as often as I could, but nothing seemed to help. Even the clothing touching my body began to feel unbearable before long.

By the second day, my body ached like it never had before. It felt like the worst cold I'd ever had. I was having some digestive distress by then, but the aching pain was far more of a concern. I wanted to move around, because I was burning up, but moving hurt. Lying down hurt. Everything hurt.

That second night, I did sleep, but only in flashes, and what woke me wasn't just the fact that I was overheating. It was the nightmares. Vibrant, overpowering nightmares, that were as real as when I'd been there. I woke with a yell more than once, hoping no one had heard me. I was supposed to be mute.

But soon my concern for all of that began to fall apart, because I was blacking in and out of consciousness regularly, even throughout the day. I saw people sometimes in the fleeting moments of lucidity. Puck... maybe Ransom, or some other canine... and then people I thought for certain were dead. More than once, I thought I had woken up, and I had my baby in my arms, or I could smell Grant beside me, and feel my hands moving over the soft fur along his shoulders, held in his arms.

But then that would all dissolve away into another nightmare, and I'd be there again, watching them die. I saw things I knew I'd never seen. Methoa'nuk, carrying our screaming young child under one of his arms, as he cast him into a gorge in the mountains along the Anukshen border. My baby, lying in a thicket of dead, crumbling leaves, crying as the night air began to freeze him...

Grant, playing with his little sister in the slums, letting her ride on Helios in the small lot beside their house.

A black vixen, standing over the fallen figure of my husband, his hands bound behind his back, fresh scars oozing blood down his shoulders as she kicked him in the gut, and grinned at the humiliated man.

My parents cooking a meal near their longhouse, when the first shots came. My mother was struck first, my younger brother next. Arrows lit with burning pitch rained down on the longhouses.

The cascade of terrible imagery repeated, again and again, until the memories flickered by too fast for me to follow, and I drifted into blackness. It was almost a peaceful reprieve.

But then I opened my eyes, slowly. I felt something cold on my eyelashes. Snow. And the breeze smelled like pine and mountain air. I flexed my toes into the earth beneath, and felt lichen. The skies above were a tapestry of stars, shining between the thinning clouds. The mountain stone was cold behind my back, beneath my hands, and it felt familiar. This all felt familiar. The shape of the rocky outcropping, the view of the valley rolling beneath, the rocky ledge ahead.

I looked suddenly to my right when I felt someone's presence there, and I saw Grant. He was staring back at me, silently.

I remembered this place, now. It was where I'd stood with him, after we'd found Ransom. Thirty paces away was our camp, between the two enormous rock faces, and past the small pines. I'd talked to Laesom on that edge, afraid he was going to end his life.

Grant was saying nothing, but I realized at that moment that he was not alone. A few paces ahead of me, I saw my parents, and my siblings. And past them, Methoa'nuk, holding our child.

And at the very edge of the cliff, sitting in the branches of a ragged pine, was a dark bird with glowing eyes.

I stepped forward, making my way out across the lichen-covered earth, towards the cliff face, passing the people in my life that I'd lost, as I went. They all watched me, but none spoke.

But Crow... Crow spoke.

"Everything..." Crow said, in that deep, otherworldly voice, with the barest hint of a roaring, crackling fire beneath it, "everything that ever meant anything to us is behind us. There is nothing ahead. Just emptiness."

I stood at the edge of the cliff, looking out over the sheer drop, and the dark world beyond. I couldn't even tell from here if what lay beyond was the valley, the Otherwolf lands, or somewhere else entirely. It was like a void. The winds swept up around my body, nearly buffeting me back. Whatever lay beyond this place was terrifyingly unknown.

I looked back at the people standing behind me. They were still silent. They couldn't give me answers any more. They couldn't make this decision for me. For better or for worse, they'd all helped lead me to this point, each having their own impact on my life. And I wanted so badly to stay here. This place was familiar. What lay beyond was—I couldn't possibly know.

I looked to Crow. He stared back at me. I could see the fire inside him, licking out from his eyes, and beginning to crack through his black body, like embers beginning to break apart. He was being consumed from the inside out. Slivers of black fell from him even as he opened his wings, and leered down at me.

"If you go ahead, you will fall," he warned. "Stay here! Burn with me, as you promised. We will light the sky one last time, as the fires consume us, and then it will finally all be over... and we can rest. At last."

"Would your loved one want you to die as she did?" I asked the enraged spirit, quietly. "In pain, and anger?"

"There is nothing else ahead of us!" the spirit cried. "What can we do but fall?"

I looked out over the cliff, into the dark night beyond. And I knew Crow was wrong. Something was there, past the edge of the rocky outcropping. I could see vague hints of the world beneath us. I couldn't see what they were, or where they were, but it was more than just emptiness, it was the unknown.

The spirit inclined its head towards the people standing behind us. "They cannot help us anymore. We are alone, if we leave this place."

"We'll have each other," I said, looking to the people I'd lost. "And they aren't even really here, Crow. We have to let them move on, as well."

As I said it, I saw them begin to fade. I focused on Grant in particular as they started to disappear, since this had been our place, and the memories of the time he and I had spent here were still so painful, and so fresh...

But he was smiling at me, now. And I saw the promise there.

I looked out over the cliff again. "Whatever lies beyond here," I said to the spirit, "it's my journey, not theirs. But all of our paths lead to the same destination some day. I'll see them again."

"We will fall," the spirit repeated, and I heard something I had never before heard in the spirit's voice. Fear. He spread his wings again, and I saw how badly they had begun to erode.

The feathers were crumbling, hot orange embers licking at his cracking form. He would not survive much longer.

"Have faith," I said quietly, as I stepped up to the edge.

"I don't know what lies beyond here..." The spirit admitted.

"That's what faith is for," I said, closing my eyes, and trying to be brave. "Belief, in something you cannot see."

"What are we believing in?" The spirit asked, as it settled on my shoulder.

I began to step forward, uttering one last word as I felt my foot hit open air.

"Ourselves."

The next time I opened my eyes, I felt hazy, and in pain, and I knew that unlike the last few times, this was likely reality. My vision was cloudy, and my eyes felt crusted over, like I'd not opened them in ages. My body felt much as it had when I'd first come to in Puck and Ransom's camp. Stiff, and aching. In a strange repeat of that memory, the first person who came into focus in my line of sight was Ransom. My life seemed cyclical at times.

Only this time, he wasn't glaring across an unfamiliar campsite at me in distrust, he was looking down on me with concern, and his spirits seemed to lift when I blinked my eyes up at him.

"Shivah, goddamn," he said with a long sigh, running a hand over the tousled fur along his neck, in relief. "We were getting' worried. H-how're you feelin', kitten?"

Before I could really think about it, I ran my tongue along my dry muzzle and gave a slight cough, murmuring, "My throat is dry... I-I'd really like some water."

"Shit, sorry," the coyote apologized, ducking out of sight for a few moments. While he was gone, I blinked my eyes and tried to make sense of the ceiling. It didn't look like the one in sick bay. The wood here was dryer, less worn, and the room was bright, like there were a lot of windows.

I forced myself to sit up slowly, and realized the stiffness and pain were nowhere near as bad as they'd been when I'd been suffering the disease at its height. In fact, most of the discomfort I was experiencing seemed primarily to be from lack of movement. My throat was dry, and I still had some residual aches, but overall, I felt well-rested, and just... well, in general. Like the last day of a cold.

Ransom returned as I was looking around the strange room. It was large for a room on a ship. There was a heavy wooden table in the middle of it, strewn with maps, a variety of strange nick-knacks, a few tankards, and a plate or two. There was furniture about the place, most of which was nailed into the walls. A lot of cabinets with small doors and drawers that could be locked down, as was the style on this ship, I'd been noticing. Some clothing hanging on brass hooks near a large door at the end of the room, and what looked like someone's sleeping quarters, beyond.

And a variety of just... the only word I could think of to describe it was 'stuff'. It wasn't junk, at least not all of it. It ranged in value from precious trinkets hung from the walls to colorful feathers tied in bunches, exotic-looking fans and a small collection of dangling metal baubles that made soft tinkling noises as the boat swayed, or wind blew in through the windows. There were also a lot of different pistols hung along the walls. More than I'd ever seen in one place.

I stretched my arms above my head and cracked my back with a wince as Ransom brought me a cup of water. I drank it gratefully, downing the cup before rubbing at my head and murmuring, "Where the hell are we?"

"Sort of a long story," the coyote said, uneasily. He sat down on the bed beside me. "Alright, so," he sighed, "your secret's kind of out."

My eyes widened. "What?" I demanded, then looked down at myself. I was only wearing the loose cotton shirt, my trousers and my under-wraps. Not the vest or overcoat I'd been wearing to obscure my figure.

Ransom held up a hand. "Look, if it makes you feel any better, it wasn't your fault. You were doin' fine 'til the inoculation. But, we sort of forgot the patchouli oil when you got all feverish, and the disease got you real bad."

I gave him a dismayed look. "It was that bad?"

The coyote nodded. "Yeah, sorry, sweetheart. It's worse for some folks than others, and Puck said it probably didn't have nothin' to do with your health. He thinks it's 'cause you were from the valley. Isolated, y'know. Not a lotta diseases hit the tribes there. Your body wasn't real resistant. It weren't your fault."

"How are you doing?" I asked, concerned.

The coyote gave the slightest of guilty grins, "Ah... I'm immune, as it turns out. I guess that's why I didn't get it in Serahaven."

I sighed, leaning back. "Lucky bastard," I muttered.

"Hey, I ain't exactly led a blessed life," the coyote said with a chuckle. "Honestly, I think it's about time I got cut a break."

"What about Magpie?"

Ransom waved a hand. "Rat's fine. Mosta' the rats had it pretty easy actually. I ain't gonna go talkin' about stereotypes, but y'know, rats and diseases..."

"But you wouldn't ever infer that," I said, rolling my eyes, then looking around the room again. The place was just so strange. "Where are we?" I asked again. "I don't recognize this room."

Ransom sighed. "This's the Admiral's quarters."

I blinked, looking back at him, stunned. "Why are we here?" I demanded. "Does he—"

"Yeah, unfortunately," the coyote sighed. "Listen, like I said, it wasn't yer fault. But we kinda' forgot to obscure your scent while you were in th' throes of the fever, and his lion caught on. Bastard's sharp. Probably got a nose for feline women in particular, too. I dunno when he snitched on us, but he did, and Reed sent the man down here to 'retrieve' you before you started a panic on the ship. I told him we had to be here with you, and Puck's been looking in on you."

"What's he going to do with me?" I asked, more than alarmed, now. Why would he want me in his cabin? Gods, please. I hoped the answer to that wasn't as obvious as I thought it was.

"Well fer the moment, he just seemed t' want to keep you away from the other men, before someone else found out," the coyote said uncertainly, but I could hear the suspicion in his voice. He was a canny man, and I knew he suspected the same thing I did. This was going to end poorly for me, in one of two ways. And I honestly wasn't certain which plank I'd rather walk.

"But he did say he wanted t' talk to you when you woke up," the coyote said, "and who knows? Man might be more reasonable than we think. We've had some time t' talk since I've been lookin' after you here, and he's an odd fellow, but I tried bondin' with him a little. He's real fond of Puck. Granted, I think it's almost entirely 'cause the fox fixes his hangovers, but..."

I went silent, my eyes falling to the blankets gathered in my lap, as I carefully considered my options. Unlike Ransom, I didn't think for a moment the wolf had any honorable intentions towards me. I had to think very hard on what I would and wouldn't do to stay alive, and spare my friends any punishments these men might take out on them for bringing me on board. It wasn't just my life on the line here. Magpie's words from back in the city were beginning to come back to haunt me.

I didn't have much time to consider it unfortunately, because at that point, the door was thrust open, and the man of the hour himself came strolling in, long coat, dreaded mane, eclectic collection of weapons and all. His blue eyes settled on the two of us and a grin split his face when he noted my condition, and he headed inside with a long peel of laughter, followed closely behind by Puck and the discoverer of my secret, that bloody lion.

Puck dashed towards me almost as soon as he got into the room, and the lion locked the door behind us. Grayson hung his coat on one of the brass hangers near the door, spreading his arms in the fashion he often tended to do, I'd noticed, as he stepped towards us.

"Thought you could pull the wool over my eyes, did you now, you sly little thing?" He chuckled, leaning against the wall beside the small bunk I was on, resting against his forearm. He stared down at me, and I did not like the way he was looking at me now, as opposed to the disinterest he'd shown me in the past.

"Shivah, how are you feeling?" Puck asked worriedly.

I glanced briefly at the fox, but primarily kept my eyes on the leering black wolf. "I'm fine," I said, firmly. "I feel very recovered, actually. Just a bit sore."

"And she talks!" The wolf exclaimed. "Amazing. Gone from a mute man to a woman with an enchanting voice, just like that. I am intrigued. In all my years at sea, I've never seen such magic."

Ransom stayed at my side, narrowing his eyes at the two men, his posture defensive. Puck, however, looked up to Grayson plaintively. "Please," he said, "I don't need any payment for my services here. I'll keep working for you, and making your potions, and helping your men, but please let her stay on. We can disguise her again. No one needs to know."

The wolf scratched at his chin, considering the fox's words for a few moments, with a low "Hmmmnh..."

"It will be very hard to keep it a secret for such a long voyage," the lion spoke up, and I noticed for the first time that he had a vague accent, not one I recognized. "And if the men find out, it won't just make for bad morale, it will be dangerous for her."

"You've sort of put me in a bind here, lovely," the wolf said, shaking his head. "I'd hate to just toss you overboard—"

"You can't!" Puck said, frantically. Ransom stiffened, his hand over his knife, the only weapon he had on him.

Grayson held out a hand, chuckling. "At ease. Believe it or not, even Privateers have a code. I don't even enjoy putting my own men to death, let alone a woman. We're not barbarians."

"Then what are you going to do with me?" I asked, as stoically as I could. I had to face this without fear. I couldn't appear weak. Men like this preyed on weakness.

The wolf was silent for a further few moments, before gesturing offhandedly at Ariel. "Show them out, would you? I'd like to talk to her alone."

"Like hell—" Ransom snarled, before the lion clapped a large paw on the coyote's shoulder, and yanked him up. Puck looked around wildly, and gripped my hand.

"Please," he begged again, "she's my friend! If you hurt her, I-I won't... I won't work for you any more," he tried to threaten, but he mostly sounded scared.

"No one's going to get hurt," the wolf said in a smooth, soothing tone. "Have I not been good to you all so far? Now come on. Don't make a fuss."

"I ain't lettin' you touch her!" Ransom snapped, trying to wrest free of the lion's grip. The coyote was barely armed, and the lion was probably one and a half times his weight, and far stronger. But I knew he'd fight the man, regardless. He'd fight, and he'd get hurt.

And Puck would get caught in the middle of it, trying to help us both.

"Stop!" I bit out, getting to my legs a little unsteadily. I put my arms out, and looked between the wolf and Ransom, and then Puck. "Please," I pleaded, to everyone. "This isn't worth a fight." I looked over at Ransom, who was gritting his teeth, on the verge of doing something that would doubtless bring the lion's wrath down upon him.

"I want to talk to him," I told the coyote. Ransom's eyes widened, and I saw the wolf smirk out of the corner of my eye. I focused on the coyote instead. "I want to handle this myself,"

I told the man, reaching forward and putting my hand on his shoulder. "I'm the cause of this issue, and I... I want to help find the solution to it. By myself. It's a matter of pride." I looked Ransom in the eyes. "Can you please just respect that?"

"Shivah, please..." the coyote begged. "Don't... don't ask me to leave y' alone with this man. I'll never forgive myself."

"I made a choice to come along on this trip," I said, addressing both men, now. Puck was looking up at me pleadingly, as well. "I can handle myself. I can... I can handle this. It's alright. Just please don't get yourselves hurt on my account," I leaned in, and hugged the both of them, individually, "And I promise, I won't let myself get hurt, either. Just let the Admiral and I work this out."

The coyote shut his muzzle, and looked me back in the eyes for a long while. I knew how he felt about this. And I knew why he was so monstrously angry at the concept of the wolf using me. But he also respected me, and my choices, and I had to hope that right now, that was enough that he'd leave this room willingly. Because any other way it went down was going to end poorly for the man.

When Ransom finally relented, and shrugged free of the lion's grip and began to make his way towards the door, Puck gave me one last trembling look, then slunk off in Ransom's wake. I hated that this was hurting my friends, but I didn't really have any other choice. And besides, I was prepared to do what was necessary, but I had been honest about what I'd told Ransom. This was a matter of pride.

I waited until I heard the door close behind them, then turned to address the dark-furred wolf. He was still leaning against the wall, regarding me with that long-muzzled, lazy smile. He reached up and pushed a few dreads over his shoulder, lifting his gaze to mine, and slouched a bit in his stance against the wall.

"So much drama," he said with a low chuckle. "And for so little reason. You know, I've actually been told by many a woman that I can be quite pleasurable company."

"How much did you pay them to tell you that?" I asked, deadpan.

The man laughed, and leaned forward. We were fairly near one another, so he was quite literally leaning over me. He had a head and then some on me, but I tried to show him I wasn't intimidated.

"You know," the wolf said, leaning in enough that I could feel his breath on me. He smelled like rum, a scent I'd gotten to know all-too-well on this ship over the last few weeks. "I really do hate to make difficult decisions like this, believe me. I'd prefer it if everything in life were easy. But like I said, you've put me in a bad spot, here. I can't risk returning you to the ranks, lest someone else discover your little..." his eyes swept down me, settling somewhere south of the border, "secret. It would be hell on morale, and dangerous for you, besides."

"So I've been told," I muttered.

"Sailors have their beliefs, love," the wolf said, "and like it or not, most believe having a woman aboard a warship curses the voyage."

"They're your men," I pointed out. "They have to abide by your rules."

"Do you know what the greatest threat is to an Admiral, or a Captain at sea?" The wolf asked, pushing away from the wall and walking towards the table, where he plucked up one of the bottles there, and tugged the cork free.

I blinked, realizing that he actually wanted me to guess. I couldn't even begin. Other ships? Sickness? I'd probably be wrong no matter what, and that was the point he was trying to make. How little I knew.

"Storms," I said at length. I'd heard a lot of the sailors talk about their fear of the terrible weather in the tropics.

"Mutiny," the wolf said, narrowing his eyes. "No man is loyal to a fault. And you never know just what will push each of them over the edge. I have to keep up a certain reputation, just inspiring enough to follow, but just feared enough to make commands and be certain they're followed."

I crossed my arms over my chest, deciding for now that I'd hear the man out. That had actually made some sort of sense, unlike a lot of what left his mouth.

The wolf held up a hand, gesturing towards the window, as he brought the bottle to his muzzle. "The whole foundation of my fleet is built on my reputation. It doesn't just affect how my men see me. It affects my contracts, it keeps other fortune hunters at bay. I can't appear soft, can't appear weak, or I'll be preyed upon. That's how this game works."

"So throw me in the brig," I said, casting my eyes down. I'd seen the brig, and I didn't relish the thought of spending the next month and a half in it, but I'd do what I needed to do. "You said yourself you don't want to kill me, but wouldn't that be enough punishment?"

"Many of my men would consider that cruel," the wolf said, swigging from the bottle again. "And I'm counting myself in that statement."

"Then what would you suggest?" I asked, sighing, because I was all but certain I knew what the answer was, and he knew I knew it. I could tell by the grin. I hated being toyed with.

He put the bottle down, and un-slung his bandolier from over his shoulder, hanging it on a nearby chair. He'd already dispensed with his coat earlier, which made this the most undressed I'd ever seen the man. He moved towards me, and I slunk back against the wall until there was nowhere else to go. He put an arm out, bracing it with a hand on the wall just over my head, and leaning down to look me in the eyes. He was close enough that I could feel the heat coming off his body, and smell more of that rum.

When he began to lean down, I twisted my muzzle away and put a hand against his chest, shoving him enough that I got him about an inch further away from me, and I knew I'd only made that much progress because he'd let me. He looked down at me like the gesture amused him.

"How does this help your predicament?" I demanded, trying to keep from yelling. I wasn't trying to antagonize the man, exactly, just reason with him. If he could be appealed to at all, I had to try.

The wolf chuckled, leaning in again, and this time even with two hands, I really couldn't push him away. He was nosing at my mane where it fell over my shoulders, like he had the right to. "Because," he murmured, against my neck, "the men won't question my keeping a woman around for womanly purposes nearly as much as they would if you were living below-decks with them."

"Oh, that is just the most paltry excuse!" I snapped, shoving at his muzzle. The man was definitely getting amusement at my sake by now, rather like he thought we were playing. Except I definitely wasn't. Every time I pushed at him, he just went right back to what he was doing, and then some. His hand was working its way along my hip now.

I sighed, frustrated, and let my head thunk back against the wooden wall, trying to figure out what to do. When he nipped at my neck, I growled, and shoved him hard, as hard as I could. Putting a bit more muscle into it actually got him entirely off of me, at least for a few moments, the man catching himself after taking a few steps back, and grinning at me.

"I like a woman with spirit," he smirked.

"You do not want to meet my spirit," I growled in a warning tone. "And you don't want to do this. Trust me."

The wolf chuckled, spreading his arms. "Come on now, lovely, why not? I swear, I'm not a bad toss. I've even been told I can be quite considerate."

"I would rather be thrown in the brig," I snarled.

The wolf put a hand over his chest, like he'd been injured. "You wound me. I've been nothing but kind to you and yours. What's with all this venom? I don't think I've earned it. At least not from you. I've been a right bastard to a few folks in the world, but..."

"Well for one, you smell like brine and rum," I muttered, curling my lip up. "And I'm... vile, myself, right now. I'm barely over the illness. I smell like sick and sweat, and I might still be contagious. How could you possibly even want to—"

"Oh, don't be so self-conscious," the wolf said with a smirk, moving back in quickly, and pinning me against the wall before I could prevent him. I kicked at his legs, to no avail. "I haven't smelled a woman in half a month," the man murmured, in what he probably thought was a sultry tone, "you smell fine to me..." he leaned in, going for my neck again, "and I've been inoculated..."

I groaned. "You are such a pig!"

The wolf just chuckled again, against my throat. Despite all of his unwanted advances, though, it was becoming clear to me that even though he easily could have man-handled me by now, he hadn't. And he hadn't begun to tear at my clothes. I think he honestly wanted me to want this. A man like this liked to have his ego stoked.

I still wasn't certain how far I was willing to test that. He'd probably push until I relented one way or the other, or maybe not. I honestly wasn't sure.

But I was beginning to formulate a plan. I just had to hope he was stupid enough that he'd let me do it.

I sighed, jerking my muzzle away from him before he got any closer to it. "Listen," I said, trying one last plea, "I'd really rather not do this. Is there any way I could appeal to your decency?"

The wolf stared blankly at me for a few moments, which I suppose was my answer.

I sighed again. "We could pretend you were doing this, instead. Make the men think you're keeping me like your bloody pet. That would save your 'reputation.'"

The wolf smirked. "Now, honestly, that's not much of a bargain for me, is it?" I opened my mouth to say something, but he interrupted me, jovially, "Come now, I'm a fair man. I don't think a bit of company is much to ask, in comparison to any other punishment we could cook up on this ship. You did lie to me."

I narrowed my eyes. "You ought to know, every man who's enjoyed my company in the past is now dead. Some would say I'm cursed."

"My men are superstitious, love, not me," the wolf said, still smiling. "I'm actually quite fond of dangerous pursuits."

"If we do this," I said, holding out a hand, "I set some rules, first."

The wolf rubbed at his chin, thoughtfully, then gave a slight bow of his muzzle. "As the lady wills it. Never let it be said I'm not a gentleman."

"No weapons," I said, shoving at his hip, where one of his pistols was pushing into my stomach. "First off."

He didn't seem to take issue with that. I watched the man remove two more pistols, two swords, and a boot knife, dropping them down deliberately noisily on the nearby table. The amount of merriment he was displaying at our bargaining was both irritating and promising. I had to push him a little farther...

I looked him over for a long moment, dubiously, then crossed my arms over my chest and cocked my hip, narrowing my eyes at the man. "No, I don't trust you haven't gotten something else hidden."

"Only one more weapon beneath my clothes, lovely," the wolf promised, with a wink, "and it's all for you."

I had to fight rolling my eyes. "I don't care," I muttered, "undress. Entirely."

The wolf didn't seem embarrassed in the least to do so, and went through the process of shedding his clothing like he assumed I'd relish it. He clearly had a higher opinion of his looks than was entirely accurate.

Well, I suppose were it not for the situation...

I shook my head. Definitely not the time to be letting my mind run away with that one.

He tossed his tail over his hip as he kicked off the last article of clothing, one of his leather spats, and leaned back against the table, smiling confidently at me. "Your turn," he stated, his voice a lower, more husky tone, now.

I pulled my long, white cotton shirt off, discarding it on the bunk behind me. I still wore my wraps beneath, and my loose cotton pants besides, but it gave the wolf something to look at, for now. And he was doing that with relish, his eyes sweeping over my figure. I had to fight back the urge to cross my arms over my chest, self-consciously.

"I don't," I murmured, trying to sound skittish, and succeeding, "I don't want to... undress... with you watching me."

"I'm gonna see it all eventually," the man said with an arched eyebrow.

"I know, but it's just the process of getting undressed," I stammered, looking down at the ground and doing my best to look sheepish and missish, which wasn't easy for me. "It's not proper," I said, because it sounded like something a woman might say that a man might believe.

And it worked.

The wolf shrugged. "If you insist."

"Can we use your bed, also?" I asked. "This bunk is so small."

The wolf smiled at that. "Why else do you think I have it?"

He wasn't a complete fool, though. He gathered his pistols, and his swords, and stowed them in a large chest he kicked shut beside the big table. I could only imagine every other pistol in the room wasn't loaded. It hardly mattered, though, I couldn't use a gun.

When he was done, he leaned up and sauntered over to me, and I didn't have to pretend to shy back from the man. He was a large, naked man, getting very close to me, and he was visibly aroused by now.

He leaned over me, his dreads brushing over my shoulder. "I'll meet you in bed."

It took every bit of willpower I had not to shove him again, when he nipped at my ear, but I withstood it. And then he wandered off towards his sleeping area, obscured from the main cabin by little more than a wooden screen, and I quickly went about disrobing, and sifting through the clothing he'd left behind, looking for the one thing I was hopeful he hadn't thought to hide, and I found it.

I was quick enough about it that I was fairly certain he hadn't suspected anything. By the time I made it to his sleeping area, the man was already stretched out comfortably on the bed, awaiting my arrival, and looking quite smug the moment I came into view.

I honestly didn't care that he'd seen me nude, but the effect it had on him did make me cringe a bit.

His bed was a real bed, a heavy four-poster, with a headboard like many I'd seen before at inns, and I was glad for that. I'd thought that's what it looked like behind the wooden screen, but it had been hard to tell.

"Just... let me start things off." I said, keeping up that timid tone.

"As you wish," the man smirked. "Like I said, I'm quite considerate."

I got on the bed, and slipped over him, and the wolf gave a low, content growl as my hips settled over his stomach. He wrapped his arms around my waist and ran them up my back, and I willed myself to allow it just a little while longer. I had to get him to close his eyes, lose his concentration, somehow...

I did the first thing I could think of that might work. I leaned down and kissed him. Hardly anyone kissed with their eyes open.

And he fell for it. And when I moved my hands down to his, and wrapped my fingers around his, and slowly raised his arms above his head, he gave a low rumble, but he clearly still thought it was part of the game, because he allowed it.

I'd stowed the small trinket I'd brought in in one of my hands, hidden behind my back until then, but he'd doubtless be feeling it by now, since I'd dropped it on the bed near where I was lifting his arms, so I worked fast.

Thank the gods for all the training I'd been receiving over the last few weeks from the men below decks in tying knots.

He seemed to understand something was happening, a few seconds in, but I'd learned how to do this fast enough by now that I'd gotten it most of the way done by the time he did, and when his eyes shot open and he tried to pull away from the kiss, I bit at his lip just long enough to give me those final few seconds necessary to complete the knot.

Honestly, the man might have been canny and dangerous with a fleet at his command, but I'd been right. He was a fool for a woman.

I sat up slowly, looking down at him as realization crossed his features. He twisted his head up to stare at his wrists, and the tight leather knot I'd bound them by to the bed post.

"That's my falconry lure..." He muttered, in realization and dawning shock.

Now it was my turn to laugh. And I did, my tail tossing merrily as I slowly chuckled.

"You minx!" The man cried out, tugging at the bed post. It shook with his efforts, but short of breaking the lure, I knew he couldn't get out of that knot. And the lure was made of tightly-wound leather. He'd have to be awfully strong to break it. He gave a growl of frustration, and glared up at me. "You're not going to get away with this, you know. My man's right outside."

"By all means, call for him," I said, putting my hands on my hips. "I'll help. I'll make sure I make enough noise that half the upper gun-deck comes to see what's going on in here."

The wolf's eyes widened at that.

"But that might not be wise," I pointed out, raising one eyebrow. "I hear the foundation of an Admiral's fleet is his reputation."

The wolf gave me a look mixed with indignation, and grudging respect.

"Now, I'm new to life on the seas, so perhaps you can educate me a bit on these subjects," I cleared my throat. "What might the men of your crew think of a man who was bested by a woman half his size?"

I hopped off of him, and sauntered back into the main area, to begin donning my clothing again. "Not hearing an answer!" I called over the screen. "Well, let's find out, then..."

"No!" I heard the man call back. Then, "no, damnit. Just, let's talk about this..."

I popped my head back around the screen. "Oh, you want to talk now?"

The wolf gave a sound somewhere between a frustrated groan and a chuckle. "Yes, alright? You're a bloody clever little thing."

"Aren't I just," I murmured, heading back into the room with at least my wraps and my pants back on. I flopped back down onto the bed beside him, and propped my chin on one hand, looking down at the man. "So, now that you're interested in talking, how about we revisit that whole 'you tell the men you're bending me over' deal, and just abide by that? You still get to be the big man on deck, and I get to keep my clothes on. It works out for both of us."

The wolf arched an eyebrow, chewing on the inside of his cheek. "You know," he said at length, "nothing says I have to abide by that once you set me free. I run this ship."

I looked at him curiously. "Are you telling me not to trust you?"

The wolf gave a crooked grin. "Oh, absolutely."

"That's not much incentive for me to set you free," I pointed out.

"That was precisely what I was inferring," the wolf said. "So this plan of yours, it's really only a temporary solution. You can shame me now, and ensure I have to replace... most of my crew, and then I'll have to throw you in the brig just to keep order. Or I say I'll follow your plan, but there's nothing really keeping me to it."

"Answer something for me," I said, in a far more serious tone. "And try to be honest. Because I want to hear you say it." I leaned down, and looked him in the eyes. "Would you really have forced yourself on me?"

"I hardly consider it 'forcing,'" the wolf reasoned, "more 'bargaining'. You want something. I want something..."

"Say it," I snapped. "Say you would have raped me."

The wolf twisted his muzzle up for a few moments, and averted his eyes.

I leaned back, slowly. "You can't," I said, at length. "Because you wouldn't have. Would you?"

"You can't be certain of that," the wolf insisted with a grunt, "I'm a bad, bad man, lovely."

"But you're not a rapist," I said with certainty.

"How can you be certain?" he replied.

I leaned in close. "Because I've known rapists," I said, lowly, "and they don't hesitate."

"Like I said before, miss," the wolf sighed. "Even Privateers have a code."

I looked down at him for a time, assessing the black-furred canine splayed beneath me... really looking at him, and taking stock of him. I still didn't really know what to make of the man. He was a bizarre mix of vile, irritating and occasionally charming, if I was being entirely honest with myself. But I'd yet to get a real grasp on the man's moral compass, and that was what truly mattered.

"You'll honor our agreement," I said, at length. "For two reasons. One," I held up a finger, "because you know I could just do this again, if you let down your guard. Women make you stupid, and I think you know it. Or you at least have to be coming to grips with that reality now."

The wolf gave a begrudging laugh at that.

"And two," I said, and for this I paused, because it was a bold proclamation to make, even for me, "because if you let me stay here with you on your ship, and you honor our arrangement and don't lay your hands on me..." I sighed, "One of these nights I might let you."

The wolf's features split into a slow grin, at that. "'One of these nights'?" He echoed. "So that's not even—"

"A guarantee? No," I told him point-blank. "Just a possibility. You'd need to earn it. You'd need to impress me. And I am a hard woman to impress."

"Long odds..." the man murmured, in consideration.

"I'm worth the gamble," I said, trying to sound confident and alluring when I said it. I'm not sure I managed it, honestly. Playing this role was new to me.

"I'm not a bad catch myself," Grayson said, flashing his ivory canines as he said it, and giving a far more practiced smoldering gaze.

I just gave a derisive snort. "My last lover was twice the man you are," I assured him, my eyes sweeping down his figure, "Possibly literally."

The wolf followed my gaze, and gave a nervous chuckle. "Ah, he's just a little timid at the moment," He glanced back up at me, and tugged pointedly at where his wrists were bound. "I don't much like being tied up on my own ship."

"Tell me we have a deal, and I'll untie you," I said.

"You drive a hard bargain, lovely," the wolf said, but he grinned. "But hell, I like your style. You've got a deal."

The arrangement with Grayson made for one of the most bizarre months of my life. The news that I was a woman spread throughout the crew like wildfire, just as we'd known it would, and Grayson himself reinforced the rumors by being particularly blatant about his 'attachment' to me when we were on deck together. Namely by putting his hands on me, in non-invasive but very lewd ways. I had to fight my constant urges to hit the man, or at least restrain them until we were behind closed-doors, and remind him what our arrangement had been. But apparently, according to him, 'groping' had not been covered under our deal. Nor had 'fondling', or grabbing, or being a disgusting pig.

And then there were the constant attempts every night to get me into bed with him. I'd kept to the bunk that was reserved for a cabin boy apparently, when he had one, but every night he reminded me in more colorful and elaborate ways how much more 'comfortable' I would be if I'd bed down with him. The man was remarkably eloquent when he was being lewd.

And the fact that I had to go about most of my private life in the same room with him was just maddening. I tried to change only when he was gone, but more than once he'd insistently stuck around in the mornings, pretending he was looking over maps, until I got sick of waiting and just went about my morning routine.

And then there was the fact that he insisted on being naked all the time! Apparently when he was enjoying his own private time in his cabin, which was quite often while we were on calm seas, he eschewed the very thought of clothing. I couldn't go a day without seeing the man's sheath. It was unavoidable.

Living with the Privateer was an exercise in endurance and tolerance. I honestly wasn't certain if he was always this crass, or if he was escalating his behavior specifically to make the arrangement harder on me, but either way, I was at my wits end after barely a week.

It didn't help that for that entire week, I hadn't really been allowed to leave much. I saw Puck, Ransom and Magpie once a day. I'd told them by then that everything was fine, and let them know about the arrangement Grayson and I had reached, and Ransom in particular was leery, but they went along with it for the same reason I did—we had to. Even still, they thought it best I not spend a lot of time out of the cabin. The crew was apparently getting used to the idea of there being a woman on board, but just like Grayson had said, some of them were none-too-fond of the thought. Apparently some Captains and Admirals did keep a woman around for pleasure in some fleets... Grayson hadn't made that up. But a lot of the time those women serviced the entire crew, and... Well, that certainly wasn't happening. I wasn't even really servicing the Admiral.

Grayson assured me the discontent would die down eventually, and that I'd be able to spend more time out as the voyage went on, but for now, I could only really leave when he did and stay close to the man. It at least allowed me to wander parts of the ship I'd never been allowed on before. I got to see where the officers ran the ship from, watch the sails being operated, meet the wheel man, and learn a thing or two about how the ship worked. Grayson was more than happy to tell me all about her. In fact sometimes he'd spend hours at a time boasting about 'his girl', as he put it. I wasn't sure how much good all the information was going to do me in the rest of my life, but I honestly found it fascinating, so I listened. I liked that there was a reason everything on the ship functioned, and a rationale behind how it was built, and how it was controlled.

As time passed, and I was able to leave the cabin more often, I even began to look forward to my strolls with the Admiral. I had very little to occupy my time, he still insisted it was best I not work with the men, a fact for which I felt guilty... but gradually, he began to give me more freedom to wander, and occasional tasks above-decks to do. The men up here didn't seem to mind my presence, and were fairly patient with me when Grayson told them to show me a thing or two about what they were doing. I got the feeling they took a lot of pride in their work, and liked to show off to a female.

Some nights I would accompany Puck and Ariel on their runs below-decks to check up on the men, and I'd visit with Ransom and Magpie. Gradually, Ransom had begun to get over most of his sea-sickness, but it was clear the coyote was still miserable at-sea. Magpie seemed to be taking to it a lot better, and had told me he'd even worked his way up to work on the upper gun deck already. His knowledge of firearms and gunpowder had caught the eye of the ship's Master Gunner, a massive badger who went by the name 'Ogre'. He spent most of his days learning from the senior Gunners now, learning how to maintain and operate the cannons. He actually really seemed to be enjoying himself.

Personally, I liked the masts and the sails. I can't even entirely say why, but I found the massive, billowing sails in particular to be quite beautiful, especially when the sun set on them and lit them up with fiery hues. I wanted to climb the rigging like the men who worked on them did and see how far the ocean stretched.

And one day, about a month and a half into the trip, Grayson gave me a chance. I'd asked him numerous times about what sorts of training and what sorts of abilities he expected of the men who worked on the rigging. And one day, he simply stated, "Grit. It's all you really need. Grit, and a good hand at tying knots," he glanced down at me, at that. "And I know you've got that."

"I have small hands," I said with a smirk, then swept my eyes up the largest central mast of the ship. At the very top of it was a perch, sort of a basket of some sort, which I couldn't see much of even from the top deck, but I knew a man was usually posted there. Grayson had told me it was called a 'Crow's Nest', which I'd chuckled at, even though he'd never understand the irony.

"That mast," I said looking up it. "It's—"

"The main mast," Grayson said, his eyes following mine. "Usually the biggest hurdle for men to climb."

"It seems simple enough to climb," I murmured, looking along the many routes up the mast. There were even pegs set into the mast specifically for climbing, by the look of them.

"It's not the physical climb that's the issue," the wolf chuckled. "It's the fear. And not just because of how tall it is. You get tossed about like a rag doll up there. Every little wave sways the topmost points of the ship far more than down here." He glanced down at me, and gestured up. "What?" He smirked, "Do you think you could handle it?"

"I think so," I said, my eyes on the distant, currently empty sentry's post.

Grayson chuckled. "Many men do, until they get to the top. That's that midway platform there."

"I can do it," I said, setting my mind to it now.

"By all means," the wolf said with a smirk, stepping aside. "Show me what you're made of, girl. If you freeze up, I'll send a man up to get you."

"That won't be necessary," I snapped at him. Grayson just put his paws up, chuckling.

I made for the mast. Two rats who were working on a sail nearby watched me as I went, one of them chuckling and muttering something to the other. He pulled out a flask from his belt, and they watched me as I made my way for the shrouds, the webs of net-like ropes that would take me as far as the top platform. Farther if I wanted to climb them at their narrowest point. I'd see when I got that high.

The shrouds shook the most when I first began climbing them, near the deck. They swayed slowly with the boat as it was, and the weight of my body only worsened it, the shifting seas and winds making it an unsteady climb.

I'd never really had much of a fear of heights, but once I started reaching the midway point, the sheer scale of what I was doing started to occur to me, and I began to hesitate. I made the mistake of looking down, at the enormous ship, which was beginning to look remarkably small, now.

My heart froze in my chest, and I willed myself to push forward while I still could. I made it to the top, the broad platform that was about two-thirds of the way up the mast, and after scrambling onto it and gripping at the wood of the broad mast, and digging my claws in, I took a long, shuddering breath, and closed my eyes for a little while. Up this high, all the noise from the deck seemed distant, far away. All I could hear was wind, and the sea. The view was spectacular, but also terrifying, and I wasn't even all the way up yet.

I looked back at the shroud in loathing. It began to grow more and more narrow, the closer it got to the top, and it was looking less and less appealing. The winds up here seemed fiercer, and I just wanted so badly to stay closer to the mast.

Apparently this was a common thought for the men who came this high, because there was a ladder, small but firmly set in to the mast that went up the rest of the way. I wasn't even certain if using it would be safer than the shroud, but it felt like it would.

I gripped the first few rungs and mentally pushed myself to climb, and I did, and I made it probably ten feet or so, before I had to look at my footing to assure myself I was really standing on the ladder, and the dizzying reality of how high I was above the world beneath finally hit me like a lightning strike.

My body froze. I just went still, gripped by some primordial fear that wouldn't allow me to move any further. Even my heart seemed to have stopped. I was certain, absolutely certain, that I was going to fall if I so much as moved my arms. I clung to the ladder, terrified, not knowing what to do. I had to go back down. The crow's nest was barely twenty feet away, but I had to go down, or I'd die.

I heard the sound of claws on the planks of the top platform beneath me, and registered that there might be someone else coming up to get me, but I didn't want to look down. Gods, this was humiliating...

"You're doing good, lovely," a voice said soothingly from immediately beneath me, and I instantly recognized it as Grayson. I felt his presence beneath me on the ladder, and one of his hands slipped up to settle on my back. "Come on now," he urged, "just a bit further. You're not gonna fall. But if you do, you can fall on me, alright? Come on now."

I held fast to the ladder, and nodded quickly, swallowing back the lump in my throat.

"Focus on the basket," he said, calmly. "Think of how much better you'll feel when you're safe inside it."

I narrowed my eyes, and willed my shaking hand to release one of the rungs of the ladder, and move upwards, to the next. And once that first seal was broken, my body began to respond to me again. I thought back on everything I'd overcome, everything I'd conquered in the past, and in comparison, one small ladder wasn't so much of a challenge. I'd wanted to do this. I'd told myself I could. I would do this.

The remaining rungs went by in a blur, and then I was grabbing at the edge of the basket, scrambling up over it as quickly as my body could manage, and tumbling down inside into the safety of the enclosing, firm wooden planks. I gasped and just lay there for awhile, willing myself to stop shaking. At some point I heard the thunk of two heavy paw-pads landing on the wood beside me, and felt the wolf lean down over me. He was offering me his hand.

"You know," he said, with a slight smile, "almost no one makes it up here the first time. I'm honestly impressed."

I took his dark-furred hand, trying not to show how much I was shaking. He lifted me, and I swayed some, which he used as an opportunity to grab me around the waist. The gesture brought me back to reality somewhat, and I glared up at him. He just smirked back down at me.

"I'm fine now," I said, shoving his hands off, and moving slowly towards the edge of the basket. I placed my hands over the rim, and slowly lifted my eyes from my feet to the horizon beyond. And it nearly took my breath away.

It was late into the day, far from when the sun would set, but it was beginning to dip in the sky, sending sparkling currents out over the waves, like rippling rivers of gold. The clouds sweeping in from the north were sparse and wispy, catching perfectly yellow along their undersides, like someone had painted them across the sky. And the horizon looked like it went on forever.

"Why does the ocean look curved?" I asked the wolf, noting the oddity only now that I was this high up. I thought it was a trick of the eye, at first. It was so slight.

"The world is round," the wolf said, from over my shoulder. I looked up at him, shocked, and he just nodded. "They've proven it," he informed me, "sailors have been able to travel from the eastern Huudari lands and the Kadrush to Carvecia. There are even talks of establishing a trade route between our east and your west, but I don't know the seas there. It's a brave new frontier. There are even some who say there's another continent, somewhere to the south between the two continents."

"There's so much I don't know..." I said softly, my eyes returning to the horizon.

"The world is a vast and wondrous place," Grayson agreed, in a remarkably introspective tone, for him. "And there's only so much of it you can see, landlocked. Especially amongst the tribes, unfortunately."

I looked up at the wolf, at his dreaded mane and the beads strung along it, and I narrowed my eyes a moment, before saying in Katuk, "Where do you really hail from, wolf?"

The man eyed me, not responding for some time, but I saw the recognition there.

"You understood me," I said with dawning realization. "Were you a tribesman before you began this life?"

"I'm not an orange, lovely," the wolf said with a sly smirk, "you don't just get to peel me back and get at the sweet center just like that."

I gave a frustrated sigh. "Why not? I'm curious about you. Shouldn't that stoke your ego some?"

"It does," he agreed, "but you ought to know by now, I don't believe in giving something valuable away for nothing." He leaned back against the railing casually, still smirking at me.

I crossed my arms over my chest. "Is there anything you want other than sex?" I asked, dryly.

"Just trust," the wolf said, evenly. "And that can't be bought. Like you said yourself, it has to be earned. And I'm a hard man to impress." He smiled knowingly at me, smugly returning my own sentiments.

"You walk around naked all day, boast about all your lawless conquests, and I found you unconscious and drooling under a bar table," I pointed out. "What could you possibly have to hide that's worse than that?"

"Personality flaws?" The wolf offered.

"Being a pirate—"

"Privateer," he corrected me.

"—a drunkard, a shameless letch, and an all-around asshole aren't personality flaws?"

"At sea, most would call those assets," the wolf smirked. I sighed, and he waved a hand at me. "Everyone has secrets, lovely."

"Please just call me Shivah," I muttered.

"I would if I thought for a moment it was your real name," the wolf replied with an arched eyebrow.

I snapped a finger at him, "You are from the tribes, or you wouldn't know that!"

"Ah, damn. Tipped my hand," the wolf lamented, playfully. "Well in any case, you can hardly blame me for keeping secrets when you're doing the same."

"Would you at least tell me one thing?" I asked. "Why are you really going to this continent? You know why we are. You already said this trip wasn't worth the risk to you, so why are you doing it? I want to know what we're in for, especially since all my friends are on your crew," I said pointedly. Grayson gave a deep sigh, and looked out to sea.

"I'm going down to that god-forsaken place because I have shite friends," he muttered, at length. "One in particular, who's in desperate straits."

"I hope he's a good man," I said, "if you're putting your mens' lives on the line to help him. And for our sakes, if we're going to have to trust him..."

"Hardly," the wolf snorted. "The only difference between men like him and Privateers like me is the uniform. But I owe him. My life and my fleet. Like I said, old debts." He didn't seem to want to linger on the subject much after that, so I let it drop, but he had another distraction in mind. He tugged something from beneath his coat, where I swear he could have kept a few cannon balls, if he tried hard enough. He'd produced so many bizarre trinkets from the 'coat realm', as I'd begun to refer to it, I often wondered if there was a doorway there that led to another world.

I recognized this particular item, though. It was a spyglass. I'd seen him use it before. I looked at it hopefully, and he smiled. "Go ahead," he said, handing it to me gingerly, "just be careful. Don't drop it."

I held it tightly, and squinted to peer through it, sweeping it first down to the deck, where I was able to see the men moving about as clear as day. I laughed, giddy at how marvelous the strange thing was and wondering at how it worked, then I swept it up over the horizon, watching the waves in the distance. It was hard to believe how far away they were, looking at them through the glass.

And then I saw something bizarre. Something I hadn't expected, considering we were two weeks away from land, as far as I knew.

"Are you certain we're two weeks from landfall?" I asked Grayson, curiously.

"Ten days maybe, with these winds," the wolf mused, "Why?"

"Are there any islands nearby?"

Grayson got an inquisitive tone. "Not on the charts, although sometimes we stumble across unexpected landmasses. Not usually this far out, though. Why?" He leaned over my shoulder. "The waves can create the illusion of land sometimes, perhaps—"

I shook my head, still keeping my gaze on the bizarre specks I'd noticed. I was fairly certain now... I could see wings. "It's not land," I said, "it's birds."

"What?!" the wolf suddenly snapped, and grabbed the spyglass out of my hands. He looked through it for a few moments, searching for what I'd seen, and then he froze. I watched his expression shift from concern to outright alarm.

"Could they be coming in from another ship?" I offered. I wasn't sure if that was good or bad.

"They are," he grit out from between his teeth, and thrust the spyglass back into my hands, reaching over to the mast to a long rope that was dangling just a foot or so above our heads, and tugged on it. A bell, which I hadn't seen until now, began to ring out, fiercely loud. I saw the specks of the men beneath begin to scurry around in a frenzy, and soon, answering bells were ringing out over the entire ship.

"What's going on?" I asked, alarmed.

"Those aren't birds," the wolf growled, looking down at his ship, and back to the horizon, as he hefted himself back over the edge of the basket to the ladder.

"What are they, then?" I called after him.

"Drakes," the wolf said, in dread and revulsion. "Look again. Tell me, does it look like any of them are carrying anything?"

"'Carrying anything'?" I echoed, confused.

"Just check for me, please!" the wolf snapped.

I looked into the spyglass again, hurriedly seeking out the specks on the horizon again. Although by the time I did, they had grown far larger, and Grayson was right. They did *not* look like birds. In fact, I could see what looked like long tails, now, silhouetted against the sun. And they were coming in fast. They were already four times larger than when I'd last seen them.

And what had once looked like two of them was beginning to solidify into a bizarre silhouette. A round ball of some sort, dangling beneath one of the strange creatures.

"Ah... y-yes," I said, "I think so. Maybe... looks like two of them are carrying something..."

"Bloody bombers!" Grayson growled, real fear in his voice now. I quickly stowed the spyglass and hefted myself over the edge of the barrel, following him as he went hurriedly down. For some reason, with the wolf so frantic and concerned, the last thing on my mind was my fear of being so high, and I was able to follow him without freezing up.

"What are they? What are they carrying?" I asked, as we dropped down onto the top platform, and the wolf stopped there, grabbing at the edge of it and screaming down at one of the rats far beneath us, "Bring the sails in, damnit! Now!"

I made it to his side at that, and the wolf pulled out his pistols, one by one, checking them. "Drakes," he growled, "carrying fire bombs. Baskets of burning pitch and tar, and whatever else they feel like loading those blasted things with. They sunk my fourth boat a few years back. The Leverage." He snarled, shoving the last of his pistols into his bandolier. "We have to take them down before they get close."

"I thought you set fires to your own boats all the time..." I muttered.

The wolf gave a shake of his head, and a dark laugh. "Not when my hold is stuffed to the brim with gunpowder, lovely."

My eyes widened. "A-all of those barrels..."

"Like I said, love," the wolf growled, irritated, "we have to take them down before they get close."

CHAPTER 4

New Enemies, New Allies

I watched the wolf clambering down the shroud to join his men, and set my mind. I swung down into the interconnected network of ropes that made up the shroud and began dropping down, quickly, catching up to Grayson and landing on the deck almost the same time he did. He was already shouting orders at his men, and the flurry of activity on deck was impossible to follow, but the men all seemed to know what to do.

"I need my bow!" I shouted at the wolf, as he was in the middle of a hurried conversation with the big badger, our Master Gunner. He held up a hand while he finished with the large man.

"I want a dozen of the best teams on the twelve pounders!" he shouted over the din of the noise on-deck, "And I want you and your three best men on the swings! Keep the carronades manned, too, I know they've got ships nearby and they'll try for a ram if they get near—"

"The bloody fliers are too fast," the badger said, shaking his head, "even for the swings..."

"I don't care!" Grayson shouted, and then a sound like thunder rang out, and the boat shook.

"We're just wasting shot, at this range!" The badger roared, over the wake of the deafening noise. I had no idea how the men could hear anything after that, but it had hardly seemed to bother them. I still had my hands over my ears.

"I gave the order to fire a volley," Grayson said, clapping a hand over the man's shoulder. "I have reason to believe we'll be expecting company!"

"What?" the badger and I both said in unison.

Grayson pointed skyward, to where a bird was circling the foremast. It looked like his falcon, judging by the coloration. And it was grasping something long and red in its talons, trailing in the wind behind it like a scarf.

"I want it raining iron, you hear me?!" Grayson shouted, as another volley fired off into the sea towards the approaching creatures. "I don't care if you're missing! Just keep them circling until we can pick them off!"

At that, he strode off, ducking under a line of flags, as they were being raised by the signal lieutenant, an exotic-looking spotted yellow feline. I followed his long strides as quickly as I could, shouting again, "I need my bow!"

"You'd have to be an incredible shot to hit those beasts," Grayson called back over his shoulder, as he strode down the staircase from the quarter deck towards the main gun deck. "You can't shoot them anywhere in the torso. They've natural armor, nothing but harpoons pierces it. Have to hit the head, legs or wings. And I mean somewhere that counts, you can tear the hell out of the webbing and they'll still fly! Bloody beasts never stop until they're dead."

"I can do it!" I shouted, insistently.

He turned to look at me for a moment, then dug into his pocket and pulled out a ring of keys, tossing it at me. "I locked your weapons in my chest," he said. "They're yours if you want them. Best of luck. I'll be with the wheel man."

"Doing what?" I asked, confused.

"Making sure he doesn't get killed," the wolf growled. "These beasts understand our boats. They're smarter than you'd think. They'll go for the swing cannons and the wheel first, save the ones guarding the bombers. Do you really think you can bring one of them down?" He asked, intently.

I nodded, even though I wasn't certain. I could damn well try.

"Prioritize the bombers," he said. He turned to leave, and then, as an afterthought, said, "And take care of yourself. You still have an almost promise to fulfill to me." He grinned and showed his fangs as he said that, then took off for the stern.

I made it to his cabin faster than I think I ever had, unlocking the door and heading inside, going for the chest immediately. Inside it I found everything the Quartermaster had taken from me when we'd come on-board, and I double-checked everything to make sure it was still intact first, then slung my gear over my shoulder and hurried outside again.

On my way out, I thought I saw Ransom... The coyote was tall and tended to stand out, and I moved my way through the throngs of men on the upper gun deck to get to him, nearly bumping into him as he attempted to shove his way past Ewan, our Master Lieutenant. The two seemed embroiled in an argument, and I noticed that Ransom also had his bow on him.

"Ransom!" I called out, and the coyote turned and regarded me with relief.

"Damn, there you are!" He exclaimed, then grabbed me by the shoulder. "Shivah, I don't know what the hell's going on, but the Quartermaster gave us back our weapons, and I don't think that bodes well, seein' as they ain't done that yet—"

"There are enemies coming in!" I shouted, as another volley rung out, this time followed by four punctuated smaller shots. "Flying enemies!"

"What in the blue blazes tha' flies could threaten this behemoth?" The coyote asked, confused, but by that point I'd seized his arm and was yanking him away from Ewan.

"I told you t' get to your post!" The rat yelled, then finally seemed to notice me. "Ah..." he paused, "unless th' Admiral's needin' him."

"Yes, that exactly," I said, nodding.

"Aye, then, go!" The rat muttered.

And we did. I half-dragged Ransom towards the main mast, asking as we went, "Where's Magpie?"

"With the gunners!" the coyote yelled back. "He made friends real fast, I guess. They said they wanted him with that badger!"

I nodded, glad to know the rat would be somewhere shooting at these creatures. No matter how hard they were to hit, if anyone had a chance at hitting one of them with a cannon, it was him.

When I began climbing the shroud, the coyote stopped in place. "What 'n the hell are you doin'?!" he demanded.

"Getting somewhere they'll have trouble reaching us!" I shouted down. "Come on!"

The coyote followed me, a bit uncertainly at first, but the man had never been shy of climbing trees, and though he managed it a little slower than I did, before long, we'd made it to the top platform.

"Nice view..." the coyote muttered, gazing out over the ocean and the crew beneath. Apparently for all his issues with seasickness, he had less issue with heights than even I did. "Alright," he admitted, "this's a good sniper post, I'll give ya that."

"All the rigging should make it hard for them to come in after us, too," I said, as I pulled an arrow, "they looked big, Ransom."

"Like how big?" The coyote asked, concerned, as he pulled his own. "Like bigger 'n a vulture big?"

"Like bigger than a person big," I said, looking to the horizon. I could see them with the naked eye now, and there were a lot more of them than I'd even seen with the spyglass, before. A veritable flock.

The coyote whistled, and nocked an arrow, raising it to the skyline, "Remind me t' get a trophy," he said with a bit of a grin, "boys back home won't believe this."

"Aim for the ones carrying those big baskets," I said. "They're full of fire, somehow. Grayson said they're going to try to light the boat up."

"What?!" the coyote balked. "How'n the hell does he know that?"

"Apparently he used to have four ships..."

"Shit," the canine snarled, squeezing one eye shut as he tried to focus on the incoming beasts. "I swear to god, Shivah, if I die on this rottin' boat—"

"Is Puck safe?" I demanded.

"In th' hold with the other non-coms," the coyote nodded, then focused back on the approaching, strange winged creatures. "Hell. They're comin'."

As the strange beasts began to solidify into our true range of sight, I saw why it had been so difficult to make them out, before. They were blue, nearly the same color as the sky. Had they not been silhouetted, we may not have seen them until they were much closer. They looked like absolutely nothing I had ever seen before. Their wings were almost like a bat's, but they had long necks, and perhaps bird-like heads. It was hard to tell. It was clear they all had talons much like a bird, but their legs seemed longer, and they had tails that were nearly the length of their body trailing behind them as they flew.

And they were enormous. Again, it was hard to tell just how large just yet, but by the look of it, they had to be somewhere near as tall as a man if not taller, and their wingspan was thrice that. An eagle's talons could do enough damage... I was terrified to consider what being caught by one of these beasts might do.

"I see one 'a the ones carryin' something!" Ransom shouted, training his bow on one as he tried to line up a shot. I followed his line of sight and aimed for the same creature, but there were three others flying beside and in front of it, and they were not going to make the shot easy. To make matters worse, just as they got within range, the creatures peeled off into two different formations, their movements in unison, yet organized, like a flock of birds, but far faster.

And as soon as they changed from coming head-on to sidelong, aiming for them became a lot harder. I'd never tried to shoot at something that moved so swiftly.

"I can't line up!" Ransom shouted, as another volley rocked the boat beneath us. It split the formation of drakes up, but I didn't see a single one fall from the sky.

"It doesn't matter, take the shot while we have it!" I shouted at him over the sound of my ears ringing.

We both fired into the same formation, aiming for the one we could see carrying the basket, which I could now tell was visibly trailing cinders and smoke in a dark line in the sky. I'm not sure which of our arrows struck one of the drakes, but one of the ones flying interference screeched—a sound I could hear even from where I was—and bucked in the sky, its wings floundering as it lost altitude. It stabilized too late, and juked down towards the boat, aiming for the stern, just as Grayson had said they would.

I heard the sound of the heavy creature striking the deck, and another piercing screech, followed by the sounds of the men beneath shouting and screaming as they engaged the beast. I saw Ransom's eyes dropping to the melee beneath, and the coyote uttered, "Bloody gods below..."

"Stay on target!" I commanded the man, already lining up my next shot. The cannons were doing their job, forcing the flocks to circle around the rain of gunfire, and stay at a distance for now. I circled the top platform and tried to catch sight of the bomber again, and at length, I did. Irritatingly, another of the drakes from its flock had filled in the gap the fallen one had left, closing the hole. I cursed under my breath, and tried to line up another shot.

But then I saw the second, finally, coming in in a third flock, from the stern of the ship.

"Ransom!" I shouted.

"I see it," the coyote said between grit teeth. "She's mine. You take th' other."

I loosed my arrow, aiming for my bomber, but the shot went wide entirely, the drakes splitting their formation at the last moment to avoid fire from below us, likely the swing guns by the sound of it.

I nocked an arrow quickly and aimed for the bomber while its brethren were out of formation, and I heard it screech and turn its wings, lifting up higher on an updraft. I was all but certain I'd hit it, but it wasn't going down like the other had.

"Damn!" I growled. I must have hit it in the torso. I could vaguely see the fletching on my arrow catching in the sunlight, protruding from the creature's chest, but it wasn't slowing down.

"Aim for the wings!" I shouted behind me to the coyote. "If we can at least take them down—"

"Hard with 'em turned to the side like tha'!" The coyote replied.

"I know..." I growled, then swept my eyes down to the deck, where the crews were hurried re-loading cannons. I suddenly had an idea.

"Wait for the carronades and the swings to fire!" I told Ransom. "They cut formation when they do, and when they turn into the winds, they're a larger target!"

"Right," the coyote nodded, and we both nocked our bows, waiting.

One of the flocks was cutting through the barrage of much-less accurate cannon fire from the gun decks, and using the chance to beeline for the deck while the swings and the carronades were re-loading. I knew the men behind them saw it, and would be highly motivated to aim at the charging flock, but it was the only flock that didn't have a bomber in it, and I suspected that was their plan. They were a diversion.

I had to hope Grayson saw through it. Letting them through would mean heavy casualties on deck, but it would give the two flocks with the bombers and opening to come in. And it would mean we'd have no opening to shoot at them.

We waited with baited breath for the shots to come, and they never did. The flock of drakes bull-rushed into the front line of men manning the upper decks. I heard pistol shots ring out, and the roar of men as they intercepted the massive creatures. But when the cannons finally came, they were aimed at the two circling flocks, just as I'd hoped. I was glad that call hadn't been mine, but it had been the right call.

"Wait for it!" I shouted to Ransom, as the drakes broke formation to avoid the hail of cannon-fire. And much to my shock, someone hit one of the defense-line drakes protecting my bomber, blowing a hole through its wing and sending it spinning down into the ocean. I saw it wheel and twist in the air, trying to no avail to land on the deck instead, which would have been a death sentence regardless, but it might have landed on someone.

The single act took my breath away. These beasts were beyond determined. I wanted—needed—to know what compelled a creature to fight with such desperation, to its dying breath. But right now, I had to focus. The drake carrying my bomb had to turn into the wind to reconnect with its flock, and when it did, its body was briefly vertical. I aimed, and fired.

I didn't see the arrow hit from so far away, but I saw the creature's left wing jerk downwards, curling up and sending it into a spin. It tried to force its wing back open, but I was fairly certain I'd hit it near the joint where it connected to its body, and it couldn't right itself. In a last, desperate effort, it swung its legs forward and released the chain holding the brazier, the flaming metal basket plummeting forward as far as it could throw it towards the ship. My breath caught in my chest, terrified my shot would ultimately mean nothing, but the brazier only succeeded in striking the soaked outer hull near the bow, banging off of it and falling into the ocean with a blast of steam and sea foam.

I heard Ransom hoot from beside me, and turned just in time to see his own bomber plummeting from the sky. It looked like he'd caught it in the wing as well, although closer to the middle joint. Our celebration was too soon, as it turned out. One of the drakes near to the bomber swept in, and as if they'd timed it, the plummeting beast released its hold on the chains to the brazier, just as the other snapped them up.

"Ruttin' hell, that ain't bloody fair!" The coyote yelled in disbelief.

"It's coming in!" I shouted, terrified but trying to steady my arm as I lined up another shot at the new bomber. I knew the swings wouldn't be firing again for at least a few seconds, and the beast either knew it as well, or didn't care. It was headed right for the center of the ship, where the upper gun deck was open to the air. I knew they kept gunpowder there, a lot of gunpowder... And if that brazier fell on a barrel, one explosion was all it would take to penetrate down through to the next deck, and the next, until... The hold.

I had one shot at this, and it had to count.

Ransom and I both stood on the edge of the top platform, lining our shots... And then I heard one rifle shot, amidst the hail of pistol fire and the clashing, screeching sounds of melee below, and the bomber just stopped, mid-air, its body seizing and a spray of red erupting from its head. Its momentum carried it straight down into the water in an explosion of spray, and there was an eruption of cheering from the men on deck.

"Ten t' one says that was Gabriel," Ransom said with a toothy grin, reaching for another arrow as he leaned down over the platform. I went with him, finally taking stock of the melee beneath.

And it was a disaster.

There were five of them on the deck, two of which looked too overwhelmed to last much longer, but the other three had effectively carved a circle around them of bodies and terrified men keeping their distance, as the beasts snapped and screeched. And those were only the drakes who'd been brought down. The ones still flying, of which there were still many, were coming down in droves, and tearing swaths across our decks, until they caught one of our hapless men and smeared them across the deck with their sharp claws, or more frequently, just picked them up and took off with them.

"I'm low on shot," Ransom admitted, lining up a shot at one of the downed creatures and taking careful aim. From here, we had an excellent vantage point, but we had to shoot down through rigging and try to avoid our own men, and it wasn't easy. His shot struck one of the beasts in the back, but it looked to have taken many such injuries already and was fighting like a caged Dyre. I narrowed my eyes and took aim at the same beast, taking the chance at a head shot.

I hit, and the beast gave one last fading, gurgling roar, before pitching forward onto the ground and being beset upon by sailors desperate to ensure it was truly dead.

"I'm low, too," I said, reaching into my quiver to check. Three more arrows.

"We need to make these count," I said, shouldering my bow and grabbing at the shroud, beginning the trip down. Ransom wasn't far behind me.

But on the way down, we unfortunately made very visible targets of ourselves, and I saw one of the creatures coming in, fast. Ransom saw it, too, but there really wasn't much we could do. It was still too far down to jump, and we couldn't climb any faster than we already were.

The coyote pulled his large hunting knife and gripped the ropes, staying in place near the outer edge of the shroud.

"What are you doing?!" I called up, in shock.

"Just go! I'll catch up!" Ransom shouted back down.

I wanted to tell him he was insane, that we couldn't take these beasts on in mid-air, but at that moment he kicked my hand and I had little choice but to drop it to the next rung of rope below. As expected, the drake went for the higher target, and I could do little but watch.

Ransom waited until the beast was almost atop him, his body tense and poised, and then, just as it closed in on him, raising its talons and diving down for him, he leapt from the shroud and fell, holding on with one hand to the outer rope edge, and letting the momentum swing him around to the other side of the shroud, while the drake ran into the side he'd been on not moments earlier, its legs tangling in the ropes, and very nearly still grabbing at the coyote on the other side. Ironically if its talons had been smaller, they might have fit through the squares of ropes, but instead the beast caught in it like a net.

And then Ransom gave a roar, and drove his knife into any part of the beast he could reach through the shroud, clearly trying to aim for its neck, and succeeding several times. It snapped at the shroud and frantically tried to disentangle its talons, but the coyote fearlessly drove his knife into the beast's flesh again and again, until its motions began to slow and it gave a blood-curdling screech.

And then the coyote drove the knife up through the roof of its mouth, and the drake finally slumped and went lifeless. Its' body swung down towards me, and I hurriedly leapt down a few rungs of the shroud as it nearly swept me off into the ocean.

Ransom and I made it down to the deck amidst a sea of chaos. I immediately drew and nocked an arrow, and took a shot at one of the drakes that was most up and moving, and causing a sizable amount of harm. It was an easy shot, but when they were on the ground, though less graceful, it was harder to debilitate them unless you shot them in the head.

I managed to hit mine somewhere near what was their 'clavicle', which it certainly didn't seem to like, but it didn't drop it. Ransom aimed and fired at the beast right after I did, though, and his shot hit its neck, briefly stunning it enough that one of the men on deck, a massive bear who was fearless enough to charge it, got past its defenses and ran a sword up through its chin into its head.

"That was my last," the coyote said regrettably, pulling his knife again.

"I'll cover you with what I have left," I said. "We have to get to the stern!"

We took off past a crew of men manning one of the carronades, the air around us erupting into a cloud of noxious smoke as it fired. I could see the silhouette of one of the drakes working its way towards the stern, towards the wheel.

"Where the hell's your lover at?!" Ransom yelled, over the ringing in both of our ears.

"Oh my gods," I growled, in disgust, "he is not my lover!"

"Whatever you say, precious," the coyote said, then gave a shout and fell to the deck, as one of the drakes strafed by us. I just barely avoided being its target as well. It closed its talons around a fleeing canine, and I heard the man scream in terror as it began to lift him into the air.

I narrowed my eyes and lined up a shot, determined not to let this happen right in front of my eyes. I didn't even know the man, but it didn't matter. I caught the beast in the meat of its thigh, and it screeched and made to retreat, but more importantly, it let go of its prey, the man tumbling and rolling across the deck.

That's when I heard Grayson's voice over the din, shouting at the men who were trying to barricade the one drake who was determinedly cutting a path towards the wheel. I pressed forward through the masses towards the melee, just in time to see the wolf leaping down from the railing on the quarter deck, and giving what I swear sounded like a laugh as he descended onto the beast like he was trying to ride a bull.

He landed atop it, and slammed a stiletto down into the meat of where its shoulders connected to its wings. There looked to be a lot of muscle there, and I was all but certain he'd been going for the spine, but it didn't look like he'd penetrated through.

The beast tossed, but the wolf held fast to the knife he had embedded in its back and hung on, gripping his sword in his other hand and swinging the saber down towards the creature's neck. He was being tossed back and forth, though, and it looked like he was having trouble getting a clean blow through.

"That man is bleedin' crazy!" Ransom shouted from beside me, as we neared the fight.

But at that moment, I caught sight of something over the railing of the ship. I hadn't been looking out to sea for quite some time, and now that I was, I saw something that could have been terrifyingly bad for us. Or a gift from the gods.

There was another ship, closing in on us. It looked large, maybe not as large as the Manoratha, but definitely not one of

Grayson's two small frigates. I could see them, far closer to us and trying desperately to aim for the drakes remaining in the air, while still skirting our line of fire, but having as little luck as the cannons on our ship were. The drakes seemed to be ignoring them entirely.

But this new ship was coming in fast, riding the winds by the look of the billowing sails, and I could only hope this was the 'company' Grayson had eluded to, or this fight was going to tip decidedly not in our favor.

I heard a distant, crackling boom, and one of the two remaining flocks that was wheeling farther out to sea had to break apart from a V formation into a chaotic, loose mob. And then there was another, far more subdued series of booming noises from the ship, and three of the drakes fell from the sky.

I let out a breath. I had absolutely no idea what they were firing. They didn't sound like cannons, but they were clearly here to help.

We got to Grayson just in time to watch as his men finally overwhelmed the beast making its way for the wheel, the wolf swinging once more down at its neck as it was bogged down and less able to move, and with a spray of gore, its neck fell forward halfway like a partially severed log, and it slumped and fell over, its head dangling limply from the stem of its spine.

"And the cavalry arrives!" The bloody wolf hollered, plucking his knife from the drake's back and leaping back down onto the deck. He shook off one of his swords and called out over the railing, as though the distant ship could possibly hear him. "Better late than never, ey old boy?"

He chuckled, making his way over towards me, shaking his head. "Amurescans," he said with an exhilarated grin, "always late to the party!"

"This party ain't over yet," Ransom growled, his point accentuated by a scream, as one of the still-circling drakes tried to swoop and grab at a man, and just struck him instead, pitching him overboard.

Grayson winced, then nodded. “Aye. Well, let’s polish this thing off, then, shall we?” He looked to me, and flipped up his short sword into his hand, offering it to me.

I took the blade somewhat uncertainly. I didn’t want to tell him I’d never used a sword before. I’d used a knife, though, so at least I knew some of the basics of using a blade. And the tiny boot knife I had would do nothing against these beasts, so it was better than nothing.

“Stay close, lovely,” he said.

“Why aren’t they retreating?” I asked, watching as the creatures wheeled around us. At this point there was no way they could sink us. The most they could do was kill a lot more of our men before they were all killed themselves. It was almost sad.

“I’m guessin’ they don’t have a boat to return to,” Grayson said, darkly, “and this far out at sea, if they retreat, all they’ll do is exhaust themselves and die in the ocean before they get home.”

“What makes you so sure their ships’re gone?” Ransom asked, watching the macabre suicide battle play itself out. At this point we just had to wait for another one of them to dive onto the deck to take out.

Grayson gestured to the ship coming towards us, becoming more and more clear as it did. “That’s the Fenrir,” he said, with certainty, “If she’s out this far, she was following something. I’m guessing the boats those drakes came from. And Denholme doesn’t turn his back on Cathazra unless they’re on their way to the bottom of the ocean. Good way to die.”

He made his way towards the wheel man, and we followed. I heard another bang from much farther down the ship, where they’d either dropped another drake, or one had landed. Grayson put a hand on the wheel man’s shoulder, commanding him, “Hard turn to starboard! Let her come alongside.”

He looked back at us, pointing out towards the approaching galleon. “Look for red,” he said, as if we were to know what that meant, “if I know him, he’s going to play lure, and get the rest of those beasts down so we can finish this.”

"They attack red?" I asked, huffing as I hurried after the wolf on his way to the quarter deck.

"They attack him," he said with a loud laugh. "Lord, those beasts hate him... Ogre!" He shouted at the large badger, as we passed him, "get all the swing cannons turned to starboard. Expect a charge."

"Aye, sir," the man said, gruffly, then began to shout at his men. I saw Magpie re-loading one of the swing guns and taking aim.

We waited barely a minute or so more, during which time the drakes were quiet, mostly circling the two boats now, as they came up alongside us, and the sailors brave enough to go to the railings began tossing ropes between the two boats, and pulling us together. As we waited, I looked to the men moving about on the other ship, and the sails of the galleon. Unlike the Manoratha, almost all the men on-board this ship seemed to be in similar, if simple, uniforms. All of them had the red sashes across their waist. The sails had a strange design either sewn or dyed into them that resembled a red shield, with three stylized canine heads above it, and three crossed swords in front of it.

And then I saw red. Coming into sight from somewhere near the ship's stern, a man wearing a bright scarlet coat moving amidst a group of other soldiers, and making his way down towards the gang plank. As if on cue, there was a chorus of screeching from overhead, and I looked up just in time to see the loose mob of remaining drakes circling together into a hastily-gathered formation, and diving down towards where the boats were joined—and more specifically, the man in red.

I was out of ammo, so I simply followed Grayson, Ransom and several of the other braver sailors, including the lion and a few more of Grayson's officers, towards the boarding party. We got to them at almost exactly the moment the drakes descended, and the scene erupted into chaos. Every man who'd had enough shot left to load his pistol or rifle loosed a round at the beasts, the swing guns and the twelve-pounders dropped several of the desperate drakes from the air, and what remained crashed down onto the deck, atop the group of men we'd been hoping to protect.

I ducked and wriggled my way through the mob of men collecting around the boarding party. Three of the drakes had overshot and were trying to fight their way through from the outside, but at least two were in the melee.

I managed to get into the circle of carnage just as Grayson broke through, mostly traveling in his wake, and caught my first sight of the strangers. They were almost all canine, save one gray rat and a fox. The man in red was pinned down by one of the drakes, its talons digging into his leg, as it tried to snap down at him like a bird pinning down its prey. He had his sword held up, shoved up against the corners of its mouth, just barely holding it back from his face. The rat beside him fired into the beast's ribs with a crossbow, but it didn't seem to care. It was single-mindedly focused on tearing the canine's head off.

Grayson charged into the fight, swinging at the beast's head while it was distracted, and raking its sword across one of its eyes. It shrieked and threw its head up in pain, momentarily relieving the canine it was pinning, and he used the chance to flip the sword to his right hand, press his left palm against the end of the hilt, and thrust it up through the creature's chest, which I'd been told was nigh on impossible to penetrate.

But he seemed to know just where to strike. There was a spot at the clavicle, where the armored plates came together, and his sword sunk into the creature like a knife through butter. It clamped its talon around his leg in its final spasms, and he grunted as he was yanked under it.

My eyes widened. It was about to fall on him.

I dashed forward with Ransom and Grayson, and the gray rat who'd been trying to shoot at the damned thing, and together, we managed to catch the beast before it crushed the canine pinned beneath it.

Grayson gave a growling yell of exertion, and my feet scrambled against the deck as I tried to help them. Slowly, we shifted the weight of the beast, lifting its body up enough that I could a least see the canine again. He was hacking at the talon gripping his leg, until it finally released, and then he hurriedly rolled free. At last, we were able to drop the creature, and I groaned, clutching at my shoulder. It had been all I could manage to lift my share, and it still felt like I'd pulled something.

But all around us, the sounds of the battle were dying down, and I was beginning to hear it replaced with something far more exhilarating—cheering.

I'd never been in a battle I'd felt so satisfied to win before. My eyes swept the deck as men dropped their weapons and gave their victory cries. Many knelt down to pray, and others began singing triumphant-sounding sea shanties. I slowly began to smile, sharing in the joy of the men all around me, and the jubilation at our victory. But life was about to teach me that no battle was ever entirely what it seemed.

A burbling, hoarse, strange voice was what stilled my joy. I turned slowly towards the sound, not certain I was truly hearing what it was I thought it was. But I was. The drake I'd thought felled was, in actuality, still alive, albeit bleeding out on the deck. I felt a shiver work its way up my spine as I heard the beast speak... really speak. It was the first sign I'd ever had these creatures were intelligent people. Not just beasts.

And it was speaking in rough Amurescan. Which meant they weren't just somewhat intelligent, they were able to learn foreign languages. Its eyes were clouding over as death approached, but even still, it wasn't looking at any of us in particular. It was just speaking, in its dying moments.

"leave... ." it said in a guttural, rattling hiss, "our... home. Demonsss... ."

But at that point, the man in red had limped his way around the body, and stopped beside the creature's fallen form. He looked down at it impassively for a moment, then thrust his sword down through the soft spot at the base of the drake's spine, and it went entirely still.

I closed my eyes, wincing back. The beast would have died, regardless, but something about the entire scene just made me feel wrong.

"Denholme, you dandy bastard," Grayson proclaimed, making his way towards the injured canine. He was shorter than the wolf by a bit, and had the bearing and build of a warrior, and strangely speckled fur. He was handling the bloody injury to his leg fairly well, all things considered, and even gave a mild smile at the wolf as he approached. Grayson chuckled as he slapped a palm into the Otherwolf's hand, and gave it a hearty shake. "You could have come around a little sooner, you know. We really could've used those harpoons earlier on."

"Yes, well," the canine said in the far richer accent I'd realized belonged to Amurescans by now, "we were a bit busy sinking the rest of the fleet. My apologies for your losses, though. We did attempt to chase them to the west, so they'd be coming in from the sun. They're all but invisible unless they're in silhouette."

"Nothing's ever just luck around you, cattle dog," the wolf chuckled. "I swear, you'd claim you planned out where the stars appear in the sky, if you thought I was gullible enough."

"I don't like to rely on luck," the Otherwolf said with a far more subdued, but equally cocky smirk as the wolf's. "Mine tends to be nothing but bad."

"Aye. What in the hell were these bastards doing out so far?" Grayson asked with a long sigh. "I didn't even have a sentry posted. I thought for sure we had a week more before we were into enemy waters."

The Otherwolf sighed. "They've been going farther and farther out to ensure they've thoroughly cut off our trade lines. And their fleet's blossomed to thrice its size in the last two years since this new Warleader took charge, so they can afford to. Bloody creature is organizing them, bringing in other clans." He looked to the sky. "I'm guessing you got spotted by a drake patrol some time back and didn't even realize it. We were headed out to escort you in when we saw the drakes ourselves."

"You came this far out for an escort?" the wolf whistled. "Must be bad times, cattle dog."

"Tell me you have the cargo..." the Otherwolf said, belaying some of his desperation, beneath the calm mask.

"Aye, every barrel," the wolf replied. "And after this one, Denholme, you owe me. This is the craziest bloody thing I've ever put my crew through, and you know that's saying a lot."

The man in the red coat gave a long sigh. "Actually, I might have further need of your help, since you're here."

"I see how it is," the wolf muttered. "You drag me into all of this, then trap me in a warzone."

"It wasn't intentional," the Otherwolf said intently, "I swear, Reed. I earnestly just needed powder, and I knew you'd be able to get it through to me. But things have changed since I sent the messenger. We're losing control, I..." he suddenly glanced around, and put a hand on the wolf's shoulder. "We'll talk later."

"Aye, sounds like it'd be for the best." Grayson agreed, his eyes flicking about to the surrounding crew. I thought he'd set his gaze on me, when I heard a familiar voice call out from behind me, over the loud din of the crowd.

"Shivah!" I turned, and saw the small fox hurrying as well as he could through the throngs of men. "Ransom!" he called out, a vastly relieved smile spreading over his small muzzle when he got close enough to us to smell us. He rushed to our side and made for the coyote, but paused a foot or so from him, and knit his paws in front of him. "I'm... I'm glad you're both alright," he said, his small frame trembling. "I was so scared for you. I-I just felt so helpless down there, hearing the cannons, a-and... gods, not knowing what was happening. They said it was all clear now. Are we safe?"

I gave him a soft smile and went to embrace him, but at that moment Grayson barked from nearly over my shoulder, "Fox! I've need of you!"

Puck's ears perked and he looked up, even though I knew he couldn't see the man. "Oh," he paused, "yes. There must be people hurt. I-I have to go work."

"It's fine, fox," Ransom said, putting a hand on his shoulder, his thumb subtly caressing the small creature's neck for a moment, before he released him. "Go do your thing."

I followed Puck towards Grayson, but Ransom seemed less interested in the wolf's company, and went off to join the men, instead. I saw him join Magpie and a few of the other gunners, and I gave a wave to the rat, who smiled at me and waved back. I hadn't for a moment been worried for the rat, I knew he was a survivor, but it was good to see him nonetheless.

By the time I reached the gathering of Officers, Puquanah was already unshouldering his pouch and hurriedly taking out his supplies. I heard the wolf and the Otherwolf leader arguing quietly as I approached.

"—because you have to maintain the chain of command, damnit," Grayson growled. "I'd think that'd matter even more to you. Officers get treated first. Stop being so bloody stubborn."

"I'll live," the canine shook his head. "Treat the dying men first."

"That's actually a very bad wound..." Puck murmured, catching both men by surprise. He was kneeling beside the Otherwolf, running a paw gingerly over the seeping, deep gashes in the man's leg.

The grey, speckled dog seemed to notice the fox for the first time, and limped backwards a step or two, arching an eyebrow down at the small vulpine. "I don't remember this one, Reed," he commented, curiously.

"Aye, he's a new hire," the wolf muttered.

"What happened to the stoat?"

Grayson cleared his throat. "You don't remember?"

The Otherwolf blinked. "Right. Basilisk."

"Mmnh."

"In all seriousness, though," the man—Denholme, Grayson had called him—said, "you have men on deck who are missing their legs, Reed. My wound can wait."

"Those men are already dead, Denholme," Grayson sighed, "I think we both know that. But fine, be a stubborn ass. You excel at it."

"You need to sit down," Puck said, again interrupting the two men. His tone was remarkably firm and commanding, considering he was speaking to two Admirals. I suppose the fox didn't really care much about rank on this ship or any other. Especially when it concerned healing.

"I'm fine," the Otherwolf repeated his sentiments from earlier.

"No you're not," Puck stated, standing and thrusting a wrapped poultice into Grayson's hands. The wolf blinked and looked down at it, confused. "He's going to pass out if you don't put pressure on that, and get him off his feet. He needs to elevate his leg." He gathered up his pack, "If you won't let me treat you before the others, at least do that. Your pride would be far more wounded if you fainted right here on the deck, wouldn't it?"

His statement managed to make the impassive, stoic-faced canine actually look moderately worried. As Puck headed off, I moved up beside Grayson, uncertain where else at the moment I should be. I couldn't help Puck treat the wounded, honestly... I'd just get in the way.

I wasn't bad with a poultice, though. I'd treated some of Ransom's wounds, and my own, and I was familiar with Puck's poultices and how to apply pressure to a bleeding wound.

"I can help," I spoke up quietly, a bit nervous about addressing the man. He had a very powerful presence about him, despite the fact that he wasn't exactly a large, intimidating man. He was half a foot shorter than Grayson, in fact.

"Let's head to my cabin," Grayson offered. "We need to speak privately, anyway."

The man nodded, flicking his gaze briefly down towards me. "This your cabin..." he paused, "girl? You've a woman on-board, Reed?" He got an odd smirk at that, and I was momentarily concerned. "Well, now. Flouting all traditions these days?"

"There are benefits to going independent, cattle dog," the wolf grinned and winked, "I keep telling you. You should give it a try."

"I might not have many other choices, when this whole mess is over," the Otherwolf sighed and winced, as we began to make our way to the gundeck, where Grayson's cabin was located.

"No rules, no restrictions, no judgment," the wolf said, emphasizing the last part, for some reason. I saw the cattle dog's eyes lower at that. "This is freedom, Denholme." He chuckled, spreading his arms as he walked down the stairs to the gundeck. I followed behind the two of them.

"Well, I congratulate your... open-mindedness," the Other-wolf said, politely. "And I'm all for flouting traditions. Even though I'm fairly certain that being progressive wasn't your primary motivation in keeping a woman on-board."

"Aye, she's a fine little piece, ain't she?" The wolf grinned.

"I wouldn't know," the grey canine muttered.

"Excuse me," I spoke up, irately. Both men turned to look at me, and the Otherwolf seemed surprised. "I'm right here. And I'm a competent member of his crew. I shot down one of those 'bombers' today."

"She speaks Amurescan?" the Otherwolf queried.

"I already—" I stopped at that, then sighed. I'd spoken to him in Katuk when I'd offered to help treat his wound. I'd gotten so used to speaking in Katuk to Grayson, since he understood it and it was my natural tongue. I hadn't even thought.

"My apologies," the man said, stopping at the foot of the stairs. "I thought there was a language barrier. Excuse my manners." He gave the slightest of bows at the waist, and my eyes widened a bit in surprise. "Luther Denholme." He extended a hand, gracefully, and I was momentarily taken aback. "It's a pleasure, miss... ?"

I paused, then tentatively reached a hand out to shake his. He didn't seem to expect the gesture, or perhaps the strength of my grip. "Shivah," I said at length. "Well met."

His look of surprise turned into a genuine, and I daresay impressed, smile. "Indeed. Well met. I apologize for my comment earlier. I didn't understand the situation. You're an archer?"

I nodded. "You shoot?"

He actually chuckled at that. "Very poorly, I'm afraid. Never had the knack or the eyesight for it. The best use I ever got out of a gun was as an improvised club."

I arched an eyebrow. "I'm not overly familiar with thundering weapons, but I'm fairly certain that's not how they're meant to be used."

The man, Luther, he'd said, and I made a mental note to try to remember the foreign name, shrugged. "It worked," he stated in his defense.

"Blast! I've never heard that one!" Grayson exclaimed from beside us, chuckling. "You'll need to share that story over a bottle sometime, Denholme. Sounds amusing as hell."

The Otherwolf's expression went humorless. "It really wasn't."

"We shouldn't dawdle," I said, pressingly, mostly to the Otherwolf, "if Puck said you're going to pass out if you stay standing too long, that's what's going to happen. We need to do as he said."

"'Puck'?" the Otherwolf queried, sounding somewhat amused and curious. But he got moving again, nonetheless.

"Yes, the fox. The healer," I stated, "he's a friend of mine. And he knows his trade."

"Cute name." the canine murmured, passing me on his way down the stairs. I let him go, and stared after him in befuddlement. It seemed an odd comment for such a serious man to make.

When we reached the upper gundeck, I realized that the scene here was almost no better than on the higher decks.

Several of the drakes had apparently targeted the hole in the center of the ship that led down to this deck, and their suicide charges may not have involved igniting gunpowder and destroying the ship, but they'd still done plenty of damage. There were four or five of their corpses strewn over the deck, one of which had scraped full across half the length of the deck and left much of its viscera in its wake. It had probably died on impact. The rest looked to have died in combat with the gunners and A.B.'s on the deck, though, and there were twice as many of our bodies as theirs.

We passed the corpse of one of the massive blue creatures as we made our way towards Grayson's cabin, and I saw the wolf stop, and stare at the disturbing scene for longer than I would have wanted to. This one seemed to have killed three of his men, and by the look of it, had done so with its toothy, beaked mouth. One man's chest was chopped meat, he'd probably died quickly, but one's leg was dangling partially off the side of the deck, and he had probably bled out.

But the most disturbing by far was the canine who was still moving. He wouldn't survive much longer. That much was very clear based on the bloody swath cut across his midsection. I saw shreds of nameless organ meat unfurled at his side, and he was twitching, and choking.

It certainly made me think twice about my pity for the similarly disemboweled drake who'd spoken on the upper deck. This whole thing made me feel so conflicted.

I couldn't look at the sight for longer than a few seconds, but Grayson was just staring. At length, I shifted my eyes back up to him, murmuring, "Grayson, we... we should go..."

He didn't respond, and another few worrying moments passed. I'd never seen him go this quiet before, and when I looked up into his eyes, they looked blank, like he wasn't even really seeing what was in front of him.

The canine beside me seemed concerned, too, and limped over to the wolf, putting a hand on his shoulder and dropping his voice.

"Reed," he said, in a quiet tone, "are you seeing lines?"

The wolf didn't respond, and I didn't know what to make of the question. Before I could ask, though, Luther spoke again, "Nod or blink twice if you can hear me..."

I watched Grayson intently, slowly coming to the realization that something was happening here I didn't entirely understand. But when the canine's words got no reaction whatsoever, the Otherwolf Admiral got a grim, worried expression and worked his shoulder up under the wolf's armpit, jerking his head back at me. "Get his shoulder," he instructed. "Help me get him to his cabin."

"What's wrong?" I asked, lost. "Can't he walk on his own—"

"Just do it, and do it quickly," the canine almost snapped. "We have to get him somewhere safe."

I rushed to the black wolf's side and tried to take his other shoulder, but he was heavy, and the Otherwolf had a limp, and moving him proved slow going. I was slowly growing terrified, as I realized the wolf wasn't just horrified or in some kind of shock. He wasn't responding at all. We all but had to drag him.

"Damnit," the Otherwolf cursed, "where's his bloody bodyguard?"

"Ariel?" I asked. "With... with Puck. He watches him when he's on rounds."

We reached the door, and found it locked. The Otherwolf cursed again, and I went to Grayson's belt, fumbling through the various trinkets he kept there until I found his key ring. I pulled it off and found the door key, grateful that by now, I knew which one it was. And then at last, we'd pushed the door open, and began to drag the heavy wolf inside.

And that's when he jerked in my arms, and I thought for a brief moment he was coming to, but he wasn't.

"Don't let him fall!" the Otherwolf Admiral growled, wincing as he took on most of the weight of the man and had to stand on his injured leg. I fumbled with my grip on the black wolf's body, but it was hard to keep a good grip on him. He was shaking. Violently.

Slowly, and primarily with the Otherwolf's help, we set him down on the wooden floor, and once we had him down, Luther looked back at the open doorway, pointedly. I dashed over to it and shut the door. When I turned back to look to the two men, Luther was pushing the chairs and Grayson's strongbox away from the wolf's fallen form. He grunted as he shoved the heavy strongbox, muttering to me, "Just get everything out of his way, or he'll hurt himself on it."

I grabbed up a few discarded items near the wolf's shaking form, a clay jug and my own pack of belongings, and looked down at him, mildly terrified. He looked like he was in pain, and I didn't see any injuries, which only made it that much more unknown and frightening. His head thrashed to the side with one particularly powerful spasm, and I went to go to him, to at least hold him so he didn't hurt himself.

"Don't," the Otherwolf said, putting a hand up. "Don't touch him. Don't hold him down. It's worse if you do."

I looked to him, wildly. "What's happening to him?" I demanded.

The man ran the back of his grey hand over his muzzle, sighing. "I don't entirely know, myself, but I've seen it happen to him before. The lion usually handles it, but there was a time Reed was on one of my ships for awhile, without him. He told me a bit about what to do if it happened."

"Is he hurt?" I asked, feeling more fear for the canine than I'd really thought I ever would. I suppose despite his salty, crass demeanor, I'd grown begrudgingly fond of the man.

"No, it's an illness, I think," the canine shook his head.

I looked back down at the wolf. "He's sick?" I asked quietly. He'd never said anything. Not even to squeeze some pity out of me. Whatever this was, it must have been intensely personal to him. This was a man that used the piss pot in the same room I was in, whether I was present or not, and liked to grade his belches like they were a sporting event. And he'd never once told me about this.

The tremors began to subside, slowly, punctuated now and then by a few last powerful twitches. At length, though, the wolf's body went slack, I saw his eyelids tremble and he blinked hazily a few times. I sat on my knees tensely, watching him and waiting for recognition to return, but eventually, even when his eyes had opened entirely, they didn't focus. He didn't speak... and he still had that lost look about him, like he was half-asleep or delirious.

The Otherwolf Admiral blew out a sigh and sat in one of the chairs near Grayson's table, putting his leg up and wincing as he began to roll up the pant leg of his britches. "I think it's passed," he muttered. "But the last time I saw this happen, he wasn't himself for a time. You can go to him now if you want, though."

I did. I scooched over carefully towards the fallen black wolf, and gingerly reached out to the tangled, tousled dreads of fur strewn beneath his head. I slowly lifted his head in my hands and straightened his neck out some. It looked to be so painful, twisted the way it had been. I stroked my paws through the tangled knots of fur, and untangled them some, resting his head on my thigh and hoping what little I could do, it would bring some clarity back to his eyes. I didn't know what else to do.

The wolf's blue eyes were open but unfocused, and he looked lost and confused for some time. I felt helpless, but I tried speaking to him in Katuk to at least let him know I was there, hoping I'd eventually get a reaction. I don't know how long it was until I finally got one. But it at least confirmed he was coming back to his senses.

"Shit..." He muttered, at length, blinking heavily. "Tell me I didn't piss myself this time."

CHAPTER 5
SERWICH

That night, the two men sat over a score of maps strewn across Grayson's table, speaking lowly about the matter of—what I could only assume was—a war. At least that's what it sounded like. The 'troubles' the colonies on this new continent were having were apparently worse than we'd been lead to believe. The more the Otherwolf Admiral spoke to Grayson about it, the more concerned the wolf became. We were sailing into a warzone. I was concerned, myself. Could this really be worth Puck's research? And what of Shadow? Had she even made it this far?

Everything that had happened in the valley seemed a lifetime away on this ship so far from home. And in some ways, even if I was guilty about the fact, that was comforting. The sting of every memory I'd left behind was still there, haunting my dreams as well as my waking life. But out here, a world away, the unknown that surrounded me and the strange lands ahead of me weren't a subject of fright, as they rightly should have been, but curiosity. Concern of course for the well-being of my friends was always there, but as for myself...

After everything I'd been through, the insanity of this trip didn't seem nearly as daunting as the concept of leaving my valley had been to me, not a year earlier. And that personal transformation was hard not to recognize. It wasn't an easy or pleasant sort of transformation. It felt like I'd been ripped apart, changed beyond what I once knew, to become what I was becoming. It was a metamorphosis, but it had hurt. I'd walked this terrible, terrifying gauntlet, and many times it could have destroyed me. But the fact that I was still standing now, in spite of everything that had happened, had toughened me as surely as the mountain trails had toughened my paw pads.

I missed the people I'd lost every day. That ache was there, and it probably always would be. There would be no replacements for the people who had passed. There never could be. But the new experiences, and the new people I was meeting were becoming a new chapter, if one could put it that way. And even if it was happening achingly slowly, I was learning to live with my losses. It wasn't like flipping a switch. There was no moment of clarity, no sudden, emotional release. It was slow, and arduous, and hard, but I was living day by day, and seeing what came next. And every day it got a little less hard to sleep, and to will myself to rise. I wasn't certain if this was 'healing', as Puck had called it, but it was something other than constant anger and pain. And that was an improvement, if nothing else.

I hadn't been paying much heed to the mens' conversation. I'd deduced by now that what they were discussing was beyond me in many ways, and probably not my business. I had little interest in matters of war, except in terms of protecting myself and my friends, and that I would do on a far more personal scale. Troop and fleet movements were not of any real interest to me.

But Grayson had been unusually weak and vulnerable since his episode, and even with Ariel back with us now, (the lion seemed severely angry at himself for not having been here when Grayson seized, even though the wolf himself had ordered him to escort Puck) I felt I should be near him, in case the incident were to repeat.

Puck had joined us an hour or so after the seizure, while Grayson had still been exhausted and slipping in and out of confusion. Apparently, Puck knew about his illness already, a fact which didn't surprise me, but did frustrate me some. The fox had told me privately that the wolf had sworn him to keep his confidence, but I had lived with the man for the last month. What if it had happened while no one else was with him? I felt very strongly that I should have been told.

But I didn't complain. For one, I had to accept that some people simply preferred to keep their secrets. I had many of my own, and friends with secrets a-plenty.

For two, one of the things Puck had told me quietly while we spoke was that it might be more likely for the wolf to slip into another seizure if he were upset now. So I was trying to be as calm around the man as possible. It was so odd to think of the crass, rugged wolf as being so fragile, which I suppose might have been why he didn't want the crew knowing of his illness.

"Is it dangerous?" I asked the fox quietly in Katuk. We were both sitting on Grayson's strongbox, cutting new bandages. Puck had run out, treating all the wounded on deck.

"Yes, but," Puck sighed, "not in the way you'd think. The seizing itself generally doesn't kill. It can, but it's rare. People with this illness more frequently die from falling, or hurting themselves while they seize. And there isn't always much warning, or reasoning behind when it happens, so..." his ears twisted towards Grayson, "It makes a lot of normal things a lot more dangerous."

"What do you mean?" I asked, confused.

"Imagine what would happen if you lost control of your body while you were standing somewhere high in the air, or swimming," Puck said pointedly.

"Why in the hell is he a mariner?" I whispered fiercely, shocked as I realized the implications of what Puck was inferring.

"His choice in profession is not wise," the fox admitted. "But I've already told him the dangers of his lifestyle, and he seemed to be well aware of them and didn't particularly care." He tipped an ear back, quirking an eyebrow at me. "Are you honestly surprised by that?"

"No," I muttered, glaring at the wolf. And I'd been worried about the bastard.

"Honestly," Puck murmured, tipping his muzzle towards the direction of the wolf. "I try not to question personal decisions made by people with illnesses like this, or judge how they choose to live."

"I understand that you try to be empathetic, Puck," I muttered, "but this is just asinine. I was standing with that man in the crow's nest just a few hours ago. If this had happened a few hours earlier..."

Puck gave a soft smile. "Shivah, he could die in a bath. There isn't really any way to be entirely safe when you have this illness. You can certainly live a more sheltered lifestyle, but," he sighed, softly, wrapping his tail around his feet. "This isn't something one contracts. He was born with it. He's had to live with it. He can't change it. It's his choice how he lives with his own condition—"

"Puck," I murmured, "it's fine... I-I understand."

The fox stopped, and cleared his throat softly. "In any case I've told him he should at least stop drinking so much. He could aspirate in his sleep. But, he—"

"Doesn't listen," I filled in.

"For what it's worth, he considers it self-medicating," Puck stated. "And it might be. I'm not certain, honestly. So little is known about this illness, but he claims he seizes most when he's tense or stressed. So, I suppose alcohol could work as 'medicine' if that's true."

"Or he just likes to have a ready excuse to get drunk," I muttered.

"Or that," the fox agreed.

"Well, I still think it's asinine," I said with a sigh, "but it's his life."

Puck smiled. "I think that's the point."

I looked to the two men, taking special note of the wolf's posture and the grim way he was setting his jaw, looking down on the maps as the Otherwolf spoke with him in low tones about the situation at the colony. I could see the tension in the wolf's shoulders, and it worried me.

It was somewhat shocking to me how quickly the realization about the man's illness had changed how I thought about him. It wasn't that it had made me somehow fonder of the man, but more protective, I suppose? It was almost a motherly instinct. It filled in a lot of gaps in the man's rough, unlikable personality, with the realization that he was suffering something he was entirely powerless to stop. It had to be terrifying. It was hard to fight the urge to sympathize, especially when the big, black wolf was visibly trembling.

"Should he be shaking?" I whispered softly to the fox.

"Sometimes. Small tremors following the seizing aren't uncommon," the fox murmured, "but it might also just be nerves. I've never endured one, myself, so I don't know how conscious he was while it happened, but..."

"I'm just worried it will happen again," I mumbled, tightening my fingers over the edge of the strongbox we were sitting on. "Whatever they're talking about, it looks grim. Shouldn't he be resting right now?"

Puck blinked at me. "Well I'm glad the Admiral has won over your concern, Shivah," he cleared his throat, and I almost glared at him, "but to be honest, I don't know exactly what causes them. No one does. He did claim stress was a factor for him, so... Maybe? It certainly couldn't hurt for him to rest. I think we all could," he muttered with a yawn, arching his back and stretching his tail out. "Mnh, but first thing's first."

He gathered up a fresh bundle of bandages and stood to head towards the men. I was silently grateful he was about to interrupt their intense conversation. Grayson really didn't look well. Couldn't the damned Otherwolf go over his war plans later?

"Sir?" Puquanah said softly, stepping up beside the two men. He was specifically addressing the 'Denholme' man, though. The foreign admiral's ears twisted towards the fox, and he glanced over at him, inclining his head slightly and leaning on his elbow.

"'Puck', was it?" he asked.

"Ah, yes sir—"

"Luther. Please," the canine put out a hand. "It's fine. I get enough formality from my own men."

"Alright," Puck said after a few moments, sounding unusually shy. Not that I blamed him. This man had an oddly intimidating aura about him. I wasn't certain I liked him. Grayson certainly seemed to consider him a friend, but the wolf didn't exactly have the best judgment.

"Well, I— I have to stitch, and re-wrap your wound," the fox said, gesturing towards the canine's leg. "I don't mean to bother you, but I have to be returning below-decks soon, and I need to do it before I go."

"Ah, of course," the canine nodded, glancing briefly back at the maps, and sighing, "Not a problem. Honestly, I'm not really certain what more we could go over, tonight. We're just circling back around to the same problems again and again at this point, anyway."

"Aye," Grayson muttered. "And I'm tired of hearing it. Right mess you got yourself in here, Denholme. Thanks for inviting me to the party," he said dryly.

"It wasn't this bad when I contacted you," the Otherwolf said again, "I swear it, Reed. I needed powder. I didn't intend to trap you here."

"You'll pardon me if I'm dubious about that last bit," the wolf said with an arched eyebrow. "I know you, dog. Nothing's an accident with you. Always a plan."

"You can feel that way if you want, Reed," the Otherwolf said flatly, and I listened carefully and watched for any signs of truth or dishonesty in the man's tone. But he was maddeningly hard to read. I watched as Grayson's own brows lowered, and I felt the fur along my neck prickle. If even the jovial wolf was doubtful of his friend's honesty, I was all but certain he'd been manipulated. Old debt or not, a lot of Grayson's men were now dead or badly injured, and the 'drakes' that had come for us had nearly sunk his ship. If he'd been lead into this situation without knowing the full extent of what this 'Luther' knew, those lives, and that blood was on the cattle dog's hands, as far as I was concerned.

But Grayson said no more, only slumped somewhat in his chair, closing his eyes and running his pawpads over his brow. Luther slid his chair back and stood, leaning against the table for support.

"Alright, then," he murmured, "where—"

"The floor is fine," the fox said, stepping back, "anywhere you can stretch out your leg."

The Otherwolf apparently wasn't above sitting on the floor, and did so without complaint, stretching out his leg and rolling his pant leg up gingerly over the wound Puck had wrapped with a poultice an hour or so earlier. It looked to have bled through quite a lot. He likely did need stitches. I'd had to endure them before, and watched Ransom endure them. Puck had very able hands, but the process was still unavoidably unpleasant. I didn't really want to watch.

"I normally don't suggest alcohol for anything except disinfectant," the fox said, settling to his knees beside the canine and carefully pulling the things he'd need out of his small healer's bag, "but if you'd like to drink, I won't stop you. I'm going to be sewing very close to the bone."

"I can handle it," the canine muttered, sounding truly unconcerned.

Puck gave a slight breath of a laugh. "If you say so. There's no need to be tough about it, though. This will hurt. I'm just warning you."

"I have a high tolerance for pain," the man said, waving a hand dismissively. "Don't worry. There's very little your needle can do to me that life hadn't already."

Puck actually laughed at that. "Alright, then."

The cattle dog got an odd look about him as he took the fox in, while he prepped his needle. "You're not a colonist," he remarked at length. "Neither of you. Carvecian Natives, yes?"

Puck nodded, distracted. "I'm from one of the northern tribes. You wouldn't know of us."

"I know very little about the Native Carvecians," the canine admitted. "To be honest, I've hardly ever met any. I didn't even know there were families of foxes with your particular pelt."

Puck sighed, muttering, "This just happens during the summers. My people are normally entirely white."

The Admiral got an odd smile. "That is a pity."

I moved over towards Grayson's slumped figure, and pushed the bottle near him towards his bowed muzzle. His dark blue eyes opened and he glanced sidelong at me. He grabbed at the bottle, and leaned back in his chair.

"You're always lecturing me about drinking, and now you're enabling me?" he muttered curiously.

"If it helps you, it's fine," I said quietly. "I didn't know about your condition," I pointed out. "If you'd just explained..."

"Keeps me calm," the man said with a lull of a nod, finishing off the bottle and thunking it down on the wooden table. "Which helps. I think. It happens a lot when," he gesticulated in the air, "when I... when..."

I arched an eyebrow at the man. He had to be tired, or upset. The wolf had never seemed at a loss for words before.

"When your nerves are rattled?" I offered, gently. "That dying man was... I was disturbed," I admitted. I gently reached a hand to his shoulder, and settled it on the shoulder of his coat. I almost never willfully touched the man on my own, and he took notice of it. "It's alright to admit it," I murmured.

"Is that what set it off?" he snuffed. "I can't remember. I never remember. I saw lines... Then it all went—well, you saw. First thing I remember was coming to seeing you above me." He forced a grin up at me, "Not an unpleasant way to wake, I have to say."

"Stop," I said with a sigh, shifting my hand on his shoulder to grip him a little more firmly. "You don't need to act like an ass right now just to cover the fact that you have a weakness. I already saw it. You can't hide it from me anymore."

The wolf's grin disappeared. "Are you going to tell my men?" he asked in complete seriousness.

My eyes widened. "Wha—no," I said insistently. "No. I wouldn't do that to you."

"You weren't above shaming me while I was naked and tied to the bed," the wolf reminded me, and he didn't bother dropping his voice. I saw the cattle dog's ears twist towards us on the last bit, and vaguely caught the hint of a smirk on his muzzle, before I glared back at Grayson.

"You were threatening to violate me," I growled. "I take issue with men who threaten to violate me. You're lucky you're alive."

He gave a low, gravelly chuckle, and leaned into my hand, shifting his shoulder so that it forced my fingers beneath the thick trellises of his dreads. He gave a rumble and glanced up at me, expectantly.

"What?" I muttered.

"I thought you came over here to comfort me," the wolf said with the vaguest of smug smiles. "You sounded concerned. A woman's touch would certainly comfort me, help ensure I don't seize again."

I gave a disgusted sigh, and threaded my fingers up through the thick, warm bundles of dreads that began along his scalp and the nape of his neck, where any self-respecting tribesman would have had a mane. They had an odd texture to them, but they weren't unpleasant to the touch, exactly, just strange.

"I see you're already not above using this for sympathy," I muttered. "That was fast."

"I was hoping for more than sympathy, actually," the wolf smirked, leaning back in his chair and closing his eyes.

I rolled mine. "Don't get your hopes up. My charity extends only so far, no matter how sick you are. And it certainly won't include anything indecent."

"Darling, I couldn't enjoy 'indecent' affections tonight even if they were forthcoming," the wolf muttered, his eyelids drooping. "I was just hoping you'd scratch my scalp. Bloody dreads make it itch like you wouldn't believe."

I paused. "You don't have fleas, do you?"

The wolf chuckled. "Not since your fox came on-board. He's got this soap—"

"You bathe?" I had to ask, shocked. I knew his cabin had a bath, but I'd never seen him use it. I'd made use of it several times since I'd been living here, and it had been a true relief from the dirty conditions below-decks.

"Don't assume just because I don't flounce about in the tub when you're here means I don't ever," the wolf snorted. "I'll reek of alcohol and brine all day, those are good seafaring smells, but I won't smell like a mangy stray. An Admiral that smells like a slum dog wouldn't get much respect, you know. I'm a bloody gentleman," he brushed his hand over his coat, as if to accentuate his, as he saw it, posh clothing and respectability.

I sighed and pressed my claws through the thick dreads, scritching at the back of his neck. The man gave a happy groan, and his beaded tail tossed where it hung over his chair. "I assumed if you did, you wouldn't hold back just because I was present," I stated. "You don't have any shame about doing anything else while I'm here."

"It's not about shame," the wolf said. "I have to have Ariel about when I wash. Would have been a bit strange to explain that away. Although now, I suppose, it doesn't matter anymore."

My brow line softened at that. Puck's words returned to me, and I actually felt momentarily bad for giving the wolf grief about washing himself. It was hard to consider a life where something as simple as a bath could kill you.

"In any case, keep doing that," Grayson murmured thickly, his eyes slipping closed as he leaned his head back over the chair. "Your claws are so sharp."

"Still got a knack for flattering ladies who don't want you, eh Reed?" the Otherwolf spoke up from the floor. He honestly was bearing the process of having the stitches done without flinching. So at the very least, he hadn't been lying about his pain tolerance.

"Still got a knack for marrying women you don't want, Denholme?" the wolf fired back, and I actually saw the canine blanch, glancing aside.

"Actually," I spoke up, "I do consider any compliment about my natural weapons to be flattering. Compliment my ability to claw up your face or my skills in battle more often, and you might actually get somewhere. At least farther than the compliments about my ass are getting you."

"Oh, I like this one," Luther chuckled. "Keep her, Reed. You need a woman who can tame you."

"No woman can tame me," the wolf muttered back, then winced as I used a claw to untangle two of his dreads, perhaps with a bit more of a yank than was strictly necessary.

"I thought that once, too," the Otherwolf Admiral said with a sigh, then glanced at Puck, who was now wrapping his leg. "Then I saw my daughter for the first time."

"When did you get boring, cattle dog?" Grayson snorted.

"I'll be forty in a year," the canine said with a sigh. "Time has a way of showing a man what's important, and what's really worth being foolish for. You tell me where your priorities lay when you're my age."

"I plan to be dead when I'm your age," the wolf chuckled.

"So did I, at one point," Luther said, sagely. "When you've the responsibility of others resting on your shoulders, though, you begin to weigh and measure what risks you take a lot more carefully."

"And yet here you are, across the whole damned world, as far from your family as you possibly can be, in a bloody warzone," Grayson snorted. "Well done there, Denholme."

"I came to Serwich for the same reason you did, Reed," the canine murmured. "An old debt. At this point all I want to do is get my people out alive. I abandoned the hope of holding the colony a long time ago. I've done all I can. All that's left now is retreat."

"They want you the hell out," the wolf pointed out. "If you're willing to go, why not just tell the bloody lizards you're going, and call off all the damned fighting? They'd probably be ready and willing to just let you pack up."

Luther shook his head. "That might have been the case some time ago, but not any more. This new warleader, Reed..." he shook his head, "He wants blood. He doesn't just want us gone. He wants us eradicated, so we can't ever return. His tribe came down from the north. I think they were chased out of Fulwynheim."

"The mining colony?" Grayson hummed, sounding pleasantly distracted by my ministrations.

"Aye," Luther nodded. "Lord Kristoff reclaimed it three years ago. If Zakkra's tribe was already chased out of their lands—"

"They sure as hell aren't gonna risk that again," Grayson muttered. "So you can't even run."

"They're determined to kill us to a man," the Otherwolf said, bitterly. "When they advance, they're ruthless. They're smart. They don't fight on if they're losing, like they always have in the past. They fall back, they regroup..." He sighed. "They have the river. They have us cut off and backed into the settlement. When they attack, they target civilians. Their drakes bomb our streets, their guerrillas stalk the outskirts, pick off those who flee and poison our water supplies."

He was silent for a moment, his muzzle drawn into a grim line. "We had a smaller settlement built downriver, where they did a lot of logging, sent the lumber down to us. Nice little town." He shook his head. "But poorly-defended. It was one of the first places Zakkra targeted. They didn't stand a chance. When we found the wreckage those beasts left behind, I saw..." he gestured at the air, silently poised at a thought he couldn't seem to vocalize, for some time. "Childrens' bodies. Gnawed to the bone. They are eating my people, Reed."

"Gods," Grayson muttered, his shoulders shaking somewhat as he ran a paw over his forehead, again. I watched him bow his head, his brow knitted, and felt another quiver work its way through his body.

I looked to the Otherwolf. "Maybe talk about this another time," I said softly. "He's tired."

"I need your help, Reed," the canine pressed, clearly not heeding my request. I narrowed my eyes at the man. I was certain he was doing this on purpose, pressuring him when he wasn't feeling well, so that he'd yield.

"Please," the Otherwolf pleaded, emphatically. "The Crown is asking the impossible of me, Reed. They won't send me aid. They don't believe these creatures are as capable as they are, they don't understand the gravity of our situation, or they don't care. They've abandoned us, but I can't abandon the colonists I'm supposed to be protecting. I need help. Or everyone in my colony is going to die."

"Alright, dammit," the wolf snapped, lifting his muzzle to address the man. "It's not like you've given me much choice in the matter. If I drop my cargo and leave, I'll be forging these waters again, which just makes me a good distraction for your retreat, anyway. But then you already knew that, didn't you?"

The Otherwolf was noticeably silent. And my protective urges were in full swing. Grayson might have been a right bastard sometimes, but I understood full well what sort of a position this Luther Denholme had put him in and even just having met the man, I suspected just as Grayson had, that it had been intentional.

And that wasn't right. No matter how you sliced it. Grayson had his own fleet to look after, his own people. It wasn't right to arbitrarily sacrifice lives that weren't your own, even if it was for the good of others. That should have been each man's individual choice. And Grayson, lout though he often was, probably would have given his men that choice. Now, though, none of us had a choice.

I didn't want this to turn into a fight, though. I looked down at the wolf again, and curled my fingers around the soft edges of his ears, hoping the simple gesture of affection would calm him down. It did, some.

I looked to the Otherwolf, sternly. "I think you're done here," I said icily. "Don't you have your own ship?"

"I do," the Admiral sighed, and glanced down at the fox, "and I should be getting back to her. Your healer seems like he's almost done."

"Nearly," the fox nodded. "Thank you for being so still."

"Thank you for being so skilled," the Otherwolf replied. "I've had this done poorly before. It's even less pleasant. You have very good hands."

I didn't miss when the fox's ears flushed. "I've been told that before, yes." He leaned down and bit at the thread, snapping it, then smoothed his pawpads over the wound, slowly, feeling the stitches. "All done," he said at length. "You should be fine until they have to be removed. I'll see you again then. Until then just keep it clean, let me know if the wound starts to smell or the pain becomes unusually strong—"

"I know the drill," the Otherwolf nodded. "Thank you." He stood slowly and pulled his pant leg down gingerly over the stitched wound, then offered a hand to the fox. Puck was struggling somewhat to find a handhold in the unfamiliar room. He was without his walking stick at the moment.

I moved towards him to help, but he found the Admiral's hand before I could get to him, and stood with his help. I tried to make sure the cattle dog caught my protective glare, but he didn't seem to be regarding me anymore.

And Puck, apparently, wasn't as put-off by the man as I was. Didn't he realize the Otherwolf's manipulations had essentially trapped us in this foreign land? Well I suppose he wanted to be here, and the longer the better, to accomplish his goals. but still.

"Thank you again," the man said with a slight bow. "And Reed..."

The wolf glowered at him wearily from where he was slumped on the table.

"For what it's worth... I'm sorry," the man offered, quietly.

"You did what you had to do," the wolf muttered. "But don't think I won't remember that mindset whenever I have a difficult choice in the future."

The Otherwolf sighed. "That's only fair." He reached down and hefted his belt and scabbard from a nearby chair, strapping it across his waist and shifting experimentally on his bad leg. "We'll get back underway tomorrow. Sleep well, Reed." He nodded to the man. "I'm glad you have people who care for your well-being these days."

He headed out, and Puck gathered up his things fairly quickly after that, moving past me with a soft paw on my arm and murmuring, "You didn't sustain any injuries, did you? I don't smell anything—"

"I'm fine," I assured the fox, putting my own hand on his shoulder to assure him. "You look tired, Puck. You should get to sickbay and get some sleep. Maybe stop below-decks first," I said pointedly.

"Maybe I will," the fox nodded. "Ariel's outside if anything happens again..."

"Gods, just tell him to get some rest," Grayson said, irritated. "I don't need to be babysat, dammit. It's enough that she's here."

"Alright," Puck nodded at length. "I'll communicate that to him."

The fox headed out, the door shutting behind him, and then I was alone with the wolf in his cabin. He was still slumped over the table, every remnant of his good mood and jovial manners entirely gone now. He just looked tired. Exhausted, even.

"You really should sleep," I said softly.

"Going to be hard, considering..." the wolf muttered.

I knitted my hands together, and stood in the center of the room for a time, thinking back on the last several months of my life, and all the trials and terrible acts I'd seen and endured. I took stock of it all and carefully considered what I was going to say, before I did.

"I haven't lived a very long life," I murmured, "but over the last year, I've seen a lot of people—people that I don't think ever thought they had bad intentions—do terrible things, because they thought it's what they had to do, to save the people they cared about."

"I know this might sound strange, coming from a man like me," the black wolf sighed, letting a hand fall heavily on the table, "but as far as I'm concerned, I don't give a damn what your intent is. If you're being a shit for any reason, you're still a shit. I built my fleet on the concept of freedom. Real freedom. A place where men could make a living without being beholden to an unfair chain of command, or having to die because someone who thinks they know better tells them what to do with their lives. My men follow me because they want to. We work through majority rule. We vote," he emphasized, "before we target a convoy, or take a contract. No man matters less on my crew, no matter his position. I respect personal freedom. That's what this life is all about. We make our own choices, and prosper or suffer by them."

"I understand that," I stated, feeling a slight swell in my chest. "And I... even though I'm not always fond of your mannerisms... I like it here. I like that you're honest. I like that you're uncomplicated. I've begun to understand why your men like it here. And I agree with you. I don't like men who do whatever is necessary to accomplish their goals. I judge a man by what he does, not what he meant to do. And it's hard to do good through doing wrong. Maybe impossible. I've seen too many good people suffer and die because a few people thought they had to, for the greater good. I..." I paused, looking to the ground, "I can't for a moment believe their deaths were necessary. The world could only be a better place if they were still here. I have to believe, therefore, that there had to have been a better way. It just wasn't the easiest way."

"You mean like what your fox is trying to do," the wolf filled in.

I nodded. "Maybe... maybe if the people who'd been trying to treat this disease hadn't given up so quickly, maybe if they'd buckled down, and tried to do what Puck is trying to do now, a lot of unnecessary deaths wouldn't have happened. I know it's dangerous. I know getting to this land, to where this plague came from, and doing the sort of intense research Puck is hoping to do was a hard prospect. But we're doing it. There was another way. I'd like to think there's always another way—a way that doesn't turn you into a monster."

Grayson gave a thick sigh. "Denholme's not a monster. He's just pragmatic. It pisses me off sometimes, but—"

"Will you be saying that if, in a month from now, all of your men died for him?" I demanded.

"If all of my men die in this damned colony, I'm going to hell with them," the wolf said, his eyes snapping to mine.

"I believe you," I assured him, softly.

"So what's your point in all of this?" the wolf sighed. "What am I supposed to do? He put me in a no-win, here. The stage is already set."

"There are always going to be men like that," I said. "Men who claim they had no choice, who defend the things they do with self-righteousness. You can't let people like that pull you down, though. I almost did, once..." I swallowed, leaning against the table. "It's a hole. Easy to fall into, hard to pull yourself out of. Harder the deeper you go."

"I have no idea what you're talking about," the wolf said with the barest hint of a smile, "but you're even sexier when you get all intense like that."

"I'm saying," I sighed, "let's keep our options open. I think I understand a lot of what he said, and I don't think we have a choice for now. We'll have to stay at this colony and do what he says. Protect his people." I looked at him pointedly. "But nothing says we have to do that his way."

"You think we should cook up a few of our own plans to get out of this, beneath his nose," the wolf said, putting a few fingers up over his jawline in consideration. "Alright. I'm following, so far."

"I can't say any more until we see the situation up-close, and get the lay of the land," I said. "But I intend to get at least the people I care for back home, safely, no matter what awaits us at this colony. I'm not going to be fodder for this man and his people, to assure their safety. But, maybe we can do both."

"You don't know Denholme," the wolf sighed. "He's sharp. If there was another way, he'd've found it."

"I don't care who he is," I stated firmly. "That man has no dirt beneath his nails. Just blood. He might be a warrior, but he doesn't know the wilderness like I do. He said that's where these people are besting his men. I think I could do better."

"You're a ballsy woman," the wolf snorted in amusement. "And yes, I realize that statement makes no sense." He paused for a few moments, taking me in. "Did you really bring down one of those bombers today?"

"I did," I said, with a bit of a growl in my tone.

"Damn, woman," the wolf blew out a breath, leaning back in his chair and giving me a sidelong look. "Everything you say just makes me want you more."

"Do you agree with me or not?" I pushed.

"It's fine. It's a good idea," the wolf conceded, waving a hand. "I know a man we can talk to at Serwich when we dock. He's close in with the men in command, but he's not afraid to be cloak and dagger if it means getting shit done. Always found him a bit slippery for a church man, but that might be to our advantage in this."

I nodded, and leaned in as he winced and rubbed a hand over his head again. "You really should sleep," I said again, more quietly.

"Hard to, after..." he gestured at nothing. "You know. I don't like having blanks in my life. It's disturbing. And I never feel right, afterwards. This thing, this illness is like..." he was silent for a few moments, "my God. My own personal God. It does whatever the hell it wants to me, and I have no control. It scares me sometimes," he admitted, almost beneath his breath.

I looked at him sympathetically for a little while, before murmuring, "We don't have to talk about it, Grayson. You should get your mind off of it."

"You should come to bed with me," he retorted, doggedly.

"You said you couldn't enjoy my company even if it was forthcoming," I reminded him, with a good-natured glare.

He leaned back on his elbow, lazily. "I could summon the strength, I think."

I rolled my eyes. "Do you really want me to sleep with you out of pity? Wouldn't you rather earn a woman's affection?"

"I think you are vastly over-estimating my pride when it comes to bedroom conquests," the wolf said with a soft snort.

"I think you don't know me all that well if you think calling me a 'conquest' will work."

"It would get my mind off of things," he said with the barest hint of a fang in his grin.

"You have a long way to go," I assured him. "I will sleep near you, if it will comfort you. That's all."

The wolf grumbled, rising slowly and shucking his coat off his shoulders, draping it over the chair he'd been sitting at, and tiredly making his way across the cabin, towards his bed. He removed his weapons as he went, and I followed him as far as the wooden screen that separated his four-poster from the rest of the cabin.

"You know it's not particularly fair that I'm being compared to this man I never met," the wolf muttered, flopping down on his bed and pulling off his leather spats.

I narrowed my eyes at him, the sting of his bringing up Grant so casually hurting me in ways he probably couldn't comprehend. And for some reason, that bothered me even more.

"I don't even know his name," he pointed out.

"Grant Wickham," I said, stone-faced. "And I never said you had to be him, or measure up to him. As far as I'm concerned, for you, that would be impossible."

"That's an Otherwolf name," the wolf said with an arched eyebrow. "You got a thing for canines?"

"Just the one," I assured him, icily.

He shrugged, "Well I just assumed..."

"I was married to one of my own kind before then," I stated, before he could ask. "He's dead now. The world is a better place for it."

"So one bastard, and one angel," the wolf rubbed at his chin. "What if I fell somewhere in the middle? Would that pass?"

I crossed my arms over my chest, sighing. "That's an idiotic question. You should strive to be the best man you're personally capable of. Whatever that is. And you shouldn't just be doing that to sleep with me, or you're not actually improving yourself."

"Yeah, but this is the man you hold up to this golden standard," Grayson said pointedly. "I just want to know what your standards are. You know. How far I've got to go."

I knew the wolf was trying to be cute, but the more this conversation dragged on, the more it was making me angry. It felt like a betrayal of the memories of a person I'd cared for deeply to be talking about him in this way. It wasn't cute. It wasn't funny. It just hurt, and felt wrong.

I lifted my chin, and looked him dead in the eyes.

"You want me to compare you to him?" I questioned. "Fine. You're a canyon-width apart, and you will never be the man he was. You don't deserve to be breathing the same air."

The wolf cleared his throat. "Well, technically we aren't, anymore."

That anger flared up inside me again, and I crossed the two feet between us, and shoved him forcefully enough that it seemed to shock even the large wolf. He fell back onto the bed, and I leapt over him, pinning him down by fisting a hand in his collar, and bringing his face to mine.

"I don't care if you're sick," I snapped. "You don't get to insult the memory of a man I loved! Do you understand me?"

The wolf's ears tipped back, and he honestly looked intimidated by me. What's more, he looked ashamed?

Yes. I'd never seen shame on the man's face before, so it was hard to recognize, at first. But I was certain, when he began speaking in a soft, docile tone.

"I'm truly sorry," he said, at length. "I didn't know."

I gave him a confused look. "Didn't know what?"

He glanced aside. "That you loved him."

I blinked, leaning up slowly, and staring at the wall. Had I said that?

I had.

"I-I told you I cared about him," I said defensively. "And he was a lover."

"You never struck me as the sort to give your heart away," he admitted, abashedly.

I had to go silent at that, because I didn't know how to respond. He was right. I'm not even certain why I'd said what I'd said. I hadn't been in love with Grant while he was alive. Had I?

"I'm sorry," the wolf repeated. His dark blue eyes fell away from mine. "I'm... I'm just sorry..."

I swallowed, looking away, myself. For the first time since I'd known the wolf, I had to admit to myself why I was so conflicted around him. When I'd lost my son, I'd thought I could never feel the warmth and the love I'd had with my little baby boy again. But then I'd met Puquanah, and Ransom, and Grant. I'd nearly lost Puck, and now Grant was gone... The pain that had nearly caused me to give up on everything, to live my life for rage, to burn from the inside out, was the fear of caring about others when I could lose them. I'd endured it too many times already.

It was hard to tell myself it hadn't been worth it, though. I couldn't honestly think about Grant and wish we'd never met. The time we'd had together, the things we'd accomplished together, I wouldn't have given it up for anything. So did that mean it was worth risking it again? This wasn't a matter of romantic love. I was afraid to love at all. I was afraid of the fact that I cared about Puck and Ransom. Terrified I'd lose them, as I had my son and Grant. And I was afraid to forge bonds with anyone new, as well.

I shifted up slowly and lifted myself off of the wolf, moving to the side of him, and dragging my knees up to my chest.

"I'm sorry I was so aggressive with you," I murmured, leaning my cheek against my knees.

"It's been a bad night." the man said at length.

"It has," I agreed softly. I was silent for a long while after that. We both were. After some time had passed, and I'd tossed through the many conflicted thoughts in my mind again and again, I came to one final conclusion.

"There are enough reasons to be unhappy in the world," I murmured. "I don't want to have petty squabbles with my friends."

The wolf's ears perked at that, and he turned to regard me. He was silent, but the childish hope in his eyes was almost amusingly heartwarming.

"Don't let it go to your head," I mumbled.

"I'm trying not to, but it's hard," the wolf smirked.

"And move over," I said, shoving him with my hips. "I'm tired of that cot."

Grayson chuckled and did as I said, giving me plenty of room to settle in, and a respectable amount of space between us I could use to keep my distance. Or try.

"I warn you, I snuggle," the man said with a satisfied grin as he settled in, himself.

"Of course you do," I muttered.

I spent most of the night shoving him off of me.

I would like to say that when we, at last, neared this faraway land, this Serwich, that I was greeted with sweeping, exotic, breath-taking landscapes, the likes of which I had never seen before. I would like to say that. But the reality was, my arrival on this 'Dark Continent' lived up to its name. Murky, dismal, a bit frightening, and very, very dark.

The day Grayson's falcon returned with word that we were nearing the shores of the Colony, an acrid, choking fog was creeping over the tumultuous seas, blotting out even the sun from the sky. I couldn't see any other ships in our fleet, even though my ears told me quite well that they were near. And we'd had clear skies not a few hours earlier, as the sun rose over a cloudless sky.

The fog was not natural. It was unlike any mist or obscurement I'd ever seen in the valley, or in any of my other travels. It seemed almost black as it slithered in from the distance and enveloped us, and as soon as the man in the crow's nest gave warning of its approach, Grayson's men began donning cloth over their muzzles, wetting them and covering their noses and mouths, much as I'd once seen Grant's men do before we entered the first infected village Rourke had decimated. But when Grayson eventually explained the source of the choking fog, I was even more stunned than I had been upon seeing the wreckage of the village so long ago.

"On the Dark Continent," the wolf said, as he used unusual care to tie a moist handkerchief around my muzzle, "the mountains burn."

"What?" I asked, my eyes widening. He couldn't mean literally.

But the wolf nodded slowly. "The earth itself. It burns, from deep within. Like a fire has been lit in the depths of the mountains somewhere, and is seeking to vent its fury. Some of the peaks are bereft of a... I suppose you'd call it a 'chimney', and when the fires build inside," he gestured with his paws, spreading them wide, "the earth shakes, and bursts forth, and the fires of hell are unleashed."

"You've seen this?" I demanded, shocked.

The wolf chuckled. "Only the remains. There was a colony some ways down south from here, established twenty years ago. It was something of the older sister to Serwich. Nostafarath, I think it was called. Kadrush and Amurescan settlers together. They built it in the valley beneath an enormous mountain, far larger than the ones that preside over Serwich. It's all part of one long ridge of mountains," he gestured again, (the man gesticulated often), "the first settlers called 'The Dragon's Ridge'. In any case, it was a successful colony for a time. The Cathazra, the native peoples, they hadn't settled near that area, which is why it seemed a good location, I suppose. But then, fortune like that often has its price. The natives simply knew more than we did."

"Were you a part of this colony somehow?" I asked, curiously. The wolf seemed well-informed.

Grayson laughed. "I told you, no. How old do you think I am? I was a boy when this all happened. No, it's just a great tale the people here tell, and a terrifying one, at that, so it made its way through the trade lines fast."

"You mentioned remains," I murmured, looking to the distant, approaching fog. It was coming in as fog did, first slowly obscuring our sister ships, then muddying the air in slowly increasing degrees aboard the Manoratha. Except, unlike a fog I'd experience in the valley, I could feel more than just moisture. It felt like the air was thick, like someone was kicking up dust. I found myself blinking rapidly, and my eyes began to water. An unsettling smell was permeating the winds, as well. It reminded me of something I'd smelled in Otherwolf towns, but what in particular, I could not put my finger on.

Grayson nodded. "When we heard that the colony had been destroyed, it was nearly a decade after it had happened of course, but details were sparse, and we did as many others, stopped by to see what could be salvaged. We were in the area as it was, and I was hoping the port would be a good place to wait out a troubling fleet in the area. I expected a colony destroyed meant the Cathazra had come in and driven the colonists out, or simply killed them all. But there are goods they don't seize, things their people have no use for I suppose, like spices and cloth, that are of great value if you can pick them from the wreckage."

I arched an eyebrow, and then blinked rapidly again, running my paw over my closed eyes. The air was beginning to honestly burn them. "So what happened?" I asked impatiently. "What did you find?"

"Absolutely nothing," the wolf said, in a strangely haunted, yet reverent tone, "it was like the earth itself had reclaimed the colony. And the mountain that had once stood there was no longer there."

I snorted, partially because the man was telling a tall tale, and partially because the fog was beginning to sting the inside of my nose, even with the handkerchief on. "I thought you were being serious," I muttered.

"I am," the wolf replied, and he sounded it.

"Mountains don't disappear," I insisted, although even as I said it, I knew I was refuting one of my people's own myths. Did the legends not say the great mountains that surrounded our valley had once been gods that walked the earth, before settling down to protect and enclose us? Perhaps if mountains could walk, they could disappear—or burn.

I'd always thought these sorts of myths were just metaphors, meant to stand for concepts, not meant to be taken entirely literally. They seemed, even to me, to be unrealistic. Impossible to prove, or defend to a non-believer. The sorts of things that had likely made men like Puquanah doubt his faith, eventually. But could they be real?

"The mountain... erupted," the wolf said with another explosive hand gesture, his eyes sparkling despite the clogging fog in the air. I noticed now that several of his men around us on deck were listening to him, as if he were a storyteller. Well that's essentially what he was doing, if in a different fashion and a different setting than I was accustomed to. But it was no less fascinating.

"They heard it as far as Serwich," he said with a toothy grin. "Like thunder that shook the earth. I heard that at least five other colonies felt the tremor beneath their feet. No one from Nostafarath survived, so it's impossible to say exactly what happened there. But when the first ships arrived, all they found was what we found. A mountain turned crater in the earth, an entire forest knocked down, as though some great god had blown it all over, and what had once been a colony with several thousand souls living within it reduced to ash and rock. They say not a single structure could be found. We certainly never found any."

"Aye," the black rat with the chipped ear chimed in from where he leaned on the railing nearby, "I was there. You wouldn't have ever known people lived there. It was like someone cut a swath outta' the earth an' wiped it clean."

"The mountains near here belch smoke and this... acrid fog, from time to time," the wolf said with a slight cough, which I could only sympathetically mimic. Even with the wrapping, the 'fog' had settled entirely over us now, and it was getting increasingly hard to breathe. "But this is nothing, compared to the fury they could one day unleash, if Nostafarath is any indication."

"It feels like ash," I said with another cough, wrinkling my nose beneath the wrapping. It didn't really smell like any fire I'd ever smelled on a mountain before. But then, I'd never smelled the earth burning, only trees and brush. I blinked blearily up at the canine. "Can stone and earth really burn? I've never seen a fire that hot."

"I'm certain you've seen at least one forge by now," the wolf countered.

I blinked. That's right. That's sort of what this smelled like. With something additional, something awfully close to the smell of thundering weapons.

"If we weren't being constantly beset upon by those blasted beasts," the wolf sighed, "I'd take you by the islands along the coast. There are places the stone bubbles up from the earth, red hot like the hearth of a fire, but pours like water into the seas. It is a sight to behold."

I stared at him, in part in wonder, in part in disbelief. I watched him stare out over the fog-choked waters, and wondered at the strange man; at the things he must have seen, in his travels. The incredible places he must have been, and the very real wonders he spoke of. In my little world within the valley, I'd only dreamed of chasing butterflies, of pursuing the unknown and the beautiful things our legends spoke of. Things I'd literally thought up until just this past year our people could only see in dreams. But this man, and his crew, had truly done it. They'd seen the earth burn. They'd seen mountains move. Things even the sages could only tell tales of.

Honestly, it made me envious. And regretful. I'd had the chance already to see and experience so many new places, to find wonders like these men spoke of, and I'd been too singularly focused on my past to simply look around. See what there was to be seen.

The world hadn't stopped being incredible, just because my loves ones had left it. Life may have stopped for me, but it had continued churning about, all around me. Things were happening everywhere. Things I could never imagine. And my little life did not compare to earth tremblings, or mountains moving. It made me feel small, but it also made my pain feel small. It was a hard feeling to describe. I knew one thing for certain in that moment, though.

I needed to see the earth burn. I could feel Crow inside me still, his own fires burning, subdued but simmering like coals. He was coming apart, and I had promised him we could make it through this together, if we took the leap to continue living together. I had brought us this far, to this foreign land. This foreign land, where even the mountains burned.

I think, even as far as we were from home, and as mad as this whole journey felt, that we were finally nearing what would be the end of our time together. What would happen when it ended, I couldn't be certain. But staring out into the black, ash-choked sky, I knew we had been drawn here, as an ember on the wind, towards a great inferno.

When we at last made landfall, some of the new continent began to reveal itself to us, cascades of dense forest disappearing in gradients into a haze of fog and ash. Here, rain was falling, or was at least threatening to. The air was so thick with moisture, and the spray crashing up from the beach so ever-present, it was honestly hard to tell. I felt somewhat choked by the sheer amount of water in this place, like I was very slowly drowning.

We disembarked alongside the Admiral and his bodyguards. That, I was realizing, was what they truly were. Ariel, the lion, and another cat I'd seen working amongst the A.B.'s until now, a small leopard with an unusual pelt and a very foreign dialect. I could barely understand him, but Grayson had told me that since Ransom, Magpie and I had agreed to be part of what he called his 'trackers', the group of people he apparently kept at his side and sent out into the brush the most when his crew made landfall, we were going to get to know the two other cats a lot better in the future.

I didn't mind the concept of getting to traverse this new, foreign countryside, but if what I'd heard amongst the crew was any indication, it was not an enviable position. Ariel was the only man who'd been amongst Grayson's 'trackers' for terribly long and survived, the strange, tiny leopard was a new hire like us. It was generally a position given to cats, Ariel had told me, Grayson trusted them the most as scouts and for their subtlety and acute senses while we were on guard duty for the wolf. Ariel was our senior officer in the odd 'squad', and he'd been dubious of Grayson's decision to include my companions. Ransom and Magpie didn't fit into the mold as well, but I'd assured the lion they had their own skills in the brush, and Ransom in particular couldn't be beat for intimidation factor. That much, at least, had gotten a rumbled agreement from the lion.

It was by no means an appointment where any of us were comfortable yet, but all we had to do was wait it out while Puck did his research here, and then we could be on our way home. Chasing down the shadowy vixen seemed a goal so far removed from reality, here on the other side of the world that I was barely considering it any longer. And that may have been for the best.

We'd heard at least that the ship she may have come here on... and I say may, because we weren't even certain of that, hadn't made it to port. In fact, we'd run into the bobbing wreckage of one of its sister frigates an hour or so out at sea. The Admiral here assured us that if we searched enough, we'd find the debris field of what had once been the massive trade vessel. Even Grayson had been horrified at the news. She'd been a large, well-armed ship, and she'd been bombed and destroyed not an hour from the port at Serwich, most of the souls on-board and the supplies she'd been carrying sent to the bottom of the sea in a flaming wreck. It was easy to see why the Admiral here had been so desperate to escort us to safety, personally.

If Shadow had been on-board that ship, it was highly likely she was dead, now. Apparently some survivors had made it to shore in boats, or been picked up by the Admiral's fleets, floating on ashen wreckage, but it had been a very small portion of the people who'd been with the fleet to begin with. The chance was still there, of course, but I was trying not to think about it. I knew what lay down that road, and I'd made a promise to Crow that we were going to live a different life, now. A life not consumed by vengeance.

It was hard not to remember the hate and the anger, unfortunately. I still dreamt of Grant dying in my arms every single night. More than once, I know Grayson had seen me choke back a sob, or pretend I hadn't woken with tears in my eyes. Every night, I had to contend with that anger again, fight the fires inside me threatening to well up, and the fierce indignation and fury that accompanied them. I wasn't certain if I was fighting Crow, or myself in those arguments, but it hardly mattered. I'd accepted by this point that we were all but one. I had to redeem him to redeem myself. Or this thing, this sickness of hate, would burn us both alive.

I couldn't think about Shadow, not now. I had to remind myself that not that long ago, I had pursued Methoa'nuk just as I wished to pursue her, to avenge the deaths he had caused, and it had accomplished nothing. It hadn't quieted the fires, nor had it prevented future pain. Almost immediately after killing him, I had lost Grant. Wiping my husband's existence from the world had not made the world a kinder place. Pursuing a more peaceful life may have, and Grant may still have been with me now. Or perhaps, he was fated to die fighting the demons he himself pursued. It was impossible to say. But, one thing at least was certain, vengeance had not given me peace. Hard though it was, that was a fact I would have to learn to accept. I could only hope it got easier with time.

The docks were a noisy, bustling place just as they'd been in Arbordale, but that was primarily due to our own men beginning to offload our supplies and the chaos that came with making port. The ports themselves were nothing like what I'd seen in Arbordale.

Were it not for us, this whole place would have been eerily quiet, as compared to any Otherwolf settlement I'd seen in the past. The docks here were visibly newer, or at least the wood was, and lead to newly-paved roads and the first hints of wooden structures beyond, jutting out through the thick fog, hinting at the small city beyond. Everything I could see looked less worn, less moldering and battered down by decades of use, at least as compared to the older settlement that had been Arbordale.

But if this settlement was a child, it was a beaten child. There were scars of blackened earth across the paved roadways that lead from the docks up towards the settlement beyond, the remnants of what must have once been the original dock, now shattered beyond recognition, lying further down along the coast, and several collapsed wooden structures once built into the rocky, forested hills beyond that the forest seemed to be hurriedly reclaiming, already. They may have been watchposts or battlements once, but they were nothing but wreckage now. Two skeletons of new structures were clearly in mid-construction further up the twin hills that flanked the docks, but they were far from complete.

It was easy to imagine that if one had wings, the small stretch of beach along the inlet that made up this colony's port must have been pockmarked with these black scars, testament to the devastation that had been visited upon this one contested piece of territory.

"Bombers," I heard the rasp of the coyote behind me before I turned to see him. He snuffed, finally tugging the soaked bandanna down from over his muzzle, and fishing about in his pocket for a cigarette. I didn't want to point out to the canine how difficult it would be to light it in this weather. He looked as frayed as I felt.

I nodded, pawing softly at the blackened earth along the roadway we were walking, following in Grayson's wake as we slowly made our way towards the settlement itself. Offloading would be up to the men from our crew, and the dock workers from Serwich. I was thankful I'd at least grown enough in the Admiral's estimation that I wouldn't be carrying crates again.

The buildings I'd seen in the distance, as it turned out, were just warehouses for the docks, and there weren't many of them. What's more, they seemed abandoned. Likely because, as we soon saw, most of them had sustained similar damage from above, and were no longer useful. One that had seemed sound proved in fact to have a gaping hole through the roof and a collapsed wall in the back.

"Looks like they pulled back from the shore awhile back," Ransom noted, as we passed another caved-in building. "Boys are gonna have to haul that shit all the way up t'the settlement? Hope they've got wagons."

"I think I saw some," I said, trying not to show how much this place put my nerves on edge. Just seeing an Otherwolf settlement at all had been new to me not a year ago. Seeing a town bereft of people had been eerie, when I'd first witnessed what became of the towns Rourke hit.

But this was more than just the result of a twenty-man raiding band. This was devastation on a scale that I hadn't imagined existed. To destroy a tribe, or a settlement, was a daunting enough prospect for most of my people. To level what had once likely been a thriving port, built by the Otherwolves, who were nothing if not industrious...

This was war. I hadn't really comprehended the sort of concern Grayson had, coming into all of this, until right now. I'd registered that a warzone was bad, and not somewhere we wanted to be, but to see it...

Ransom cursed, apparently having given up lighting his cigarette, and shoved it back into his pocket. "Rutting soaked," he growled. "Everything I own is moldering. Fuck that boat. I swear to god, if I didn't have to get back on it to get home, I'd never step foot on one ever again."

I saw Ariel glare over his shoulder at us, but if Grayson took any insult to his beloved ship from Ransom's comment, he didn't speak up. The wolf seemed intense, gaze focused down the road, towards the settlement coming into view. And I soon saw why.

"Hell," the wolf stopped in his tracks, and we all did the same, forming up at his sides and following his eyes as they swept up the towering structure before us. Well, I say structure, but in reality, what it truly appeared to be was a wall, or a fort. It was hard to tell, because it seemed to go as far as my eye could follow towards the sides of the steep mountain ravine the colony was built into. The towering mountains rose on either side of us, sharply, the fog blocking what looked to be unnaturally jagged peaks from view.

The mountains here were nothing like back home. The rock was dagger sharp and black, the dense forests breaking away as the stone rose up from their clutches to impossible heights beyond. Nothing like the soft, tree-covered, sweeping curves of the beautiful mountains I knew back home. No gods had laid down here. It seemed more like they'd erupted from beneath the very earth itself, and brought the mountains up with them in their fury.

The wall we were facing was enormously tall, made from the trunks of trees that must have been great giants in life. It looked to have walkways at the top, if the distant, silhouetted figures walking along it were any indication. The fog obscured much of it from view, but I could only guess the wall reached as far as the mountains that encased this... I hesitated to call it a valley, because it was so unlike my home, but that seemed to be what it was. I suppose you could call it a basin. The inlet the port was set into seemed to be part of it, and I'd been told there was a river that flowed through it, which meant somewhere at least, the wall had to break. But it wouldn't have been a very effective wall unless it either encircled the colony beyond, or went as far as the mountains.

I was again amazed by the ingenuity and sheer industriousness of the Otherwolf people. And apparently, so was Grayson. Or at the very least, he was shocked.

"Was this here before?" Ariel said aloud, the lion staring gape-jawed at the massive gates.

"No," Grayson murmured, then shook his head. "This is desperate," he sighed. "And Denholme never gets desperate. Things must be worse than he let on."

"Reed!" a voice called down from the ramparts above, and we all looked up, towards a slender, tall figure standing above the gate. He looked to be wearing a coat much like the Admiral's, but so far as I knew, the Fenrir was still patrolling the port, while we offloaded. I couldn't make out much about the man except that he was likely a canine, but Grayson squinted for a moment, before shouting back.

"That you, old man?" He called up with a mirthful chuckle. "Never thought I'd see the day you'd be rolling out the welcome mat for me. How much did he lean on you to make this happen, this time?"

"I've stopped being choosy, these last few years," the canine called back down, and I heard the first creak of the enormous wooden gates beginning to open. "I've learned to trust in his decisions. They've kept us alive this long."

"Oh, now that's disappointing," the wolf snarled back. "That boy needs a leash, Knight. Even I can see that. He's one hair from being a worse man than me, if he thinks it's worth his while. I can see why he pulled this shite now. If even you aren't reigning him in..."

There was a long pause from the top of the gate, before the canine finally replied. "Never assume I've lost my bite, Reed, or I'll show you I haven't. But it was never my job to morally police him, especially not where sell-swords are concerned. You know if I'd had my way a decade ago, you and all of your men would have hanged on the beaches of Grenadd. Before you complain about my deferring to his judgment in the future, I'd suggest you remember that."

The wolf gave a 'tch' in the back of his throat, and resisted a low growl, but I wasn't certain if he was honestly angry, or just annoyed. What's more, I had no reference for the conversation, or the man he was having it with, to know how much of this was serious, or playful taunting like he'd shared with the Denholme man. That was settled in a moment, however.

"We have a job to do here, Reed," the man stated. "All of our past squabbles aside, I don't care what we have to do, or whom we have to do it with, to see our task here done. If you're here to aid us, I'm glad to have you."

Grayson gave a fierce smirk. "I brought your powder, Johannes."

I could see the man on the wall put a hand to his brow, even from where we were. "God be praised," he said, so quietly I almost missed it. Then, far louder, he shouted, "Keep the gates open! Harpoons to the skies! They'll target the wagons first!"

"I ain't seen any of them flyin' critters yet," Ransom said a bit nervously, his own eyes on the murky, grey skies.

"The fog is our ally today," I heard Ariel murmur from beside us, and looked to him. His eyes flicked towards mine when he noticed me looking at him quizzically, before he explained, "The drakes. They need the sun to fly. They are weak and slow without it. As it is, they cannot fly for long burdened down with a cauldron of burning pitch. I doubt they could manage it today, at all."

I filed that away in my mind for future reference, but kept my eyes peeled on the sky, nonetheless. We all did, choosing to remain outside the gates as the first of the wagons arrived.

Grayson himself had made no move to go inside yet, and I respected his conviction. He wanted to see to it that his goods made it safely inside, and I shared that sentiment. We hadn't come this far to fail now.

That was quite literally the last thought in my head, when I felt a slight pinprick, like a bee sting, in the side of my neck and all at once, the world began to spin. Noise erupted around me, but everything—the sights, the sounds—everything suddenly seemed to look as though I were seeing it through water. I felt the almost disconnected, dull ache as my body hit the ground, and heard the barking yell of a man's voice from above me.

Dimly, my vision swiftly fading to black, I managed to catch sight of a canine over me, but I couldn't tell if it was Ransom or Grayson. Some sort of unknown, musky smell entered my nostrils, and I thought I felt the unkind grasping of foreign hands at my ankles, yellow eyes... and then the smell of blood...

But it all happened so fast, I hadn't even enough time to process if what was happening was real, or some bizarre daydream. And then blackness.

'Confusion' wasn't a sufficient enough word for my panicked mind in my waking moments. I would have woken with a start, and grabbed for a weapon, but my body was receiving the messages my mind was sending it like I was shouting across an ocean. Even opening my eyes proved a great undertaking.

Comfortingly enough, the first person I saw when I woke was Puquanah. And I won't lie, that alone set me more at ease than nearly any other sight would have. The arctic fox was looking down on me, concern, but not real worry, in his features. The sort of expression he gave most of his patients who weren't critical. Whatever had happened to me, I realized, I was going to live.

But what the hell had happened to me? My last few moments awake had been so frantic and the whole chaotic event had come upon me so suddenly, I hadn't even had the time to process it. It reminded me far too much of the clearing where I'd lost Grant, except this time I hadn't even caught sight of my attacker.

And, I was sluggishly coming to realize, I didn't actually feel wounded, not at all. Generally speaking, when I had even a minor injury, I could pick it out, even if I were drugged, or half-asleep, or... whatever I was right now. It didn't really feel like Len'sal. Despite the terrible events of the night when I'd been drugged with a low dose of Len'sal, the effects of the berries themselves hadn't been entirely unpleasant. I'd just felt drowsy, and overly relaxed.

This was different. It wasn't even that my body was slow to respond, I realized. My body couldn't respond. But unlike when I'd first felt it, my mind now was sharp, racing.

"You've been paralyzed," Puck said softly, as usual coming to my mental rescue. Although his words didn't exactly alleviate my panic. I'd never been so awake, and so unable to move. It was... fairly terrifying.

I felt the fox's paw on mine, and struggled to move my fingers. I think I managed to twitch them, which the fox gave a soft smile at and squeezed my hand in return. "The sedative, at least, seems to have worn off. Blink if you can think coherently."

I did, and he sighed, reaching over to somewhere beside him that I couldn't see, and producing a cool cloth, which he ran over my forehead. "Good. Whatever they used to sedate you... I'm guessing an herb I don't know... some of the others had a poor reaction to. But you don't feel feverish. So, just the venom to contend with now."

I tried to move my mouth, and managed a hoarse, "... nhhuhh?" but little else.

"Everyone's alright," he assured me. "The men on the wall, and Admiral Reed, managed to take care of the creatures before they got anyone. A lot of people got shot up with darts, though, so I've had my work cut out for me."

I tried to make my face resemble the utter confusion I wanted to portray right now, so the fox understood I required more of an explanation, but I remembered belatedly that he wouldn't see it even if I was managing it, which just made this whole situation even more frustrating. Communicating with Puck had just gotten twice as difficult, and it wasn't always easy to begin with.

Whether or not he could tell what expression I was making or not, though, he filled in the gaps for me. "It was more of the natives," he murmured, "the... 'Cathazra'. I think one of the Otherwolf men called them 'Wyrms'. I couldn't really make out much of the fray, unfortunately, but apparently they struck from ambush with blow pipes and darts, with a mixture of poisons on them. It's a fairly brilliant concoction, actually. A paralytic for the body, and a sedative for the mind. Neither lethal, but both extremely fast-acting. I'd be fascinated to know what sorts of herbs and vipers they sourced."

"Don't..." I managed, and the fox's ears perked, "... sssou... nd...too... ex... cited."

Puck laughed at that, and smiled down at me. "Just like you to recover quickly, Shivah. Ransom and Ariel are still out. And don't worry. I'm far from hoping for diplomacy with these creatures at this point. We've barely made landfall, and they've already attacked us twice. My sympathy is running thin."

"Ran... som... alright?" I asked, weakly.

The fox nodded. "One of the two poisons really didn't agree with Ariel, though. He's had a bad fever. But we've kept him cool, and he's doing alright. He just needs to get through it."

"Magpie?" I asked, amazed at how painful it was to move my jaw. It seemed like the more feeling came back into my body, the more I was beginning to ache. Almost like my entire body had fallen asleep.

"You and I both know that rat is untouchable," the fox smirked. "He's fine. And so is Admiral Reed. Although he wouldn't have been, if Ransom hadn't been there. The wolf said he took a shot for him."

I tried to nod, but failed. I wasn't surprised Ransom had taken his job as a bodyguard seriously, even for a man he, based on what little interaction they'd had, wasn't terribly fond of. The coyote was nothing if not loyal to his 'pack', or whatever it was we were calling our small circle of friends these days.

"What... happened?" I finally managed to use a difficult word. Progress.

"The Admiral, and an Otherwolf he's been talking to... I think, it sounds to me like the one who was up on the wall, earlier," the fox explained, "they both seem to think their intention was simply to take a prisoner or two, and flee. There weren't many of the beasts, from what little I could gather, and they aren't large, like the drakes. I touched one's body. It felt about my size. And odd. I'm fairly certain they don't have legs. Only arms."

I blinked, confused. The 'drakes' we'd seen were nothing like that. They were enormous, and had most certainly had legs.

"The Cathazra are four different people," the fox said, speaking of the whole thing like he found it fascinating. Which, irritatingly enough, I'm sure he did. I was getting tired of surprises, myself. "We've only encountered the two thusfar. There are two others. Ones built more like us, with two legs and two arms, who stand upright, and another fourth variety no one seems to want to talk about. I gather they're rare, but very dangerous. I haven't been able to glean much more just yet."

"Why... take us... alive?" I asked.

Puck just shook his head. "I don't know. But apparently, they've done it before."

I tilted my head some, only realizing then that I could. Something about the way the fox had said that last bit sounded dark, in contrast to his clinical tone throughout the rest of the conversation. He knew something I didn't, and it bothered him.

I spent the next few hours regaining the ability to move, painfully. As sensation returned to my body, it brought with it a burning in my muscles, like I'd over-exerted myself. Eventually, though, I was able to sit up, and even drink some water. Puck had to tend to the others, but once I was upright I was able to get a better look at my surroundings, and spent my time in recovery taking in the new sights.

The new sights were limited, unfortunately. We were in a large room, but it was still just a room. It reminded me of a sickbay on Grayson's ship, but larger, less cramped, and with far more occupied beds. I counted at least twenty other wounded or recovering people, almost all of which were Otherwolves. I couldn't really tell what afflicted most of them, save the obvious injuries... lost limbs and bandaged wounds... but the place was filled to capacity, and the few people I saw tending to the patients were always busy. There were two women in white smocks and simple, utilitarian dresses who mostly seemed to be bringing around water and food, changing out dressings and pans, and taking orders from a tall, unusual-looking Otherwolf man in black britches and a grey vest over a long-sleeved white shirt. He wore spectacles, something I'd rarely seen, but knew aided in vision somehow, and had one of the most unusual muzzles I'd ever seen. But other than that, I couldn't discern much about the odd man except to guess that he was likely the Physician here, since the woman attendants seemed to be deferring to him.

Puquanah stayed at the four beds the people I recognized were resting in. Ransom and Ariel hadn't been the only ones hurt in the Wyrm ambush, apparently the small leopard and one of Grayson's men who'd been escorting the wagon had also been shot with the poisoned darts.

"Shivah!"

I looked up immediately when I heard the wolf's elated, booming voice, and saw that the Physician had noticed the Privateer's entrance, as well. As had half the room. Grayson made a scene wherever he went.

Although actually, it was the second man to enter the room that truly garnered the most attention. In Grayson's wake was a familiar, speckled cattle dog, in a dark, rain-slicked coat much more humble and less flashy than his crimson one, but he was still unmistakably the Admiral. I saw the Physician stiffen, and drop his muzzle, raising a hand vertically to the bridge of his forehead. I wasn't certain what the gesture meant, but a few moments later, many of the men who were physically capable in the room did the same.

"Admiral—" the Physician began, but the cattle dog silenced him with a tired wave of his hand.

"At ease, please," he muttered. "Back to your duties. Don't mind me."

The Physician dropped his hand, but he didn't relent, turning on his heel to follow the small group of men on their path towards us. Grayson had come accompanied, as usual, with a small group of hangers-on. Magpie, first and foremost, whom I was glad to see was well and, apparently, still continuing his body-guarding duties, but also a few other sailors and an extremely tall Otherwolf with a long blue coat, and wiry grey fur.

"Sir," the Physician spoke up again, tailing behind the Denholme man. He was clearly taking note of his limp. "You're injured..."

"It's being treated," the cattle dog said with a reassuring nod.

"Not by me," the Physician insisted.

The Admiral finally stopped, and put a hand on the man's shoulder. "You're overworked enough as it is down here, Forrest," he said, giving a mild smile. "Don't worry about it. I'm fine."

The Physician let him head off, looking perturbed. The entire party made it to us eventually, after crossing the hall of beds. I saw the Denholme man's eyes linger for some time on one particular patient, a sleeping, malnourished-looking canine who was missing both feet and one of his legs to the knee. Whatever was afflicting him, it must have been wasting, and the sight of him seemed to pain the cattle dog most especially, for some reason. I could only assume he knew him particularly well.

But at that point Grayson had made it to me, and sat on the corner of my small bed, looking me over. I blinked up at him, mildly alarmed by his level of concern. The wolf wore his feelings on his sleeve, and he was looking at me like I'd been dying.

"I'm fine," I interjected before he could say something stupid and entirely inappropriate. "Stop with the face."

"We didn't know what was in those darts," the wolf insisted. "I thought I'd just lost half of my closest men. And you, sweetheart."

I arched an eyebrow at the man. "I'm sure you would have soldiered on just fine without me, wolf."

"I'm a resilient man," the canine admitted, putting a paw to his chest, beneath his coat, "but my heart would have borne the scars until the day I died."

I glanced at Magpie, who was chewing on the nub of a nearly burnt-out cigarette. The rat just shrugged down at me. "I knew you were fine. They told us 's soon as we got inside the gates what was on the darts. The natives use poison-tipped arrows when they wanna kill. So I wasn't worried. Th' wolf here's been all mopin' about it, though."

"If by that you mean he 'moped' his way straight to the nearest tavern for a drink, then yes," the tall canine muttered dryly, in a thick accent I could only assume was another Otherwolf variant.

"I drink when I'm depressed!" the wolf insisted, biting out the retort at the tall, wire-haired man. "And who asked you to interject, Johannes?"

"As if I'd help you lie your way under a woman's skirt, Reed," the Otherwolf snorted. And then, surprising me somewhat, he addressed me, in a strange, almost fatherly-like tone. "I'm not certain what your connection with this man is, miss, but let me assure you, he is a lout, a criminal, a drunk and a whore-monger, and whatever your station in life is now, or will ever be, you are too good for him."

I had to fight the urge to smile, and instead forced a glare in the black wolf's direction. "Trust me," I stated, "I know."

"Attacked from all sides," the wolf sighed. "Can't a man express his concern for an injured companion without meeting with all this speculation and character assassination?"

"Save your concern for your lion," Puck spoke up. "Everyone else will be fine, but he's having a poor reaction to the sedative... or the venom. I'm not certain. He's been feverish for some time now."

That got everyone's attention, and I saw a flash of real concern on Grayson's features. The Physician, who'd been standing back but keeping his attention on our group, also perked up at the fox's words, and began to hesitantly make his way towards us. Grayson stood, looking to Puquanah.

"Is he going to pull through?" the wolf asked, worriedly.

"He should be fine," the fox said, "I'm keeping an eye on him. But I'm not entirely certain why he's having the reaction at all, so—"

"It's an allergic reaction to the sedative," the Physician spoke up, diverting everyone's attention. Even the fox looked to him, despite the fact that he couldn't see. I saw his nose and his ears twitching, clearly trying to get a mental picture of the new voice.

The strange-looking Otherwolf moved through the small crowd of men around my bed, towards Puck and Ariel's slumbering form. He looked down on the lion as he drew close, and gestured above his head, calling out to one of the women in the room.

"Alicia! Bring the anaphylaxis serum. Quickly," the canine snapped, before brushing past a suddenly pensive-looking fox and kneeling beside the lion. I'm not certain why, but he leaned down beside the sleeping, paralyzed man's muzzle, listening for a moment, then pulled something strange from around his neck, inserted two ends of it into his ears, and pressed the other against the lion's chest.

A long few moments of silence passed over all of us, and Puck in particular looked like he'd stopped breathing. The fox's ears were tipped back, his body stiff. I knew him well enough by now to see shame in his body language. I couldn't imagine why he felt that way, though.

At length the canine leaned up, then stood. He glanced back, past Puck, at Grayson and the Admiral, murmuring, "He'll be fine without the injection, but I'd still suggest it. His breathing isn't labored, but the fever can still have ill effects. You're lucky the reaction wasn't worse. Some men's throats close up."

At that point, a woman with a strange glass vial on a tray made it to us, and the Physician thanked her lowly and took the odd implement, before leaning back down beside the lion and pressing what looked to be a sharp, metal tip protruding from it into his arm. While he was doing so, he spoke in a sharp, unpleasant tone, not diverting his attention from his work.

"Why wasn't I informed about this man's condition?" he demanded. The reactions amongst our group ranged from simple confusion on Grayson's part, to a flash of anger from Puquanah, who looked about as uncharacteristically defensive as I'd ever seen the fox.

It took us all a moment to realize the question wasn't directed at us, but rather at the female aid who'd brought the vial. It seemed to take her a moment, as well.

"Alicia?" the man persisted, finally looking up at the female Otherwolf, with a glare that could have melted glass.

"Oh, I..." the woman stammered.

"You have to have seen us here with the patients," Puquanah spoke up, in an equally hard, displeased tone. The canine seemed to notice him, at that point, perhaps for the first time. He gave the fox an inquisitive look, and made to say something, but Puck interrupted him.

"I was told," he stated, "when I came here with wounded, and said I needed beds for them, that you were 'much occupied' with colonists, and that we could take up on cots in the back until you were free to see to us. I informed your aids that I could treat the wounded on my own, but that I'd never dealt with the poisons from this land before, and I could use a second opinion. Since that was never forthcoming, I'd assumed we'd been left to fend for ourselves."

"They came in with the Privateer, sir," the woman said, defensively. "I thought—"

"Admiral Grayson Reed is part of my force," the Denholme man spoke up, in that deep, commanding voice that almost didn't fit his stature. "His boats sailed in with the Fenrir, and his fleet will be aiding our force in defending this colony for the foreseeable future. From now on, you're to treat his men with the same respect, and afford them the same services you would my mariners and soldiers."

I don't think I've ever seen a woman disappear into herself quite so much as I did in that moment. The Otherwolf woman shrunk like a turtle into her shell, ears tucking back and tail curling around her leg. I had to admit, even I'd been somewhat cowed by the force in the man's words, and I didn't even like him, much less respect his authority.

"And that's beside the point," the Physician muttered, placing the strange, now empty vial back on the woman's tray with a clatter. "You know damn well I hadn't approved another Physician to manage any sort of treatment within these walls. I thought these men were here for simple bedrest. I never saw them come in. If anyone in this infirmary dies because they're receiving incompetent treatment, if it's under my watch, it's still on my head."

I physically leaned away from the fox at that, because I saw him bristle, and I'd seen Puck angry before. It was a rare occasion, but all the more terrifying for its scarcity.

"I was managing his care!" the fox grated out. "I'm grateful for your superior knowledge of the local poisons, and your... injection... I'm certain... will be of aid to him. But I was managing treatment of all of these people as well as I could in a foreign land, with foreign toxins and a lack of local knowledge—"

"You're not a certified Physician, are you?" the man retorted, in a gratingly dry tone. I saw the fox's ears tip back. "Or at least not from anywhere respectable. Are you educated at all?" He asked with a tilt of his head. "I know you're from the Colonies. That accent is unmistakable."

"I'm a tribal healer," the fox said defensively, without the edge of pride one might expect from someone defending their profession in life. But then, Puquanah didn't truly respect his profession in life. Or even believe in it, most of the time. And watching him try to defend it was painful.

I remembered that long ago, he'd spoken of his dealings with Otherwolf healers. These 'Physicians', like the one who'd refused to treat the people of Serahaven, despite his superior knowledge of medicine. The way he'd spoken about them was almost bitter, and yet also somewhat yearning. He'd said it was hard to gain respect, do trade with, or learn from any of them, because of his heritage. Yet at the same time, he wanted so badly to know what they knew. To use the tools they used, and have access to the medicines and learning they had. But he'd been rejected at every turn, because of the very reasons he himself doubted the Shaman arts. Because faith healing required faith, and not even a faith the Otherwolves shared. Or Puck, for that matter. Not anymore.

To judge him so harshly as an inferior healer seemed unfair to me, though, and made me bristle. I'd been treated by, and had my life saved by Puck a number of times now, and watched him put his life on the line to treat others. People he hardly even knew. He may not have had the advanced knowledge that the Otherwolf healers learned across the sea, but he was, at his heart, what every healer should be. He had an earnest desire to cure any who were ailing, even at the expense of his own safety. I was about to speak up to defend the fox, but he beat me to it.

"But—" Puck said, with a bit more strength in his voice, "that doesn't mean my methods are mystical, or spiritual in nature. Don't assume that simply because my people rely on spiritual healing sometimes, that that is all we do. I believe in physical healing above all else. I may have less knowledge of the world than an educated man, but I know the body well, I have a steady hand, and I am eager to learn. My knowledge of herbs may even surpass yours. And for what I lack, I..." he raised his jaw. "I would be very willing to study, and defer to a more learned man. If any would deign me worthy enough to give the chance."

"Aye, Forrest," the Otherwolf Admiral spoke up. "I honestly was hoping you'd be able to make use of the lad. I know how overworked you are down here," he patted his calf, "and he stitched me up like a pro while I was aboard the Manoratha. I was actually going to have him check the wound today, to make sure it's healing proper."

The Physician's ears shot up at that, and he gave a shocked expression. "You let him stitch up a wound on you? God above..." he gave a frustrated sigh, and pushed right past Puck towards Denholme. I don't think he'd even heard the fox's words.

The Admiral balked at the Physician's approach, especially when he knelt down and tried to tug up the man's pant leg to inspect his wound. Denholme stepped away from him, quickly, and his expression went from bemused to irate.

"For heaven's sake, Forrest," he growled, thrusting the man aside with a slight shove at his shoulder. "I said it's fine!"

"You let a blind man stitch a wound on a filthy ship!" the Physician insisted. "Begging your pardon, sir, but how can I be expected to keep you well and on your feet when you're being this reckless? At least let me inspect it. For God's sake!"

"I might have, if you hadn't been so damned pushy about it," the cattle dog muttered. "Now you get to live in suspense for a few days. I'll let you know if I start turning green."

"This isn't humorous!" the Physician all but sputtered.

"I don't honestly see what your problem is, Forrest," the Admiral sighed. "You're the one who insisted we change up the P.O.W.'s meals and elevate their holding cells—"

"They were starving to death on cooked meat," the Physician retorted, "They don't metabolize it as well. And wet mud causes disfiguring fungus on their feet—"

The cattle dog gave a disgusted sigh and gestured at the man with a hand, "See, that tripe. That's what I mean. You worried so much about the damned lizards. I never saw you as a specist."

The Physician bristled, defensively. "I'm not."

"Then let the damned fox help you in this God-forsaken place," the Admiral growled. "You need the help, the patients here need the help. God knows you could help more people with a few more able hands. What does it matter what his lineage is?"

"My issue isn't with his lineage," the Physician stated, "it's his lack of education—"

"Education comes in many forms," I spoke up, unable to remain silent any longer. "Who are you to say he isn't an experienced, able healer? Puck has treated me and the people I travel with more times than I can count, and he's saved many lives, just in the last year I've known him. What proof do you have that he's incompetent?" I challenged him, brows knitted.

The man looked to me, letting out a soft breath through his nose, before straightening up and replying. "Because," he said evenly, "he has advanced, untreated cataracts in both eyes. I can only assume that if he were educated, he would have had them treated. Long before they became so debilitating."

The air went still, and silence fell over our entire group. I stared at the man, tossing between confusion and a desire to respond—somehow, anyhow—to what he'd said. But I just didn't know what to say.

Puck was a statue, for the entirety of the frozen moment. But at length, he lifted his hands slowly to the level of his eyes, and blinked blankly down at them.

"This condition is treatable?" he asked, in a rasping whisper.

The Physician looked down at him, the first real notes of pity becoming evident in his features. He gave another quiet sigh, and reached up to pull off his spectacles, wiping them on the edge of his shirt sleeve.

"Yes," he said, at length. "Although yours are quite advanced. How long?"

"Ten years..." the fox said, so softly I almost didn't hear him.

The Physician re-donned his spectacles, his muzzle twitching. "Have you any vision remaining whatsoever?"

"Just... shapes," Puck said quietly. "It's like seeing through a dark cloud. It's gotten worse as I got older."

"It's a common condition in cultures with inadequate nutrition," the Physician murmured, then as an afterthought, as though we were all simpletons, "in communities where food is often scarce."

"My tribe is from the frozen wastes," Puck murmured.

The Physician only nodded. He was again silent for a time, before speaking again. "I didn't mean any insult," he muttered. He lacked what I would call a good 'bedside manner', but there was a hint of real empathy there. This was a hard man with a strict exterior, but I was beginning to think I may have leapt to conclusions in judging him as harshly as I had. There was something similar enough to Puck in his demeanor now, that concern I heard in the fox's tone when he was treating someone. It was just not as evident in him.

"I think it's a travesty that basic knowledge like this hasn't made it to so much of the world," the Physician said. "A lot of peoples from settlements that haven't the benefit of higher learning suffer unduly, often throughout their entire lives, when the solutions to their maladies exist, and are often so simple. It's an injustice I'd see undone if I had a few hundred lifetimes to do so myself."

"Is it too late to fix this?" Puck asked, and I could feel the quiver in his breath on the last word.

"It's not an easy operation," the Physician said, stoically. "And I've only performed it myself twice before. But, no. It's not too late." He looked back down, staring the fox in the eyes.

"That's the incredible thing about medicine. So long as you're still alive there is always a small chance."

CHAPTER 6
Whatever Necessary

The office of the 'Seneschal', an odd word in Amurescan that was apparently a title for what we would have otherwise called a 'keeper', in my tribe, was a modest two-room domicile in a large, if nondescript building near the center of the settlement. It was in the area of town where they bothered to keep up the roads, there weren't very many personal residences, and I'd by now established that this was where the Otherwolves ran their tiny, stranded 'kingdom' from. A center of government, for governing one isolated, lonely little settlement, deep in enemy terrain, in the midst of a war.

Nowhere in the city was safe, ultimately. We'd been here only a week now, and I'd already experienced two more fire-bombing raids from the 'drake' creatures. I was beginning to associate their distant silhouettes with the same sense of terror and foreboding that everyone here seemed to hold for them. And that made everyday life immensely unsettling, because they were never far. I'd frequently see them circling high in the distance, too far for the defensive harpoon cannons to fire at, but just close enough to strike fear into the hearts of everyone on watch. Which I suppose was the point.

In addition, I'd been keeping up with Puquanah, who was spending most of his days at the hospital, doing what little the Physician would allow him to. Despite their first meeting turning into such a clash, they'd apparently since put their differences aside enough that the man, Forrest, Puck was calling him, was allowing the fox to work with him, at least in some small way. Enough that Puck seemed satisfied for now.

And from what little I'd understood from him on the few occasions we'd had to speak since then, the place was badly in need of help. Aside from the many natural dangers this land presented to the colonists, the 'Cathazra', the native peoples of this place, (whom I was learning bits and pieces about, but had yet to really form a complete picture of) were fond of using poison in their assaults on the community and all outlying residences. And they didn't discriminate. Puck had told me a story just a few days ago of a three-year-old child who'd happened to stray too far from the fishery her parents worked at, and had been shot with the same sort of dart that Ransom and I had. Except this one had been meant to maim or kill, smeared with a mixture made from crushed, poisonous ants found in the forests here. If you were bit by them normally, they could cause welts that would swell and wrack a man with pain for days, possibly become infected, and in some of the worst cases, cause the loss of a limb. But the dart mixture was somehow worse, because of the sheer amount of poison. Even most grown adults would be reduced to days of feverish pain and agony. The little girl hadn't made it an hour.

My sympathy for these creatures had long since worn thin, and I was beginning to understand the anger of many of the colonists here. Ransom, Magpie and I were often stationed on the walls as part of the watch, since I'd offered our services at the outset of our journey for scouting details. I didn't mind the work, it was dangerous to be sure, but at least it wasn't boring. Ransom actually didn't seem to mind it either, or was just so glad to be off the ship and back on dry land that he was more content than before. He'd also said more than once that despite it being a foreign forest, it was good to be amidst the trees again, even if we could only see them from our side of the wall. I had to agree. I'd enjoyed the sea, but the forest, any forest, was more my natural element. Although the scent of leaves, of fresh rain on grasses and the floral aroma of pollen in the wind made my mind wander to the past, to places and people I'd left behind.

But, I'd tried to focus on getting to know some of the other men on watch to distract me from dark thoughts. For the most part, the Otherwolves here were a frayed, if decent lot. Unfortunately they were far too accustomed to death, to the point where the only way the men seemed to cope with it anymore was through dark humor, and alcohol. Those in charge of the patrols along the walls didn't keep the drinking in check, I noted, and while that was probably a mistake on one hand, I could understand why they didn't on the other. Being positioned on the wall was the most dangerous job a soldier could be assigned in this settlement, for obvious reasons, and many of these men might not have summoned the courage to come to their post every day, were it not for the poison water.

The general rule seemed to be, a man had to stay on their feet. If they no longer could, they were first replaced, then reprimanded. There didn't seem to be enough men on any shift to keep as many eyes on the sky as were probably needed, but we rotated, we took short breaks at the guard towers so our eyes and our feet didn't tire, and the whole of the garrison did their best to make it work.

As a newcomer, and a crewman from a Privateer vessel, I'd been warned I might not be warmly greeted. We'd all been warned of that. Grayson had even given me an out—just me personally, of course, not the other men. He wasn't ashamed of favoritism, and he was, after all, still doggedly attempting to court my favor. But I'd declined the offer. Both of them. And not just because I wanted to honor the deal I'd made with him when we'd come aboard his vessel. I'd wanted to stay beside Ransom and Magpie, and all the other men risking their lives for this settlement. And that fact, perhaps here more than any other battlefield, seemed to weigh with far more importance to the men on the wall than anything else about me. My allegiance with Grayson's Privateer fleet, the fact that I was not Amurescan, the fact that I was a woman, even... once the soldiers here realized I reported to my post on time each day, and we'd weathered one of the bombing raids together and I'd showed I was not afraid to fire on the beasts, or remain standing on the wall when they strafed our lines... I'd found acceptance quickly. Almost more readily than I had aboard Grayson's vessel.

The men here, the Amurescan men, were of different stock. Better in some ways than the Privateers, and worse in others.

Quieter overall, more disciplined—which made sense, they were in the military. Harder for men like Ransom to warm to, he found them too stoic, too 'stuffy', as he called it. Whatever that meant. The word I knew in the Otherwolf tongue seemed to make no sense in context. But apparently, these Amurescan men were, from families with wealth and consequence, or at least all the canines from the Denholme man's fleet were, and they were usually the men he trusted to defend the walls. So dignity in the face of death meant a great deal to them, especially around outsiders. The few rats and felines I'd seen along the walls were less concerned with putting up a front, and Ransom and Magpie kept company with many of them.

All the same, I didn't feel disrespected by these men the way I had aboard Grayson's vessel. I was still treated as an outsider, to be sure, and spending time aboard one of their vessels would probably be uncomfortable and awkward, but they were civil. Over time, some of them even spared a word for me now and then. They were always polite, and a few of them had even asked me if I wanted to drink with them after a shift. I wasn't fond of poison water, so I'd turned them down, but I took it as a good sign that I was growing more accepted, and that gave me some peace. I might have been sorely out of my element in this place, but I was determined to fight beside these men now that I was here, and I couldn't do that if they didn't accept me amongst their ranks.

My original intention in coming here had been... I hardly knew anymore. It seemed in retrospect, I'd just been swept up in a flood of anger, and a desire for vengeance so furious as to be almost unrecognizable, now that I looked back on it. I'd even taken it for granted that Shadow would be here, to begin with. On the word of a madman. For all I knew, she was still somewhere in the wilderness in my homeland. We'd honestly lost her trail before we'd even really found it. The only reason we suspected she was here at all was for the same reason we were. And I hardly knew the woman, except as some specter who'd killed my lover, and many others before him.

She could be dead. In Carvecia, or in the waters surrounding Serwich. The concept of finding her now seemed so hopeless, and I was almost glad for that fact. I was here, in this settlement, for a reason. My path had brought me here to serve a purpose. But it wasn't the purpose I'd set out for.

It was Puck. It had always been Puck, all this time. The fox was the only one amongst us who had ever truly had the right goals in mind. And we were here now to support him. To keep him safe, and keep these people safe, until he accomplished what he'd come here for.

Whatever had started me down this path, all the pain and terrible experiences I'd endured, I'd at last begun to accept that it had all happened for a reason. I was meant to walk it, and finally I felt I knew why. And it wasn't just for the fox. It was because of what we'd come here to do. If Puck could find out why the Seer's Fever was spreading, we could do a lot of good, for a lot of other people in the world who were suffering. They may not have been suffering the same way I had, or my child had, or Grant had, or even for the same reasons, but that didn't mean righting this wrong was any less important. It was certainly more important than vengeance.

Puck's goals here were in jeopardy because of this war, and that was the bottom line. Whether or not these creatures were in the right to force the Otherwolves off of their land, they were killing their people, cruelly and without consideration for the lives of the innocent. My sympathy for another tribe of peoples being oppressed only went so far. I wasn't off the fence entirely about what was happening here, but I was determined to defend myself, and my friends. And right now, that meant defending this city.

And ultimately, that's what had brought me here, to this freshly-painted wooden building. It was innocent enough in appearance, it would have gotten lost amidst the other white-washed structures in this bizarrely 'new' settlement, where everything was less than a generation old. But, the reason I was here was less than innocent, and I knew it.

A few days ago, approximately a week into my stay here, I'd been approached while I'd been on wall duty, by Grayson, and a man I'd only met in passing until now. A tall, grey, wire-furred dog who apparently bore some sort of position amongst the elites in this settlement, because I'd seen him at the side of the Denholme man more than once, especially when he came to visit Grayson aboard his ship. Which, alas, was where I was still staying, preferring it to sleeping alone in some empty, unfamiliar room in an unfamiliar inn, in the unfamiliar community. If barely, as I still had to put up with the wolf.

I didn't know the man well, couldn't even remember his name now if someone had asked me for it, didn't know his position or what it was exactly that he did here in this community, but he'd sought Ransom, Magpie and I out specifically. Had gone so far as to come to Grayson personally to have him introduce us. And he'd given me his name again, and I'd, again, forgotten it. It was ludicrously exotic and complicated.

He hadn't told us much at the brief meeting except that he wanted to speak with us privately at some point about work he needed done, scouting work, he'd said. It was certainly something we could do, but I had no clue exactly what he intended, or why he needed to meet with us in private. Let alone, as he'd later insisted, separately. Ransom was to come and hour after I, and Magpie had come and presumably gone an hour before. I didn't see him here now.

It was all very cloak and dagger, and I didn't trust it. The man had never actually given me any pangs of concern before now. And he had told me not to trust Grayson, which was sane, rational advice if ever I'd heard any. So I wasn't certain what this was all about. But it was odd. It definitely didn't feel innocent.

I sat nervously in the Seneschal's office, feeling once again dirty in the immaculate furnishings the Otherwolves seemed to prefer. It wasn't especially fancy, like the Mayor's house had been, but the wooden furniture here was all polished and clean, the drapes were white, the desk in the corner of the room neatly arranged with a few stacks of papers, a quill balanced on a wooden peg that seemed to have been made specifically for it, its ink corked beside it. The shelves were immaculately well-organized and stocked with books, none of which I could read, but it was clear by the colors and sequential, similar writing that they were all in their proper place. If this was how the Otherwolves kept track of their supplies, it was no surprise they had such an eloquent name for their keeper.

But I wasn't here to meet him. This was just the place the tall, grey Otherwolf had told me we'd meet, and when I'd made it here, a woman had let me in and told me to wait. And so, that's what I'd been doing, nervously. To say I was out of my element in this place, and this entire situation, was putting it mildly.

The door suddenly opened, no louder than any other door, but for some reason it startled me to my feet. I saw the tall man duck inside and tried to calm my nerves, smoothing down my leathers as I attempted to look like standing had been an intentional move. He barely looked up as he entered, so he hadn't noticed. I tried to calm down.

The man took stock of me before long, and cleared his throat, walking into the room and tugging something out from between the folds of his coat, tucked under his arm, settling it down on the desk as he greeted me. It just looked like a rolled up piece of paper, albeit a large one.

"Good morning," he said in that deep, rich voice I remembered from before. "It was Shivah, was it not?"

Great. He remembered my name.

"Um... yes," I stumbled out. "Sir."

He arched an eyebrow a moment, then said, "Cuthbert. Johannes Cuthbert. If the name's too difficult for you, 'sir' is fine, but you aren't under my command so I won't require it."

I let out a breath I hadn't known I was holding, while the man turned his back on me and made his way over to the desk he'd dropped the rolled paper on, deftly undoing a ribbon that tied it closed, before pushing a few of the things on the desk out of the way, and unfurling it entirely.

"Oh," I said, making my way slowly towards the desk. It was a map. Well, what had I really expected? Apparently this was in fact about scouting. So, perhaps there was nothing sinister going on here at all. I might have been worried for nothing.

The Otherwolf traced his paw-pads over the map for a little while, ostensibly to flatten it out, but I could tell he was deep in thought as he did so. I looked it over, seeing if I could pick out any land-masses and make sense of it. The mountain and the coastline were obvious, but the rest was a blur. I didn't know these lands well, and we hadn't left the walls since we'd first entered them—for the best, considering what lay beyond.

The canine tapped a corner of what must have been the wall, a dark, red-lined area in the basin of the mountain range Serwich was pushed up against. There were other scrawled red marks across the map, and several blue as well, punctuated by symbols I could only guess the meaning of. A war map, perhaps? I'd never really seen one before, but Grayson was fond of collecting maps and I'd often considered pawing through his collection, even though most of it would make little sense to me.

"This here," the man stated, "is our line of defense. These are the few way-posts we have in enemy territory," he pointed to red triangles spread throughout the map, "and these are the few enemy way-posts we know of," he pointed to blue triangles, at that. Fairly simple. I was following so far.

"The latter are always in flux," he said with a barely-hidden edge of irritation in his tone. When he took a moment to glance down at me, and noticed I was staring up at him vacantly, he explained. "I'm sorry, second language, I know. 'In flux' means 'changing', essentially. They are always changing where they keep their sentries, their skirmishers... their guerrillas. Keeping us on our toes," he sighed. "So this map is more guesswork than anything else. Take nothing for granted. The blue indicates areas that should just generally be avoided, if possible."

I nodded and silently felt a wave of gratitude towards the man for being so patient with the language barrier between us. It reminded me again of the 'fatherly' air he'd had about him when I first met him. Patient, willing to explain, not judging me for not following him entirely. Again, I was almost unconsciously starting to feel comfortable around him, and I didn't know why. I usually kept up my defenses around strange men, but he just didn't feel threatening.

"It seems like these creatures hunt much the same way our people do, so the concept of 'guerrilla' warriors, my people would call them 'Tokshan', 'stalkers', isn't as foreign to me as you might think," I said. "It's your people who fortify with your stone buildings. These creatures' tactics are almost more familiar to me. Save the flying."

The man gave me a thoughtful look for a moment, then leaned back, one hand still on the desk, as he looked down at me. "Might I admit something, miss?" He asked, ever polite.

I blinked. "You may."

"I didn't know the tribal people of Carvecia allowed female warriors," he admitted. "It's strange enough that the Privateer enlisted tribal folk, it's been something of a guessing game between the Admiral and I how that came to pass, but you're an even stranger anomaly."

I stared up at him expectantly.

He sighed, "Apologies again. You're an oddity. Amongst oddities. I mean no offense—"

"No, it's fine," I said, unable to stop from giving a light, breathy laugh, "I hardly understand how I came to this point in my life, myself. It's been a long and winding path, that is for certain," I looked up at him, sighing, "I was never a hunter in my tribe, but I've experience hunting others who worked similarly."

The Otherwolf arched an eyebrow, and for a moment I got a flash of something I hadn't seen from him yet—distrust. And it was intimidating.

"Not your people," I tried to insist. "I mean, I don't think so. Some of them were Otherwolves—"

"'Other'..." he blinked, "ah, right. That's a term your people use for us, isn't it? For all non-native canines."

"Ah, yes," I murmured, suddenly conscious of the fact that the term might actually be offensive to these people. I'd been using it on them since I'd emerged into their society, without even considering that. Was it derogatory, to them?

I was about to apologize, when the man interrupted me, "Never you mind, miss," he said, casually waving a hand. "I don't intend to pry into your past. I'd already accepted that any of the men Reed brought in might have... colorful histories. We aren't in a position to be picky at the moment, which is why I'm tolerating him, at all."

"You really dislike him," I said quietly, feeling at once a slightly defensive flare for the wolf, and then a wave of revulsion that I was even considering that. I was still extremely confused where that man was concerned.

"Well," the canine said, running his fingers over the mustache of fur along his muzzle, "he is a murderer."

"What?" I blinked. General character-assassination, I had expected, but—

The man gestured towards the window. "Oh, come now. You strike me as a woman of the world, miss, not some sheltered lily. You must know what the canons on his ship are for, at the very least. How do you think the man makes his living?"

"There's a difference between murder and fighting for your life," I insisted.

"Yes, and," the canine began to shrug off his blue coat, hanging it over a nearby chair. He looked very different without the coat on, somehow. The garment made him look older. I hadn't really any idea how old the man actually was, but I could tell once he was down to a shirt and vest that he was no scarecrow. The Otherwolf had the bearing and the build of a warrior, if a lean one. And he wore a chest harness with several hidden, sheathed blades between his shoulders, and one neatly tucked along his left breast, covered by the coat and the cravat he tugged free as he continued speaking. "That difference is what? How the killing is done? Killing in the heat of battle, versus killing in cold blood. Yes?"

"Yes," I said, without question. "I've killed in the heat of battle. I wouldn't consider myself a murderer."

"Grayson Reed is a Privateer, miss," the man said with a sigh. "And I'm guessing you simply haven't been a part of his fleet long enough to know what that means. The man is a pirate with a license. A thief, who is paid by countries, by men of the law, to steal from others. Usually enemies of that country. And merchants don't generally part with their wares good-naturedly. He spills blood to plunder those ships. He's sunk more than he's spared, in fact, if the reports I've seen are true."

I bit at my lower lip. I knew, of course—I'd always known what it was the wolf did. I suppose I just hadn't forced myself to think about it much. And that's precisely what this man was attempting to make me do. Just once in my life, it would have been nice if something was black and white. But something in the canine's claims didn't connect.

"I don't understand," I said. "He can't profit from a ship he sinks. I'd always thought he did his theft more through... a show of force."

"Oh certainly, for those who haven't the spine to stand against him," the canine snuffed. "But many merchant vessels, especially these days, have armed escorts. Frigates, usually hire-ons to support the vessel with the goods. Pirates—'Privateers'—whatever you want to call them, they're all the same to me... have no issue sinking defense vessels. Besides miss," he sighed, "cannonballs don't always discriminate. I know for a fact he's sunk at least a dozen Amurescan navy ships, and three merchant ships I know of in pitched battles, rather than sink himself. A loss for him, I'm sure, but the man is reckless in his pursuits. His ships are well-armed, but a hodge-podge of pieces he's scrounged over the years. Last I saw the inside of that man-of-war, baling out the hold was an everyday necessity, even at port."

I sighed. Having worked below-decks, I could attest to that. The old vessel was a mess.

"Anyone who sails in a decrepit beast like that," the Amurescan man shook his head," that sort of attitude leaves a lot of wreckage in your wake. If you've been with him any amount of time—"

I ground my teeth, and bit out an irritated, "I know what kind of a man he is."

The canine looked mildly taken-aback, but not flustered. He crossed his arms over his chest. "Then I'm curious why you'd leap to defend him, is all."

"I'm curious why you called me here to talk about scouting, when we've been spending most of our time on a tear about Reed," I replied, pointedly.

The canine's eyes narrowed. "You're fond of him, aren't you?"

My own eyebrows shot down. "I fail to see how that's any of your business!"

"It isn't," the man said with a wave of his hand, "but you denied it before, so it is a lie, if nothing else."

"I am no more fond of that man than I would be a lame horse... that bites at me," I growled. "He was a means to getting here, and a troublesome one. That's all."

The dog's grey eyes gave me a quizzical look at that, and he murmured, "Interesting. We'll come back to that."

"I fail to see how any of this is on-point," I reiterated, with more force behind my words. "You brought me here to discuss a scouting job. A job I'm only considering, I'll point out, because of Reed. So no matter what you think of the man, he's the only reason I'm here right now to help you. At the very least—"

"I am grateful that the man came here," the canine said, surprising me. "I'm thankful to have him, his ships, and his people, here. I wish there were some other way we could have requested aid, but he truly was the only option left available to us."

"So, then—"

"That being said, I wouldn't have called him in," the canine muttered. "That was Luth—," he paused, "Lord Denholme's call. And it was the right call to make. I wouldn't—couldn't—have made it. But then that's where my lord excels. Making the hard calls..."

He went unusually silent at that for long enough that I arched an eyebrow, until his eyes at last flicked down to me. "Reed is a wild-card," he continued. "As it is, we had to lie to him, and trap him here to even ensure he would still be here when the fighting occured. The only way we could be certain of that at all is to give him no other choice. 'Flighty' does not begin to describe that wolf. And he owes my Lord a great deal. The bastard should come whenever he snaps his fingers."

"I don't care if your 'Lord' dragged him from death's door!" I snapped.

"The gallows, actually," the canine muttered.

"It wasn't right to do that to him and his men!" I argued, over his muttering. "I have friends amongst his crew!"

"Who signed on willingly, I can only imagine," the canine shrugged, then, as though thinking the better of it, asked in curiosity, "or were you press-ganged?"

"Enough of this," I growled. "If you don't get to the point of this meeting soon, I'm leaving. You called me here, away from my post and apart from my friends, and I took it on good faith that I could trust you. But all you've done is shown me a map, and questioned me like I'm some sort of prisoner. I'm here to help you."

"Why?" the canine asked, leveling his grey eyes down at me, and suddenly, in the one word, all of the fatherly compassion and concern I'd thought I'd seen there in the man drained away. This really was an interrogation.

I began to look for the door.

"It's a simple enough question," the man said, not bothering to move from where he stood as I turned my back on him. I made it as far as the door, but his deep voice somehow compelled me not to leave. "Your rat comrade found my questioning uncomfortable, as well. He chose not to hear me out, but I figured you for having stronger bones, miss."

I turned on him with a venomous glare at that. "Gabriel has his right to his privacy. We don't deserve this."

The man arched one eyebrow. "'Gabriel'? You see, that's not even the name I was given. Some kind of bird. I saw it for an alias from the outset, but—"

I blanched. I hadn't meant to give that away.

"The scouting mission I have in mind, miss," the canine said, "and the sheer concept of working beside me in my endeavors in general, requires a certain level of trust. The tasks I need completed, more specifically the information I need gathered, is of a nature that cannot be disseminated to the public at large."

"Use. Smaller. Words," I snapped, done with waiting for the man to break things down for me, now. It had lost its charm.

The tall canine moved towards me, not in a threatening matter, but with his arms folded behind him, taking slow steps. "I gather information for my Lord. Information relevant to this community, and more specifically of late, the war. Some of the things we've learned over the years have enabled us to prevent raids, to cut off enemy reinforcements before they reach Zakkra, the Cathazra's leader, and to find more effective ways to defend our settlement. But these secrets would be no good to us if they got out."

"Why?" I asked, baffled. "I've seen these 'Cathazra'. Surely you don't think they're here in your community, spying on you?"

"No," the canine said with a soft sigh, "but some of our own people are."

"For what?" I asked, shocked. "What do those beasts have that your people want?"

"Gold," the man replied simply. "It's what first brought Carvecians here to this land, and then later my own people, and what's kept us coming back time and again. The lumber is our primary export, but gold is the real reason the colonies here were built. The Cathazra have it in excess. They wear it, they use it in their holy vestments and charms, it festoons their temples," he said it all with an edge of ire.

"Riches are no good to the dead," I muttered. "I just don't see how it would be worth it to anyone who lives here to sell out their own safety."

The man shrugged, "Many of them likely think they can escape. Some of them probably even have. In all the chaos over the last few years, keeping our trade in check hasn't been high on the list of priorities. We're happy for any vessels that make it in or out of port, especially of late. This place is rife with criminals, believe it or not. Like maggots on a corpse."

"You speak like you're giving up on the place," I stated.

"We have," the man replied, stoically.

And that's when it all fell into place.

"Your 'Lord' mentioned something along those lines," I said, realization dawning. "You're planning to abandon this colony, aren't you?"

The dog was silent, but that was enough confirmation for me.

"You trust me enough to tell me this?" I asked, quizzically. Surely the population hadn't been told yet. I would have heard about it from the men on the wall.

"Well, despite the fact that our back-and-forth here seems to have put you ill at ease," the Otherwolf stated, "I do believe you've been honest with me the entire time we've spoken, which was the point of all of this questioning. You're poor at concealing your emotions, miss."

I glared at him.

"Deadly," the canine replied to my icy look, with the barest hint of amusement. "You could run a man through with those eyes."

"Don't play with me," I growled. "I don't play nice. And I haven't had good dealings with men who keep secrets, so I might be the wrong person to keep yours."

"Even if it could help this community, and the friends you have protected by its walls?" the canine countered.

"Even if you believe I'm an honest person," I replied, "which I am. I don't think I'm right for your work. Like I said. I don't like secrets."

"Nor do I," the man said in an even tone that was beginning to grate on me. "That's why I flush them out. I'm in the game of gathering information, miss, not concealing it. We just don't need our enemies knowing what we know. If that makes sense."

It actually did, and I gave a soft huff. "But what more information for your war here do you need, if you're surrendering this place anyway?" I asked, crossing my arms over my chest. "Just flee. It seems to be what they want, anyway."

"Don't fool yourself," the canine said darkly, "they don't intend to let us leave this place alive. They may not be able to stop a mass exodus, but they would sink most of our fleet before we got away, as things stand. Zakkra's longships wait at the south and north end of the coastal range like predators in wait. They will show no mercy, even after they've won."

That troubled me more than I cared to admit. I'd thought at the very least, once we were ready to leave this place, fleeing would be no issue. I'd overheard the conversation the Denholme man had had with Reed, of course, but somehow, hearing it reinforced by this man, with such conviction, really affirmed it.

We were trapped here. In the middle of a war-zone. And so was every soul in Serwich, right down to the most innocent. And most of them didn't even know it yet.

"Do you grasp the gravity of our situation?" The man asked.

"I do," I said softly, "but, what can we do? What is it you need me for? You asked for Ransom, Magpie and I specifically. I can only assume you need us to do something that involves our skills in the wilderness. You said scouting, but—" I paused, "scouting what, exactly?"

"This is the point where I need a yes or no," the canine said quietly, leaning back against the desk the map was strewn over. He leveled his grey-eyed gaze at me.

"On what?" I asked, an edge in my voice.

"On whether or not you're willing to work with me," the man replied simply.

"I can't know that until you tell me what I'll be doing," I grunted, giving the man an indignant look.

"Then our conversation ends here, unfortunately," the man said with a shrug.

"This is why Magpie left, isn't it?" I snarled. "You expect us to sign on for a job you won't even tell us the nature of?"

"I've told you what the nature of it is," the man replied. "I've told you I need you to gather information for me that will be essential to the safety of this city. Considering you're residing within it, I would imagine that's of interest to you—"

"You won't say what, or why," I persisted. "Which means—"

"It means that once I do that, you'll already know too much," the man said in a hard tone. "I need to know you're within my circle of trust before I can do that, miss. If this gets out at all, the Cathazra may have an inkling what our plan is, and I can't have that."

"Who would I tell?" I said, exasperated. "I just got here!"

"We don't know where the leaks are, so I can't take any chances," he responded, calmly.

"Fine!" I bit out, suddenly. And for the first time since we'd begun our conversation, I seemed to have caught him off-guard.

The man blinked at me. "Fine?"

"I'll do it," I growled out, my mind on Puck, on the hospital, on everything we were trying to do here. "Whatever it is," I said, with more strength in my tone. "I'll do it."

The tall Otherwolf looked across the room at me for awhile, his eyes gauging me. When he finally spoke, after an irritatingly long pause... I wanted to punch him.

"Just like that?" He asked, scratching at his chin.

"For the love of!" I stomped a foot forward, thrusting my arms down at my side. "Is this another test of some sort? Did you want me to say no, or someth—"

The canine actually chuckled, putting out his hands. "No, no, please. Calm down. I just expected you'd ask me more questions."

One corner of my muzzle twitched up. "I'm not killing anyone for you," I snapped, "if that's what this is about."

"Well, there's always the chance we have to defend ourselves against the Cathazra out in the field," the man said, "but no. I'm hardly looking for an assassin."

"I have no issue defending mys—" I paused, "'We'? You're coming on this excursion."

"This is important enough that I need to personally oversee it," the man nodded.

I let out a breath I hadn't known I was holding at that. Well that at least meant this probably wasn't suicidal. I was marginally more willing to trust a man who was putting his own life on the line beside us. Connall had always conveniently been absent whenever push really came to shove, dealing with the raiders. And, of course, there had been a reason.

I didn't actually get the feeling this man had been lying to me about anything we'd spoken of thusfar, though. In fact, if what he was saying was accurate, and I only had his word that it was, mind you, he was something of a mirror opposite to the sorts of men Connall had kept company with. We were searching for information, not trying to cover it up. But what?

"What is this mission?" I asked, my voice steadying a bit as my nerves settled down.

"How about I answer that," the man said, holding up a hand, "if you answer one more question of mine?"

I sighed. "You like to ask a lot of questions," I muttered.

The Otherwolf gave the barest hint of a smile, and this one seemed genuine. "This is strictly personal curiosity this time, I assure you."

"Go ahead, then," I said.

"You said Reed was a means for you to get here," the canine said. "That means your purpose aboard his ship was specifically to travel here, not simply to loot and plunder and find employment with his men."

"Hardly," I mumbled with a shrug. "Does that make you feel better about hiring me, or something?"

"Yes," the man replied off-handedly, "but that's not why I was curious. If you don't mind my asking, miss... Why did you come so far to be here? This place is hardly on most maps, it's certainly not a destination for sight-seeing, and it's worlds away from your homeland. I'd have to wager it's something very specific that brought you here." He paused for a few moments at that, as I looked contemplative. "If you don't wish to answer," he said quietly, "I understand."

"No, it's..." I sighed. "It's not as though we're hiding it or anything. It's just, this is an odd thing to say..."

The man waited quietly, patiently giving me as much time as I needed to answer.

I sighed. "It just sounds ludicrously noble and naive when I think of saying it out loud, and I don't think you'll believe me. But you'd have to have walked our path over the last year to really, fully understand how we came to this point. Why it's so important to us."

"Is it anything I could help you with?" the man asked, and I was forced to look up at him, at that. I needed to see for myself if his expression truly matched the earnest, guileless tone of his voice. And it did.

"Maybe," I conceded softly, and even a bit hopefully. "But, tell me about this mission, first..."

"So what's the old codger want?" A familiar, rough voice broke through my thoughtful reverie as I stepped out into the early afternoon sunlight. I turned to regard the tall, scarred coyote where he stood leaning against the porch railing that wrapped around the white-washed wooden building.

I sighed at Ransom, crossing my arms over my chest and letting my body fall back against the sun-drenched wood, closing my eyes. "I have been 'instructed not to speak on the specifics', at least until after you talk to him."

"Shady," the coyote said with a snort and a chuckle. He hopped down from the porch without using the stairs, and loped towards the door. "Well," he casually waved at me as he opened the door, "if'n I don't come out 'n an hour or more, send help."

The door closed solidly behind him, and I let out a breath, remaining right where I was. I wasn't on duty for another four or so hours today, so I'd already decided I'd be waiting to see whether or not the coyote reached the same outcome with the man I had. As it turned out, I hardly needed to wait an hour to find out.

Roughly five minutes or less after he'd entered, the coyote stepped out again. The short wait had me jumping when the door clattered open beside me. My eyes snapped open, taking in Ransom's expression and expecting to see him angrily storming away, the way Magpie likely had when he'd walked out on the meeting earlier.

He actually looked extremely casual. He even struck a match on the paving stones along the entrance as he stepped out into the street, lighting a fresh cigarette dangling from his muzzle.

I blinked at him. "Well?" I asked, the curiosity gnawing at me now.

The canine turned his long muzzle towards me and blew out a breath of smoke between his teeth. "I'm in," he stated simply.

I tried to keep my jaw from hanging open. "Just like that?" I asked disbelievingly. The man had barely been in there long enough to make introductions and be briefed on the plan.

"Ah don't see we've got much option but t' work with th' blue bloods here," the coyote shrugged, so casually it annoyed me. "I don't wanna get ate, d'you?"

I just shook my head, mute.

"They know the terrain, they know what needs git done," he waved a hand, shaking one of the enormous horse flies that seemed to flourish in this place off his shoulder. "So, if they tell me t' jump, ah'm askin' how high. Simple as that. B'sides," his eyes swept past me, towards the city line beyond. "My fox is here."

My gaze on him softened at that. Sometimes the coyote had a way of boiling down what seemed like very complex decisions to an almost absurdly simple level. And most of the time, I tended to agree. We'd come to the same decision on this in the end, and for the same reason. He just came to his decision a lot faster than I had.

I guess that's what you'd call living on instinct, as opposed to thinking through everything. I suppose it had its merits and flaws, as his track record showed. Honestly, it might have behooved me to give it a try myself from time to time. I was prone to over-thinking, even though I'd never considered myself a deep thinker. Well, there was probably a middle-ground I could walk, if I could ever figure out how.

I let out a long, deep breath. "So he explained the plan to you?"

"Yeah," the coyote said, his pupils going small in the sunlight as he looked to the horizon. "Find somethin' to burn."

"It's a little more complex than that," I muttered. "And I can't say I really like it, but it's a solid plan, and it's probably better than the alternative."

"If by 'alternative' y'mean throwin' a buncha' our boys' lives away in some kinda' distractin' attack on one 'a their outposts, then leavin' them here t' die, then... yeah... I'd say it's a hell of a lot smarter," the coyote snuffed.

I set my jaw. That really was the alternative, wasn't it?

"The ships this place's got t' use for the evacuation ain't armed, Shivah," the coyote grunted, putting a hand on the small of his back and stretching with a slight wince. "All stripped-down, old trade vessels, not warships. They won't make it too far if the scaled beasts ain't distracted somehow—"

"Doesn't this all just make you a bit uncomfortable, though?" I queried, growing tired of the coyote's detached demeanor. "I mean, just a few months ago, we were hunting people who were burning villages, and now—"

"Hey!" the coyote stabbed a finger in my direction. "Don't compare this 'n that, a'ight! This's a war, Shivah. Like it or not, people're gonna die. Ain't no avoidin' that. But these ain't innocents we're talkin' about here. These people are tryin' to obliterate us! If they'd just let all the people here pull up their roots 'n leave, that'd be one thing. Ain't no reason to kill 'em in that case. But they ain't even givin' us that option. They're the ones who're keepin' this goin'!" He spit on the ground. "We gotta do what we gotta do, and that's that. Stop analyzin' it."

"But don't you think there's probably a reason?" I pressed. "They wouldn't be this angry, unless—"

"I don't ruttin' care!" The coyote snapped, and I went silent. He didn't even sound angry at me. He just sounded final. "Look, cat," he said, dropping his tone somewhat and moving towards me, making a rare gesture for him, and putting a paw on my arm. Despite the fact that we were arguing, I was glad for the comfort. I raised my eyes to his.

"I didn't want nothin' to do with this place, or this war," he said quietly. "I doubt you did, either. But we're here fer Puck. To help him do what he came t' do. An' that's important, yeah? Hell, I tried t' talk you all outta it, but even I know if he can figure this fever out, it'd be a real good thing. For a lotta people. Right?"

My eyes fell to the ground, and I nodded.

"So stop twistin' yerself up over a buncha' folk we don't even know, who want us all dead, anyway," the coyote said. "These people, th' Otherwolves and these lizard folk, they got their own fight goin' on here, and it ain't ours. Let's just do what we gotta to survive, and get the hell outta here. And don't worry if we're tippin' th' balance somehow. We're on this side of the wall. Ain't no way to be neutral here."

His hand slipped away from mine, and he leaned back, seeming to consider something for a moment before giving a disgruntled grumble, "B'sides, yer fond of th' wolf, right?"

My eyes shot back up to his. He didn't look like he'd liked admitting that. Not a surprise, really. He was still intensely distrustful of Grayson, and hadn't in any way hidden his ire for the man. And I couldn't even blame him, really. The man had tried to blackmail me into sleeping with him, and Ransom had issues with people taking advantage of others in that regard.

"One," I grated out, "I am getting tired of people accusing me of that. And two, how is that relevant to this conversation?"

"If we don't find a target fer these blue-bloods to burn, to distract the lizards long enough fer our people t' flee," the coyote said pointedly, "they're gonna hafta' send ships t' busy all them boats the lizards got along the coastline. Who d'you think these men're most likely to throw away on something like that?"

My breath caught in my throat. He was right. I'd been thinking they'd be sending men over-land to distract the Cathazra when the time came for the exodus, but the lizard people were hard to find within their own forests. That's why we were going to scout their lands for important sites—holy sites, is what the 'Cuthbert' man had said—where we could set fires that would consume their time and manpower to quash, while our people fled. Keep them away from their ships long enough that the citizens here had a real chance at escape. If we couldn't do that, we would have to fight them at sea. And the boats that would go out to fight them, while the less-armed ships full of civilians fled would be...

I didn't know this Denholme man or his people well, but it wasn't much of a jump to think he might throw Grayson to the predators at our backs, if it meant he and his people could escape. Hell, that could be the whole reason he'd brought the wolf here to begin with. As a contingency plan.

"We gotta do this, Shivah," the coyote said determinedly. "Fer everyone's sake."

I nodded, stoically. I turned towards the city sweeping up the side of the basin beyond us, shielding my eyes against the sun. "It puts Puck on a bit of a deadline," I stated.

"He's always been on a deadline," the coyote muttered. "Ah think he knows that. He's really pressured, now. Ain't seen much of him since we got here. And when I do, he don't want t' talk much."

I winced at his words. I knew there were more reasons for that than Ransom himself was aware of, but the fox had absolutely forbade me to speak on it to him. I hated keeping secrets from my friends. Secrets that people really ought to have told their lovers.

The coyote glanced at me out of the corner of his eye suddenly, with a wry expression, and I made a face at him. Did he suspect I was keeping something from him? Puck had absolutely sworn me to secrecy about the possible fix for his eyesight. As much as I thought he should have spoken to Ransom about it by now, though, I wasn't going to betray him.

"I jes... tell me y' ain't actually into that wolf," the man muttered, pleadingly.

I narrowed my eyes, "I keep telling you that, and no one seems to believe me!"

"Yer still bunkin' with him, Shivah. Even here at port."

"I don't have any coin!" I snapped at him. "And, before you say you'd give me some... to do what? Sleep alone in some inn, surrounded by these people I don't know? You and Puck have each other—"

"I said I was barely seein' him anymore, didn't I?" the coyote said bitterly, his shoulders slumping somewhat, and I felt a pang of depression at his words. He honestly looked upset by the fact.

“He’s working,” I said, uneasy that I’d brought out such depression from the coyote. “He’s doing what he came here to do. You said yourself, it’s important.”

“I know,” the coyote muttered. “I jes... didn’t see much ‘f him on the ship, and now we’re here, and it’s even worse, somehow. I ain’t like you, Shivah. I don’t get on well left alone with my thoughts.”

I almost laughed. Almost. “And you think I do?”

“Is that why yer fond of the wolf?” the man said with a glance my way, throwing the burning stub of his cigarette on the ground and stomping it out. “Tryin’ to move on?”

I felt my fur bristle defensively, but he actually didn’t look accusing. More hopeful.

I looked away from him. “No,” I said, quietly.

“Ain’t a bad thing if you are, y’know,” the coyote murmured. “Ah’m sure he wouldn’t ‘a wanted you pinin’ for him fer the rest o’ your days.”

I arched an eyebrow up at him. “Are you now telling me I should pursue the Privateer?”

“Aw hell no!” the coyote growled. “That bastard’s a piece o’ shit, Shiv. He don’t deserve yer time, let alone yer feelings. You know how I feel about him.”

I chuckled. “What are you, my older brother? Protecting me from unworthy suitors? You did this same thing with...” I went silent. So did Ransom.

I wrapped my arms around my midsection, hoping if I squeezed hard enough, I’d stave off the heaviness that threatened at the back of my throat. These days, I could stop myself from crying when I thought of him. Most of the time.

At length, I felt the coyote slide one of his long arms around my shoulders. I leaned against him somewhat, and we stood in the quiet street and looked to the mountains beyond.

“I ain’t one to lecture,” the coyote murmured. “I went off th’ deep end when I thought I lost Puck. Yer fairin’ better than I would’ve.”

“I’m just quieter about it,” I whispered.

"Grant was a good man," the coyote said, respect laced through his words. It still lanced through me when he said his name, though. "Ah know you cared for 'm, and I understand why. Ain't many men like that who walk th' earth."

I shook my head, silently.

"But that's why he wouldn't want you spendin' the rest o' your days alone, Shivah," he said, his yellow eyes flicking down to mine. "I ain't sayin' you oughta' leap int' the first man's arms y' find, specially not that bloody wolf, but y' also don't need to feel like you won't find no one else again. That's all I'm sayin.'"

"I know that," I said softly. "But, Ransom," I looked up at him, "I have you, and Puck, and Magpie, and a widening circle of friends. And to be earnest with you, I'm not really certain I ever needed to be in love. The fact that it happened was..."

I averted my eyes from his at that, because I didn't want him to see that they'd grown glassy. I stared into the sun, instead, letting the tropical warmth of the blossoming day bathe over me, and sink into my bones. The heat in this place had been a good distraction, of late.

"I can't imagine ever being happier than I was for the short time I was with him," I said, my voice small. "If that's all I'm allotted in life, it's enough. I don't feel unloved, these days."

"I'd be pissed if ya did," the coyote said with a wry smirk down at me, ruffling my head fur.

I smiled up at him. "It was hard for me to let love in when you first met me. I was too angry. Too hard. He helped me accept that sort of feeling, again." I swept my eyes back up to the sky. "Now that I've remembered how, I don't think I'll ever be without it again."

"Yeah," the coyote said, kicking at the dirt idly with one of his footpaws. I arched my eyebrow at the childish gesture. He looked nervous about something. "I guess," he muttered, "the fox sorta' had the same effect on me."

"'You guess'?" I asked, in an amused tone, bumping his elbow with my own.

"I love him," he said, only sounding mildly awkward these days when he said it. It still sent second-hand warmth through my chest every time I heard it, though. "Ain't, like no doubt'a that. I jes..."

I looked at him curiously, turning my entire body to regard him, now. Something was really eating at him regarding the fox. It couldn't just be that he'd been absent a lot, I'd never exactly known the coyote to be clingy. Did he suspect Puck was hiding something from him? Well, he was. I again considered telling him, biting at my lower lip.

"He's been gettin' angry at me a lot, lately," he finally admitted, with more nervousness in his tone than I'd heard yet. "Since th' whole thing in Arbordale. We've been fightin' about it a lot."

I rolled my eyes. "Ransom," I growled. "Honestly. Can you not see why?"

"I ain't simple," he muttered, "but it wasn't ever a problem before. They're just whores—"

"Ransom," I said with an exasperated sigh.

"—which I know, it don't matter who they are, he wants me t'be loyal... I get it. Like I said, I ain't simple."

"Then I fail to see why you're still confused about all of this," I muttered, crossing my arms over my chest. "If you care enough about him that you want to honor his wishes, you'll be loyal. He doesn't ask a whole lot of you. I'd say it's a small concession to make."

The coyote splayed his ears and looked anywhere but me. "But bein' with a woman every now and then makes me feel more... normal."

My mouth dropped open, and my tone grew more demanding. "Tell me you haven't said that to him!"

"'Course I have," the coyote said, sounding wary, "it's kinda' the whole crux o' my argument."

"Ransom, what the hell!" I bit out, physically batting him in the back of the head. He lifted a paw in protest, looking baffled.

"Do you have any idea what that sounds like to someone like Puck?"

"I don't— What?" He blinked down at me.

"You're telling him he isn't normal!" I pointed out, and the coyote's ears immediately drooped. "That's what everyone's told him, his entire life. It's why he was exiled! How do you think that makes him feel?"

"Oh," The man was silent for awhile, before muttering, "shit."

"Yeah 'oh shit'!" I scoffed.

"But... but that's honestly how I feel," the canine reasoned. "I don't like thinkin' I'm jes into men. Makes me feel like—"

"You're not Dominick," I said, forcefully. The coyote grimaced, averting his gaze. I hated seeing him like this, his tall frame stooped, his whole posture bent inwards, like he was nursing a wound. He really was. But right now, that just wasn't a good enough excuse anymore. Puck had feelings, too. And this was something I knew for a fact could tear them apart, despite everything else they'd gone through. Puck was dead serious about his concerns with Ransom straying. And he had legitimate reason to be.

"Is it true you got him sick?" I asked, my voice hushed.

The coyote's ears still flushed. "Jes... fleas," he insisted. "And I dunno, men get issues sometimes... I-I dunno where they came from—"

I held up my hands, groaning. "Please, please! No more. Gods. I already know more about the two of you than I ever wanted to know."

"Weren't nothin' serious!" The coyote insisted, defensively. "And b'sides, he fixed us right up. I kin be more careful in th' future—"

"It's not just about that, Ransom!" I growled, frustrated with the coyote's thick-headed attitude. "And I know you know that! He loves you! It hurts him to see you with other people. Especially since you tend to ignore him whenever you're around those women!"

"I won't do that no more, then!"

"Then you're just rubbing his nose in it," I said, shoving at his chest. "How would you feel?"

The coyote's gaze flicked down to the ground. "Ah've told him he's got the same freedom."

"No, I'm with Puck on that one," I said. "You only say that because you know he literally can't look for companionship elsewhere. If he ever actually found someone else, you'd be livid. You're a possessive man, Ransom. This situation's only unfair to him."

The coyote gave a ragged sigh. "You're entirely takin' his side—"

"Because he's right!" I bit out. "I'm sorry, Ransom. But I honestly can't even believe we're talking about this! It would be one thing if you both agreed to this, but the fact of the matter is, just because he allowed it back when you were treating him like a convenience rather than a lover doesn't mean you should expect him to accept it now. He expects more from a man who says he loves him!"

"I always loved him!" The coyote suddenly shouted, and I actually took a step back from the man. His body was rigid, his fur on end, hot air escaping his nostrils in a long-withheld breath.

I closed my muzzle for a few long moments, before sighing softly. "I know, Ransom."

"I'm so damned frustrated!" The coyote spat out, thrusting his clawed fingers through the rough fur between his ears, and turning in a partial circle where he stood. "It ain't even about this whole thing with the women!"

I looked at him curiously. "Then what's it about?" I asked, lost.

"We can't really ever be t'gether, the way most folks is," he said, his words coming out staggered, like he tended to do whenever he was stumbling through something that was difficult for him. "I mean not normal-like. I mean, wouldn't that be strange? It ain't somethin' you see. Gods, I don' know if I'm crazy t'be even thinkin' about this, it don't matter none, but that's why I see th' women, 'cause... 'cause I can't really ever be sure he ain't gonna just walk away, 'cause we can't do what most folks do—"

I held up my hands. "Ransom, please slow down." I gave him a few moments to do just that, and it didn't really seem to help any, but he stopped talking, at least. "Alright," I said at length, "I have no idea what you're trying to say," I admitted. "Could you be a little more clear?"

He gave a soft, frustrated whuff of breath, before he thrust a hand into his pocket, and yanked something out of it. It looked like a bunched-up wad of cloth, an old handkerchief, perhaps. It wasn't folded all that expertly, but it was definitely bunched many, many times around itself, like he'd taken great care to wrap up whatever was inside. He grabbed my hand and dropped it into my palm, before walking a few paces away from me with his back turned, running his hands over his muzzle and his face.

I looked down at the wad of cloth, turning it over a few times in my hands. Whatever was in it wasn't very big. I began to unwrap it carefully, noting that he'd finally turned to look at me, albeit out of the corner of his eye.

"Be careful," he muttered, as I finally uncovered the two solid, metal items within. "It's been tough keepin' those safe on that bloody ship, with all we been through..."

I looked over the two links for a moment, not certain what to make of them, before a sudden memory struck me. A conversation I'd idly had with Grant once, when we'd been talking of Otherwolf society.

"Oh... Gods," I murmured, my jaw falling open. Then I looked up to the coyote. "Ransom, where in the hell did you get these?"

"Veronica," the coyote said, his voice a rasp. He didn't seem to know what to do with his hands, at the moment. He was just running one of them back and forth over his ragged neck scruff, the other fiddling at his belt. "I think they belonged to her and a man o' hers awhile back, before he died. I'm sure they was important to her. I-I don't even know why she gave them t' me. They been burnin' a hole in my pocket. I don' know what t' do with them."

I swallowed slightly, before handing the rings back to him. He took them, then quickly bunched the handkerchief around them again, tucking it up as carefully as he could before he thrust them back into his pocket. Some measure of realization struck me, as I began to untangle what he'd been saying.

"So," I said, uncertainly, "this is why you've been so upset? Why you went and saw that woman in Arbordale?"

"I know she probably gave 'm to me as some kinda' gesture for the fox and I," the coyote muttered, "and that's sweet and all, but damnit, Shiv. I can't— I can't be with him like most people can. Like everyone else can, with someone they..."

I remained silent, not certain what to say to the man. I had a few thoughts, but they might be better left until he'd gotten this all out of him.

"It's so bloody simple fer normal folk," the man said, that bitterness returning. "But it can't ever be, fer us. Ever. Is it wrong t' want t' feel normal once in a while?"

"No," I said, trying to measure my words. "But Ransom, have you ever considered this is normal for you two?"

"How 'm I s'posed to feel that way, when every other bleedin' soul says it isn't!" The coyote insisted, sweeping his hand over the city beyond. "Just considerin' this made me realize it. And I mean it ain't like I didn't realize it before, but—" He gave an angry growl, and averted his eyes from mine. "This ain't even like we're from two different tribes, or types o' people. There's a place even fer people like that. Yer looked at as odd, but..."

I gave a soft sigh. "I could have married Grant if I wanted to."

The coyote cast a sympathetic look my way. "I didn't mean t' bring that up again—"

"It's fine," I said softly. "And you're right. You're in a hard place, Ransom. Both of you."

"Anyone else who loves someone," the coyote said in a hoarse voice, "they can promise themselves t' each other, somehow. We can't ever do that. I can't ever really have him, Shivah."

I swept my eyes back up to the coyote. "You have him now," I said, with an edge in my voice. "And you're chasing him off by trying to find 'normal', or whatever it is you find with those women. I'm not sure how any of that makes sense in your mind, Ransom. And honestly, I'm not going to try to understand it. I do, to some extent. But it's irrational. And I think you know that. You just have no self-control."

"I don't—" the coyote began, but I cut him off.

"No," I said, firmly, and reached up to grab him by a suspender, yanking him down so he was eye-level with me. "You listen to me, alright? You know me by now. You wouldn't have told me this unless you wanted some sense talked into you."

The coyote was just silent at that.

"Right," I nodded. "So here it is. You love him. He loves you. No vow you can take under any God, under any spirits, is going to change that. But your behavior could. Puquanah has put up with a lot of your shit over the years, and the fox is a near endless well of tolerance and sympathy, but every well has its bottom. You've gotten over the biggest hurdle between the two of you, as far as I see it. This just has you all tangled up because you're a coward about admitting your feelings, and this is sort of the ultimate admission."

"But—" the coyote began, and I yanked on him again, silencing him.

"If it's that hard for you, then take the coward's way out," I snapped. "Throw the rings into the ocean. Get rid of them. Puck would never expect you to want this, anyway. Especially considering his lack of faith."

The coyote gave a long sigh. "Yer right there," he muttered. "Besides, ain't no holy man would do it for us."

"I don't think that's true," I stated, my words clearly shocking the man. "I said he'd never expect it," I continued, "not that he wouldn't want it. Honestly? I think this is one of the only things on earth that might actually restore his faith."

The coyote's ears flattened at that, like I'd dropped a mountain on his shoulders. I released him, but he barely stood straight afterward, anyway. "Your choice," I finished.

"Fer the love of..." the coyote stared down at me, disbelievingly. "That's a lotta' pressure, Shivah."

I shrugged. "Don't ask me for the truth if you don't want it, Ransom. You know that."

The coyote hung his head, seeming exhausted. "Ah'll... think on it," he murmured, his brows knit.

I elbowed him in the gut.

"And stop seeing whores!" I snarled. "Dumbass!"

The hospital was, as ever, a bustling hive of activity. I slowly made my way through the throngs of people out front, standing or sitting near the entrance, awaiting their chance to be seen inside. It was very clear, the more I came back here to visit Puck during his work hours, how badly they were in need of more able bodies to help people here.

Most of the people out front didn't seem to be horribly ill or injured, the worst cases I could only suspect they brought in ahead of the rest of the flock, but it was clear there was more of a need here than one Physician with a few nurses could possibly cover.

I was able to make my way inside without too much fuss. Most of the nurses here knew me by now, and I'd been given something when I'd first 'enlisted' with the Amurescan men, some kind of long red cloth, which I'd been instructed to wrap around my midsection. It was apparently a way for the people here to identify me as belonging to the defense force, without having need of a uniform. It certainly earned me a lot of odd looks, (likely because I was a woman wearing it, I'd seen no other women in the military here) but so long as it got me in to see the fox every day, I didn't care.

I couldn't see him anywhere in the immediate area near the front desk or the first few beds beyond, but that didn't surprise me. This was the time of day he usually took his one meal, so it was the usual time of day I came to visit him. He was probably somewhere in the back.

The nurse at the front greeted me politely with a warm smile, and I smiled back at her, moving my way around a man in crutches and beginning to head down the triage line until I quite-literally bumped headlong into a man I'd honestly hoped to have as little to do with as possible since I met him.

The grey, speckled canine blinked gold eyes down at me, before giving a distracted smile down at me. "Afternoon again, miss Shivah," he said in that smooth voice. "Here to see your friend?"

"Yes, sir," I grated out, trying not to appear as put off by the cattle dog as I was. Or as annoyed as I was that he remembered my name.

"Oh," he blinked, suddenly turning his gaze back to mine. It again occurred to me how artless, how charming this man could appear. But I knew better. "You're just from that meeting with Johannes, are you not? My second?"

I blinked, then nodded. Clearly, bent on secrecy or not, the tall Otherwolf had seen fit to tell his 'Lord' about our meeting. Hardly surprising, I suppose.

"I take it you're on board, then?" The canine asked, knowingly.

"Yes, sir," I said, trying to keep the stiffness from my tone, but preferring to keep my answers short with this man. I didn't trust him as far as I could throw him, and I was honestly afraid to have anything but the most brief of conversations with him. He was far too canny for my liking, and I didn't want him to know any more about me than he already did. He'd already used his history with Grayson against him. He seemed completely undeterred by my clipped attitude, though. Almost determined to be friendly, if I was being suspicious about it—which I was.

He glanced past me again, to where I knew not. "Well I really must be off," he said, before bowing slightly to me. "I'm here to visit an old friend as well. Oh, do one more favor for me, before you go?"

I tilted my head at him, uncertainly. "Ah, I suppose."

"Do take care of Johannes while you're in the field," the man asked, so earnestly I couldn't bring myself to dislike him in that moment. "He's a good friend, and he has a wife and nine children awaiting his return back home. It would destroy me—and them—if anything were to happen to him."

He rose from his bow and headed off, and I was left standing in place, shocked by the request. It had seemed so personal, from a man who, for one, barely knew me, and for two, hailed from a country full of men bent on formality, like he'd been asking a friend.

But at that point I heard Puck call out to me, and shook the odd encounter from my mind. I saw the brown and white-furred fox waving at me from a nearby corner of the room, sitting on the edge of an empty bed. How he'd known I was here over the din in the room, I didn't know. Smell, most likely. The fox continued to amaze me.

I made my way over to him and felt myself smile despite the environment around us, and the unfortunate encounter I'd had on the way in. The fox seemed to be spooling bandages, and a metal tray beside him with several used ones, neatly folded for disposal, suggested he'd just been working. It smelled like the cattle dog here, so I suppose he'd been treating him again.

"Forrest is letting you do a few things around here, huh?" I asked, leaning on my hand and looking down on the fox as he worked.

"Just the basics," the fox said with a bedraggled laugh. "But, he has no compunctions about talking to me. I'm actually learning a great deal. The man's brilliant, Shivah. Personality flaws aside."

I chuckled. "I've noticed those two traits often coincide, company notwithstanding."

The fox laughed. "You're too kind. But in all seriousness... I honestly feel like I'm really making some progress here. I mean, nothing ground-breaking yet, but I at least know a lot more about the disease than I did before. And that's nothing if not helpful."

I looked around the room. "They really could use your help here, Puck. I still don't see why he won't let you work."

"I do," the fox said quietly, and my ears perked, turning towards him. When I looked back at him, his tail was twitching, uncomfortably. "And honestly, Shivah... he's right. I've made do over the years, I've managed. I have a lot of little tricks that allow me to perform medical services when the need is dire, but—"

"You've saved our lives more than once, Puck," I said, knitting my brow. "Mine. Ransom's. Almost every soul in Serahaven."

"A blind man shouldn't perform surgery, Shivah," the fox said soberly. "When there's no better option, perhaps, but it is a fact that I put every patient at greater risk, because of my condition. There's no reason to do that with a more skilled, more able Physician present."

"The man can't be in twenty places at once," I pointed out.

"We're managing," the fox shrugged. "We haven't yet been put in a situation where a slight delay could cause the loss of a patient. If we ever got to that point, if we had many critically-injured men, and not just a small mob of people suffering digestive issues and minor wounds, I think he'd honestly consider having me work. There's little to lose in that situation. But as things stand..."

"I just don't like that he doesn't think you're good enough," I muttered. "You've been good enough for all of us, for quite some time now."

"He's told me he'd let me work if I went through with the treatment to restore my sight," the fox murmured.

I sighed, softly. I knew how much this topic had been weighing on Puck of late, and of course, it had been on my mind a lot of late, as well, because he wouldn't let me tell anyone about it. I still wasn't entirely certain why. I didn't see why it was all that complicated. Was the fox attached to his disability, somehow? Was he afraid to have his sight back? He had yet to explain to me. He'd just made it clear, since I'd first heard Forrest talk to him about it, that Ransom couldn't know. And that he'd figure things out on his own.

I couldn't really know what was in the fox's head, and it had been a week already. Was he already receiving treatment and just didn't want to tell us, for fear we'd all get our hopes up, and it wouldn't work in the end?

I was about to just end the frustration and ask him, when his ears suddenly perked, and he looked up at me with an unusually mischievous expression on his face, considering the mood from just a few moments ago.

"What?" I asked, warily.

"The Admiral," Puck murmured low enough so as to only be heard by the two of us, "shares my predilection."

"What?" I blinked, too shocked by what he'd said to point out that he was obviously changing the subject on purpose. My gaze drifted briefly in the direction of where the canine had got to. I could barely see him somewhere across the room, sitting near an injured man's bed.

I looked back to Puck, dropping my voice. "How on earth do you know that?"

"Do you really want to know?" Puck whispered, looking particularly amused at himself.

I paused, suddenly not so certain I did. The little fox had a mysterious and sometimes frustrating habit of being right, but even if he was right about this, how was it my business? It had been sheer chance we'd even met the Admiral of the colony, Grayson had made no mention that we'd be under his command at any time while we were on our way here, and I still wasn't, technically. So far as I was concerned, our loyalty was to our own people, not the Amurescan colonists. And even if we did have to work under his men, and by proxy him... What would his 'predilection' matter?

There were other, far more important things about the man that had allowed me to shape his character, of late. Whom he took to bed was hardly my concern, nor did it affect how I'd think of him from this point on. In fact, I really, really didn't want to think about it. Still, Puck had that impish smile, and curiosity was just gnawing at me.

I sighed. "Alright, how?"

"There's a particular item I needed to find a purveyor for in town." Puck murmured, lowly. "Something mostly used only by men of my persuasion."

"What?" I asked, then immediately regretted it.

Puck cleared his throat. "It's a sort of oil for personal use that..." his muzzle twitched, "You know, this is one of those things that you probably don't want me to fill in the—"

"—gaps. Yes, fine," I groaned. "Please don't."

"Right. So, there's a man in town, specifically a man who works at the local brothel," he paused, "Who works at the local brothel, you understand?"

"I understand," I sighed.

"Well, he also uses, and sells, this oil. He's the only man in town I've found who sells it, actually."

"So you smelled the oil on him?" I filled in for him. "Isn't it possible he's just using it for other purposes?"

"No. I smelled the man on him. On his muzzle, in particular," Puck said with a coy smirk.

"Well, that's..." I paused, "There could be a lot of reasons for that. Maybe he brushed against him on the street. Maybe the man served him a drink while he was there buying a woman. Maybe the man brushed against him there at the brothel."

"With his cock?"

I balked, and Puquanah visibly had to stop himself from laughing. It was so rare I heard language like that from the fox, it had taken me aback.

"Well that's harder to explain... " I floundered.

"Trust me, Shivah." Puck finally gave a quiet chuckle. "I'm fairly certain on this one."

"Well even if it's true, what does it matter?" I asked.

"It doesn't." He shrugged, his ears turning to regard the canine behind him, tail swaying. "It's just... interesting."

I narrowed my eyes at the fox, dubiously. "Puck..." I warned. When all I got from him was continued efforts to fight that impish smile and telling silence, I gasped. "Puck, don't you dare. Don't even try. You wouldn't."

"Ransom strays," the fox said defensively. "It would serve him right. Taste of his own medicine, as it were. He's always said he wouldn't care."

"Two wrongs don't make a right."

"Oh, live in the real world, Shivah." Puck grumbled.

"You hardly know the man," I insisted.

"That could be remedied."

"This isn't a good time to be stirring the pot, Puck!" I insisted, trying to be as convincing as I could despite the fact that really, none of this was any of my business to begin with. Despite the fact that I knew things, things that were arguably as important as what Puck was keeping from Ransom, that would have turned this entire conversation around right now. And of course, my mind was immediately going back to the conversation I had just had with the coyote—about this very subject; about their tumultuous relationship of late. About two rings the coyote had in his pocket that the fox was not aware of, and might never be aware of.

"Gods," I groaned, tipping my head back, and hating my life and my luck in that moment. I had two of the best, and most infuriating friends in the world. If they ever talked to one another even remotely as often as they spoke to me, they'd probably solve every problem between them twice as fast. Or kill each other.

"Calm down, calm down." The fox sighed, rolling his eyes. "Like you said, I hardly know the man. We don't even interact much, save the times he comes here to have me treat his wound."

I made a face at that, something occurring to me. He'd specifically been coming here to see Puck, to have that wound treated. If the fox was right about him...

Oh, hell. This could get bloody.

"We'll probably see very little of him in our time here," The fox shrugged, but he was smiling too much for me to think for a second he believed that.

"Actually, Grayson says the Admiral likes to get his hands dirty." I muttered, thinking back on what little the wolf had told me about the Amurescan Lord. "So we actually might. He certainly wasn't shy about joining the fray aboard the Manoratha... and Ransom and I are—" I paused suddenly, remembering our work with Cuthbert was supposed to be kept secretive, for now. From everyone. "—serving in his forces," I finished. It was the truth, but it certainly wasn't all of it.

"Well, then. I may not be able to avoid a more personal acquaintance." Puck said with far too coy a smile for my liking. "Since he'll be working with you, he's a friend of a friend, so—"

"Behave yourself." I growled, quietly. "Or you're going to get us in trouble. And he is not my friend. And trust me, if Ransom knew what you just told me—"

"Is he handsome?"

I paused at that, honestly not certain how to respond. I couldn't help but glance at the man again for a few moments, trying to ensure I did so subtly, so as to not be noticed. But the canine was sharp. His eyes flicked over to mine after barely a few seconds and I had to look away.

"He has a piercing gaze." I replied almost in a whisper. "Unnerving, even. Reminds me of a Dyre, or Ransom, sometimes."

"Interesting."

"And I suppose he's handsome. In that way Otherwolves can be. He's not that tall, though, and he looks rough, for one of their elite. Closer to someone you'd see in the settlements back home, and what does it matter to you, anyway?"

"Hm?"

"What should it matter to you whether or not he's handsome?" I questioned. "You can't see him."

"I can imagine."

"You could do that regardless." I said with an arched eyebrow, then glared as the fox got a glazed-over expression. As in, more glazed-over than usual. "You're imagining right now, aren't you?"

"Mm-hm."

I rolled my eyes. "I'm leaving," I announced, standing.

"We haven't even had lunch yet!" the fox protested, between laughing.

I glared down at him, and somehow even without seeing it, the fox seemed to sense my dark mood, his ears tucking back. "Puck," I said, as emphatically as I could, "you need to talk to Ransom. Really talk. You two have a lot of things to work out, and a lot to tell one another, and I am tired of being the mediator, and your keeper of secrets."

"Ransom's keeping something from me, too?" the fox asked, suddenly sounding worried.

"Oh, no," I shook my head. "You do not get to interrogate me today. I've had enough of that already."

The fox's eyes dropped, his tail tucking up around him. With his ears flat and his small, soft form all subdued like that, he—

"Stop it!" I snapped, running a hand over my face. "I don't care how cute you look! Talk to him! I'm so tired of being the conduit for you two to work out your issues! You need to do it yourselves this time!"

"Damn," the fox muttered, his pose relaxing. "That usually works."

"Tell him what Forrest told you," I demanded. "About your eyes. He deserves to know. I'm pretty sure he'll have a few things to say about it."

“That’s exactly what I’m worried about,” the fox murmured.

“Why?” I asked, exasperated. “Why is this even a question? You want to see, don’t you? Are you opposed to his kind of medicine, or something?”

“Shivah, you know I have no issues with any kind of medicine that works,” the fox said emphatically. “I’m not hung up on spiritual healing. If methods are sound, any methods, I’ll put them into practice.”

“Then why are you so hesitant to accept what I know you’d suggest to a patient, for yourself?” I asked, baffled.

“Because it could kill me,” the fox said, softly.

My ears fell flat at that, and I stared down at the fox in silence for a few moments.

“Puck,” I breathed, at length. “Then... then don’t do it. It’s not worth it.”

“That’s exactly what I’m afraid he’ll say,” the fox said with a soft exhale.

“Probably,” I agreed. “Your sight isn’t worth your life.” I could imagine the coyote saying exactly that, in fact.

“You two can only say that because you’ve never known what this is like!” the fox said, in such a plaintive tone, it hurt to hear it. He stared up at me blankly, his shoulders quaking. “You’ve never experienced waking up to complete blackness in the mornings. Seeing nothing but milky, dancing lights when you stare up towards the sun! Remembering what colors used to be like, but knowing you’ll never see them again!”

I bit at the inside of my mouth, stopping myself from saying anything placating. I knew it would only come out patronizing, in the end. Puck was right, of course. I couldn’t understand what he was going through. Not really.

“Shivah, I remember what it was like,” the fox intoned, desperately. “I wasn’t born this way. I used to be able to put pictures to the world. Color and shape, to faces, to people I knew and loved. I have never seen Ransom. Never!”

I winced, balling my fists at my side and averting my eyes from his blank gaze, even if he'd never know it. I could feel the pain in his words, and see it in his eyes, and it was like staring straight into the sun. I couldn't bear it.

"Why..." I let out a breath, "what is this treatment? Why is it so dangerous?"

The fox gathered his legs up beneath him, tucking his tail around his knees. "It's," he sighed, "it's hard to explain to someone who doesn't understand medicine. And yet, absurdly simple." He was silent for a few moments, obviously deep in thought. "The eye," he continued, at length, "has a lens over it. Like skin, but much thinner. And it's clear, like glass."

I didn't want to admit to him how confused that made me, but he seemed to sense it. "Alright," he murmured, "it's like... like the skin around the outside of a berry. That thin. Except it's not there to keep the eye in, it's there to help us see. You know when things at a distance are blurry, but you have to stare intently for a moment, to bring them into focus?"

"Yes," I nodded. That made sense to me. "Like when I target."

"Right," the fox sighed. "Well that lens, that skin over my eye is clouded. I don't entirely understand why it happened, but Forrest says it can happen to a lot of people who don't eat well. I grew up in an area where food was extremely scarce, most of the year. A lot of us went hungry fairly often, especially during the winters."

I felt a somewhat guilty pang at that, for every time Ransom and I had teased the fox for over-indulging in biscuits or other food. Despite all I'd endured growing up, both of my tribes had usually had enough food for everyone. There were lean times, but...

"So how do you un-cloud it?" I asked, uncertainly. Could that be done? Like cleaning glass?

The fox shook his head. "You can't. It has to be removed. Like peeling a berry."

I twisted my muzzle up in horror, and suddenly, the reality of this 'treatment' became a whole lot more clear to me. Forrest was going to peel his eye?

"It's a very painful, dangerous operation, and one requiring a lot of focus and skill," the fox said softly. "Forrest himself says he's only done it twice before, and he warned me it isn't his specialty. And especially in this place, the risk of infection afterwards, even if it goes well, is very high..."

"Puck, that sounds terrifying," I said, bluntly. "Don't do it. How would you even remain still for something like that?"

"There's a plant that grows here, and in other tropical areas, that can be used to dull pain and subdue the senses," the fox said softly. "But, I'll have to be bound down, as well. The medicine only does so much."

"Gods..." I said quietly, knitting my brow. "Well, you're right," I murmured, "Ransom would tell you not to have it done."

"I'm considering not giving him the option," the fox admitted softly.

"You have to," I said fiercely. "Puck, if you're not going to have this done, that's one thing. But if you are, you have to tell him. If you could die, he deserves to know beforehand."

"He'll stop me from doing it, then."

"He might try," I agreed, "but that doesn't mean he doesn't deserve to know. If you don't talk to him about this soon, I'm going to."

The fox's face tightened at that, but I refused to go back on my words. Some secrets, you could only keep so long.

I put my hand on the fox's, though, and sat down beside him. "Look," I said with a sigh, at length. "You two have been through hell together. Explain your feelings to him. I sat here and listened, and I... understand, to a certain extent, why you think it's worth the risk. I wouldn't stop you. If it's what you really wanted."

The fox turned his muzzle towards me, whited-out eyes imploring.

"Ransom will understand, too," I promised him, and only because I believed it. "He loves you. He's a hard man, but he's got a soft spot for you a mile wide. If you tell him you want something, he might bite and kick and scream, but in the end, I know he'll relent. You'd just better not die, because I will not be able to handle that man if you do."

"The chances are low," the fox said, as if he wasn't entirely certain. "Forrest says it rarely goes wrong. But in this place, with all the unknown diseases here, and with mine being as advanced as they are..." he sighed. "And there's also what to do afterwards."

I blinked. "What do you mean? Afterwards you'll be fixed, won't you?"

"It takes a long time to grow re-adjusted to life after so long without sight," the fox said quietly. "But that's beside the point. That would only take time. The real issue is, I'd need to replace the lenses. With something I really can't afford."

"What?" I asked, confused.

"Spectacles," the fox murmured. "Like what Forrest has."

"Oh," I said, the answer seeming absurdly simple to me now that I thought about it. Right. Clearly men wore those odd glass panes on their faces for some reason. "Well that's not a huge issue," I reasoned. "We'll just get you some of those."

"They're incredibly hard to come by, and expensive," the fox said. "Forrest says there's only one man left in Serwich who even makes them anymore, and they'd literally cost more money than I've ever had in my life. More money than Ransom would make in five years of trade."

I gave an irritated grumble. I really didn't like it when material wealth even entered into the equation when it came to helping my friends. I'd gone literally my entire life without having a use for coin, and the rest of the world seemed to absolutely revolve around it.

"Don't worry about that," I said, waving a hand. "Just decide whether or not you want to do this, and I'll figure that part out for you."

The fox gave a soft whuff of a laugh. "You don't have a crown to your name, Shivah."

"I'll figure it out," I repeated, vehemently. "I'll do whatever I have to. Just focus on the important issues, for now. Alright?" I stood. "And talk to Ransom. Please."

I left the fox after we'd shared our meal for the day, and had a few more words. I tried to keep the topics lighter, and so did he, and we managed to have a relatively relaxed meal, despite all the heaviness that still permeated the air between us.

Any longer and I'd be late for my post, though, so I headed out with more than enough time to make it to the wall. We wouldn't be reporting back to the Cuthbert man for at least a week, when he had a more concrete plan of where we'd be going. Apparently he and his men were deciding between a few specific areas now, where we were hoping to find 'holy sites', areas the Cathazra considered sacred. My own people had sacred grounds, so it turned my stomach to considering defiling theirs, but...

It was just earth, I told myself. Foliage, trees and soil. It could grow back. It was better than attacking one of their actual settlements, and safer for the men we sent to accomplish the deed, as well. The Cathazra's main protection for their lands was the jungle itself, and the fact that they hid their holy grounds well. Also, according to Johannes, their shrines and holy land didn't really look much different than the rest of the forest, to most outsiders. He said he'd found monuments from time to time, but mostly the Cathazra built mounds in the earth, rock gardens and carvings in the stone. They apparently didn't even build many structures in their actual 'villages', save for meeting areas, and the large stone ziggurats that served as temples. These were a people that lived as a part of the land and the water. Moreso even than mine. They sheltered in caves, natural inlets and burrows, in their everyday life.

Despite the fact that the air always felt thick with water here, I'd noticed that it actually hadn't been raining much. According to Johannes, this was the dry season out here, and there were large swaths of the forest where vegetation was going through a yearly die-out. Especially along the cliffs, which was a lot of the terrain out here, seeing as we were on the uprise of a mountain. I'd been dubious at first that burning this tropical place would be a sound method, but he'd assured me, unless we had an early rain, it would work. Forest-fires here burned slow, but they burned for ages on reserves of dead vegetation built up over years of die-offs. A substantial fire would take a lot of manpower to put out, and if it was in an area the Cathazra considered sacred, they'd commit their people to putting it out, over any war—which would provide a window for the people in this colony to escape unassailed.

It was a good plan, and probably the best way to accomplish it without substantial loss of life for either side. It still made my stomach coil and churn, for some reason I couldn't put my finger down on, but I was committed to it, now.

My ears twitched as I walked down the triage line, past the worst cases in their beds, and the nurses and visitors gathered near. I hated this part of the wing, so I tended to keep my head down and my eyes off the badly mangled men, but something caught my attention, this time.

The cattle dog was here visiting someone. Specifically, the badly emaciated man missing a leg, and a foot. One of the worst cases here. For the first time since I'd seen the bedraggled, clearly dying canine, his eyes sunk in deep, his patchy, unkempt fur hugging his body like a tattered, old cloak... he was sitting up. And he was gripping the cattle dog's arm, raising his voice loud enough that I even caught part of the conversation as I passed.

"—has to be another way!" the man bit out, his voice a croak. I'd hardly ever seen the canine eat, or give a damn about anything, until now. He lay around like he was already a corpse, staring at the ceiling with lost, vacant eyes. But right now, he looked so passionate, so pleading.

"You know if there were, I'd have found it," the Admiral said, far more quietly. I stopped where I was, standing nearby at the nurse's station and pretending to look over the charts, listening in. I wanted to know more about this man I was working for.

"Would you?" the dying canine replied, bitterly. "You won't even listen to me—"

"I have come here, every day for months now, to listen to you, Finn," the Admiral said with a soft sigh. "You've been all twisted up by them. I don't know what to say to you any more. It's frustrating trying to get through to you day after day, getting nowhere."

"You didn't feel what I felt..." the canine said in a deeply haunted, and somewhat unhinged tone.

The Admiral was silent for a long while, and when I risked a glance back at him, he was only staring at his lap, sadly. I'd never seen the confident man look so defeated.

"They're not interested in talking anymore," the cattle dog murmured, so quietly I almost missed it. "They just want blood, Finn. I would give them anything, to make all of this stop, but I can't give them my people's blood." He stood slowly, wincing as he put weight on his bad leg, and re-shouldered his coat. "I didn't even ask for all of this, and you know it. I'm just trying to serve the crown. Serve my people."

"She feels the same," the dying man said in a hoarse, quiet breath.

"Who, Finn?" The cattle dog asked, tiredly. "You're not making sense, again."

The emaciated canine just turned over onto his side slowly, turning his back on the Admiral. And then he went silent, that vacant stare returning. I saw the Admiral shake his head, running a hand up over his muzzle, then stepping away from the bedside.

"I will do whatever is necessary to protect my people, Finn," he murmured. "Because it's my duty. Not because I take pleasure in it." He walked around the bed, putting a hand briefly on his friend's shoulder before letting it slide off. "You should eat. This is a miserable way to die. Think of your family back home. Please."

The man was about to turn in my direction, which sent a wave of panic through me. He was canny enough to know I didn't read Amurescan, I was certain, and I just knew he'd realize I'd been listening in if I didn't get out of his range of vision, and quickly.

I stumbled through two nurses, and made for where the density of people in the room was largest, near the admission desk, when I saw her. Or at least, I think I saw her.

She wouldn't have stood out to me, not really. She was dressed nondescript, in a white smock and pilgrim's dress like many of the women here, carrying a basket under her arm that seemed empty at the moment, her head wrapped in a worn green scarf. Except she was the first vixen I'd seen here in Serwich who was clearly from my continent. Her fur was dark, almost black, with hints of silver in what little of it I could see along the back of her neck and ears. Every other fox I'd seen in this settlement was rusty red, or some variation thereof. And it's not that silver foxes back home were all that rare. But here, she was the first I'd seen.

The air left my lungs, all caution and reason thrown to the wind for that moment in time. So much so, that I ended up pushing my way through several unsuspecting people near the front desk, including a man on crutches. His wife shouted at me, aghast, and it was only his cry of pain that broke me from my charge.

I turned around, mortified, before quickly murmuring an apology, and continuing in my sprint for the door. By the time I got there, she was gone. And that in and of itself was suspicious. I'd expected at least to see her still walking along the road. If she was just an innocent civilian, my mind told me, that's what she'd be doing. She'd be right there, for me to catch up to, to spin around, to confirm for myself that it wasn't her.

But, like a phantom of my imagination, there was no trace of her. It was as though she'd never been there at all.

Was that possible? The thought horrified me somewhat, but I had to accept to possibility of it. Was my mind truly so haunted by this woman, this creature who had tortured my friends, killed my comrades, then disappeared off into darkness like her very namesake, that I'd imagined seeing her? Or, more likely, had it just been a silver vixen who lived here? Someone come to visit a loved one? If it were Shadow, why would she be here?

"Are you mad?" A voice asked from behind me, snapping me out of my reverie. I turned on my heel to see Forrest, standing in the doorway behind me with a writing board in hand, looking extremely irate.

"Wh-I..." I stammered, honestly uncertain how to answer that question right now.

"This isn't a battleground," the dog muttered, blatantly ignoring my distress. "It's a hospital. Walk softly here, and do try not to further injure the people I've gone through such labors to treat, would you?"

I swallowed, my throat feeling parched. "I'm... yes, sir. I'm very sorry, sir."

The canine gave me an odd look, then made to head back inside. Before he could, I moved forward to grab at his sleeve, then thought the better of it, clearing my throat, instead. He turned to regard me, impatiently.

"That woman," I said, "the silver vixen. Does she come here often?"

"Who?" The canine arched an eyebrow, just looking confused.

My tail drooped. Well, there went that. If she were a frequent enough visitor, I'd hoped he might know her and set my fears to rest.

"I don't have the time to keep track of well-wishers and wives," the Physician said at length, when he'd grown tired of my silence. "Ask the nurses, if you're that curious."

He headed off at that, and I did as he said, despite the fact that it would doubtless make me late for my post. I asked every single woman who was working there that day if they'd seen the fox, that day or any others. I got a lot of blank stares, and a few who said they thought they'd seen a vixen or two, but nothing specific. I left feeling lost, frantic, and somewhat frightened... of myself.

Puck had long told me my visions of Crow might have been the result of some damage done to my mind, when I'd been stoned by my tribe. I'd never believed him, before. Crow was as real to me as the ground and the sky, and even now, I couldn't bring myself to doubt his existence. But if I was seeing more than just spirits, faith alone couldn't describe that. The Physician's words rung through my head, the whole walk to the wall. Was I mad?

CHAPTER 7
Dangerous Knowledge

"He's got you working with the old priest, does he?" The wolf murmured lazily, his claws moving through my mane as he patiently worked out the knots. I was still violently opposed to the Privateer touching me, lest he get ideas, but I couldn't deny that he had skill with—of all things—tending a mane. You wouldn't think so, looking at his own ragged dreads. But he was actually fairly meticulous about grooming them, twirling them and waxing them so they remained fairly uniform, and beading them with different trinkets and baubles he'd collected throughout his travels. And for all his skill at keeping purposeful knots, he was also pretty good at getting rid of them.

"He's a priest?" I asked, curiously.

The wolf shrugged. "I don't know, something like that? I always got that church-y impression from the stuffy sod. He certainly talks about God a lot."

I turned and regarded the black wolf at that, lowering my brow. He blinked his dark blue eyes back at me, trying to appear innocent.

"You're bad at lying while you're drunk," I stated.

"That would make me bad at lying near every moment I'm awake," the wolf pointed out with a crooked smile, "which I know isn't true."

"Fine, then this time you wanted me to know you were lying," I said, rolling over onto my side facing the man. We still shared the same bed, even though that's as far as our 'relationship' had gotten. And was likely to, at the rate the wolf was going. I knew thanks to Magpie that he'd been no more reserved in visiting the local establishments here than he'd been in the port we'd met him in. That wasn't going to fly.

"No," I said, peering at him curiously, "you know something, and you want me to know it, but you want me to ask, first."

"That's a leap in logic," the canine said with a snort, but there was a teasing tone there, just beneath it all. Like a child taunting a pet with a scrap of meat. He wasn't bothering to hide the sly smile.

"What is it?" I pushed. "What do you know? Is it about the... Johan... man?"

The wolf scratched his bare chest, idly. "I dunno, you haven't been all that nice to me, of late—"

"Grayson!" I bit out. "This is important! I'm working for the man! What is it?"

"Nothing that would put you in danger," he said with the wave of a paw, tossing his tail. Then, a moment later, "I don't think."

I groaned. "What do you want for it?"

The wolf just chuckled.

"Other than that!"

"You could scratch my back," he said, rubbing his shoulder-blades back against the bedspread. "I've been itching like a dog with mange since we got here. I think the weather's doing a number on me. So muggy—"

"Or you have fleas from the whores in port," I growled.

"No fleas, I promise," he said, clapping his hands together. "The fox fixed me up with something for that, awhile back. I'm keeping up with it. I even bathed this week!"

"Ugh," I groaned, "just... fine. Roll over."

The chipper expression he gave at that was almost worth the dirt I knew I'd be digging out from under my nails later. He rolled onto his chest, and I climbed up over his hips, settled in, and began. The man was groaning almost as soon as I gave his shoulder-blades the first rake. I made sure to press extra hard, just so he might regret this later, but this wasn't the first time we'd exchanged this favor, and damn the man, he only seemed to like it more the harder I did it.

"So?" I pressed.

"Huh? Oh, right," he buried his muzzle in the bedspread, and I could tell from the way he spoke that his tongue was probably lolling contentedly out of his mouth. Like the suave, charming gentleman he was. "The wolfhound," he muttered, around another groan, "is some kind of... I guess you could call it 'assassin'? For the church."

I stopped at that. "'Assassin'?" I repeated, incredulously, then smacked him in the back of the head. "And this wasn't important enough to tell me?"

"Ow—calm down," he grumbled. "I would have told you eventually, no matter what. And besides, it's nothing to worry about. Not unless you're plotting his Lord's death."

"The Denholme man?" I snorted, getting back to scratching. "Don't tempt me."

"Anyway, they're not literally assassins," the wolf said, his voice still muffled. "More agents, for the Church and the Crown. They think a lot more of their secrets than the rest of the world does, I think. Hung up in their ancient cloak and dagger, secret society nonsense. Some lads think they've got the whole of the world on puppet wires, and I'm sure they like to think that, but the fact of the matter is, if that were true, Amuresca wouldn't have lost the last war, and they did. They can't even keep their colonies protected, these days," his words faded off into muttering, and more groans, at that point.

"Keep going," I prompted. This was interesting.

"They're called Knights, or Knights Templar, or a dozen other names, I'm sure," he said with a sigh. "I only know about them because along the Southern Islands, they used to be infamous for shutting down cartels, and hanging men of my persuasion. They usually fix one of their crazy, zealous little church boys up with a noble who owns a fleet, and make sure they manipulate things so the right routes get protected, and the right Privateers are successful, or sunk. But I think that age has mostly passed. The Church and the Amurescan Crown can barely keep any of their trade channels safe these days, save the most major. Their fleet's spread too thin."

He turned his head to the side, and let out a long breath. "So, I don't really know what that man's goals are, these days.

He's fiercely loyal to Denholme, though. That might be all there is to it, now."

"Mnh, I guess you're right," I said, shrugging. "None of that is really likely to affect me."

"I told you," he sniffed, then turned his head enough to look back up at me. "Just take care around him, is all. Old hound can't be trusted. And he's a wicked shot. I'm not saying he's shot me, but..."

"He's shot you," I finished for him.

"Yep," he said, with a rueful chuckle. "I'm only walkin' around because he wanted to see me hung, not because he missed, neither." He was silent for a few moments, then asked, "What are you doing for him exactly, anyway? Not that it's a huge surprise, but he didn't give me too many details."

"Oh, I'm not supposed to say," I said, conspiratorially, leaning over his shoulder. "It's a secret."

"I told you mine."

"That was his secret, not yours," I chuckled. "And I'm really not supposed to say."

"Old bastard always does Denholme's dirty work," the wolf muttered. "But, then I guess that's what they do for their Lords."

"If it was something that directly affected you, I'd tell you," I promised the man. "But, for now, it seems better if I keep my mouth shut. We aren't even heading out until the end of the week. And I believe I'll be serving the good of the colony. And potentially you, so..."

"I trust you," the wolf said, with complete sincerity.

I smiled somewhat, and eased up a bit with my claws, switching to rubbing at his shoulders. The wolf's tail tossed, beads sparkling in the low candlelight. I didn't mind him so much when he was docile and agreeable like this.

I don't know why, but at that moment, something completely different popped into my head, and I felt the need to voice it. It had been bothering me since I'd spoken to Ransom about it, and seeing as I couldn't discuss it with Puck, the wolf seemed the only other option.

"Strange question," I murmured, feeling the need to preface it that way. "But, you seem like a worldly man, if nothing else."

"I am that," the Privateer grunted.

"Can a Priest," I paused for a moment, trying to figure out how to say this, "marry himself?"

The wolf slowly turned his head at that, and gave me the oddest look.

I sighed. "I-I don't mean like can he marry himself. I mean, can he perform the ceremony to marry himself to someone else."

Grayson laughed. "Well, damn. That is a strange question, I'll give you that."

"I just," I stammered, "I met one, recently, who— It would be difficult for him to find anyone else to do it, is all—"

"I'm guessing this has to do with the fox and the 'yote, love, you can skip the run-around."

"Oh my Gods how," I stated, rather than asked. "How? How did you know? They were barely ever even together on your ship—"

The wolf's shoulders shook with a laugh, although he'd buried his muzzle in the bed again, so I barely heard it. "Sort of thing's more common at sea than you might think, lovely. I've gotten so I know when two men are buggering. So... what? They want to get hitched?"

"Well, no," I said quickly. "I don't think it really matters to either of them, honestly. I mean maybe a little, to... I just, it was mentioned, in passing, and I was curious if it was even possible, is all."

"Well, sorry to be the bearer of bad news," he muttered, "but it ain't. Not like that, anyway. I mean tribal traditions are all different, but I'm fair certain I don't know a one that allows a priest to oversee his own ceremony. And the Amurescan priests don't even marry. So no. He can't. Sorry."

My shoulders fell somewhat. The wolf turned, the hint of a smirk tipping the edge of his muzzle.

"But I could," he said.

When we met at the gate the morning of the first scouting excursion, I was surprised to see both Ransom and Magpie waiting for me, as well as a small cadre of others I didn't know. They all looked to be soldiers from the Amurescan force. But it was the rat who caught my attention first.

I heightened my pace to a jog, the humid air moving sluggishly through my lungs. It seemed like it never rained here. The water was just, somehow, stuck in the air. Clouds threatened every day, but according to the locals, during this season, the 'dry season', they all dumped their reservoirs on the other side of the mountains. Things just got progressively drier on this side, the marshy areas of the woods slowly drained, vegetation died off, and game began to get more scarce.

But the humidity certainly hadn't gone away. I'd thought I would get used to it, but after nearly a month here, I was mostly just fed up with it. It was like I was slowly drowning.

"Magpie!" I said, huffing as I made it over to my two friends. The men were passing a cigarette back and forth. The rat tipped his head at me when I approached, and handed it back to Ransom.

"Don't exhaust yourself just yet," he said with a toothy smile. "Gonna be out in the field for awhile."

"What are you doing here?" I asked, confused. "I thought you turned down the offer."

"Yeah, well," the rat spat on the ground. "I didn't think you'd be fool enough to accept. But, here we are."

"Please don't do this if you're opposed—" I began.

"Shivah," the rat said, seriously, looking me in the eyes. "I ain't gonna let you two do this alone, alright? We've come through a lot together. You were there for me through some bad decisions. I'm hopin' this doesn't turn out to be another, but if it does, I'm your brother-in-arms. We deal with it together. Alright?"

I smiled. The rat had never been much of a talker, not open in the way Ransom or Puck were, but when he did, it was to say something important. And I got the impression he always said exactly what he meant.

"Eyes up!" A strong, authoritative voice snapped from somewhere near the gate. I turned, as did most of the other men, albeit in a sharper, more orderly fashion. The man who'd addressed us all was none other than the wolfhound; that's what I'd heard him called a few times now, which seemed to fit, he had the appearance of a dog, but the bearing of a wolf; who was overseeing this mission. The tall, wiry-furred man was not wearing the blue coat I'd come to associate with him now, but he was armed and armored. He had on leathers, and he and many of the other Amurescan men here had long brown coats with hoods, which looked like they'd seen a lot of travel. The cloth they were made from was strangely mottled, with threads of dark green and yellows woven in, likely to fit in with the vegetation here. I'd never seen garb like it, so it must have been specially made by their forces here for this particular group.

He and most of the men here were also armed with crossbows, and hand weapons. Johannes seemed to be the only one amongst them with such a long blade, though. A sword, although not like the ones Grayson kept. It was broader, heavier.

"You've all been briefed," the man said, his eyes sifting through the small group. "So I'll keep this short. We'll be traveling in our usual pattern. The advance group will be led by me, and I'll be assigning the few in that party at the start of each excursion. The rest of you will take up right and left flanks. Right will be in charge of cartography and marking, left will have your eyes on the sky, and will investigate possible burrows. It's the dry season, so most of the Basilisks will be upstream, but all the same, we'll be avoiding the river as much as possible."

A noticeably uncomfortable air settled over the men, at that. I saw several of the soldiers shifting on their feet. It probably would have meant more to me if I knew what he was talking about, of course. I'd heard the term 'Basilisk' passed around amongst the men, and some had attempted to describe them to me, but I'd thusfar only ever seen the Drakes and the Wyrms, not the two large bipedal Cathazra species remaining. The 'dragons', as they were called, were apparently the most intelligent and usually in most of the positions of leadership, and I'd not even seen one of them, yet.

Johannes continued on, but at that point Magpie's low murmur caught my attention.

"Be wary o'that one," he warned me. "Keep yer eyes on 'im."

"I keep hearing that," I sighed. "I don't trust anyone in this place, Magpie. I figured you knew that by now."

He nodded. "Good instinct."

"What's 'at now?" Ransom muttered out of the side of his mouth, glancing our way surreptitiously.

"Grayson says he's some kind of... assassin, or something," I whispered. "From some secret society?"

"For once, the wolf ain't spoutin' bunk," the rat said. "They ain't all assassins exactly, though, more agents for the nobility, and the church."

"What the hell does that even mean?" The coyote muttered, annoyed.

"Could mean a lotta things," the rat shrugged. "Some of 'em's just glorified bodyguards, like battle priests. 'Cept they do some shady shit. The shit the nobles don't want to dig their paws into, y'know?"

"This doesn't feel 'shady', exactly," I said, looking around at the men. "Just... important, but not something the public should know. Did he tell you about how people were—"

"Sellin' out their own? Yeah," the rat nodded. "Once I agreed t' talk to him. He don't seem that bad. Might even be on the level. Jes' keep in mind, sweetheart," he looked to me. "The Knights are what the Carvecian government based their Secret Operatives on. They use a lot of the same techniques. Hell, there're probably some Knights working with them."

My eyes widened. “You mean like...”

He nodded. “Connall. Yeah. That whole plot, with him ‘n the otter, and that vixen. That was theirs. That’s what organizations like this do. It’s all acceptable risk, and acceptable loss. Do whatever necessary to accomplish their goals. So just stay sharp, a’ight?”

I swallowed, and swept my eyes forward again, as the tall canine finished speaking to his men. There were salutes all around, and then the enormous gates began their monstrous, slow yawn as they were opened to the steaming jungle beyond. My eyes inadvertently, and perhaps by habit, moved skyward as the forest loomed ahead. No drakes, for now. But I was learning to fear them just as much as everyone else in this place. I was so caught up in the moment, I nearly didn’t notice the tall canine who’d made his way to me, until he was standing right beside me.

When he said my name, I nearly jumped out of my skin. So much so that it seemed to shock even him.

He glanced down at me apologetically as I turned, putting one of my hands to the back of my neck, awkwardly. “Apologies,” he murmured, “I hadn’t meant to frighten—I thought you would have heard me approaching—”

“It’s fine,” I said, letting out a breath, and forcing a smile. “You are very quiet, for a man your size.”

“Force of habit,” the wolfhound muttered, then cleared his throat. “Miss Shivah, yes?”

I nodded. “But ‘Shivah’ is just fine, sir.”

“I don’t—it seems more proper to—”

“It’s fine,” I said with a good-natured huff. I was more amused by the stuffy formality of the Amurescans at this point than anything else. ‘Assassin’ or no, this man seemed just as hung up on it as the rest of them.

“Right, then,” the wolfhound nodded. “You’ll be with my unit. If that’s acceptable to you?”

I paused. Magpie and Ransom were already being corralled by one of the men in charge for the left flank unit, and I’d just automatically assumed I'd be with them. I glanced their way, and the wolfhound followed my gaze.

"We'll all be close," he assured me. "But I've heard from the men on the watch that you're both an excellent shot, good at spotting drakes, and Grayson assures me you're quite the climber, as well. We lost our last feline scout two missions ago, and I badly need a good pair of eyes on the sky in the forward unit. Do you think you can handle it?"

I tensed my jaw, uncertain if I wanted to go against an order just to be closer to my friends. But in the end, it wasn't a very difficult decision. I wasn't the sort of person who put my personal agendas over the safety and protection of an innocent population. I'd dealt with people like that, and I was determined not to become one.

This mission felt important, and for some reason, despite everyone's warnings, I trusted the man in charge. I can't even exactly say why, it was just an instinct. I didn't feel that he'd lied to me yet, and he didn't strike me as the sort of person who did. Of course, I could have been wrong. I turned, and nodded crisply. "Yes, sir," I said. "I'll do my best."

The following week was full of excursions into the foreign jungle. Into enemy terrain, and a world of dangerous, more natural threats I wasn't accustomed to.

Serpents as thin as an arrow shaft, but more dangerous than a Dyre, were amongst some of the more common threats. One of the men in the forward unit pointed them out as we went, and we frequently had to check branches for the small vipers whenever I was sent up into the trees. For the most part, they kept to themselves and wanted as little to do with me as I did with them, but some of them were the same color as the leaves, and I very nearly stepped on one once.

There were ants and other insects that lived in the trees, as well, that could be outright deadly if they bit the wrong person.

The ants, in particular, were a recurring issue. I'd been bitten by one on one of the first expeditions, and had spent an hour in agony. My only consolation was that I was not the only one. I actually weathered it better than the three other men who became victims to the small creatures. I'd had to see Puck that night, to have the bite inspected. Apparently, some people had lost limbs to infection that could follow the ant bites. It was horrifying to think such a tiny creature could do so much damage to us. Most of the time, we couldn't even see them. We just had to know the sorts of areas they usually to nested, and avoid them.

In some of the areas where the marshes had receded, the ground became a tacky, muddy soup of dead vegetation and sticky earth, which I'd been told could swallow a man whole if he weren't vigilant. Thankfully, some of the men on our expedition were veterans of the terrain, and seemed to always know what areas to avoid. Johannes in particular was always mindful, and kept on the men to wash and clean their feet as often as we possibly could. The earth wasn't just dangerous if one sunk into it, it was dangerous to leave caked in your fur, and between your paw pads. Some of the veterans bore the scars of previous infections and untreated insect bites, in the form of missing toes. I scrubbed at my feet feverishly whenever we had a chance to rest, determined not to suffer the same affliction. I needed all my toes for balance.

And then there were the natives, and their traps. I'd spotted several drakes and whistled the warning for our men throughout our excursions, and we'd always managed to get to cover and avoid being spotted, but that hadn't protected us from the ground-based guerrillas. The 'Wyrms', the same creatures who'd shot us up with poison when we'd first entered the city, were everywhere. They never moved in large groups and we'd rarely actually seen them, but we found their traces constantly, and more than once had walked into an ambush. I'd managed to take down one of the creatures from a perch over them, but the other two had escaped, and one of our men had been shot, forcing us to retreat back to the city for a day.

But they didn't even need to be present to cause us trouble. Their traps were spread sporadically throughout the forest. There was probably a logic to how they placed them, but Johannes and the others had apparently been trying to track their patterns for years to no avail. We had a map with likely trapped areas, but they were always creating new ones. We dismantled or filled in any we found, but the fresh ones we found were always an unwelcome surprise. They were especially fond of pitfalls with pungi sticks, a sort of covered pit with sharpened bamboo inside, the sharp ends smeared with poisons, mud and what smelled like the creatures' own waste. A man impaled on the sticks, even if the injury wasn't critical, would quickly succumb to an infection.

We'd been very careful to avoid those, but we'd still had a lot of near misses.

After two weeks of missions, we'd successfully inspected three of the five sites, and found very little, unfortunately. Johannes had been right, these creatures didn't leave much of a trace to give us any real idea what areas they'd be most fiercely protective of. We'd seen signs of them here and there, of course. Stone carvings into the mountainside, intricate formations of rocks, boulders and terrain that had to have been man-made, the men referred to them as 'rock gardens', and many, many strange, terrifying fetishes left as warnings throughout the forest. Usually, they were skulls adorned with feather headdresses and macabre hanging collections of bones and red rope dyed and lashed to ancient trees, with gold coin-shaped pendants strung along them.

One of the men in our unit, a foreign species of fox I couldn't identify with oversized ears and a nervous, skittish personality, took notes on almost everything we saw, and often pointed out what something we encountered might mean. Apparently he was a scholar of some sort, but seeing as nearly every fetish we found was usually also found near traps or ambushes, I was less interested in what he had to say about their significance, and more concerned with what Johannes had to say about what dangers we should expect to face in that neck of the woods.

We'd determined at least that the three sites we'd been to were still in use, although for what purpose, we could mostly only guess at. The scholar with us confirmed one was a holy site of some sort, like a shrine. But it was small, and we didn't find many recent tracks there, which meant it probably wasn't often used. We'd had totems like that back home, to spirits whom our people rarely prayed to, or to spirits one tried mostly to avoid incurring the wrath of.

One of the other sites was likely a graveyard. Although apparently, the way the Cathazra dealt with their dead was significantly different than how our people, or the Amurescans, or nearly any other people I could think of did. Johannes had confirmed for me that the rumors of the lizard people being cannibals were not just myths. Apparently the creatures found the destruction of a body through burning, or through leaving the dead to rot, even under the earth, as sacrilegious. They ate their own dead, provided they had not died of illness or poisoning, as part of a holy rite. Their 'graveyard' was little more than a bone pit inside a basin, where the peat swallowed up most of what could be seen... but here and there, the distinct, ivory protrusions made evident what the ghastly place was used for. If one looked down into the surface of the water from a distance, it was like looking at the tangled roots of a marsh tree. Except upon closer inspection, it became clear they weren't roots... .

Even if the graveyard was valuable to them, we couldn't burn it. So it wasn't an option. And I was glad. Going to the place once had been enough for a lifetime.

These people weren't like our people. They weren't like the Otherwolves. They weren't like any people I knew. The gap between them and us was so massive, so unreachable, it was starting to become clear to me why the Amurescans here had so little pity for them. I was trying very hard to be objective, reminding myself again and again, this wasn't my war. But it was so difficult not to be completely terrified of the Cathazra. They weren't just a culture apart, they were... worlds apart.

The Otherwolves had come here and taken their land, the same way they had to my people. The main difference seemed to be, there was little either side had to gain from one another, so no negotiations had been found to ease their presence here. The locals' way of life was so inherently different than how the Otherwolves lived, and vice versa. Neither side wanted to bridge the gap, and to be fair, it would have been a massive bridge to build. I could somewhat understand why these people couldn't tolerate living together.

The bottom line was, though, the Cathazra had been here first. No matter how much I was repulsed by them, terrified by them, I had to keep reminding myself they were only defending their lands.

But on the other hand, most of the people in Serwich were innocents, only here to scrape a living from the difficult terrain, while some distant government pulled the strings. Mistakes had been made, but ultimately, a lot of innocent people on both sides were suffering for them. And now, most of the people here only wanted to live long enough to leave.

And that's all we were trying to do. Find an escape route that promised the smallest loss of life. I had to keep telling myself that. This wasn't my war. But it was both so hard, and so easy, to empathize with either side. It had me all twisted up. I couldn't even imagine how the men in charge felt. I saw it on the wolfhound's face, all the time. That pensive, tenuous, exhausted stress, etched in every feature, every time we found a new site and it was a dud. The weight of what we were doing with these missions was just beginning to sink in for me, but for him, it had been years of this. The Admiral, too, had to be feeling it.

This is probably what Connall and the heads of state in Carvecia had felt, in trying to deal with the disease. And we had to be careful not to go the route they did. In times of tension like this, with so much on the line, it was far too easy to take the low road to accomplish what needed to be done. But there was always a better way, I was convinced. And this time I had a chance to help them find it.

Because the alternative to us finding a site was to sacrifice a few ships worth of men, to draw away the Cathazra while the citizens fled. And that would mean many, many people dead, on both sides. And Grayson's fleet would likely be one of the sacrifices.

So we kept looking. Risking life and limb, quite literally. Every expedition left me exhausted, and we went out for two days at a time on some trips. I could tell Magpie and Ransom were growing as weary and paranoid as I was, spending so much time in the jungle. But we all knew we had to.

At the beginning of our third week we found something. Something beyond what we'd all expected.

It had been a particularly hot day, and we'd had to take more breaks than usual, since the site we were going to investigate was fairly high up in the cliffs. That also meant there were less places to take cover from Drakes, so everyone was on edge. Johannes called for all of the units to group together, in case of an attack. If we couldn't hide from the beasts, there was no need to be scattered. Drakes usually couldn't clear the tree line, even this high up, but they would circle an area and shriek whenever they spotted us, which drew in their ground troops. If we were spotted on the cliffs, we'd not be able to avoid that, but being spread out just made it easier for the guerrillas to pick us off one by one. We still weren't keeping in tight formation, because Johannes wanted to avoid giving the Wyrms a large block of men to shoot at, but we were keeping within eyesight of one another, moving over the rocky terrain.

It was a bad place to be, with no real good solution to deal with an attack. I saw the drakes in the distance probably at about the same time they saw us. I gave a shrill, sharp whistle, imitating one of the jungle birds here. Masquerading the warning call was useful when we'd been in the jungle and could hide easily enough, but out here, I knew it was pointless. We all went for cover, skidding under rocks and the low, gnarled trees that managed to grow this high, but I knew they'd seen us.

As it turned out, it hardly mattered, because so had someone else. The roar that cut through the late-afternoon heat literally echoed off the cliff face, bouncing through the sharp, jagged rocks so that I couldn't tell which direction it was coming from. It wasn't like the roar of a big cat, or a Dyre, it was... sharper, like a hiss cut with the screech of a bird. I saw Ransom nearby, an arrow already nocked as he straightened from his makeshift hiding location, and I took that as a sign that it wasn't worth it for any of us to hide any longer. Ransom was a far more seasoned hunter than I, and still, even after all the experience I'd had over the last two years, I trusted his instincts more than my own.

If he'd given up on avoiding this fight, then it was happening. Even before the creature came into sight, I knew it wouldn't be Wyrms this time. The small, snakelike creatures never made a noise. I wasn't certain if they were incapable of it, or if they simply didn't speak when they were hunting, but they'd certainly never roared.

The first thought that crossed my mind when I saw my first Dragon was utter confusion that something so brightly-colored could have snuck up on us. The beast was bright crimson, and close to eight feet tall, sporting a thick, ropy tail and just as much natural armored plating down its body as the Drakes had, if not more. It was barely clothed, save a loincloth loosely slung over its lean hips, and golden jewelry hung about its neck and wrists, sparkling in the sun. It had a crest that straightened into a raised frill as it leapt from a nearby ledge with a long spear, landing upon and impaling one of the Amurescan soldiers, one of the veteran Otherwolves who'd taught me about the vipers, I think his name had been Sam.

The beast straightened with a low growl, plucking the weapon from the now dead man's back, and for a moment I was almost too shocked at the brazen display to respond.

Thankfully, some of the more seasoned men hadn't been, and a small volley of crossbow fire, and one arrow from Ransom's bow, rained down on the exposed, unafraid creature. Ransom's arrow at least struck home, lodging in the beast's midsection through one dense, armored chestplate scale, but if it cared, it didn't show it. Another arrow seemed to have caught it across the shoulder, and that one at least drew blood—I could smell it on the wind. I vaguely remembered a soldier talking about crossbows having better penetration between these creatures' scales.

The beast bellowed at us, swung its spear into both hands, and charged, bounding over the rocky terrain as easily as a horse across an open field. Its broad, powerful clawed feet were at home on these cliffs in a way none of us could hope to be, and it closed the gap between the man it had killed and its next intended victim in less than a few seconds.

What's more, its red scales reflected the stark sunlight up here on the red stone cliffs, making it hard to follow as it moved between the rocks... and all at once, its color made sense.

I tried to train my arrow, but I knew the second I let it loose that I'd missed. I cursed, grabbing for another, and wondering if I'd even be able to strike this creature, let alone penetrate its hide. Ransom, some thirty feet to my left, seemed to be contending with the same realization, and was hastily unshouldering his rifle. He had to have a shot packed, but it was far from a precise weapon. If he was lucky, he'd get a shot at the Dragon only after it killed another of our men. When it was moving, it was hard enough to follow even with a bow.

I set my jaw grimly, convincing myself at that moment that I had to give him a chance to down the creature, if we could possibly find one. There was only one of the beasts that I'd seen, but there were probably more in the surrounding area, and the longer this fight took, the better our chances were of attracting more. We had to end this fast.

I fired the arrow I had nocked just as the Dragon closed into combat with another of our men, and realized in horror, just at about the same time I was aware that I'd missed once again, that the rodent it was about to hit head-on was Magpie. He was swearing and had dropped his rifle, making for a nearby tree, which could only mean it had misfired or jammed. He was exposed, unarmed save his hunting knife, and by no means faster than the far larger beast. He was in trouble.

My heart leapt into my throat and I raced across the rocky terrain, as fast as my paws could carry me over the sharp-edged rocks and coarse soil. The boulders on these cliffs jutted from the earth with blackened edges, and could cut into your pawpads like glass, but right now, I didn't care. I wasn't about to watch as another of my companions was killed right in front of my eyes. I wasn't even certain what I'd do when I got there. My arrows were literally one of my only efficient weapons, I'd never been in a situation before where I couldn't kill a person with them if need be. I'd even managed to shoot down the Drakes with my bow.

But these creatures had thicker scales, and what areas looked vulnerable on them were too small a target to shoot accurately when they could move like that. I could probably nail one of them in the chest the way Ransom had if I were trying, but I'd been aiming for limbs, since I'd seen how much effect the torso hit had made. Namely, none.

I was practically as ill-equipped for this confrontation as Magpie was with a jammed gun. All I had besides my bow were my claws, my teeth and one old knife. Nonsensically, I wished for a moment that I'd brought along Grant's gun. I still didn't know how to use it, or how to keep and store the powder, let alone target the foreign weapon accurately, but at least it would have given me some other option.

Just as it came to mind, I heard the familiar crack like thunder echoing through the cliffs, and the Dragon bucked in mid-step of his charge, pitching forward and half-sliding, half-tumbling down a slanted expanse of jagged rock and loose soil. He fell a good five feet before he was out of sight, over the edge of one of the nearby cliffs, and by then I'd made it to my friend, who wore the expression of a man who'd looked death in the eye.

"Magpie!" I cried, nearly out of breath from even the short sprint. I all but fell into the rat, clutching at his shoulders. For some reason, it was so hard to breathe up here...

The rat was still staring at where the beast had been not seconds earlier, and as I turned to look as well, both of our eyes fell on the splatter of blood cascading over the rocks.

"Who—" I began.

"Role call!" A familiar voice boomed from nearby, and I saw the wolfhound leaping down from a nearby vantage point, an outcropping of rock slanting upwards towards the sky. He was in the process of re-loading a pistol as he walked, making his way towards us. Some of our men began to call out their names and emerge from where they'd taken up hiding, or in the case of people like Ransom and I, had been preparing to fight. As the small group of men re-gathered, Johannes stepped up beside the two of us, briefly putting a paw on Magpie's shoulder. Ransom made it to us at that point, equally out-of-breath, if not moreso. His lungs weren't as strong as mine, and even I was struggling up here.

"Holy hell, rat!" the coyote whuffed. "That was a close fuckin' call! I couldn' a gotten a shot off before he got t' you, that bloody bastard was fast!"

Magpie still hadn't spoken, and I could tell he was trying to shake it off, but I wasn't the only one who'd noticed. I saw the wolfhound's paw tighten somewhat on the rat's shoulder, and he leaned down, dropping his voice. "Are you alright, son?" He asked, quietly.

Gabriel was visibly shaking, and I swallowed. I'd rarely seen him like this, nor did I know what triggered these episodes for him, but I hadn't forgotten what Grant had said a long time ago about the rat's problems. Perhaps it had been the gun malfunctioning that had him so shaken up? I'd seen him face monsters before without balking. It was hard to say what shook the man up. He was so private, most of the time.

I was about to say something, I don't really know what, anything I could think of, when the wolfhound spoke again. "You're not alone right now," he said in that calm, even tone. Like a man who did know what to say. "Wherever your mind is at, you're not there anymore. You have comrades all around you. Come back to us."

The rat turned his head at that, blinking for a few moments at the wolfhound, before giving a thick breath in the back of his throat, and nodding. "Ah'm... alright. I, uh..." he glanced past us, as though lost for a moment, "Where's my gun?"

"I'll get it," I said quickly, darting off towards the abandoned rifle. Ransom followed me, glancing back at the rat and the wolfhound once more before he fell in step behind me.

"Spooky," he muttered.

"I wouldn't talk if I were you," I reminded him.

The coyote shook his head. "I meant the beastie. Eerie how it just came up on us like that. Wouldn't think something so big..."

"I know," I said grimly. "But, all of the men have been saying the Dragons are the worst to contend with."

"Worse than the big'uns?"

"I think that's up for debate," I muttered, as I bent over to pick up Magpie's discarded long-rifle.

"I dunno, it'd be hard to top somethin' I can't shoot dead with an arrow to th' chest," the coyote said with an annoyed sneer. "Seriously. Fuck this place. I hate that boat, but we can't get outta here soon enough."

"Anyway, don't get comfortable yet," I said, sweeping my eyes back to the skies. I could still see the drakes circling, distantly. They were sounding an alarm we could hear even from here, the distant screeching eerie in a way that sent chills down my spine.

"They ain't comin' down," Ransom said, sounding uneasy. "They could, too. Ain't much tree cover up here."

"It's like they know someone on these cliffs will hear them," I said, picking up my pace and jogging back over towards the collecting group of men. “That Dragon wasn’t alone. Come on, hurry!”

The coyote groaned and jogged after me, muttering something about quitting smoking.

By the time we made it back over to our gathering group, the wolfhound was back to giving orders, and Magpie was shakily lighting a cigarette, looking like a man who was trying to maintain his composure.

“O’Brian,” the wolfhound said, even as his eyes swept the horizon again. Just like I’d been. He was minding the drakes with just as much concern. “Get Samuel,” he ordered the large canine. O’Brian was something of a mule for our unit, the largest soldier who could keep up with us. He’d helped carry several other men home when they’d been wounded by traps or vermin.

“Sir?” The brindle-furred canine said, raising his brows and glancing back to our fallen comrade. “I... Sam... He ain’t with us no more...”

“I don’t care,” the wolfhound said sharply. “We don’t leave our dead to the Cathazra. The man has a family back in the settlement. They deserve to bury him, not have nightmares over what the beasts will doubtless do with his corpse. Now go.”

“Yes, sir!” the large canine said, seeming to catch the wolfhound’s meaning with a grim set to his jaw. He headed back towards the fallen man.

“We’ve hit a nest of them,” Johannes stated, staring once more to the sky. “I’m certain of it. I don’t think this is a random temple, or simply holy land. I think there’s a tribe nearby. There wouldn’t be Dragons here otherwise. We need to pull out.”

The mood amongst the small group of men shifted dramatically at that. Even being here for as little time as I had, I knew that was bad. A tribe meant protected lands. It meant we could be near the real warriors these ‘Cathazra’ had, deep within the heart of their own civilization. I’d thought the cliffs were supposed to be unoccupied land, but perhaps our information had been wrong. If we were actually on their land right now, near where their people's 'villages' were, we were encroaching. We were literally in a warzone.

"We're splitting into threes again," Johannes stated, as several of the men shifted on their feet uncomfortably, their attention rapt on their leader. "Priority now is getting down the cliffs as fast as possible, and getting this information back to Serwich. If there's another tribe this close, we have bigger concerns than sniffing out a holy site."

"You said the drakes an' these 'dragons'll pick us off faster if we split up up here," Ransom, ever brazen about expressing his opinion, stated. "What 'n the hell's the point in makin' it easier on them?"

"Priority," the canine repeated, his grey eyes settling hard on the coyote, "is getting this information home. Is that clear? If one group is cornered, if even two, provided the third makes it home, we've done our job."

The cold words settled on us like a frost. I saw Ransom's face twist up, but I knew he was thinking of Puck back in Serwich, and that's the only thing that stayed him from fighting the wolfhound any further.

No one else disagreed. All of these men had someone back home to protect.

"Left flank, use the game trails we found earlier," Johannes ordered, gesturing to the three remaining members of that squad, two of which were Magpie and Ransom. "You're the fastest on the ground, I want you to have the best chance—"

"Like hell!" the coyote bit out, proving my pride for him staying his tongue misplaced. "Let the boys with the stiff and the supplies take the easy way down—"

"Maximizing our chances—" the wolfhound began to say...

I saw the battered Dragon pulling itself up over the cliff edge in the split second before it swept its claws out and swiped them at the first reachable person it could, Johannes.

The swing was wild, and the rock the creature was barely clinging to gave way almost as soon as it tipped its weight into it. But it was enough. It was enough to knock the wolfhound off-balance, especially with the Cathazra Dragon gripping at his leg, and pull the man forcefully over the edge with it.

Almost as soon as the horrifying sight had come, it was gone, and so was Johannes. And I was running to the edge of the cliff, alongside several of the others, and skidding to a halt at the edge, rocks raining down the precipice.

It wasn't a sheer drop, and it wasn't a long one, but it was long enough. By the time I'd gotten to the edge to see what had happened, the tall wolfhound and the Dragon were nearly done tumbling end over end down the sharp-toothed cliffside, thirty or forty feet down, it was hard to tell, and the beast fell hard on its back, blood pooling where it crumpled, but it was still moving, shaking its head slowly—impossibly.

Johannes had managed to roll with the fall, likely he'd rolled the whole way down the cliffside, or at least tried to get his footing, because he fell gracefully in comparison, but I heard him cry out as his arm caught between two wedged rocks and jerked in a motion I knew was bound to have caused an injury. When he finally came to a halt, he was struggling to his feet far before the Dragon could, which was to say not quickly at all, but he was still alive.

His arm hung at his side, and he was battered and bleeding, but he was alive. And he still had a packed gun.

I called out to him, as did several of his men. The man wrenched his gun from his holster with his off-hand, took about one second to aim at the beast slowly swaying to its feet before him, and fired. And missed.

The beast wasn't even moving particularly fast, but I knew the man was right-handed and firing with his left, and he'd just suffered a bad fall. It still made my heart sink to watch. He seemed a world away. I heard several of the men readying crossbows, and even Ransom was pulling his bow, but down an inward-facing cliff...

And the beast was already roaring, its bloody maw snapping like a whipcrack as it sluggishly but determinedly charged the wolfhound. The man pulled the large sword I'd seen him carrying from his hip, the steel catching the late afternoon sunlight as it cut across the hazy ocean below us, and for a moment, just for a moment, I knew for a fact I was about to watch a man die. Unless I did something.

"Go!" the wolfhound screamed hoarsely, as he raised his weapon to the eight-foot-tall monster coming for him. The beast had lost his spear in the fall, but it still had claws, and even parried, the first blow nearly blew the wolfhound off his feet.

I'd been so absorbed by the battle taking place beneath us, it didn't occur to me until that moment that there was a more present threat to our own lives closing in. But at that point, I heard the roars echoing down the mountainside from overhead, and a man behind me shouted, "Drakes!"

Ransom aborted his impossible shot down the cliffside at the last minute, swearing viciously as the shrieks of the flying creatures closed in. His arrow sung into the air, and one of the blue, winged beasts veered off-course, but avoided being struck. I felt his paw grab at my shoulder, and he snapped, "C'mon sweetheart! We can't do nothin' for him!"

But I was already shouldering my bow, looking for the best way down. The wolfhound was fending off another impossibly strong blow from the dying Dragon, but the creature seemed immortal. Nothing had killed it yet. I didn't know what I could do, but I had to try.

"Damnit, listen t'the man's orders!" The coyote yelled, as I began to scramble down the cliff. "Shivah! He's willin' t' die for 'em... do what he says!"

His protests faded when I leapt nearly six feet down to a lower ledge, because right then, I'd hit the point of no return, and the coyote must have known it. There was no quick way back up, now. I heard him shout my name once more, and then I could barely hear anything over the sound of the wind buffeting the cliffside, and the hellacious noise of the Dragon below me. I pulled my knife as I skidded down the remaining broken terrain, careful not to lose my footing, but unable to stop running, lest I topple end over end. It was a controlled charge at this point.

When I at last made my way to the wolfhound, he'd managed to fend off another attack, and the creature was reeling back, clutching at a bloodied eye. Madder than hell, of course.

"I told you to run, damnit!" The canine swore, which was, to say the least, unusual for him.

"And leave you to die?" I said with a huff, catching my breath.

"I expect no less of my men," the wolfhound said, around a labored pant, "my life is no more important than theirs—"

"Yeah, and we can talk about how 'bloody' noble that is and all, later," I said between grit teeth, "once this thing is dead!"

The beast came at us again, choosing to swipe its tail out this time, which very nearly caught me in the legs, since I was slightly farther forward than the wolfhound. Fortunately, it took it some time to turn from the swing, and during that, Johannes shouted to me, gesturing with his sword.

"Can you get past it—around it?" He shouted over another frustrated roar from the beast.

"What?" I called back, uncertain what he meant.

"Flank it!" He bit out. "You're faster than I am—"

"Got it!" I said, springing forward just as the beast pitched itself forward into a run towards us. I charged it head-on until just the last second, then juked to the side and tumbled to the right of it, skidding along the unusually slippery rocks on the cliff face, wet from the mists and lichen, and probably the creature's blood, and narrowly avoiding its tail again. But I was behind it, just as it was closing in with Johannes again.

This time I knew the creature's claws had caught the wolfhound, at least partially. I smelled fresh blood, heard him grunt and half-stumble, half-dodge the beast as it snapped at him. But I had my opening.

I coiled my legs beneath me, gripped my knife as tightly as I could, and leapt. The beast happened to be bent over at that moment, and that made clearing enough air to land on its back fairly easy. It was the next part that was hard.

I used the force of my fall to sink the blade in, as deeply as I could between its shoulder-blades, hoping and praying I'd plunge it in deep enough to hit something important. But the Dragon was enormous, layered in thick, ropy muscle and scales, so it was far from guaranteed.

My blade sunk in deeply, at least, and once I had it in, I clung on for dear life. The Dragon reared back, nearly throwing me off as it tried to buck me free. I held fast to my blade, using every ounce of strength in my body to try desperately to plunge it in deeper. I could dimly see the wolfhound over the beast's shoulder, staggering back with blood seeping down his chest from where he'd been hit with the beast's claws, panting from exertion and still readying to charge the creature again, despite that.

I couldn't help but remember every other time in my life I'd fought an enemy—enemies far weaker and less terrifying than this beast—whom I'd been helpless to stop: Methoa, who'd taken my son from me; Shadow, who'd taken Grant from me. It didn't matter that this man was barely known to me, barely a comrade. What mattered was I wasn't weak anymore. And I wasn't going to let this happen again. Not if I could stop it.

I began to feel the beast weaken, and it stumbled back, away from Johannes. It began clutching for me, tossing its tail at me, but I was far smaller than it, and in a difficult spot for it to reach. I clung to its back by sinking the claws of my feet into its ribs, and shoved at the dagger with all my might, until it was buried to the hilt. Yet still it was alive and moving.

If one of these 'Dragons' was this hard to kill, I couldn't even imagine facing an army of them.

"Shivah!" A familiar voice called over the din of the battle, from somewhere distantly to my right, past the Dragon, past Johannes, even. "Get down!"

I did as I was told, and ducked behind the creature's back, just as the rifle shot split the air. Something in the creature's skull popped, and it stumbled back, and at last, I felt its body go limp.

I abandoned my knife, leaping away from it before it fell. A wise decision, as it turned out, because the creature wouldn't simply have fallen atop me. The cliff ledge we were on was slightly sloped, and when it tumbled over, it also rolled, and pitched down into oblivion beneath us. A far steeper drop I wouldn't have survived.

"Damnit, cat!" The coyote growled as he skidded down the last few feet of the cliffside towards us. "Was that mah old knife? I had a lotta memories with that blade—"

He didn't get to finish his statement, because at that point, I'd thrown myself forward into his arms, and was hugging the life out of him. The coyote's body loosened up, and he gave a long sigh, settling a hand on my head. "A'ight, calm down," the canine muttered, stroking my hair, "you did mosta' the hard work, anyway."

"Thank you," I said in a small, hoarse voice, unable to really fully express my love for the coyote in that moment. I dragged in a thick breath, looking up at him, and I was absolutely certain my eyes were glassy. I exhaled sharply, trying not to laugh or cry. "When did you become a good man, Ransom?"

I swear, the coyote looked embarrassed, at that. His eyes darted aside, and he scratched at his neck. When he spoke again, it was sort of a murmur, like when he'd admitted to having fleas or something. "Yer confusin' 'good' and 'stupid' again, Shiv, and you know I'll always pull yer ass outta the fire when y'do somethin' in the latter. Yer mah girl."

I scrunched up my muzzle somewhat, but I couldn't keep from smiling.

"Not like that," the coyote muttered, rolling his eyes. "Although th' offer's still always open, y'know—"

I punched him, and he snorted back a laugh. But at that moment, I remembered we weren't alone, and shouldered gently past him, towards the wolfhound. The man was on the ground now, his sword at his side. He was conscious, kneeling, but he wasn't in the best condition. I couldn't really assess the entirety of his wounds at the moment, but I knew at least he'd broken or sprained his arm, and he'd suffered a few scrapes and bumps on the way down. More worrisome, though, were the expansive... if shallow, by the look of them... claw marks.

His eyes were still on the sky, though. Ransom was looking as well, and soon, so was I.

"My men—" the wolfhound began.

"Followed orders," the coyote responded, looking down at the wolfhound. I glanced his way, and he nodded. "Yeah, even Magpie. Else th' left flank would've been weak. I think he really respects you, oh fearless leader. And that ain't no small thing." He dug around in his pocket, looking for a cigarette, I was certain, regardless of his vow earlier. "He told me t' get you home alive," he muttered around the tobacco stick he'd shoved between his teeth, then his eyes fell on me, "Both of you. So c'mon. Them drakes don't seem to've realized we're down here yet, but one of 'em's gonna spot us eventually."

"Can we even get back up?" I asked, looking up the sheer cliffside.

"Nah," the coyote said with a heavy sigh, his yellow eyes sweeping over the jagged cliffs. "But we can crawl our way outta this. Just gotta find the right path down. Y'all are lucky t' have me," he said, flashing a fang as he grinned, and began to make his way along the rock ledge, towards the nearest trespassable path downwards. "One thing I'm good at is gettin' outta tight spots. Just follow real close. And Shiv, help him along."

I nodded, reaching down and gingerly putting an arm around the wolfhound's shoulders. I'd never be able to carry him, but I could at least help support him.

Thankfully, that's all he seemed to need. He was unsteady on his feet, but able to walk. He was being unusually quiet, though, and his eyes were slipping closed from time to time, which made me nervous. He didn't seem to be bleeding enough to kill him, but I wasn't a healer. I didn't think his wounds were life-threatening, but...

"How are you feeling?" I asked softly, even though I knew it did little good. I mostly just wanted to keep the man talking to me.

"Seeing double..." he said at length, like he didn't want to admit it. "The arm and the wounds, not the problem..."

That was bad. I'd never heard the man slur his speech before, not like Ransom did on a daily basis. My arm was wet with something from where it was pressed alongside his skull, and I drew it away for just a moment to see. It was about what I expected. At some point on the fall down, he'd struck his head. Again, it didn't look major, but I'd had enough head injuries in my life to know what they felt like.

I reaffirmed my grip on his shoulder, helping him down a particularly steep slope. Ransom had his bow out, on vigil for us, as if it would do much good if a drake showed up. At this point we just had to hope we weren't spotted.

"It's alright," I said, keeping my voice firm. "Just keep talking to me. You have to stay awake, alright?"

The man nodded, which I took as a good sign. I forced a slight laugh. "You're a hell of a tough bastard, you know that?" I said, using some of the slang I'd learned in the colony. "You fought that thing seeing two of them? How did you even know where to swing?"

"Guessed," the wolfhound said, dryly, then winced, glancing down at the rake marks on his chest. "Guessed wrong, one of the times."

"Sound strategy," I said, smiling for real that time.

"Not my preferred method for combating Dragons," the man said. "But, didn't have much of a choice in th' matter."

He stumbled, suddenly, and I caught him under the arm, forcing him back up. He stopped for a moment, probably to gather his senses or stave off a swell of nausea or dizziness, if my own experience was any indication. I held on to him and let him take the moment to recover.

"If I become too much of a burden, please—" he began.

"I didn't leave you to get eaten by a Dragon," I said, annoyance laced through my tone. "What makes you think I'd leave you here now, just because you have to take a breather every now and then? It's fine."

"We need to get to tree cover, quickly," the wolfhound said, blinking his eyes a few times as he gathered himself, "I don't want your efforts to save one life... to end up costing two more..."

"I promised your friend I'd get you back," I said, firmly. "Now shut up. Besides, it's not just your life I'm thinking of. You have nine children and a wife back home. He told me."

"My wife is dead," the man said, in a tone so flat and quiet, I barely heard it. I knew the moment he said it that I'd just heard something that, I hadn't been meant to hear. If this were any other time, if he weren't suffering from a head wound. That hadn't been a simple admission. His best friend had told me—

"What in the bloody hell?" Ransom's voice, and the fact that he'd stopped dead in his tracks, caught both of our attention. I nearly went for my bow, before realizing I still had a wolfhound to support. But the man himself was trying to go for his weapon as well.

"Ransom, what?" I asked, my heart racing. The coyote wasn't aiming at anything, though. He was just sort of standing in place, staring down at something. From what little I could see from where I was, just a mass of collected brush and dirt that was piled on the nearby cliffside.

Piled in a way that didn't look natural, I realized.

We made our way over towards him, and soon, we were staring down at the same baffling sight. Ransom glanced at the two of us, then back down into the 'nest'. That's what it was, I was slowly realizing. An enormous nest.

"What 'n the hell am I looking at?" the coyote asked, dumbfounded.

What we were looking at... I knew what they were, of course, but it was almost lunacy to voice it aloud. They were enormous. Tannish-red, leathery, and easily twenty times the size of any I'd ever seen before in my life.

"Eggs," Johannes breathed, then swept his eyes back up the cliffside, from where we'd fallen. "Oh, lord," he uttered. "This isn't a holy site. These are nesting grounds."

CHAPTER 8

FORGIVENESS

It would have been impossible for us to make it down the cliffs to the forest floor going the route we were by nightfall, even under the best conditions. But as the light began to fade, it became evident we wouldn't even come close. By the time the night insects had begun their thrumming song, we were looking for somewhere to bed down. Somewhere against the mountain, somewhere out of sight where we wouldn't be spotted from the air, even though the drakes rarely if ever flew at night. We'd been hearing them during the whole descent, and even more terrifying, the distant roars of the Dragons, likely calling to one another as they hunted us.

When we found a shallow cave, likely carved out generations ago by the sea or some other force of water, it was quite literally a godsend. Or at least, I thought it was. And I wasn't the only one murmuring prayers of thanks when we at last all slumped inside, exhausted and ragged.

The wolfhound was faring the worst of all of us, but thankfully, he seemed a lot more lucid. Just very tired. He'd lost enough blood that I was concerned, but his vision had begun to even out, or so he claimed, so that meant the head wound probably wasn't critical. Or he was lying to us, in an attempt to put up a strong front. Ransom would have done that. But this man, I believed. He didn't strike me as the type for false bravado.

"Let me see your arm," I said, hunkering down beside the tall canine as he stiffly unshouldered his blood-soaked coat. Behind us, Ransom was pulling out some rations and helping himself to his flask, liberally. I made no move to admonish the man. After the day we'd had, he'd earned whatever vices he wanted right now.

"Fair certain now it's just a sprain," the wolfhound said around a wince, as he eased his arm free of his coat sleeve. He gingerly unbuttoned the cuff of his white cotton shirt, and rolled the fabric up to his elbow. I could tell he was in pain by the way he was hissing between his teeth.

I hesitantly, gently wrapped my paw around his wrist, and moved it upwards, slowly. I wasn't much of a healer, but Puck had taught me long ago the basics of assessing a break. He didn't feel like he had one. So he was likely right... just a sprain. All the same, it was his good arm. It would put him out of commission for at least a little while as it healed.

I wanted to keep everyone's spirits up, so I forced a soft smile and dropped to my rear beside the man, letting him ease his arm back against his chest. "Considering the fall you took, that could have been a lot worse," I said, seeking out the elusive silver lining to this miserable day. The man's eyes were still squeezed shut though, and I'm not certain he really heard me. I knew from experience that as soon as you stopped moving, your body lost the fervor it had while you were pushing yourself, and the pain from your injuries could come back with a vengeance. He was probably contending with that fact right now.

"Here," the coyote's voice suddenly cut through the silence, and he padded over to us, then crouched beside the two of us and held out the flask. The wolfhound's eyes opened to slits, but he didn't take it. "It's whiskey," the coyote said, as though apologizing. "And not even good whiskey, but it'll cure what ails you—"

"I don't drink," the wolfhound stated, flatly. He winced again, then waved his good hand. "But... thank you."

Ransom honestly just seemed confused by the man's statement, like he'd spoken in another language. At length, he withdrew the flask and took a swig himself, standing. "You a priest, or somethin'?" He asked, sounding more curious than anything else. As if no one else in the world would even consider living sober.

The wolfhound shook his head. "No, I just took some of the same vows."

"To yer secret society?" The coyote asked, brazenly.

For his part, the wolfhound didn't even seem surprised, let alone concerned. "Yes," he said, unphased. "To them, and to God. And they are absolute, so it wouldn't do me much good, in any case. I haven't imbibed since I was ten years old. It would only make me sick." He shifted up against the wall, straightening his back some and eyeing the coyote, with the barest hint of a sardonic smile. "Besides, Carvecian whiskey is piss compared to whiskey from the Motherland."

Ransom laughed at that, and gave a toothy smile. "That so? I oughta' try that sometime, then." He shook his head and pocketed his flask again, stretching his back as he turned back to eye the cave mouth. "Yer not so bad, y'old codger. Bit of a badass, even. I guess I'd work with y' again, if we get outta this."

"We will," I said, certain of it. "We're far enough down the cliffs now that we'll start hitting jungle soon. Once we do, you and I can easily skirt the traps and Wyrms over the small stretch home. We'll be fine." I looked to Johannes, taking stock of his remaining injuries. "And even if you're out of commission for awhile, sir, we can continue the survey missions in your stead. Maybe Magpie could—"

"But there ain't no call for that any more, is there?" the coyote interrupted me, crossing his arms as he looked down at the two of us. "I mean... we're done. We did what we came out here t'do."

"What?" I blinked, alarmed.

"We found a site they're right fierce t' protect," the coyote said, pointedly. "We found what we were lookin' for. Now we just gotta get back home and report—"

"Are you serious?" I exclaimed, in a mixture of revulsion and horror. "That wasn't a... a holy site, or a temple, or a rock garden, it was a nursery! The nests, the eggs—"

"Yeah, place is a real omelet waitin' t'be fried up," the coyote snuffed. "And them nests will burn well—"

"Ransom, those aren't bird eggs, o-or snake eggs!" I said, gaping at the canine. "Those are babies! People!"

The coyote shifted on his feet, enough that I knew my words had made him uncomfortable, but he still looked like he was stubbornly keeping to his point. "Shivah, these people ain't like us—"

"They're still people!"

"I ain't sure they are! Did you see that damned thing?" the coyote bit back, his ears flattening. "I've seen Dyre I'd rather break bread with. Be a damned realist, Shivah, it's what yer good at. These things might walk an' talk, but they ain't people like we know 'em. And this is about survival! Our people or theirs!"

"We are not having this conversation," I said, with venom in my voice. I turned to Johannes for an ally, hoping the older man would see the wisdom in my words, but he was only staring pensively at the cave floor, looking uncertain. Something sunk inside me.

I looked back up at Ransom frantically, digging for something I knew would stick deep in him. He was a moral man at his center, I was convinced. "Ransom," I said, plaintively, "we can't... We can't even be considering this. Don't you see the parallels here? Between us and—"

"Don't bring up the pitbull," the coyote snapped, "or the vixen, or Rourke. This ain't the same."

"Isn't it?" I demanded. "What's more innocent than the unborn? You wouldn't be arguing for this if we were talking about burning down a village full of pregnant mothers! Gods, we're even talking about using fire! Just like Connall, just like the Raiders!"

"These ain't our people, Shivah! We're at war! If we don't beat them here, we die. It's that bloody simple," the coyote stated, but his voice was weakening some. I could see this bothered him at least, that the reality of the decision before us had begun to take hold. I knew I could keep working on him. I wasn't sure if I'd ever be able to convince him so long as Puck was down in that settlement, though.

I wasn't even certain it was right to convince him. To abandon our best chance?

Everyone in Grayson's fleet could die, if we had to hold off the Cathazra to protect the vessels with the citizens on them. And if we failed, they could go after those vessels as well.

Everyone in Serwich could die, because we had decided that their salvation was too morally wrong to undertake. But... But there had to be a better way. Connal, Shadow and Rourke had tried to combat the Fever with a terrible solution, and I'm sure some of them felt it had been worth it at the time. We were in a similar position now and we had the chance to find a better way out.

Except this had been the better way out. This had been the plan that was supposed to spare lives. And it would, except they would only be our people's lives. We'd found another solution, a solution that didn't involve throwing entire crews of men to the monsters at our backs. It should have been an easy choice. Instead, it felt somehow worse. Even more difficult.

The silence that permeated the air after that was thick and heavy. I looked between the two men, waiting for someone to agree with me. Even disagree, put their foot down, something. Anything. The three of us had all seen the nests. And I knew if what we'd found made it back to Serwich, made it to the Admiral, he would make the most of it. I barely knew the man, but I could tell from the wolfhound's expression that he knew the same. And he knew his friend a lot better than I did.

I couldn't stop either of the two men from going to him, if in the end, that's the path they decided to take. And maybe it was cowardice, but knowing that suddenly made this feel as though it was out of my hands. It didn't mean I felt any better about it, but it solidified for me what my own feelings on the matter were.

"I'm not going to tell anyone about what we found up here," I said quietly, breaking the silence. Both men slowly looked to me, and I looked back at them. "If either of you two do," I implored, softly, "please... please consider what you're doing. There are still other options. We can find other sites. We haven't exhausted every possibility."

"In that, you're correct," the wolfhound stated, although his voice was little more than a rasp now, his exhaustion evident. He cleared his throat, gaining back just a bit of the strength to his tone. "We'll keep trying. We'll keep looking. There is no reason not to."

That set me at ease some. The coyote was silent, but that was probably for the best. I didn't want to fight with him anymore tonight, and I doubt he wanted to, either. I turned my attention back to the wolfhound, who was trying to unstrap his blade harness one-handed. I leaned forward on my haunches and reached for the straps, but he stiffened away from me.

For a moment, my ego was bruised, until I realized he wasn't angry at me because of the conversation we'd just had, he was just uncomfortable.

I gave a mildly exasperated sigh, dropping my voice. "Would you rather I have Ransom help you with that?"

The wolfhound seemed to consider that for about three seconds or so, before blowing out a breath. "No, it's... it's fine. I need to clean these wounds, or—"

"Infection and insects, I know," I nodded. I hadn't forgotten about the claw marks. They looked shallow from what little I could see of them. I'd seen one man who'd sliced himself open accidentally on a pungi stick, whose arm had become maggot-infested by the end of one day. The insects around here flocked to wounds and laid their eggs in them. It was vile.

Hopefully we were still high enough up that the insects here wouldn't be too bad. Hopefully. We'd used maggots to treat a wound Ransom had gotten once, but the maggots here weren't the same. They never stopped eating.

The harness was easy enough to unbuckle, and he was mostly able to do the rest, although I helped him get it over his shoulder and bad arm. I looked it over a bit after I'd removed it. It was actually very handy, if one wanted to carry knives without making it obvious. The sheathed blade on the front looked as though it could be removed, sheath and all, which meant he could wear it beneath his coat, and the blades along his back would never be visible. Not essential on a mission like this, but I could imagine uses for that. I made a mental note to ask him about it in the future, and perhaps have one crafted for myself.

"Alright," I said with a sigh, setting it down. "Shirt off. And Ransom, can I have that whiskey again?"

The coyote grunted an assent and tossed it over to me as he made his way back towards the cave mouth, presumably to keep watch. I dug into my pouch for where Puck had packed a few healing essentials. Bandages, and one of his salves for healing wounds faster. I also had a clean rag in there for applying alcohol, which I tugged free and began to dab with the whiskey.

However, when I looked back over to the wolfhound, ready to tend the scrapes, he still hadn't pulled off his torn, bloody shirt. And I knew stubbornness when I saw it.

"You can't be serious," I sighed, exasperated.

"Leave me your healing kit, I can tend them myself," the wolfhound insisted.

"With your off-hand?" I snorted. "And a head-wound? No. Stop being ridiculous." I got up on my knees and moved towards him. He again shifted somewhat away from me, and I dropped my hands at my sides, the rag clenched in one of my fists.

"Fine, you can get your coyote companion," the man insisted, and I had to hold back a frustrated laugh, at the way the lanky canine was inching away from me. Like I was on fire, or something.

A better comparison might have been a young boy running away from a girl, because she was a girl, and that fact was somehow infectious.

"Trust me, you don't want Ransom treating your injuries," I muttered. "He can't even take care of himself. I studied under Puquanah, the healer who worked on your Admiral. I know what I'm doing. Now stop being stubborn and take off your shirt."

"It isn't appropriate for me to disrobe in front of a woman—"

"Oh my gods, then pretend I'm a man," I said, rolling my eyes. "Shirt. Now."

The man was tired, which is perhaps the only reason he eventually relented. It didn't really help ease his dignity crisis any that I had to help him out of that, as well, but he'd just have to deal with it. Honestly, I felt just a bit guilty, I wanted to respect the man's culture and his traditions, but I mostly found the whole thing funny. The term 'stuffy' had begun to make sense to me the more I got to know these people. They were in fact very different from the Otherwolves in Carvecia, just as I'd been told, but in ways I hadn't expected. I'd anticipated arrogant, elitist, dangerous conquerors, and I'm sure to some people, that's exactly what they were. But they were also quirky. Bizarrely polite, even when I was fairly certain they disdained me and everything I was doing here. Decent to their women, if overbearing. There was a great deal made about protecting their women from the less pleasant things in life, like they were flowers to be tended in a garden, somewhere safe away from the wilderness.

My own people must have seemed brutal and uncivilized in contrast. Even the Carvecians. But I honestly wasn't certain which society would have frustrated me more, had I been born anywhere else.

As I leaned in and began to gently clean the rake marks, and wash the seeped-in blood from the man's fur, I vaguely wondered what the Cathazra society was like, if they even had something like that. Surely there were men and women amongst their people, even if we couldn't tell them apart. And I'm certain they had religion, lived in families of some kind, or groups. They couldn't be all vicious and animalistic. Even if they seemed barbaric to me, the fetish totems we'd seen throughout the rainforest were beautiful, crafted by artisans who were capable of intricate carvings, of devoting themselves to their art, and that took passion. That took feelings. It couldn't all be instinct, like they were wild beasts.

These were people, no matter what Ransom said. They just weren't people we could understand.

"Thank you," the wolfhound's low voice cut through my reverie, and I raised my eyes to his. He still looked to be in pain, but it was easing, some. Perhaps simply from relaxing, finally. I hoped he was able to rest tonight. He'd need it. We all would.

"You're welcome," I replied simply, with a slight smile. I gently dabbed at one of the longer rake marks, making sure not to swipe with the cloth, but to be as thorough as possible while still cleaning the skin, just as Puck had always shown me.

"Not just for this, for disobeying my orders. Coming to aid me," the man murmured. "I was truly prepared to die on that cliff. I thought it was my time. A good death."

I looked up at him at that, my brows coming together. He'd almost sounded relieved when he'd said that.

"But, all the same," he said with a soft sigh, "When that beast charged me I was... I was afraid. I suppose no one is ever really ready for death."

I looked down slowly, fisting both my hands in the rag where it sat in my lap. "I've seen a lot of people die," I said quietly. "I don't think I've ever seen a death that was good. I've seen people resigned to it," I murmured, my thoughts briefly flitting back to Connall's expression, in the final seconds as he'd raised his own gun to his head. I shook my head, closing my eyes. "But I don't think it's ever peaceful. I think everyone is afraid. Because we don't really know..."

"How God will judge us," the wolfhound murmured, his gaze going distant.

I nodded. Even though my understanding of what lay beyond was probably quite different than his, it was the same fear. What lay beyond. Was I bound for suffering? Would my loved ones be there, if I truly was going to a better place? It was so hard to assess what sort of a person you'd been throughout your life, when the world was this complicated, with so many difficult choices. Had what we'd done today damned me? Would the spirits tear at my soul once I left this world, like vultures at a carcass? Would I become a malicious spirit, like Crow, because of the pact I'd made with him? Was it even all real?

This man seemed faithful, so he was probably more in fear of punishment from his God than doubting his existence. Although for what, I wasn't certain. I couldn't know what kind of a life he'd lead.

I put the rag aside and dug out the salve, opening the dried leaf package it was wrapped in, and smearing some on my fingers to begin applying it to the wounds. As I leaned in, I let my voice slip low enough to be inaudible to Ransom. He was near the cave mouth in any case, so I doubt he'd hear anything we said, regardless.

"You still have your children back home, don't you?" I asked.

The wolfhound's eyes snapped to mine at that. "Excuse me?" he uttered.

I looked back up at him. "Your children. You said your wife died, but you still have children back home, right? Live for them."

The man went dead silent at that, and a fresh wave of pain washed over his features. I doubted it had to do with his injuries.

"Am I wrong?" I asked, softly. "You said you were ready to die. Were you hoping you would?"

His response was so candid, it shocked me. "Not hoping," he said, monotonously. "Just resigned that I would. I've been expecting to die since I came here. I'm honestly shocked it's taken this long to come so close."

"I've been where you are," I said, lowering my eyes to the man's chest as I continued to apply the salve. "I know how it feels to believe there's nothing left to live for except pursuing some task that will inevitably kill you. But, there's always something—"

"Do you honestly think," the wolfhound said, "that I would be in this hellish place, if I could be with my family?"

I leaned back at that, blinking and trying to process his statement. If his children were alive, why couldn't he be with them? If my son was alive, I would sure as hell be with him right now. No matter what.

"Is it because of your commitment to... that man?" I said, cutting myself off before I could say 'that bastard'.

"No, it has nothing to do with Luther," the wolfhound muttered, leaning back against the stone and staring off into nothing. "I can't be around them. I'm not fit to live anything but a soldier's life anymore."

"Why?" I pressed.

"Reasons you couldn't understand," he replied stoically, and I suppose he expected I would simply accept that. He didn't know me very well.

"Try me," I stated stubbornly, staring him in the eyes. He looked aside for a few moments, so I pressed. "I know to you I must seem young," I said, "but in the last two years, I've gone halfway across the world, lost the people I loved, again and again, become a widow by my own hand, and chased a spirit I'm not even certain exists. Whatever haunts you, it won't shock me."

The man's muzzle had turned towards me mid-way through my speech, and I wasn't sure exactly what had caught his attention, but I had it now. "A 'spirit'?" He echoed.

My eyebrows raised. Of all the things I'd thought the canine might fixate on, that wasn't it. I wasn't even using the Otherwolf word for it, because I wasn't certain what it was. "Yes," I replied, uncertainly, "do you know the word, or are you asking the meaning?"

"You mean a 'demon,'" the man clarified, brows knit.

"Is that the word?" I asked, trying the Otherwolf word out on my tongue. It felt wrong, for some reason. I'd heard at least Ransom use it before, and it wasn't a pleasant word. But then, Crow wasn't really pleasant, when I came to think about the spirit.

The canine shook his head. "I'm not certain. I only know your peoples' religion in passing. We studied some of your traditions when I was schooled in the Seminary."

"What does it mean?" I asked.

"It's a malignant, otherworldly presence," the man said, then, as if remembering my limited vocabulary, attempted to explain further. "An evil creature, from the realm beyond this one—or beneath, in the case of demons—that haunts or possesses a person's dreams, their waking mind... even their body. They can speak directly to you sometimes, but usually they just torment you, lead you astray, bargain with you to commit ill deeds, with the promise of power or gain. If you surrender your soul to them entirely, they can claim it in the next life."

I stared at him, blank and silent. I was absolutely certain my mouth was hanging open slightly, but I was too shocked to care.

He stared right back at me, knowingly. "Does that sound about right?"

"It's like you've been in my dreams," I admitted at length, in a haunted tone.

"No," he said, with a quiet sight, sweeping his eyes to the ground. "I'm just well-acquainted with what it means to battle them."

"But," I stammered, "I don't... I don't know that Crow is 'evil', exactly. Just very... very angry," I said softly, "and alone, like I used to be. He came to me when I was at death's door, and promised me life if we could..." my words fell off at that, and I looked aside, somewhat ashamed.

"What?" The man asked quietly.

I sighed. "It's just," I ran a hand up my arm, nervously. "Every time I've ever talked to someone about this—even Puquanah, and he was trained as a shaman—they've told me I was mad. Imagining things. I did take a lot of injuries to the head, and that was right before I began seeing Crow..."

"Miss," the wolfhound said, his tone showing no hint of uncertainty, "I'm a cynical man by nature. I've even begun to question the teachings of my Order, in recent years. But if there is one thing in this world I do believe in, without any doubt, it's the existence of demons."

I let out a long-held breath, then, as we sat in the quiet darkness of the cave, the coyote keeping vigil near the starry mouth, I began to tell the wolfhound everything. Everything about Crow. The dreams, from the first moment I'd seen him, when I was buried by my husband, to the last vision I'd had of the creature when I'd been suffering from the fever. It occurred to me somewhere through the long conversation that I'd never actually told anyone the whole of what I'd been going through with the strange, dark spirit. I had tried, in the beginning, with Puck. Back when I thought he'd be the one person who might believe me. Before I knew he'd given up his faith. I'd made mentions to Ransom, but mostly, the man looked on me with pity whenever I spoke about the spirit. I wasn't sure how deep his faith ran, but he'd believed, and chased, after a spectral mountain beast. We'd even seen her. So it had always disappointed me that even he didn't really seem to believe me.

And Grant... Well, I'd told him some of what I was going through with Crow. I don't think he'd known what to make of it all. He'd been endlessly supportive when he was still with me, so I know that he wanted to give me comfort, but I don't think he'd ever known how to approach the subject. And in any case, when Grant had been in my life, Crow had made fewer and fewer appearances, which really bolstered Puck's case that the spirit was a manifestation of my anger, gone in happier times. Damn, I hated how much sense the fox made, sometimes.

"I don't know what to believe any more," I said softly, after a few moments of silence had passed between us following the end of my tale. The wolfhound had been quiet the whole while, but he had definitely been listening. Intently, even. He hadn't tried to interject, hadn't looked on me with pity or judgment... He'd just listened. I had a lot of people in my life who cared about me these days, but this was the first time I'd really felt someone cared about Crow. The spirit had almost become a private embarrassment to me, of late.

I gave a sniff, and covered it up quickly with a huff of breath. "I-I just don't know," I said, swiping a paw through my mane, "if I'm... crazy. If he's real? If... if I gave up my soul, or if I can fix things. The last time we spoke, I felt almost like he needed my help. That we could... I don't know. Heal together?" I finally looked up to the wolfhound. He seemed to be deep in thought, but his expression was impassive, otherwise. "Am I just mad?" I asked, with a nervous laugh that had no real humor in it.

"I don't think so," the man finally spoke, shifting so his arm was laying across his lap, on his bundled coat. "Everyone will have their own opinions, of course. But only you know your own mind."

I sat back, gritting my teeth inside my muzzle. The man couldn't know how terribly dissatisfied that answer had left me. I knew, of course, it was ludicrous to think so, but I'd honestly been hoping to get some kind of answer from him. He seemed to know a lot about this subject.

"I believe you," the Otherwolf stated, and something inside my chest lifted at the three simple words.

I blinked, realizing that my eyes had begun to burn. "You do?" I asked, suddenly breathless.

The man nodded. "And I do think this creature is a demon. They aren't merely evil creatures. They were good beings once, you know. Fallen angels."

"Angels?" I asked, remembering the word. It snapped into place a few moments later. "Grant told me about 'Angels,'" I said suddenly, in realization. "They're like our totem spirits, our protectors. The good ones. The ones that watch over people, and the land."

He nodded sagely. "Some of them are ascended souls. But they aren't faultless. When an angel falls from grace, they become a demon."

"Our religions are very different," I said with a ghost of a smile, "so I don't know if any of this has any bearing on me. But... tell me more."

"Look at it in the same way you would your 'spirits,'" the wolfhound explained. "They are creatures just as you and I are.

They were created differently, perhaps, but they have their own minds, their own lives, even if they are beyond what we can truly understand. They can sin, they can abuse their power, they can—"

"Feel alone, and abandoned?" I asked.

The wolfhound was silent for just a moment, before nodding, "I'd imagine, yes. There are many tales of angels who grew so saddened or angry by the holy war, that they descended to our world as men, or fell from grace and became demons. And demons want nothing more than to be in this world again. The realm they reside in now is torture. If they cannot escape it, they seek to drag mortal souls to their depths, to suffer alongside them in the pit. To burn with them."

My eyes widened. I could almost hear Crow's voice, in tandem with the wolfhound's.

Burn...

The Otherwolf seemed to sense that my mind was somewhere else, and he leaned in to bridge the gap between us just slightly, putting a hand on my shoulder. "I know this must all sound foreign and preachy to you, miss," he murmured. I blinked, wanting to shake my head, to tell him that no, this was the first time I'd ever heard anyone else saying the same things I was about the spirit, but I couldn't make my mouth work. "But," he murmured, "I've found over the years that... faith is what we make of it. The specifics of each holy book, of each person's God, or gods, or what we call the 'spirits', or 'demons', or 'angels' in our lives... none of it truly matters. What matters is that faith is the one cornerstone that every culture seems to have in common. Not the names, or the stories, perhaps, but the faith itself. And I think that's very powerful proof that these forces do exist. We just interpret them very differently."

He leaned back, the warmth of his paw leaving my shoulder, and I began to digest what he was saying. It made a lot of sense, actually.

"I don't think either the word 'demon' or 'spirit' can accurately describe what you're experiencing," he murmured, "but

I do believe this 'Crow' of yours exists, because it exists to you. And belief makes it real for you, even if others can't see it. You suffer because of this creature, do you not?"

My muzzle fell, and I gave a slow nod. There was no other way to look at it, really. Crow may have given me strength in certain moments, but there had been more bad than good. The angry spirit had tormented me when I was at my lowest, had abandoned me a great many times when I felt I needed him. Crow was an affliction, real or imagined.

"Your suffering is real," the wolfhound said, with a certain tone that had a pang of personal pain beneath it. "Let the Physicians call it 'madness' if they wish to. It doesn't matter what name anyone gives it. I would consider the forces that torment the men with Seer's Fever 'demons', as well. I've seen them drive a man to kill the Admiral he once idolized. That is what a demon does. They seize upon us in our weakest moments," the man's voice had grown strained, almost a rasp, "strike fear through our hearts, confusion and panic... cloud our eyes with visions, memories, places we wished never to remember... obscure and disrupt the present with vengeful, hateful thoughts from the past."

I remained silent, his words sinking into my bones. Some part of me knew he wasn't just talking about Crow, any more. But it was terrifying how much of what he had to say resonated with me. At length, he closed his eyes, and seemed to be collecting himself. I seized upon the moment to speak, albeit softly.

"Does your demon have a name?" I asked.

He squeezed his eyes closed more firmly for a moment or so, then opened them, slowly. "If it does," he murmured, "it hasn't told me. My demons don't take forms, they are merely demons of memories. Of places I have been. Battles. Slaughters. Things I have seen. Things no man should have to see." He cast his eyes aside at that. "Men like my late Lord, and like Luther, can contend with seeing the horrors I have. I'd always thought I was a strong man, as well. I went through extensive training to prepare me for this life. But I suppose no amount of training can change what you are at your core."

"It's not a matter of strength," I murmured, "to be affected by seeing horrible things. I have nightmares about some of the things I've seen—"

"But do they haunt your waking world?" the wolfhound replied, evenly. "Do you see them when you're at dinner? In a dark hallway, where the shadows happen to... remind you..." He shook his head slowly, and went silent.

I gave him time. I'd seen this before, I realized. Not long ago, even. The 'visions' he was talking about, the sudden bouts of panic... Gabriel suffered the same affliction. It's why he'd killed that woman. It's why he'd frozen on the battlefield just today. Suddenly, it made sense to me why the wolfhound, and not Ransom or I, had known what to say to him, to pull him out of it.

"I've hurt family members," he admitted. "Not just frightened them, not just metaphorically. Physically hurt them. I nearly broke my little girl's arm. I've struck my wife while she slept, because she startled me, or for no damned reason at all. Because I thought I'd woken in the jungle."

I tried not to let the sympathy I felt inside me make it to my eyes, knowing that wasn't what he wanted. It had never been what I wanted. I tried to simply do as he had, for me. Listen.

But a sudden thought sunk its claws into me, and I couldn't let it go.

"Your wife," I said, my mouth falling slightly open, at the horrifying concept, "did you..."

The way he looked me dead in the eyes, without speaking for several moments made my spine chill like ice. But finally, after a long enough wait that I honestly thought I might bolt, he spoke again, "Kill her?" He sighed. "Yes. But not in the way you're thinking."

I blinked uncertainly. What did that even mean?

"My wife died in childbirth," he said, in a well-practiced, forcefully even tone. There was so much strain beneath it though, I would have rather heard the emotion there than heard him forcibly keeping it down. But at least...

"That's hardly your fault," I urged.

"The Physicians warned her not to have any more children," the man said, and now I could hear the bitterness, the hurt. He couldn't keep it entirely obscured. "The last had gone so poorly, she and my son both nearly died. They told her, told me, that if she became pregnant again, she might not survive carrying the child to term, let alone bringing it into the world. We knew the risks. I knew the risks. It was my responsibility to keep my passions in-check. We thought," he shook his head at that, "thought we were being safe. But she was late in her thirties, her heats were sporadic. It doesn't matter. The point is, if I had enough bloody restraint..." he swept a hand over his mouth, holding it there, and looked anywhere but at me, "She would still be here."

"You're overcompensating," I murmured.

The man eyed me at that. "Excuse me?"

"You want someone to blame, for something that happened that was no one's fault," I said, with a soft sigh. "You're blaming yourself because there's no one else you can take this out on."

"It was the direct result of my actions—"

"And hers," I said, defensively. "I'm sorry, but you don't strike me as the type to take a woman against her will." The way he balked at that seemed to confirm my statement, so I pressed on. "You loved her, right? Your wife?"

The tall canine leaned back just enough that his back hit the stone wall, and looked upwards for a moment, blinking as though some of the dusty air had gotten into his eyes. I let him pretend.

"More than anything," he finally uttered. "I want to be with her."

"Don't blame yourself for what happened, then," I said, quietly. "You're doing a disservice to that love. Death comes for women when they bring life into the world, sometimes. It's a terrible thing, but it not something any of us can help. And there's no shame in loving your wife, and having children with her. I'm sure..." my breath hitched, "I'm sure if we could ask her, she would have said it was worth it. I know, if I could have given my life for my child, I would have."

The Otherwolf gave a long, ragged breath through his nose. "I could have stopped it."

"What?" I asked, uncertain what he'd meant by that.

"I could have saved her life," he said quietly.

"There... there isn't much you can do in situations like that—" I reasoned.

"Before then. Before it got to that point," he said.

"I," I stammered, "I don't understand, I'm sorry."

"I had an herbal mixture," he said, as though every word were a blade he was forcing past his lips. "I purchased it from the black market in Pendarest, a month or so after I found out she was with child. When I was visiting my Bishop," he said the last part with a huff, like he found it darkly amusing.

"An herbal mixture?" I repeated, confused.

"If I'd given it to her, she would have miscarried," he explained quietly. I felt a pang in my chest at the mere concept. He shook his head. "But I couldn't do it. I didn't even care that it was an affront to God, that it's one of the most heinous Sins. I would have gone to Hell for her. What stayed me wasn't that. She wouldn't take it willingly, and I couldn't subject her to it, if she wasn't in agreeance. I could have. She'd never have known."

"But you didn't," I said, firmly. "And that was the right choice."

"If I had, she'd still be alive," he stressed.

"And she'd never have forgiven you," I emphasized.

"You can't know that."

"I wouldn't have," I stated. He looked briefly over to me when I said it, then sighed. "You can't know what it feels like to have a life growing inside you," I said. "To carry that. To know you're ultimately their last line of defense. My husband punched me in the stomach once, when I was pregnant."

His head whipped around at that, and I only nodded at his look of horror. "I remember the fear I felt that day," I murmured. "Maybe some women could bear it, but... If your wife didn't want it, there is nothing you could have done to convince her otherwise. Trust me."

He didn't respond to that, only looked away, and I had to bring up the obvious parallel, or it was going to sit in the air between us all night.

"The nesting grounds..." I began.

"I know," he said, his tone dark. "Trust me, I've made the comparison in my mind. A man should never have to make this choice twice in a lifetime. God forgive me..."

I pursed my muzzle for a moment, then dropped my voice. "I don't think either choice is right or wrong, exactly," I admitted, which seemed to surprise him. "You can't compare the value of lives like that," I said, "I've seen people who did just that. It was arrogant then. It's arrogant now."

"Then there is no right choice," the man insisted. "Either way, we're in the wrong."

"Life puts us there sometimes," I said. "When things like this happen to me, and they've been happening more and more, over the last few years, I take a page from my friend's book," I gestured with my shoulder, to the coyote standing a ways away at the entrance to the cave mouth, "and go with my gut. I'm guessing that's what you did, with your wife."

"And she died," he growled, although the anger seemed mostly meant for himself.

"The important part is that you didn't make the choice for her," I emphasized. "And that's all we can do. Do as well as we can, without forcing what we think is right on others."

"Someone has to bear the responsibility of this decision," the wolfhound said, his voice strained. "We had a mission out here. People's lives are depending on it."

"I've made my decision," I said. "It's what feels right in my heart. Make a decision you can live with. That's all we can do."

"I thought I could live with the decision I made then," he put his good hand to his brow. "Then she died. It all seems so obvious until it goes wrong."

I remained silent, because I knew there was little I could say to ease that ache, but when his hand dropped away, he only looked like the same tired man he'd been before. There were still no tears.

"She was my anchor," his voice was a ghost of what I'd heard it to be before, all of that strength gone. "I could live with the demons, when I had her. Once she was gone, I... they grew louder. More powerful. Seized upon me so often, I-I couldn't even hide it from the young ones, anymore. They were frightened of me."

My eyes fell to where my raw, battered feet were resting on the dirty, red rock of the cave floor. "They grow stronger when we grow weaker," I murmured. "Drag you down with them, into the depths of your darkest feelings. Burn you up inside."

He nodded, one of his draping ears twitching weakly. I leaned forward, wrapping my arms around my knees and resting my chin on them, sitting in pensive silence for a time.

"You know," I said, suddenly, "maybe it's both."

"Hm?" the man queried, not even looking up.

"Puck, and most Physicians, I guess," I said, "think these creatures, like Crow, and your 'demons', are just manifestations of our madness, or whatever it is they claim. Holy men say they're beings that live inside of us, and compel us. But what if it's both?"

"How would it be both?" the wolfhound asked.

"What if we make our own demons?" I asked, plainly. "Before I was ever hurt, before I ever had reason to have so much anger, Crow was my totem spirit. Not the Crow I came to know, just here," I swept my fingers through my tangled mane, and showed him the carved turquoise bead, with the black etching of Crow in it. "He was in my life, before he was ever the spirit that began to haunt me. And I've always felt that his pain, that his loneliness, mirrored mine. What if he's my spirit? What if I made him?"

"It's an interesting thought," the wolfhound said, sounding exhausted. "On a better day, I'd gladly talk philosophy with you. But, even if it's true, it doesn't make them any less hellish to contend with."

"No, but," I paused, "doesn't it mean we could heal them? Heal ourselves? If they're a part of us."

The Otherwolf gave the slightest of smiles.

"What?" I said, tilting my head. "What is it?"

"Nothing, it's just," he winced a bit as he leaned back again, "you're beginning to sound like my Bishop. He said something similar to me once."

"What did he say?" I asked, curiously.

"Some Priests believe the only cure for possession is an exorcism, or to push the possessed person's body so far towards the brink of death, that the demon abandons them. That is a tradition I cannot support," he murmured. "I've seen it fail far too many times. And I've never truly seen what I would consider proof that it works. But I— When I was at my worst, I still considered it."

He looked somewhat startled when he looked into my eyes. Likely because of the obvious venom behind them. "My people have a ritual to cleanse our tribes of sin like that," I said, icily. "But no one lives through it. Well, no one is supposed to live through it."

"I'm sorry," he said, seeming to sense my meaning.

"It's fine," I sighed, pushing the anger away, as I had so many times in the past. "But you clearly didn't go through with it. Or you survived it."

He shook his head. "My Bishop convinced me out of it. He's a good man. A holy man. But even he doesn't support some of the traditions. If he doesn't believe in this rite, then I am convinced it's a creation of Canid, not God. He suspects it is, as well. But," he looked out the cave mouth, towards where the sky was growing dark beyond, "he told me, there are ways to fight the demons inside you. One true path to salvation, albeit a difficult one."

My heart lightened a bit at his words, even if I was uncertain whether or not they'd be of any help to me, coming from a holy man across the sea, who didn't even worship the same gods I did. Still, I asked, "How?"

"Forgiveness," he said, the word sounding as heavy on his tongue as it felt sinking into my mind. I knew his language well enough to know the word, but it wasn't one I used frequently, if ever.

"Some things can't be forgiven," I said quietly, averting my gaze. "There are evils in this world that have to be rectified. Even if it gives us no pleasure to do it. Someone has to put a stop to it."

"You cannot put a stop to all the evil in the world," the Otherwolf said. "You're young, so it's easy to feel as though you can 'fix' it all. You can't. And you can't even the scales by causing more pain. My friend, the Admiral, once felt the way you did. I told him the same thing, then. Evil is a force that will always exist in the world, it's not a tangible enemy. It cannot be beaten. Anger and revenge are a cycle we fall into, when we're confronted with that reality."

"That sounds too hopeless," I muttered. "I don't want to believe that."

The man shrugged. "History bears me out. And you sound as though you know the truth in my words."

I sighed. "Crow is like a mirror reflection of how I've felt, in my darkest moments. I've said things similar to what you're saying now to him. It's easier to accept when I'm lecturing someone else."

The wolfhound smiled. "Isn't that always the way?"

"I'm sorry," I shook my head, "but there are people in the world—even people who've already died—who I can't even imagine how to forgive. And I don't know what good it would do me."

"Forgiveness is the one true escape from evil," the wolfhound said, his grey eyes heavy as they settled on mine. I could see the burden of the weight in his words, wearing him down, as though they were as hard for him to say as they were for me to accept. "It is the only escape from evil. It doesn't matter whether or not it's deserved, whether or not you feel it's right. So long as we hate, so long as we regret, so long as we cling to our anger over the evils committed against us, against others we love... that evil still has a power over us. The wrongs that were done in the past live on, in the present, through us. The only escape from them is to let go. Forgive."

I looked up at him over the bridge of my knees. It had grown dark in the cave, and we hadn't lit a fire. The wolfhound was barely a silhouette now, and it occurred to me then that, staring at the black shape that was his body, leaning away from the wall now, silhouetted against the deepening blue of the night sky outside—clear for the first time in weeks—that I would probably always remember this second in time. This conversation. I couldn't say why. I just knew I would. The same as I remembered chasing butterflies through the valley, or seeing my son for the first time, or standing with Laesom on the cliff edge, looking over the other side of the world I'd once known.

Or lying with Grant in our small tent, feeling the warmth of his body against mine. Smelling the scent of his fur. That same moment in time, so little time later, resting my head against his chest as the warmth seeped from him. As he ceased to be the person I'd known, and became a memory.

For the first time since it had happened, I was able to remember that moment, and the pain in my chest eased. Because I was also remembering everything else, every other moment we'd had, coming upon me in a cascade, like I was still there. And I didn't want to remember the pain anymore. I was so tired of it. Had it really been this simple all along?

It wasn't about forgiving Methoa, or forgiving Rourke, or Shadow, or the Raiders. The person I'd been angry at, the person for whom I'd really felt all this frustration against, this rage, was...

"Sir," I said quietly, looking to the wolfhound. His eyes told me he'd reached the same answer I had, a very long time ago... and was struggling to accept it. "Who are you trying to forgive?" I asked finally, the words feather soft in the air between us.

The man closed his eyes for just a moment or so before answering.

"Myself."

CHAPTER 9
UNCLOUDED

We made it down the cliffs the following morning, hitting the forest floor before the sun had even entirely risen. We didn't want to risk being near the nests at any point in the daylight hours, since that's when the Cathazra were most active. Johannes was doing much better by then, although his arm very badly needed to be seen to by a Physician, and quickly. If I'd been wrong, and it was a break, it would need to be re-set. He bore it all so stoically though, it was hard to tell how much pain he was in.

The chest wounds at least hadn't been deep, and they looked to be healing well. And the symptoms of the head wound didn't seem to be affecting him any longer, save the fact that he'd admitted to having a hell of a headache. That was to be expected, though.

My thoughts occasionally flickered back in time to the days following Grant's death, and how different my life might have been, if he'd just had a 'close call', like the wolfhound had. But just as I began that whimsical train of thought, I remembered where we were, the very real dangers we still faced, and sharpened back on the present. Now was not a good time for daydreaming.

When we hit the bottom of the cliffs and began our trek into the sprawling, messy forests beyond, I noticed Ransom had been looking back towards the bluffs an awful lot. If he were just looking for pursuers, they were more likely to come at us from behind us, from the winding paths we'd taken through the brush along the hillside. And he wasn't looking to the skies, either. He seemed to be looking down towards where the coastline crashed into the peaks, far off in the distance. I couldn't imagine why, so I decided I'd ask.

"What is it?" I asked, as I moved up beside him, keeping my eyes on my footing. We were walking through a marshy, reedy area for now, on the outlying edge of the forest, and it was a likely place for Wyrm ambushes and traps, so I was keeping my eyes peeled.

"Huh?" The coyote muttered after a few moments, only seeming to realize I'd wanted an answer to my question belatedly. "Uh. Nothin'," he sighed.

"Thinking about the nests?" I ventured. He seemed to be looking up towards the cliffs, from where we'd come from, specifically, so that was my best guess.

"Naw," the coyote grunted. "I ain't gonna over think that'n too much."

My eyebrows knitted. "You've made your decision on that?" His silence was telling, so I sighed. "Well?" I pressed.

"Ah don't like th' Admiral," he muttered. "So you ain't got nothin' to worry about. It ain't even that I don't think we should report this. Ah just... don't wanna talk t'that man."

I nodded, even though I knew it was a lie. The coyote's morals had won out, in the end. He just didn't want to be seen as soft, and that was fine by me. And we did still have time. If things got close to the wire and it became clear that a lot of people, possibly even Puck, might die because of the decision we'd made, though... I didn't trust his resolve to hold out.

Even mine might not. I couldn't know until we got to that point. But it wasn't worth thinking about right now.

"So then what's wrong?" I asked, suddenly feeling the need to change the subject.

The coyote growled something under his breath, then, when I leaned in, sighed and repeated, "I was hopin' we'd find that beast's corpse, is all. But it must've fallen further down towards th' cliffs."

I gave him a bizarre look. "The Dragon? Why, for gods' sake? I promise you, it's dead. And there are a lot more live ones where it came from that we need to worry about." A sudden thought crossed my mind, about the coyote's profession, and I recoiled. "Ransom, you can't... you didn't want to skin it, did you?"

The coyote's ears fell back and he whirled on me with a look of disgust. "Goddamnit cat, no! I ain't depraved! That's disgustin'!"

I held up my hands. "I know," I insisted, "I know, I-I just... I can't imagine what else you'd want from—"

"That thing was wearin' gold," the coyote said, cutting me off. "A lot of it. I'd heard tell their adornments was worth a lot. I was hopin' if we ran into one of 'em, I'd be able to strip off whatever was valuable. But it fell, so I ain't got nothin' out of this whole mess."

I blinked at the statement. It made sense, of course, but it still seemed somewhat uncharacteristic for the coyote. Not that he didn't care about money at all, he'd wheeled and dealed for his furs back at Crossroads, and he liked to have enough to live on. But there was an edge of desperation to his tone right now, and I knew for a fact he'd been receiving enough to live on from the military garrison here, which was generally all the coyote wanted for. A warm place to sleep and enough food to fill his belly. And buy cigarettes and booze, both of which he'd seemed to have more than enough of, of late. Apparently they could grow a lot of tobacco in this climate, so it was inexpensive. 'The one upside to this place', as Ransom had put it.

Then again, I'd also been thinking of ways to make money, of late. Or at least trying to, I was piss poor at understanding currency or what was of value to Otherwolves. Of course in my case it wasn't for pleasure's sake, I just wanted to help—

"Oh!" I'd paused in my step, and I rushed the few feet through the grass to grab at the coyote's arm, suddenly. "He told you, didn't he?" Ransom's expression said it all.

"Oh thank the gods," I blew out a breath. "Keeping that secret was eating me up inside."

"Y' should've told me as soon as he told you," the coyote growled. "I'm right pissed th' both of you kept this from me as long's you did."

I punched him in the arm, hard enough that I saw him wince. "Have you proposed?" His ears fell at my comment, and

I snorted. "Then I don't want to hear it. Hypocrite!" A few silent beats passed between us as we continued to push through the reeds, before I asked the obvious question. "And you're going along with it?"

"I don't got much choice in th' matter, do I?" The coyote grunted. "You know the fox. Once his mind's made up on somethin', it's like tryin' t' budge a mountain. He was even too stubborn t' stay dead."

I chuckled, looking back up at the coyote, affectionately. "Ransom," I said after a few moments, in a more serious tone, "he values your feelings. More than his own sometimes, I think. If you told him you didn't want him to get the surgery—"

"Don't tell me that," the coyote cut me off. His eyes were on the skyline, vigilant for drakes or other dangers, but I knew he wasn't seeing much of anything in front of him right now. "I gotta feel I don't got a choice in this, Shivah. Ah don't..." he scrubbed a paw over his muzzle, "Ah don't want to tell him what t' do with his life. This oughta' be his choice. No matter how much ah hate it. I ain't the kinda' man who tells th' people 'e loves they ain't allowed to see, just because ah'm afraid of bein' alone again."

I was nearly staggered off my feet by the deep pang of respect I felt lancing through me at the coyote's words, and the sudden realization that he'd changed more than I'd ever given him credit for, this last year. I still had a long way to go, because if I was in his position, I'm not certain I could have made the choice he had. Not where a loved one was concerned. Even though it was the right thing to do. I was still too afraid of losing everyone in my life. Petrified, even.

"That's very brave, Ransom," I murmured, putting a hand on his shoulder.

He just shook it off. "Puck's the brave'un. I'm quakin' in mah britches. Ah'm just not interferin'."

"So," I said, quietly, "he's definitely going through with it?"

The coyote nodded. "Think so. He's talked t'the Physician about havin' it done, at least. Ah know that much. Ah don't know when, but after he has it done, he needs these... spectacles."

I nodded, "He told me." I reached down and grabbed for a loose stick, sticking it in the marshy mud a few paces in front of us before crossing the patch. It had looked a little suspect, like a sinkhole, but apparently it was just normal mud. I leapt it anyway. "Are they really that expensive?" I asked over my shoulder at the coyote. He was waiting for the wolfhound to catch up. He'd been lagging a few paces behind us the entire way, still tired no doubt, but keeping up steadily despite his injuries.

"More 'n I'd make in a year, back home," the coyote muttered, with a sigh. "And that's a good year. Out here I can't even hunt, and there ain't much of a market. My skills ain't worth bunk, here. And the military pay's just enough to pay our way to live here. Everythin's so expensive in this place. I don't know what t' do."

"I wish I had an answer for you," I murmured. But I didn't, and I'd been thinking on it for weeks now. Really, the whole thing seemed idiotic, but it was still daunting. The difficult choice here had already been made, if Puck had decided to go through with the surgery after all. That should have been the hard part.

It was somewhat cruel that, even after weighing his odds and making such a hard choice, even if he were to survive and heal from the operation, he could still be left mostly blind. Without the spectacles, Forrest had told us it would be like looking through a foggy glass, except when objects were extremely close to him. And even then...

"We'll figure something out," I promised the coyote with a firm nod. "It's not even as if it's something we have to do here. Puck's been blind a very long time now. If he has to wait until we make it back to our lands to get these spectacles, even if it means you have to save your earnings for a few years, I know you'll do what's necessary, Ransom."

"Damned straight," the coyote growled.

I smiled up at him. "Then let's focus on the present, for now. Being there for Puck while he endures this, and making certain we get out of this place alive."

"Yer bleedin' heart ain't helpin' us there," the coyote muttered.

"Our bleeding hearts."

The coyote grumbled, but he didn't bother denying it. He did, however, speak again after a brief pause. And when he did, he'd dropped his voice. "Y'know, all yer guiltin' me and yer goddamn stubbornness ain't gonna mean a thing in th' world if the wolfhound talks."

I had to briefly glance over my shoulder at that to see if Johannes had heard us, but he was busily navigating the same sinkhole we had a few moments ago, and seemed more interested in keeping up the pace despite his injuries above listening in on our conversation.

"Do you really think he will?" I asked him in a low whisper. "He seems like a good man. I think the thought disturbs him as much as it does us."

"Ah think the thought a' betrayin' his Lord will disturb him more," the coyote muttered. "But I guess we'll see, won't we?"

The thought that the man whose life I'd just risked everything to save might be the instrument of the same sort of merciless slaughter we'd seen from the Raiders sank into my gut like a lead weight. But Ransom was right. Good man or no, this wolfhound, the man whom I'd poured my heart out to last night, might be a comrade to us now, but his loyalty still undoubtedly lay with the Amurescan Lords here. Especially the damned Admiral, whom I had no doubt would use this information if he ever heard of it. The cattle dog had been willing to drag Grayson's entire fleet into this mess by way of deception and trap them here in the middle of a warzone, after all. He'd all but admitted to it.

Situations like this forced me to wonder how it was ever possible to make the right decision. It seemed like no matter what I'd done in my life of late, no matter how obvious the moral choice had seemed at the time, there was always some unintended consequence of my actions. If saving a man's life—a man who was willingly throwing himself to the monsters at our backs in a purely selfless act, to save his men—hadn't been the right thing to do, then what could be?

And yet here we were. We'd saved his life, and at the time I'd felt I was almost undoing a wrong from my past, protecting a comrade in the heat of battle, something I'd failed to do for Grant. I should have been elated.

Instead, I was beginning to wonder if I should have let him die. Because now we shared our secret with him. And unlike Ransom, I didn't trust him to keep it.

"It's all so maddening," I said, catching the coyote by surprise. And why wouldn't I? That had probably come out of nowhere to him. He hadn't been taking part in my mental conversation, after all.

"What is?" He asked, idly chopping at a jagged frond with his hunting knife.

"It's like no matter how hard I try," I said in an irritated tone, "I can never really take the right path. Every road I take finds some way to twist back into gnarled," I shoved the same bent frond out of the way, and kicked down another cracked, sharp-edged dead jungle plant of some sort, "thorny, difficult terrain. Pitfalls I never seen coming. It's shit. I hate it."

The coyote barked a laugh, "I take it yer not talkin' about the jungle." When I snuffed, he gave a surprisingly easy smile, the way he did whenever he was about to say something he knew more about than me. "Shivah, that's life. 'Specially fer people like us, who don't take the beaten path. 'S always gonna be difficult. Yer never gonna be entirely certain y'did right. Even folks who live easy, direct lives ain't got that kinda' conviction. And if they do, they're arrogant shits."

I gave a frustrated snarl. "It shouldn't be this hard to do the right thing, though."

The coyote shrugged. "So long as yer intent's good, Shivah. All 'at matters is that y' tried. Shit happens, people fuck up, gods know ah make mistakes all the time," he muttered. "Y' can't control th' world. You just get wise to it as y' get older, and make better choices as y' go."

I glanced over at him. "Since when did you become a philosopher?" I asked, mildly amused by his sudden bout of insightful rhetoric.

The coyote's fur whipped in the light breeze coming in off the ocean a mile or so away. Even this far from the shore, I could smell it. He was looking towards it as well, probably having caught the same scent I had.

"Them's my father's words, actually," he said quietly. "Old 'yote... was honestly a smarter man than I ever gave'm credit fer. I was just..." he glanced down, slowing his pace some, "a wild little 'un. Bent on not listenin' to my old man. I wish I had, more. Man had some wisdom."

I pursed my muzzle a moment, before asking, "Have you ever considered going back home to see them again, Ransom? Your parents?"

The coyote was silent for a span after that. "Yeah," he said at length. "Ah jes'... been afraid, I guess. Knowin' they're gonna ask about Dominick."

I opened my mouth to say something, but nothing came out. That was an aspect of his reality I'd never even considered until this moment, and I felt foolish. Not just for thinking the issues that might come with the coyote returning home would all evaporate in the face of parental love, although that in and of itself was a naive thought on my part, and I knew it. My own tormented relationship with my parents, who'd given me up to an abusive man, knowing who he was, should have shattered my perception of unconditional parental love. But I guess in the recesses of my mind, I still wanted to hope other people's families were the ideal I'd always wanted in mine.

But the fact was, even if that was the case, even if the coyote's parents truly did love him and had simply never gotten a chance to save him from the clutches of the man whose control he's thrown himself into... that didn't mean they'd pity him for the choice he'd made. Or that they'd accept him for who he was now. I could imagine a thousand nightmarish scenarios for him returning home, and only really one good, very unlikely one.

They could blame him for running away with Dominick. They could pity him to the point of being unable to see him as anything but a victim any longer. They could blame him for killing his cousin. They could force him to cut himself off from Puquanah, out of the same fear that had haunted him for years—that he was only in love with the fox because of what Dominick had done to him. That he'd been corrupted, twisted by his cousin, and couldn't ever have 'natural' relationships with women anymore, because of what had happened to him.

I'd known the two men long enough to know their love was real, had seen it first hand, knew it was the only reason both of them were alive right now. But they hadn't seen what I'd seen. And people had their prejudices. I knew one thing for certain. If Ransom tried to reconnect with his parents, and they opened those wounds again; if two people he'd once loved, whose opinions would stick in him like a knife; made him feel the same old doubts he'd felt before... it could tear him apart. It could tear him and Puck apart.

And he probably knew that.

"Ransom?" I said. The coyote tipped an ear back towards me, but didn't turn. "Your parents," I said softly, "even if it wasn't by their doing, haven't been a part of your life for a very long time. If when you go back home, you decide to seek them out... I think that would be great. But they... they don't need to know everything that's happened in your life over the last few years. Sometimes, some parts of ourselves are so personal, they don't bear sharing with everyone."

"They're my family, Shivah," the coyote murmured, turning to look at me. "You suggestin' I hide those parts o' me from'em?"

I hesitated only a moment, before saying, "You know them best, Ransom. Do you think there's any way they'd accept you, if they knew?"

The coyote's silence said more than any response could have.

"Pick your battles," I said quietly, but intently. "Don't give yourself that kind of pain."

"They're family."

"Then just don't involve them in those aspects of your life," I said. "Or don't seek them out again. Enjoy your memories. We're your family too, Ransom. At least, I'd like to think so."

The coyote put a calloused palm on top of my head and mussed my hair some. I batted at him. He was smiling tiredly down at me. "Aye, cat, yer right," he said at length. "Ah don't even know why I've been thinkin' about the old man, of late."

"I'd venture to guess it's because you're considering getting marr-"

"Never should've bloody told you about that," the coyote growled.

"It's sweet," I said with an impish smile. I swear, the man rolled his eyes. In that exaggerated sort of way he did out of affection. "Well you have to at least tell him about the rings," I said, jabbing him in the ribs with an elbow. "Talk about it."

"Why? It ain't even like it's possible."

"If it was, would that change your opinion on the matter?"

The coyote briefly glanced down at me at that, but then he just swept his eyes back to the horizon. "I got time," he said at length. "On that, a' least. I don't see no need t' rush, when we got so much else goin' on. All the miserable shit goin' on in my life right now... the fox a' least is a constant. Only thing now's gettin' b'tween us is death, and if that happens, I ain't exactly got no more worries, do I?"

"You're so certain of that," I sighed, shaking my head.

"Yeah, I am actually," the coyote stated, bluntly. "There ain't a whole lot I can count on in mah life, but Puck's one thing ah know I can. Only thing that'd take him away from me is the damned reaper, and I'm doin' my best right now t' make sure that don't happen. And Forrest will do his damnedest too, ah'm sure." He pulled ahead of me at that, purposefully putting some distance between us. "So don't you worry yerself about the two of us 'n our 'relationship' no more, cat," he said over his shoulder at me. "That's one bit ah think we've finally got all worked out."

I watched him plow ahead, too dumbstruck to move for a little while. The coyote was audacious at times, but this was beyond the pale. He was in no place to be that confident about Puck's loyalty to him, after all he'd put the fox through—and was continuing to put him through, if my talks with Puck were any indication. I knew full well it was only a matter of time before the fox did something about it all, too. He was a patient soul, but he had his limits. It made me more than a little irate to think the coyote considered Puquanah so firmly 'his' that he didn't realize the increasingly tenuous state of things between him and the fox. What they'd been through in the mountains must have given him a big head. As if accepting that he wanted the relationship with Puck now was enough that it would be so. Without any real effort at empathizing or showing some damned loyalty to his partner.

The maturity he'd shown at letting Puck make his own decision in having the surgery was a step in the right direction. But he had a long way to go.

I must have been standing there for some time, because the wolfhound caught up to me. I felt his presence at my side, and looked up to see the man catching his breath, the morning sun casting a shadow over me from his tall figure. He tilted his muzzle down at me, curiously.

"That looked rather animated," he said, indicating the coyote. "What was that all about?"

I sighed. "Denial."

"Oh?" the wolfhound's scruffy moustache turned up in an amused smile.

"My friend," I paused, wording this carefully, "has a very complex, unnecessarily dramatic love-life."

Strangely, the wolfhound only patted my shoulder at that. "I feel your pain," he muttered, "I have one just like him back home."

"I think we've narrowed it down to the water supply," Puck murmured, as he dug through his pouch for something, a sewing needle stuck out of the corner of his muzzle. He was in the midst of working on something that looked a lot like a wrist brace. I briefly wondered if it was for the wolfhound. They'd improvised something a few days ago when we'd made it back to Serwich and he'd come here to be treated, but I'd seen him since then, and it didn't seem adequate to me. He was mending well, but had mentioned that the brace came loose too easily. Likely because the straps were hard for him to tighten one-handed, not being sewn into the leather they'd cobbled together.

They were low on supplies in this place, though. A lot of people were going without necessary medicine, or medical supplies. From what I'd seen, that's primarily what Puck had been working on while spending his time here over the last two months. That and talking to Forrest about the Seer's Fever, as well as assisting in the few cases they saw of it here. Apparently, for all his superior training, Puck actually was more knowledgeable about how to treat the fever than the Otherwolf Physician. Likely because of his crash course in Serahaven, seeing every flavor and horror of the illness first-hand. From what Puck had told me, most of the people who'd come to Serwich had gotten vaccinated against the illness, since they'd had prior knowledge of its prevalence here. And the few that hadn't that came in from time to time were usually isolated before it could become a contagion. They knew how to look for the symptoms here, knew to expect it.

"They're paranoid about it," Puck muttered out of the corner of his mouth, before plucking the needle out, and handing it to me to be threaded. There were still some things that he simply couldn't do without sight. Re-threading a needle was one. He usually kept some pre-threaded in his bag for medical emergencies, but this was more a sewing project.

"About what?" I asked.

"The water supply," he said. "It's long been suspected that's how the disease spreads, and I have to concur. It seems likely. The question, of course, is how."

"That does make sense," I murmured thoughtfully. "A lot of the settlements in Carvecia that got the fever were along the river."

"A lot of otters, in particular," the fox nodded. "Which is another factor that makes me think it has to be in the water. There's just a few things that don't fit."

"Such as?" I asked, mostly making conversation at this point. When the fox got like this, I knew full well I couldn't keep up. But Forrest was away treating patients, and I'm sure he'd already had this talk with him, at length.

"Well here, we could say it's natural to the environment, somehow," the fox said with a sigh. "I mean, we don't really know where it comes from, ultimately. Perhaps it comes from the animals here, or the insects, or the Cathazra themselves. It's hard to say. But whatever the case, because it's endemic to this land, cases of it appearing seemingly out of nowhere can be explained. Especially with the river running through this settlement. It could be coming from anywhere upstream. The mountains, animals in the wilderness, the Cathazra settlements."

"Isn't it bad that it's that vague?" I asked, suddenly concerned. "I mean, if you can't isolate the root of it, how are we going to end the spread back home? Isn't that what we came here for? To figure out how it's spreading, and stop that?"

"Precisely," Puck nodded. "But back home, we actually have a chance. Back home it's spreading through the population, primarily. Whatever the source of it is, that source is here. We might not be able to isolate that source just yet, but presumably, unless it's coming from a population of livestock or something else that was brought to Carvecia, if we can stop it from spreading through the populace there—"

"There won't be a source for new infections," I said, understanding.

"Well, there always will be that, unfortunately," the fox sighed, "so long as people are sailing between the two continents, someone new could bring the Fever to Carvecia again. In fact, I'd say that's a fargone conclusion. All the same, if we're just treating isolated cases, and we can stop those isolated cases from spreading, we've pretty much beaten the disease."

"So that brings us back to stopping it from spreading," I muttered. "I feel like we're going in circles here, Puck."

"It has to be the water supply," the fox said with a sigh. "There's too many coincidences for it not to be. But a few things don't fit, in that case, which is what's frustrating me."

"Mnh?" I leaned on my palm.

"Serahaven, for one," the fox said, sticking up one finger. "I talked to the people who lived there, Shivah. They weren't ignorant. Mice can be remarkably meticulous. They had a town well. They didn't use the river for drinking water, only washing clothing and watering livestock. And even if that's where the disease came from, how?" He spread his hands, as if at a loss. "The only settlements up-river from Serahaven were the ones closer to the valley. Disregarding the chance that the disease somehow came from some isolated traveler we never found who somehow got his fluids or corpse in the river nearby, and that is a possibility, but every settlement that was hit by the Fever further North, especially those along the river, has to have been hit by the Raiders. They wouldn't have missed an infected town along the river, since that's how they traveled."

"Maybe it was from a settlement even further north along the river?" I offered.

"That's an awfully long way for a disease to travel, especially in the winter," Puck sighed. "It seems far-fetched. And the outbreak that hit Serahaven was acute. It hit hard, and fast. Nearly everyone in the town was infected in a very short span of time.

That's the sort of outbreak I wouldn't expect to see unless there was a massive surge of the disease making it into their water nearby, somehow."

I shrugged. "It's possible the Raiders missed a settlement," I offered.

"I have to believe I'd have heard about that," Puck muttered.

"Or didn't burn all the corpses?"

"That's more plausible," Puck sighed. "But it doesn't make figuring this out any easier. Finding the solution here is easier if I think in absolutes."

"But not necessarily true," I muttered.

"Therein lies my problem," Puck said with a frustrated snap of his teeth. "I really need to know all factors absolutely to come to an accurate conclusion, here. And that's impossible. I'm honestly just hoping for a bolt of inspiration, at this point. Something obvious I'm missing."

"Well I can't help you there," I said, sliding off the cot he was sitting on and getting to my feet with a stretch. "Nor with your sewing any more, I'm afraid. I have to go."

The fox's ears perked, and he looked a bit disappointed. "Really?" he queried. "I'd been hoping you'd stay longer today. Where are you going?"

"The Navy Lodge," I replied. "There's a war meeting there today, and for once, I've been invited. I figure that means it's not all that important, but Johannes invited me along, so I figured I'd make the most of it. Learn what I can."

The fox arched an eyebrow. "Johannes'?" he parroted.

"The wolfhound, the one Ransom and I serve under," I said, bristling a bit defensively. I hadn't told the fox about what had happened on the cliffs, or since, and he was irritatingly perceptive sometimes.

He seemed to brush it off, though. "Well," he mused a moment, "can I come?"

"Um," I paused, "I... I suppose. You're technically with the defense force here. And I don't think this is one of their secretive meetings, or I wouldn't be invited. I'm guessing they're just assuaging local merchants' fears and going over the 'hypothetical' evacuation. Although I think that excuse is wearing thin at this point."

"Yes," the fox nodded. "I'm fairly certain the people all know it's coming, now. The nurses talk about it all the time. People are making preparations."

I began shouldering my cloak, then looked down at the fox, tilting my head. "You know," I said, "if you can afford to take time off today, you should go be with Ransom. He's not stationed on the wall today, and it's a few days before our next scouting mission. Why don't you two go spend some time together?"

The fox looked away, which I'd always found to be a reminder that he hadn't been born blind, a habit from a previous life. "We saw each other this morning," he muttered. "It's... things are uncomfortable with he and I right now. Can I please just spend some time with you today, Shivah? I won't be a bother."

"Oh for god's sake," I growled, "are you avoiding him?"

"Um, no," the fox said at length, running a paw up his arm in a gesture that looked to me to be oddly guilty. "I just—like I said, things are just awkward. I'm giving him the day to think. I'm sure it will all work itself out in the end."

"I don't want to know," I said, slicing a hand through the air. "Don't involve me this time, Puck. You two need to start working your problems out on your own. I am not your fixer, and the more I help, the more it's enabling you two not to solve these things yourselves."

"That's fine," the fox said, still with that strangely guilty look about him. I couldn't put my finger on it, exactly. It was unusual to see on him. Usually when he was fighting with Ransom, he was angry. Rightfully so, most of the time. This was something else. I decided to follow my own advice, and think on it no longer. It was so hard not to mother the two men, but I really needed to stop intervening, or they'd continue to rely on me.

We headed off for the Navy Lodge, a sort of all-purpose building for the Navy men and a city center for a lot of other functions in the middle of the settlement. It was a large log building, with one main hall and several adjoining offices, although I'd only ever been in the hall before, and only a few times.

I helped Puck inside, after explaining to the door guards that he was here from the triage unit. They seemed to accept that with a disinterested nod, which confirmed my suspicion that this couldn't have been a terribly important meeting, or they'd be more choosy about who they let in. Despite that, there weren't exactly throngs of people inside. Mostly faces I recognized. The Admiral, of course, currently speaking with a barrel-chested canine in a blue coat who seemed to be missing half an arm, a few men from the wall I knew, one of Grayson's messengers (the wolf himself likely hadn't thought this meeting important enough to wake up for) and several other navy men and military types I'd seen around, but couldn't put names to.

The lodge smelled of wood, lamp oil and dogs, and by the time we got there people seemed to be settling in, which was for the best, because Puck would have had a hell of a time navigating the place otherwise. As it was, I led him to a good corner where we could stand, since the only places at the table were for the higher-ups.

I felt a familiar presence slide in beside me, and looked up to see the wolfhound giving me a polite nod. He probably could have sat at the table if he'd wanted to, but a man like him, I'm certain, preferred to watch the action from a distance. Especially somewhere where he could see the entire room at once, with an unobstructed view of the door. I'd chosen this spot carefully. Not that I felt it necessary at this meeting, just habit.

"Anything important coming up for discussion today?" I asked the tall canine.

The man glanced briefly down at me, then back towards the long table, where discussions had begun. A jowly canine of some sort had started things off, prattling away at the Admiral about something or other he seemed irate about. I was only vaguely listening, and honestly, so was the Admiral, by the look of it. He seemed more interested in idly chewing on the tip of his quill pen.

"Mostly Treasury matters," the wolfhound said in a thoroughly flat tone, like even he found this tiresome. I knew then that we were in for a long, boring meeting. "Serwich's Treasury is actually rather impressive, considering the size of our settlement," he said. "Back when trade was good, we exported far more than we imported, and we haven't been able to purchase much of anything in the last year. Not to mention the gold we've won in the war with the Cathazra. We have more money than supplies. Not that it's of any value, without the latter," he muttered. "But it is, of course, the main thing the merchants and the Pedigrees are grousing over and worrying about divying up before the exodus."

"I'll be happy to escape with our lives," I sighed.

"They don't seem to realize the peril they're all in," the wolfhound agreed. "Pedigrees take it too much for granted that we're here to protect them. They never seem to consider that we might fail."

I was about to remind him that his Admiral was a 'Pedigree', the term the Otherwolves used for their nobility, when I remembered that he'd once told me the cattle dog had humble roots of some sort. Watching him nearly dozing off in his palm now, that was suddenly easy to believe. He was only vaguely listening to the fat canine barking something about tax revenue at him, but he was still at least looking at the man.

Which is, I suppose, why I saw the threat closing in on him, and he did not.

I reached out and gripped at Puck's wrist suddenly, breathing out a soft, "No..." as I saw the coyote's lean frame step through the doorway. Even from thirty feet away, I could see the malice in his eyes, the anger boiling off of him in waves, and all of it directed at the back of the Admiral's skull.

The fox just sniffed. "Is that Ransom?" He asked, tipping his ears forward.

The wolfhound beside me must have sensed my tension, and glanced down at me questioningly for a moment, before following my gaze across the room. The second he saw the coyote stalking through the thin crowd, he seemed to catch on to the same permeating sense of impending disaster I had.

I knew even as I surged forward to try to cut the man off that there was no chance in hell I'd get there in time. This was happening, and there was nothing I could do to stop it.

Before I'd so much as made it halfway across the room, Ransom was at the Admiral's back, and without breaking stride in his step, had wheeled back a fist and connected with the side of the cattle dog's jaw.

The impact seemed to shock the Otherwolf more than anything. He staggered forward in his chair, slumping for a moment as he put a paw to the back of his head. When he slowly raised his muzzle in the moments following, he looked absolutely perplexed. Not like someone who'd just been punched in the back of the head out of nowhere. More like he'd been dumbfounded with a riddle.

The entire room went silent. And I mean that. I don't think anyone breathed. And everyone, absolutely everyone, looked as confused and shocked as the Admiral.

The cattle dog slowly blinked up at the coyote, who was standing stooped over him, a trickle of a low growl the only sound slipping past his snarl, his fists balled at his sides. I think I'd honestly only ever seen Ransom this angry once or twice before in all the time I'd known him, and that was saying something, considering all we'd endured, and how prone the man was to anger.

The Admiral gave the coyote a long, curious look before, at length, simply inclining his head and asking, "I'm—I'm sorry. Do... I know you?"

"You. Me. Outside. Now," the coyote snapped, stabbing a finger towards the doorway. He leveled that broiling snarl at

the man a moment or so longer to make his point, then turned and stalked back outside.

The cattle dog's perplexed stare followed the coyote the whole way out, before he slowly turned back to the table of merchants, dignitaries and naval men, who seemed to be expectantly waiting for some sort of explanation for the scene. He clearly had none to give.

Someone coughed, but other than that, silence pervaded for a few more moments. Finally, the cattle dog shrugged, of all things, and slowly stood, pushing his chair back with a wooden squawk. He straightened his cravat and glanced down the length of the meeting table.

"Pardon me, gentlemen," he said, excusing himself with a demeanor so nonchalant, one would think the whole previous scene hadn't in fact transpired. "Apparently, I'm wanted outside."

I felt the wolfhound beside me pushing ahead, and found myself following in his wake, towards the door. And the fox behind me. The room had erupted in murmurs, but I didn't much care what all these people thought of what had just happened, I was busily trying to make sense of it, myself. Johannes had a longer stride than me and made it to the door at about the same time the Admiral had, and was there to catch the man's red coat as he unshouldered it and handed it to him.

Meanwhile, all I could think was 'what on earth'? As far as I knew, Ransom had only had the most cursory of encounters with the cattle dog. I knew at least that he wasn't fond of him, but I'd always assumed Ransom just didn't like any Otherwolf in a position of power. Also the man came off like an arrogant piece of shit, sometimes. But still. Ransom didn't just pick fights at random, unless he at least thought he had a good reason. And he'd been angry. The only other times I'd seen him so angry, it was usually over—

I stopped dead in my tracks, and felt Puck bump into me from behind. The fox blinked up at me, trying to navigate around me to get out the door. I stopped where I was, blocking his path for a moment.

"Shivah, please," the vulpine pleaded, "I want to see... listen... to this."

"What in the hell did you do, Puck?" I growled, knowing the instant that guilt I'd seen earlier lanced across his expression that I was right. My muzzle dropped. "You didn't," I gasped. More silent guilt from the fox followed, and I put a hand up over my mouth. "Puck!" I cried, exasperated.

An elbow bumped mine, and I looked up to see the wolfhound, who looked more annoyed than concerned, now. He was patiently folding the cattle dog's red coat over his arm. "If you're going to have this conversation," he muttered in a low tone, "would you mind doing it outside, like your friend had the decency to? A public meeting hall isn't the right place for this sort of foolishness to take place in. There are a lot of ears about."

Puck pushed past me at that point and rushed outside, and I wasn't sure I wanted to follow. I gave a disgusted snarl, crossing my arms over my chest. After a few moments, I glanced up at Johannes, who seemed to be uncertain about whether or not he should go back into the meeting hall or go out to watch over his friend, as well.

"Aren't you his bodyguard, or something?" I muttered.

"I told that man a long time ago," the wolfhound said, "that it wasn't my job to protect him from the consequences of his own immoral behavior. If he wants to stew trouble with his loins, he can deal with the fallout himself."

I sighed, uncertain if I should adopt the same attitude.

"Besides," Johannes sighed, "I'm not exactly worried for him. The man can handle himself in a fight."

"So can Ransom," I warned him.

"You remember the Dragon, I take it?" the wolfhound asked.

"How could I forget?" I responded, glancing up at him questioningly.

"I've been fighting those beasts since we founded this colony," the wolfhound said. "I've six kills to my name, mostly by way of well-placed pistol shots, and I'm including that one we triple-teamed on the cliff. The Admiral has slain twenty-three of them, throughout the few years he's been here," he arched an eyebrow, "with a sword."

"Damnit, Ransom," I moaned, and jogged outside.

By the time I'd made it out to the alley beside the Navy Lodge, the fight was already underway. Judging by the lack of blood, though, I'd probably caught it before things really got bad. Ransom was all wild energy and reckless abandon, as ever, and the cattle dog was in the midst of carefully side-stepping one of his wide swings, when I turned the corner and caught the tail end of whatever it was the coyote had been previously shouting.

"Don't play dumb, you shit!" Ransom snapped, recovering fairly quickly from the swing, and launching himself at the Admiral again. "You soddin' well know what 'chu did!"

"I earnestly—" the cattle dog ducked, coming up laughing so hard, he almost seemed out of breath, "—have to tell you, I really don't!" He chuckled again, a feral grin split across his features, "But, if it's a dustup you want," He leveled a well-timed, clean shot at the coyote's muzzle at that, and I heard the crack as it connected. Ransom went sprawling to the ground, spitting and swiping a paw over his teeth as he shoved himself back up.

The cattle dog stood over him, letting him get up, but gesturing at his chest with both hands invitingly. "Give it to me good then, boy," he growled a challenge at him, smiling. "I won't deny you a good beating, if that's what gets you off."

"I can take you any day o'the week, old man!" The coyote snarled.

"Oh, lad," the Admiral gave an almost sly smirk, one that would have been more at home on a feline than a canine, "don't say that until you've tried."

The coyote gave an angry, indescribable sound somewhere between an obscene word and a snarl, and charged him again. And this time, his overwhelming ferocity seemed to catch the cattle dog by surprise. Ransom was nothing if not determined, and raw. He brought a knee up into the Admiral's gut, which he bore well considering how much it should have hurt, but it still bent him double long enough for the coyote to club his fist into his neck. He'd probably been aiming for the jaw again, but the cattle dog had had enough of his wits about him to get mostly out of the way.

I moved up beside Puck, who of course wasn't intervening, but seemed to be straining to follow the action with his ears, and what must have only been silhouettes to him with his gaze. The alley was lit by the early afternoon sun, so it was possible he could even see hazy blurs of figures, right now.

I gave him an annoyed glare until he seemed to notice me, although he didn't turn his attention away from the ongoing fight. He was standing on the balls of his paw-pads, his tail twitching nervously back and forth, but there was the hint of a smile beneath all the feigned concern, and that's what had me angry.

"Stop enjoying this," I growled. "I'm ashamed of you, Puck."

"Oh, let me have this," he whined. "They're fighting over me."

"You're awful," I sighed, my eyes going back to the fight. It was at about that moment that the Admiral looked our way, as well, and seemed to finally notice us. Including the fox, of course.

"Oh!" he said, literally snapping his fingers, and shoving Ransom off of him from where the coyote had been vainly trying to wrestle him to the ground. "Is this over the fox?" He seemed to realize, tilting his muzzle towards the angry canine.

Ransom gave a bloody snuff, his nose dripping down his chin by now. The hatred in his gaze was so palpable, I could almost feel the temperature rising from the sidelines. "That's it, isn't it?" the cattle dog crowed, and I'll admit in that moment, even I wanted to punch the smile off his smug face. "You're the other man, aren't you?"

"Ah'm his only man," the coyote growled, his tone laced with acid.

"Aye, well, past tense may have been more appropriate for that statement," the Otherwolf seemed to taunt, leaning over him. "'Were'. You 'were' his only man. Say it with me now."

Mistake. Ransom used the opportunity to catch the Admiral by surprise, swinging his head forward to crack him in the skull with his own, presumably denser one. I could only guess. The sudden attack made the cattle dog crumple to one knee, clutching at his skull with a pained groan, and a moment later, Ransom was dragging him up by the armpits, and kneeing him in the gut again. That sent him to the ground, but he managed to drag the coyote down with him after kicking him in the knees, and wrenching an arm around his neck.

And then the scuffle was on the ground, and I still wasn't intervening, and neither was Johannes or Puck, so... I guess we'd all just decided to let this one play itself out. Neither man was pulling weapons, so it didn't seem like the intent on either part was to kill. If things changed, I'd step in, but...

"This is so damned stupid," I muttered. The wolfhound beside me only nodded.

The Admiral had Ransom nearly in a headlock by now, and the coyote's feet were scrambling in the dirt, his far scrawnier arms trying, to no avail, to undo the iron lock the stockier canine had him in. He may have been shorter, but it was easy to see the cattle dog was a lot stronger than Ransom. He almost didn't seem to be taking this seriously, though, despite the fact that his nose was bleeding now, too.

"Now, the way I heard it," the man said around a grunt, as he shoved Ransom down into the dirt again, the coyote yowling in protest and struggling against him with all his might, "you're fond of straying off-course. So what's all this possessiveness about, then? Turnabout's fair play, is it not?"

Ransom shot a hurt glance in my and Puck's direction, and it sent a stab of pity through me before I could remind myself that, in fact, the Admiral actually had a point. And maybe he'd finally have to face it, coming from a third party. So I only crossed my arms over my chest, shut my mouth, and glared back down at the coyote. This was difficult to watch, but I knew intervening was wrong now. I was absolutely certain of it, in that moment. He'd quite literally made his own bed, and now he had to lie in it.

"You don't love'm like I do..." the coyote rasped, gripping at the Admiral's speckled arms, taut where they were locked around his neck and shoulder.

"You're likely right, there," the cattle dog confirmed, his voice reflecting some of the strain it was taking him to hold down the thrashing coyote, "but then, I barely know him. Give me a bit more time, and I could steal his heart away. He's a sweet, pleasant little creature. Not bad on the eyes, either. And eager—"

Ransom gave a powerful shove and a growling yell at that, rolling the two of them over once, twice, and then he was on top of the cattle dog, the Otherwolf still holding him in a lock, but forced to his back beneath him as Ransom dug his heels into the dirt and tried to scrape him free.

"My point is," the cattle dog ground out, still grinning like a maniac, "I might try. And so might others. You're a fool to not hold on with both hands."

That seemed to stop the coyote's struggling for a few moments. His whole body went limp, and he just stared up at the sky in the following silence. It was impossible to say what was going through the man's mind at that moment, but I hoped it was something profound, for once.

The cattle dog released him suddenly, and shoved him off of him, wrenching himself to his feet and shaking out a wrist. His sleeve was torn from where the coyote had been tearing into it with his claws, and he was covered in dirt, and whatever else was on these roads. He was still bleeding from the nose, the red freckled on his white cravat.

"Do you want my advice, son?" He asked, staring down at the coyote, who still hadn't picked himself up off the ground.

Ransom swiped a hand over his now bloody teeth, scrunching up his muzzle in an expression mixed between hurt and mortified. "Shove yer advice, old man!" he snapped.

The cattle dog approached him slowly, with a purposeful stride. I briefly considered intervening, because his face had fallen darkly serious, all of a sudden, and I was worried the violence was about to escalate. But when he made it to the coyote, he stopped a pace or so away from him, looked down at him, and simply spoke.

"That's right, I'm older than you," he said in a firm tone. "Probably by a decade or more. So, learn from my experience. Don't wait until the people you love are dead and gone to start treating them with the respect they deserve. The last thing you want is to spend the rest of your life regretting the things you never said." He tugged free his cravat and used it to dab at his nose, sniffing some blood back and looking down at the soaked fabric, then gave a wet snort, muttering, "Damn... You've got a hard head, boy."

Ransom had remained silent, but he'd averted his eyes by now and didn't seem to have any interest in renewing the fight. Thank the gods for small favors.

The Admiral headed back towards us, calling out, "Johannes!" as he did. On cue, the wolfhound stepped forward and offered him his coat, as he dusted off some of the dirt from his undershirt. It wasn't as though any amount of that was going to cover the fact that he'd been in a fight, but he didn't seem to be letting that fact bother him.

He looked to us once more before he strode past, back towards the Navy Lodge. I didn't miss the secretive smile he cast the fox's way, nor the wink that followed a moment later.

"Hold on with both hands!" He shouted a reminder over his shoulder in the coyote's direction. "Fate is cruel. Death comes for all of us eventually, and a grave's a bad place to realize you wanted everything to have gone differently."

And then he and the wolfhound were gone, the tall canine shooting me one last empathetic look before following his Lord inside.

I looked down at the fox, arching an eyebrow. I hadn't missed the conspiratory look the Admiral had given him at the end there. "Wait," I paused, "Did you actually? Or was this all some ruse to make him think?"

The fox only shrugged. "Does it matter?" He replied, turning his muzzle towards the slumped coyote, who was shakily picking himself up off the ground. "I think I made my point." He inclined his head towards Ransom. "Uh, I... I have to go. You know, act offended that he thought this was the proper response to something he's done a thousand times."

I nodded mutely, and the fox hurried over to his dirty, beaten lover. He admonished him in a low, hushed voice for a few moments, but I was considering heading back inside myself at that point, since I'd become determined of late to let them handle these things on their own.

But then, suddenly, the coyote was gripping the fox by the shoulder, and shoving a hand into his pocket for something, then gripping the smaller man's wrist and pressing it into his palm. And my heart leapt into my throat, because I knew what it was before Puck did.

"Wh..." the fox stammered, running his thumb over the metal band in his hand, clearly trying to make sense of what it was Ransom had just handed him. "What is—"

"Marry me," the coyote growled out. Then a moment later, as if as an afterthought, he murmured, "please."

The fox opened his mouth as if to say something, but nothing came out. He sort of mouthed something a few times, as though out of breath or just too shocked to manage words.

"I get what you've been sayin' now, a'ight?" the coyote said, helplessly. "I'll be loyal. Ah don't want you with no one else. This felt worse 'n Serahaven. Ah can't lose you t' another man."

"Ransom, I-I—" the fox stammered, "this is going a bit far to... It wasn't serious, I swear—"

"That a 'no', then?" the coyote bit out.

The fox's ears flattened, his pale eyes wide, and his tone dropped to an earnestly shy, almost demure one. "No... I mean, of course it's not a no," he said, his tail tucking between his legs, paws scuffling nervously at the dirt. "Ransom, how could I possibly turn you down?"

"So that's a yes, then?" the coyote pressed. Blood was dripping from his muzzle, one of his ears was bent over from being jammed on the ground earlier, he was covered in dirt and might not ever have looked more pathetic. Or more hopeful.

I swear, somewhere deep inside me, something long-since buried was bubbling up to the surface, and it felt suspiciously like a feminine squeal. I suppressed it, of course.

The fox gave a soft, still somewhat disbelieving 'heh' of breath, smiling shyly, "Y-yes. It's a yes."

The coyote leaned down to half-nuzzle, half-slump against him at that, the tension seeming to drain out of his shoulders. I was trying very hard not to interrupt the scene with my secondhand joy, when the canine seemed to notice I was still there.

"Hey," he growled, "d'you mind? Me'n the fox here are havin' sorta' a private moment."

"I don't know what to say," I mumbled, knitting my fingers together tensely across my stomach.

The small arctic fox looked up at me, blinking drowsily, with a soft smile. A smile I'd come to know and love over the two years we'd known one another. "You don't need to say anything," he assured me, patting my arm weakly.

I leaned over the small cot he was lying in in the back of the infirmary. This room was separate from all the others, used primarily for surgeries, births, and occasionally, for housing someone on their deathbed—a quieter, less crowded place for them to pass on.

I could only pray that this time, it would not serve that purpose.

"Puck, if this is the last time..." I trailed off, a hitch in my voice.

The fox's eyelids drooped for a moment and he shook his head against the pillow. "It won't be," he promised me.

"You can't know," I said, but I couldn't manage more than that. The last thing I wanted to do right now was bring his spirits down and I knew that lingering on those thoughts would do just that. But at the same time, the whole reason I was here was, potentially, to see him one last time. Both of us knew that. It was not a reality we could ignore.

His clouded eyes were at mere slits and his breaths were beginning to slow. I leaned over him again, reaching down and stroking a hand over his cheek. His eyelids fluttered open and he almost looked at me, smiling again. He brought his paw up to mine and squeezed.

"The medicine is working faster than I thought it would," he said, clearing his throat and sniffing. "Maybe... maybe you should send Ransom in. Before I can't stay awake any longer."

I nodded then, standing quickly. It took me a few moments longer to release his hand, though. I could feel his pulse through my pawpads, and seeing him lying there, under the effects of a powerful sedative with his heartbeat slowing, bit by bit...

It brought back a lot of memories. Painful memories of the last time I'd thought I'd lost him.

Surely, life couldn't be so cruel, twice? Could it? The fact that he'd had that one brush with death meant he was foretold to survive this surgery. It simply wasn't possible that after all he'd come through, we'd lose him to this. It wouldn't be fair. I'd come to think that when I'd allowed myself to start caring for Grant. After I'd lost so much already, lost the only person I'd ever loved, I'd thought that surely, this time, I'd be safe. Time had proven me wrong.

The world was cruel. Life wasn't fair. If there were spirits or Gods, they had larger issues to concern themselves with than my personal happiness, and I knew that now. The reality had been crushing at first, but in the time since, I'd come to accept it had been a lesson in humility. The world did not revolve around me or my wishes. I had to carve my path through it and find my happiness where I could, not expect that what I had would last.

And I had to make the most of every happy moment I had, when I had it, and not wait for everything to go wrong or waste my time mired in anger over everything that had gone wrong previously. I'd given up too much of my life to those thoughts, already. They could consume you whole. Burn you from the inside out.

So instead, today, I leaned down and kissed the fox's brow, squeezed his paw once more and left the room, hoping that my confident departure would give him some amount of the conviction he needed to see himself through this. It was all I could offer now, and it would be unkind of me to offer anything less.

When I stepped outside and saw the coyote slumped on the bench outside, with his long arms draped over his knees, his ears tucked back and his head hung, I nearly lost that composure. He was chewing on the end of a toothpick, since he couldn't smoke inside the triage building. His eyes were wide, but staring at the ground and I knew the man's posture. It was like a bowstring pulled too tight. He was slumped and ramrod stiff all at once. I think he was even shaking.

When I put a hand on his shoulder, he jerked forward, startled, until he realized it was me. And even then, he didn't look comforted.

"You can go in now," I said softly. "He's falling asleep, though, so it won't be long."

The coyote said nothing, only nodded stiffly, stood, and brushed past me into the room. The door closed behind him with a click that resounded in the narrow back hallway. I let the confidence slip from me like a sleeve, slumping down on the bench myself.

My mind was blank. I didn't look up again until I heard footsteps and saw Forrest making his way towards the room, tray in hand.

The tray terrified me. I'd seen surgical instruments before, of course, but just knowing what these would be used for added an extra level of fear. And they weren't even for me. I just... I could hardly believe that in a few minutes' time, this man would be carving up my friend's eyes. And I was allowing it. At any other point in my life, I would have fought to the death to keep a man with knives away from the vulnerable fox.

He stood near the doorway and looked down at me. I thought it would be a momentary pause, but then he leaned against the wall. We waited there in silence for some time.

"Thank you," I said at length.

"Hm?" the Otherwolf glanced down at me.

"For giving them this time," I explained. "You could have gone right in."

"It's customary to allow significant others time with the patient before surgery," the Physician said, in an almost offhanded way. "There are no time constraints on this surgery, so it's hardly as though it will affect the outcome much. It's a Physician's prerogative to give some consideration to the welfare of the patients' loved ones as much as the patient themselves. Provided it doesn't detract from the level of care afforded. And much of recovery and health is mental. The additional comfort may prove some boost to his morale."

I just blinked up at him. "I guess I shouldn't be shocked by now that people know about them," I muttered, "but I always am. It's just, the way they made it out, I figured more people would be—"

"Intolerant?" the Physician answered for me. "Men who believe in God, perhaps. I don't. Sexuality is part of our physical makeup. You could as soon blame a man for being spotted.

The Church can try to treat the condition, if they truly think they can... I don't see the point in treating something so frivolous. There are far more crippling, unfortunate afflictions one can be born with. I've seen them all. It puts things like this in perspective."

"I don't think it's an affliction," I murmured.

"It is a societal affliction," the Physician shrugged. "Just as having no interest in taking a wife, or any lover, can be. The world expects people to pair, and to reproduce. Those people who take no interest in it whatsoever are also often objects of scrutiny."

I glanced up at the man. I may have misheard him, and he would never clarify it for me, but that had sounded personal to me. Forrest was never personal, though, so maybe I'd just imagined it. I'd never know.

"In any case, I've given them long enough, I think," the man said, the tools rattling on his tray as he straightened up from leaning on the wall and reached down with one hand for the door knob.

"Wait," I said, putting out a hand hesitantly. He looked down at me, questioningly. "I mean..." I stammered. "How... How good are his chances, do you think?"

The Physician looked at me seriously. "Do you want a percentage?"

"I don't know what that means," I said, feeling ashamed for a moment. He could give me an answer, and it wouldn't make sense to me. Of course. I wasn't as intelligent as this man, or Puck. Medicine was beyond me.

"His chances are good," he said, and those four words sent a bolt of hope through me. Not just because I understood them, but because he'd said them with some confidence. So that 'percentage', whatever that was, was good. "He is healthy, his body is strong, my tools are meticulous, and we're in the cleanest room in this building. And potentially this entire fetid colony," he said with a certain amount of derision I didn't miss. Puck had told me many times how obsessively clean the

Physician was. But that could only bode well for this operation, so right now I was thankful for it.

"The biggest fear is infection," the man continued. "But that's a wait-and-see sort of issue. I trust my hands enough during the operation that I'm fairly certain he won't bleed out. Although we need to be careful he remains as still as possible, or no steady hand in the world will matter."

"That's what the straps are for?" I asked, even though I knew the answer. I'd seen them, of course. Leather belts, riveted into the side of the bed. There was even a stabilizing device for his head, and more straps that would presumably keep his head as still as possible, too. I couldn't imagine what else they were used for here at the hospital that they had to have a bed like that on hand, but... on second thought, no, I didn't even want to begin to imagine that.

"Also why I require an assistant," the Otherwolf confirmed.

I bit my lip at that. "I still don't think Ransom should be doing it."

"Oh, I agree with you there," the Physician said with an edge of annoyance in his tone. "I would have vastly preferred to use one of my nurses. Although he won't be doing much more than ensuring the fox doesn't move, so... A man's strength will be of more use to me, in that regard. But it's idiocy to have someone so close to the patient assisting in this surgery."

"Then," I sighed, "why are you allowing it?"

"He wouldn't have it any other way," Forrest muttered. "And I don't like to argue. It grows tiresome, quickly."

"If Puck tells Ransom to listen to you, he will," I promised him. I was more worried about what watching this surgery would do to the coyote. I didn't doubt for a moment he'd do whatever necessary to help Puck. But if this surgery went awry somehow, and Ransom had played a role in it at all...

"He had better," the Physician stated. "Or I'll have him tossed out and one of my nurses sent in. But he's been warned, and the man seemed determined, if nothing else. Let us hope that is enough."

I blew out a soft breath and looked to my feet for a moment, arms crossed over my chest. The man seemed to know I had more to say, and waited. When I did finally speak again, I had his full attention. "Can I just ask one more thing?"

"I wouldn't be lingering here in the hallway while the sedative runs its course, just to ignore you," the man pointed out.

"Right," I sighed. To the point, then. "Why do you care enough to do this?" I asked, directly. "I know a man like you could fetch a lot for your services. We're still trying to figure out a way to afford spectacles for him. And this is surgery. Puck told me you didn't even broach the issue of payment. Why are you doing this?"

The man stared back at me implacably. "You think I have ulterior motives?" he asked.

I thought for a few moments, before answering, "Yes. Everyone seems to, outside the world I grew up in. I have to make my judgments based on what I've seen so far."

"That's only wise," the man confirmed. "But you've nothing underhanded to fear, here. Put simply, my motives are the same as your friend's."

"Curing the Seer's Fever?" I asked.

The man was silent for a few moments, his expression mostly unreadable, but beneath his calm exterior I could see a certain sense of frustration. I recognized it because I'd seen it in Puck, from time to time. Usually when he was trying to explain something to me that I was either incapable of grasping, or didn't like his perspective on—essentially whenever we disagreed.

"Seer's Fever cannot be cured," the man finally said, the words spoken almost between his teeth.

I opened my mouth a moment, then looked aside. "Of course," I muttered, "I'm... I'm sorry. Puck's told me that before, of course. I just, well I thought you'd know what I meant. Stopping the spread, and all that."

"Miscommunication like that is precisely why treating illnesses like this are such an issue, though," the man said with a sigh. His eyes swept up to the ceiling for a moment, then came back to rest on me. "I'm going to say something here, and you must try for a moment not to be offended."

"I'll try," I said, uncertainly.

"The world as a whole, and the people that make up most of the population, are mentally inferior to the people who have to treat them," the Physician stated, like it was nothing. "People like myself, physicians and healers. And yet, despite that, a great deal of them seem to believe they know what's better for their families, for their communities and cities than we do. I cannot even begin to express to you how very frustrating that is."

"I can only imagine," I said truthfully. His words didn't offend me much. I'd long accepted I wasn't an intellectual.

"That makes treating a disease like this, that spreads like wildfire, and is, in actuality, very easily survivable if basic medical care is given," the Otherwolf gestured uselessly in the air with his free hand, "like... trying to weave fire. Difficult to handle, dangerous for the Physician involved, and more than likely, no matter what we do, it will continue to spread."

"That's a very colorful metaphor for you, sir," I pointed out. I knew he'd done it for my sake.

"Thank your friend, he once used the phrase," the Physician explained. "I'm not nearly so fanciful. But it's apt. And it's a good example of why I need him."

"Metaphors?" I queried, trying to follow the man's explanation.

"I came here to treat rare, exotic diseases," the man said, "like the Seer's fever. This place is rife with them. The Seer's fever isn't even amongst the top five of the most deadly, it's just the most prone to spread, which is why the world is taking notice of it. Your friend is right to be so desperate to find the root of its spread too, because given time in a chaotic, intermingled, dirty place like the Colonies, it can and will become a plague that could very well cripple the entire country."

I swallowed. Hearing that from this man just confirmed everything we'd ever feared. I believed him.

"Why do you want to treat the fever, though?" I pressed. "I mean, it's mostly threatening Carvecia not your country, right?"

"For whatever reason, yes," the man confirmed. "It hasn't been a major issue in Amuresca. That's part of the pathology we don't understand yet. I'm certain it has something to do with why it spreads, but until we determine that, it's impossible to say why Amurescan cities haven't had the same kinds of outbreaks. As for why I wish to tackle this illness specifically..." he looked towards the doorway. "I didn't. Until Puquanah arrived here, and I began to work with him. The fact of the matter is, miss, your friend has already done a considerable amount of the work in learning how to treat this illness. His experiences with an entire settlement afflicted by the illness, in testing an inoculation on himself, were invaluable. Others have done what he's done, of course, but none of those others are colleagues who are willing to work with me. And none of them are Carvecian."

Something clicked at that. "You think he'll be more suited to help treat the spread of it back home, because it's his country."

"Your friend is a rarity, miss," the man said. "In addition to having the background, and thus the cultural understanding, of the folk medicine practiced in your country, he also possesses a sharp enough mind to know better than to use all of it. He can converse with your people on a spiritual level, and perhaps coax them away from their foolishness, while being intelligent enough to practice true medicine."

I recoiled a little bit. "I don't like the way you talk about our Shamen," I said, defensively. "Spiritual healing is important to our people. And spirits can aid people in dire need. I've seen it."

"I'm not going to argue religion with you," the man said with a sigh. "But the fact of the matter is, having the background he does, but the intelligence to know what is true healing and what is just mystic nonsense means Puquanah may be able to cross a bridge most Physicians who've had the benefit of higher education simply cannot. And given time and better education, I believe he even has the mind to count himself amongst us, eventually. Earnestly, to be as sharp as he is, to have picked up on so much over the years without that education, he must be brilliant. He'd be a boon to medicine if he didn't waste his life in the wilderness."

"I don't think Puck wants anything so grand," I said quietly.

The Otherwolf snorted. "No. Which is foolish. I hate to see wasted potential, but it is his choice. He doesn't even want the credit of our work. A sentiment which, in all honesty, I have no desire to fight him on. Science is the only true immortality men have. In a hundred years, I want a University named after me. All your friend wants, as much as I can gather, is to educate people in the back country. It's honestly a very fortunate alliance for both of us. I can make the connections necessary to spread the word on how to tackle this monstrous illness once we're in Carvecia, to Physicians and whatever passes for learning institutions in the Colonies, and he can reach out to the people, since that's what he truly desires. If we can target the spread of this disease, we'll both make our mark in the world, in the way that suits us." His eyes narrowed. "But he won't be able to do any of that unless he can see."

"He's healed us many times," I insisted. "Being blind hasn't kept him from helping a lot of people."

"No, but it is a hindrance," the man stated. "And there's no getting around that. He will never be able to read. To research. To properly perform surgery, or assess a patient. A blind Physician may be possible, but it isn't preferable. He could do more. And considering there's a treatment for his condition, and the survival rate is actually quite good..."

I put my hands up. "It was his choice," I said with a soft sigh. "I'm not going to question it anymore."

"Yes, well," the man cleared his throat, "rest-assured, I am invested in seeing to it that he survives. You've nothing to fear."

"So you can work together in the future?" I said with a slight smile. "That's... really good to hear. Thank you for talking to me about it."

"Yes, that, and..." the man's usually calm composure stammered a bit at that, and he looked odd for a moment. Like he was uncomfortable. "Other reasons," he muttered, after a few moments.

I arched an eyebrow, but wasn't able to ask him to clarify what he meant, before the door opened again and the coyote was suddenly in front of us, looking directly down on the shorter Otherwolf. And the expression he was wearing was menacing, to say the least.

"He's asleep," he said, jerking a thumb inside. "So get t' work while that stuff's hittin' him the hardest, doc."

"I already told you, he is going to wake at least a few times during the operation," the man said, exasperated, but he seemed to be choosing his words carefully. And acting oddly polite, considering his evident derision for the coyote when he'd been speaking to me about him. "You need to be prepared for that."

"S'why I'm in the room, ain't it?" the coyote grabbed the man by the shoulder, and tugged him inside. "Now c'mon. Let's git this done. Y' ain't gonna screw nothin' up with me 'round. Now are ya?"

The Physician just gave him an irritated, if wary look, and walked in past him. Ransom looked to me once more, then grabbed at the nob, and shut the door without saying another word.

I considered briefly in the few seconds as the door closed that I might wedge my foot between it and the door frame, and remind the coyote that intimidating the Physician probably wouldn't do much to steady his hand... In the end, I only took a deep breath, and forced myself to say nothing at all. It was more important that the Otherwolf just got to work, while the sedative was still powerful. Puck had said it was made from some sort of plant called 'Coca' that grew in abundance in this region. It actually, ironically, would be less effective than the Len'Sal berries had been, and Puck said if he'd thought to have any more of those on hand, this might not have been a bad time to take a diluted mixture made from them. But we were working with what the region provided, and apparently, these leaves were it.

He'd never be able to sleep through the pain of what was going to be done to him. The Physician had warned us about that, time and again. Warned Puck, even. The medicine he'd taken would have him in and out, and dull some of the pain, but the straps would have to do the rest, because as awful as the surgery sounded, keeping him still was of the utmost importance.

Ransom was strong though, and so long as his nerve held out, I knew he could keep the fox as still as was necessary, where the straps and the medicine failed. Other than that, we had to leave it all to the Physician.

I don't know how long I sat on the bench, my nerves raging, unable to sit entirely still. The minutes moved by as slow as the currents in a mud-choked river, and not knowing what was happening behind the door that was barely a foot to my left was agony. It was nowhere near as bad as when I knew the surgery had begun, though.

I think I'd expected screams. Or something along those lines. Shouting, outbursts of pain... That's what I'd been prepared for. I'd been bracing for it, in fact. I didn't have to wait outside and hear it, of course. I wouldn't be allowed to see him until tomorrow, as it was, lest I risk infecting him with something from outside. Even Ransom had been thoroughly bathed and scrubbed down by the nurses (something he'd promised me he'd try not to enjoy) before he'd gone into the room today. I could leave at any time. But I'd felt obligated to stay, for some reason. Like my presence would ease Puck's pain, somehow.

I had been prepared for screaming. But I hadn't been prepared for quiet, plaintive, pained whines. They sounded only half-coherent, like someone crying in their sleep. And they were a thousand times more heart-wrenching.

They didn't sound like the pained noises of an adult. They sounded like they were coming from a kitten. A child. And I knew by the sound of them that they were coming from Puck, but it still pulled at every motherly bone in my body and made me want to dash into the room and make the noises stop.

I stood, swallowing back an anguished groan and forcing myself to march down the hallway, away from the doorway. I couldn't be there any more. I just couldn't. I'd wait outside.

But even once I was out in the busy commons area, the knowledge of what was still occurring in the back room hadn't left me, my hands were twitching for a bow that wasn't there and all I wanted to do was scream, and... and I just needed something—anything—to distract myself from what was happening to my friend.

Fortunately, thanks to the fact that we were in the midst of the war and nearly everyone I knew was injured or knew someone else who was, there were quite a few people in this place I knew. One in particular quite literally stood out from the rest of the crowd, due chiefly to his height.

The wolfhound looked startled when I grabbed at his coat, and with good reason. I hadn't realized my pace, and I'd nearly crashed into his back. I couldn't help it, though. I felt like I was still running from that room.

"Good God," the man said, his voice laced with concern as he turned to regard me. "Miss Shivah, are you alright?" He instantly began looking me over, suspecting I suppose that I'd been injured. Considering where we were, it wasn't exactly an odd conclusion to come to.

Before I could answer him, I felt a paw settle heavily on my shoulder, and was tugged back into a familiar-smelling mass of dreaded fur. I glanced up past the heavy collar of the brine-infused coat, to a similarly-concerned pair of dark blue eyes. "Aye, what's wrong, love?" The Privateer asked, making sure to thread an arm around my waist as he did.

I knew by only a secondary glance at the wolfhound's suddenly icy glare that I had about three seconds to diffuse this situation before it got out-of-hand.

"I'm fine," I insisted, pushing gently at the wolf's chest, and trying to extricate his arm from around my waist. "I'm just... gods, Grayson," I finally just reached down and tugged each of his fingers free of my tunic by hand. I snarled up at him, "Would you please not grab me? Especially in public?"

The wolf only gave a lopsided smile. "Ain't this exactly the sort of place we should be keeping up the ruse, though?"

"I think you've forgotten it's a ruse," I growled.

"Kindly do as the lady asks and keep your distance, Privateer," the wolfhound warned from over my shoulder.

"It's— I can handle him, Johannes," I snapped. "Don't go playing Knight right now, alright? I don't need a man defending my honor." I glared back up at the smirking wolf. "I've already proven I can best this drunkard."

"'Johannes'?" The wolf echoed with a chuckle. "Ain't you two gotten chummy."

"I don't particularly like watching a blackguard man-handle any woman," the wolfhound warned, "let alone one under my command."

"Your command?" the wolf replied in a remarkably chipper tone, despite the low set of his brow, and the teeth he was baring with his grin. "Whose ship is it she returns to every night?"

"I never wanted you here, you son of a bitch," Johannes snapped his jaws. "Just give me a reason, and I'll ready the gallows—"

"Oh for God's sake, Johannes," another familiar voice called from somewhere far to the right of us, past a small crowd of onlookers who were trying not to look like onlookers. I caught the barest sight of the cattle dog through the crowd, seated beside a cot.

"Don't let him bait you," the Admiral said with a sigh evident in his voice. He sounded tired. Very tired. "You're supposed to be more dignified than me. Let's not have a replay of last week, shall we? I never got those bloodstains out of my shirt, and you own... What? Three?"

I don't think I'd ever been more grateful to the damned cattle dog in my life. I made sure I gave both of the towering canines on either side of me a good, hard glare, long enough that both of them wilted back a bit. Then I pushed past a few still gaping people in the crowded hospital and made my way towards the cattle dog. I don't know why. His mood just seemed to suit mine better right now.

I found him where I'd almost always seen him, when he was here. Seated beside the dying Otherwolf who'd lost both of his legs, and still seemed to be wasting away. If possible, he looked even worse than the last time I'd seen him. And this time, he wasn't talking, only sleeping fitfully.

I felt a sudden and unexpected pang of sympathy for the Admiral, watching him sit beside his friend. I didn't know the man, or what exactly he'd been to the cattle dog, but I knew grief when I saw it. Grief, and helplessness.

"Apologies," he murmured suddenly, and even though I knew it was directed at me, I couldn't imagine why. I began to ask, but he clarified, "For their behavior. Johannes doesn't exactly wear his emotions on his sleeve, and Reed covers it with a mask of bravado, but..." He turned his muzzle slowly back towards the dying canine lying in bed a foot or so away. I saw his ears twitch and fall back. "Finnegan was the heart of my fleet. There wasn't a soul who didn't consider themselves kin to him. If you'd known the man..."

He dropped his head for a few moments, putting his palms over his muzzle and just shaking his head.

"He's," I swallowed, "he's not gone yet." I knew there wasn't much hope in my voice, but I tried. I didn't even know this man, but I knew pain. And especially right now, I knew how terrible it could feel... the fear of losing a friend.

"I didn't know Grayson knew him," I admitted at length. Because it occurred to me that I honestly knew very little about the wolf's previous connection to the cattle dog's fleet.

"We..." he dragged in a breath, raising his head and pulling himself together for a moment. In that moment, I realized I'd been terribly wrong about something. I'd always assumed the Admiral was as aloof as most of the Amurescans, but now I realized, he'd actually always been fairly openly emotional. I'd just never seen him in a weak moment before.

He turned to regard me, giving me a smile that was painfully obvious had been forced. "It's a long story," he summarized. "It feels like a lifetime ago. Or three. But yes. We all used to sail together. Hunting Pirates." He gave a weak chuckle. "Dangerous business. But, thinking back, it was a whole lot more simple than all of this. We knew how to handle ourselves at sea. All this..." he gestured at nothing, "Imperialism... doesn't suit me. This isn't even my colony. It wasn't even my father-in-law's colony. All of it belongs to the damned crown. We're just the hounds they sent to guard their interests."

His voice got very bitter, suddenly, "I hate this place. My father-in-law hated this place. We aren't meant to be here. All this land does is take, and take, and take. No amount of gold or lumber is worth it. They just can't see it, because it isn't the people they know and..." he looked to the dying canine at that, his words catching in his throat, "care for... that are dying."

"I'm sorry," I said softly, because it's all I could say. I didn't understand everything the man was saying, of course, because he wasn't filling in all the blanks. But one thing came through loud and clear.

These men were soldiers. Warriors. Pure and simple. The objective of this war for their people wasn't even being directed from here. I knew enough of their society by now to know their 'tribe', their elders, were actually in a country across the sea. The fact that they were stranded here fighting for their lives, for a war they weren't even directing, seemed like madness to me.

The world was so much bigger, so much stranger and crueler than I'd ever thought it could be. And it put all of my suffering in a perspective I don't think I'd ever have found, had I not begun to travel and meet all these different people.

"What happened to him?" I asked softly, looking over the canine. I think the two of us were just making conversation at this point so we weren't trapped in our thoughts. But it was working for me, so maybe it was working for him.

The cattle dog glanced over at me, tiredly. He looked like he'd slept here. Or rather, not slept here. "He..." he swallowed, "He was stranded at an outpost along the river, where we were attempting to build a new Garrison. He was there to install the cannons. Finnegan was brilliant with firearms, and any and all uses for gunpowder." He shook his head. "The Garrison came under attack, and they cut off our reinforcements along the river. They hit us hard at the gates and we had to batter down. We couldn't get to him, or the men under his command, for nearly a week. By the time we got there..." he leaned back, his back thudding heavily against the wall, "The Garrison was in splinters. I knew it was his work. The Cathazra burn, but this was... it was very clear gunpowder was involved. We found out later he improvised something, in an attempt to take down the war-band with him. It must have been a contingency if they became overrun."

"I don't understand," I said, confused. "You sound uncertain. He survived, clearly. Couldn't he just tell you what happened?"

"What happened at the Garrison hardly matters," the cattle dog muttered. "He was cornered, and he tried to do what he could with what was left of his life. It was bloody heroic, I'm certain. But it was what followed that was the true horror."

I looked to the man. The explosion explained the loss of limbs, I suppose, but as for the rest, I couldn't even imagine. Maybe an infection was what was causing the malnutrition?

"They took him," he said, his voice hard-edged. "We don't know why. He must have survived the explosion, and they must have known, somehow, that he was an Officer. I don't know. The Cathazra never take Prisoners of War. Why they made an exception this time, I can't honestly say."

"What did they do to him?" I asked, aghast.

The cattle dog gave a soft breath through his nose. At long length, he murmured, "We don't know. He'll not speak on it. In fact, not much of what he's had to say since we got him back has made sense. He's just miserable, hostile, and he seems to want to die. His body is only dying because he's allowing it to. It seems like they actually treated his wounds, when they had him."

"How did you ever get him back?" I asked, unable to take my eyes off the decrepit man, now.

"He was returned to us," the cattle dog said, and when I whipped my head around to stare at him incredulously, he only shrugged. "Don't ask me. I don't know. One of our scouts found him in the jaws of a Basilisk. They followed the creature for a time, but it was either playing with its prey, or earnestly carrying him back to Serwich. I don't know. They killed it, of course."

I opened my mouth to object, but he only shook his head. "It wouldn't have mattered if the beast had been spared. Basilisks are non-verbal. We couldn't have gleaned anything from it even if we'd tried to communicate with it. Besides, the scouts didn't know whether or not the beast meant him harm, and their prerogative was to save one of our own from—quite literally—the jaws of death." He looked down at his friend. "Not that we did, in the end."

"What do you think happened?" I asked, drawing my knees up to my chest.

"They did something to his head," he said, vaguely. "We don't know. Brain-washed him, is what the Physician was calling it. He seems sympathetic to their people now, and even I can't reason with him. He keeps asking to be returned. He even speaks in their language, in snippets. And he's grief-stricken about what happened to the Basilisk. He even calls it something. A name, I suppose, although how he got a name from the creature, I don't know. We only have two 'diplomats' here in Serwich who are still alive, and still even willing to study the Cathazra, and even they can't make sense of most of what he says."

Something crawled up my spine, suddenly, and I turned slowly to regard the Admiral. "Sir?" I asked at length. He regarded me with a flick of his eyes. "Are you..." I paused, uncertain I even wanted to voice this aloud. "You come here often to speak to him, I've noticed."

"I still consider him one of my Captains," the cattle dog murmured, miserably. "I keep hoping he'll come around. But we're on death-watch, at this point. The Physician thought there was a good chance he'd slip away last night. He actually seems slightly better now, but—"

"Sir," I interrupted, and felt bad that I had, but I had to press my point here. "Have you been talking to him about any pertinent information regarding your plans for the evacuation?"

The cattle dog's ears perked at that, and he looked suspicious. "I hope you're not inferring what I think you are—"

"You said yourself, he sympathizes with them," I pointed out. "And Johannes has said there are leaks in this colony that you can't track down."

The cattle dog gestured at his dying friend, seeming mildly irate, now. "Look at him! Does he look like he's sneaking out at night to relay information to our enemies?"

"No," I persisted, "but he could be talking to someone who is."

The Admiral gritted his teeth at that and averted his gaze, knitting his fingers tensely in his lap. "I've been careful with what I've said around him," he assured me.

"Are you certain?" I pressed. "Because that would be an easy slip to make, with a friend you hold so close, whom you used to talk war with."

The uneasy way the Admiral shifted at that made me even more suspicious, but when I opened my mouth to continue, he turned quickly and snapped out, "I think you should leave for now, miss. My friend is ill, and I don't have long to be with him today before I have to get back to work. So please. Leave us be for now."

I wasn't about to disobey a direct command from the man in charge of the colony, let alone when he was so frayed, but I had little more to say anyway, so I stood and left without any hesitation. I made my way back towards Johannes. Grayson was lurking around a nearby corner, and I saw his ears twitch in our direction. But I didn't care if he heard this.

"We thought we were going to lose him last night," the wolfhound said quietly. "It was a long night—"

I cut him off by grabbing at his collar, yanking his head down somewhat. He was startled, but leaned in, as I whispered, "Have you been watching him, when he visits with that man?"

The wolfhound arched an eyebrow, and I saw the wolf closing in behind us, curiously. "I try to give them a bit of space," Johannes replied, uncertainly. "What's your concern?"

"Your friend is a lot more open and unguarded than he should be, around a man who harbors sympathy for our enemy," I said pointedly.

The wolfhound looked briefly concerned at that, before shaking his head. "Luther's no fool. He's a bit easy to read, sometimes, but he's clever enough to keep his secrets close to his chest. Especially those concerning other peoples' lives."

"Are you certain about that?" I narrowed my eyes. "Because he seems like an open book, to me. Especially around his friends."

"You don't know the cattle dog like we do, love," the wolf assured me. "He's crafty. Sometimes he only plays like he's being candid. Th' man can lie backwards and forwards when it suits him, though. I'm sure he ain't slipping secrets to the poor old boy. Besides, even if he was, what would Finn do with them?" He scratched at his dreads, yawning. "Don't worry your pretty little head."

The wolfhound, however, seemed to have latched on to my concern. He lifted his long muzzle and stared across the room at his friend's back, eyebrows lowering. At length, he looked back down at me.

"Do you really think he could be relaying what Luther's been telling him?" He asked, seriously.

"I saw someone suspicious here a few weeks ago," I said, stammering, "I mean... I think I did. I'm not certain. But she was near your friend, Finn. You said you were trying to track down where some of these leaks were coming from, right? Don't you think it's at least possible?"

The wolfhound's expression turned pained for a moment or so. "I don't want to think that, no," he said softly. "But I'd be a fool not to. I've been a fool. I let my friendship with the man cloud my judgment. I never even considered it."

Even the wolf's tone had turned grim. "I... Finn?" His ears fell back. "I don't feel right even thinkin' this way. But..." By now, he knew about the evacuation, and knew that the fallback would likely be his fleet. His dark blue eyes fell to his feet, and one corner of his muzzle turned up in a snuff. "If that's the case, how do we even deal with that? The man's already dying. What are we going to do, lock him down somewhere?"

"No," the wolfhound said, quickly. "If he's communicating with someone, we need to intercept that person. We can't act as though anything's changed. If we cut off Finn, we've only caught one part of the chain. We need to find the messenger."

"I don't like that we're talking like this is really happening," the wolf said, uncomfortably. "We don't have any proof."

"There's no harm in finding out we're wrong," Johannes murmured. "I'll post a man—"

"No," I interrupted. "Let me." When the two men looked down at me questioningly, I explained, "I'm going to be here for a few days, anyway. Puck's in surgery right now, and then afterwards he'll be recovering."

"God Bless," the wolfhound said softly.

I smiled. "Thank you. My hopes are high. But, the point is, since I'm going to be here anyway, I can also keep an eye out. If you'll trust me to the task?"

The wolfhound didn't even pause. "Absolutely. If you need a reprieve, I'll send Gabriel for the night shift."

"You know he prefers his alias," I reminded him with an arched eyebrow.

"I don't like false names," the wolfhound replied.

I felt a pang of guilt at that, but only nodded. It had been a long time since I'd owned my real name, and this didn't feel like the right moment to grip hold of old pain and make it fresh again. There were too many other things happening now that needed my full attention.

At some point during the night, my resolve had boiled down to exhaustion and I'd sent for Gabriel. I'd been up since dawn the previous day, after all, spending time with Puck and being with the two men as they readied for the operation. And even if it hadn't been a mission into the wild, it had been equally draining.

Besides, I needed to be sharp if we were going to catch a spy, and there was no reason not to have a fresher pair of eyes relieve me. Magpie was only too happy to fill in, since we'd been grounded ever since the cliff mission, and he was itching for something to do.

All I knew of the operation was that about an hour after it had begun, Forrest had left the room and I'd caught him washing up to ask how things had gone. He'd seemed calm, and assured me that at the very least, Puck would not bleed to death. Which wasn't much of a surprise, I'd trusted the Physician's able hands. But now we were playing the waiting game, letting Puck sleep off the medicine he'd ingested and praying that the operation hadn't scratched anything necessary, or caused any kind of infection. Forrest promised me he'd been as clean as possible, but he'd also warned me that opening up the body in any way was always a gateway to infection, especially in a place like the Dark Continent. And we'd only really know by visual and scent inspection in the coming days.

"If something goes wrong in the eyes," he'd told me, "it usually sets in quickly. We should know by the morning."

And that was all I had to go on, all night. It had certainly kept me awake for most of it. But eventually I'd found myself slumping and blinking far too often, and had realized I wasn't the best candidate for keeping a vigil. So now the rat was filling in, and I'd finally collapsed on one of the spare cots.

I slept only fitfully, especially since the cot was in the common area and the place was bright and noisy come morning. When I did wake, probably only a few hours after I'd fallen asleep, I decided against trying for any more rest and opted to start my day early, instead.

I passed Gabriel on my way to the baths, and he put a palm on my shoulder, comfortingly. "You could get a few more hours, you know," he offered.

I shook my head. "I won't be able to fall back asleep once the crowds really start coming in and out," I sighed, looking towards the back hallway. Puck would still be sleeping, most likely. I glanced back down at the rat. "Keep up the vigil, would you? I'm going to clean up, and check on him."

"You should get yourself something to eat," the rat reminded me.

I only shook my head as I sleepily wandered off. The early rise and lack of hours was making me mildly nauseated, so food didn't exactly sound appealing right now. A hot bath did, though, and this place was one of the few in which you could get one in this colony.

I got permission from the nurses and made my way to the barrel out back, pulling up the water from the well myself, and lighting the first fire of the morning to heat the water. Most of the time, I'd never been here early enough to catch the very first bath of the day, and using second or third-hand water just wasn't quite as pleasing. I soaked for quite some time, letting my mind wander, but making sure I didn't fall asleep. That would be embarrassing, to say the least.

I scrubbed my hands and arms clean, specifically, since the Physician had told us that was most important. Showing Ransom how to scrub himself thoroughly enough to remove about twenty years of dirt had been an ordeal, and he'd complained the whole way through. But he'd probably never been cleaner than he was right now, and that's the only way we could be with Puck while he was recovering.

As I made my way towards the small back room, I had to fight the urge to backtrack several times. I almost didn't want to know what I'd find when I stepped inside. I knew essentially what the operation had involved, but I wasn't sure what Puck was going to look like. How badly his eyes would be scarred, or his face, or the gods only knew.

The room seemed quiet from the outside. I stood frozen at the door for—I don't even know how long. It could have been half an hour. I couldn't account for my sudden lack of courage. I was just so afraid. Could he have passed away in the night? Had the doctor missed something?

At some point, my hand managed to turn the knob, and I stepped as silently as I could into the small, dimly-lit room. The curtains were mostly pulled, but they were a light cloth and it was long past dawn at this point, so the room wasn't terribly dark, just subdued, matching the quiet I stepped into.

I first saw Ransom, because he was seated near the door, slumped over in a chair sleeping. Similarly, and proof indeed of his earnest desire to see the fox through it, was Forrest. The Otherwolf looked more like he'd planned to fall asleep, leaning back in his chair with his arms crossed over his barrel of a belly. Ransom, on the other hand, looked more like he'd passed out where he'd sat without much choice in the matter. One of his arms was entirely fallen over his knee and he was tilted at an angle I knew would prove aching when he woke.

"Is someone there?" a hoarse, soft voice asked.

I sucked in a breath and swept my gaze towards the bed, where Puck sat. He was entirely upright, his small paws gripping the edge of the blanket. His eyes were covered in two circular bandages that were wrapped tight with gauze. And for the first time since I'd known him, he looked entirely blind.

Puck had never before not known me when I entered a room. I was puzzled for a few moments, before something struck me.

"Puck..." I said softly, padding towards him as slowly as I could, so as not to frighten him. He looked very much awake, but also very wary. His fur was on end, and he seemed disoriented. Lost. "It's me," I said, reaching tentatively for his hand.

He took it, slowly, and seemed to relax. "O-oh," he murmured after a few moments. "Shivah. Good. I-I'm glad. I... the door woke me, and I heard breathing, but..."

I squeezed his palm. "We had to scrub ourselves raw," I explained. "And we're wearing clothing they gave us here. The Physician was afraid of infection."

The fox sighed, seeming somewhat relieved. "That's why I can't smell you," he murmured. With a slightly forced smile, he murmured, "For a moment there, I was afraid I'd lost another sense."

I chuckled softly. "I don't know if you can even lose your sense of smell."

"You can," the fox assured me. "Through damage, mostly, but—"

"He's awake, then?" a somewhat groggy voice asked from behind us. The Physician gave a bit of a groan and a snuff as he came to, pushing himself slowly to his feet. I heard his knees crack more than once.

I nodded at the man as he headed over towards us, and gave him some space as he leaned down, taking the fox by his chin and turning his head a few times, likely inspecting the bandages for seepage or blood. I'd already looked, and I hadn't seen either.

At length, he leaned back, dragging a breath through his nose, and... shrugging, of all things. "He smells good, to me. I think we can remove the bandages."

"Today?" I balked, my heart skipping a beat. So soon? I'd thought for certain Puck would be in recovery for a long time.

"I tried to tell you," the Physician said matter-of-factly, "it's a very simple operation, just not a pleasant one to undergo. I removed the clouded lenses. That's all that needed to be done. I'll need to visually inspect the eyes to be sure nothing was scratched, but I did that last night, and all seemed well. He doesn't smell infected. I think all went well."

Puck gave a shuddering breath, and I nearly stopped breathing entirely.

"Th-at's it?" the fox asked, trembling.

The Physician cracked a rare smile, and nodded. "That's it. Well, once you're fitted for spectacles. Your eyes won't be able to focus, as they are. And expect to be disoriented for quite some time. You haven't seen so much as shapes or colors for many years, and it's going to be startling to be barraged with it all at once. I've heard you might even see color more vividly now than you did before, though. You'll have to let me know how it compares to your vision before the cataracts."

"I can hardly remember," the fox admitted, softly.

"Make sure the curtains are closed entirely," Forrest said to me as he leaned forward to begin undoing Puck's bandages. "Best that he grows accustomed to it slowly."

I nodded and made for the thin cotton over the windows, tucking it in as well as I could. By the time I'd looked back over to the bed, Forrest had most of the bandages off, and was just removing the two remaining circular ones over Puck's eyes. He removed each pad very carefully. Puck's eyelids were shut beneath them, and he didn't open them at first.

"Slowly," the Physician cautioned.

The fox was shaking, the blankets fisted in his small paws, body rigid where he sat. But slowly, very slowly, his eyes slipped open. They were brown.

I put a hand up to my muzzle, stifling the quiet sob that threatened to escape my throat. I watched as the deep, mahogany-colored pools that had been so long obscured beneath a clouded surface revealed themselves, so perfectly fitting my friend's deep, gentle soul. I was shocked I hadn't been able to imagine him this way before.

But really, those clear, soulful eyes had always been there. I'd seen them, seen through the clouded lens obscuring them, many times. Now, the entire world would be able to see what I always had. And hopefully, so would he.

The fox gave a soft 'hah...' of breath, his dark eyes sweeping the room. They fixed first on Forrest, then swept over towards me. They were extremely dilated, and for a moment, he squinted hard, like he was trying to see something far in the distance. But it wasn't like every other time he'd tried to look at me when we spoke, using his other senses to compensate, and fake a gaze he couldn't really follow through on. I'd known then, every time, that he was only doing it for my benefit. So that his wandering gaze wouldn't disturb me. It never had, of course, and I'd hated that he felt he had to do it.

But this time, he was looking at me. Really looking. And I could tell he couldn't see me clearly, but he could see me. And that was all that mattered.

"Shivah..." he said with an amazed smile. "I... I think I see spots. It's you, right?"

I nodded, wanting to say something but knowing that if I tried, I'd probably start crying.

The fox let the breath out that he'd been holding, giving a gasping laugh. "I-I can... see... colors..." He blinked quickly a few times, sniffing wetly and looking down at the blanket he was gripping. "This is blue," he murmured, still in that awed tone. "I'd nearly forgotten what blue looked like."

I heard the creak of heavy footsteps, and so did Puck. He turned slowly, his dark gaze sweeping upwards. At some point, he'd woken, and had come to stand at the foot of Puck's bed. And this time, the fox didn't squint, or hesitate, or pause.

"I know that scar—" he said, his voice catching in his throat. Before the Physician could catch his shoulder to stop him, the fox pushed aside the blankets and stumbled out of bed. The coyote quickly caught him before he could go crashing to the floor, and held him fast.

But Puck was gripping him tighter, suddenly, and the two men were drawing one another close, the fox clinging to his shirt and pressing a hand up along Ransom's ragged neck scruff. He shakily drew it down over the coyote's cheek, pulling him closer still, until their noses were nearly touching.

The coyote was shaking, Puck was dragging in ragged breaths, and both men were crying.

"Why didn't you ever tell me you had gold eyes?" was what Puck finally chose to ask, to break the silence.

I was glad at that point that Forrest stepped out, because a few moments later, even I lost my composure. We all spent that morning happier, and more elated that we'd been in years, crying like children.

CHAPTER 10

Chasing Shadows

After everything that had happened, after all the trials and hardships the two had endured, it was good for my heart to watch the two men celebrate one thing gone right in what had been a cruel and difficult life for them both.

Two days later, I was mostly annoyed by the 'celebrating'. As far as I was concerned, it had gone on long enough.

I rapped on the small door to the back medical room, impatiently. I was three seconds away from tapping my foot, but honestly, that was almost too comical for my current mood.

"Would y'jes leave us alone, cat?" The coyote grumbled from the other side of the door, his voice muffled by the thick wood.

"No!" I snapped. "I have left you two alone for two days, now. I don't know how you apparently seem to have forgotten this, but we're at war! Johannes needs you in the next scouting detail, and I am sick to death of playing messenger and making excuses for you!" I sighed, then remembering, continued, "Oh, and Forrest wants the room back. There are actual sick people who need it."

There were another few moments of silence, before the fox spoke up, sounding at least somewhere near as embarrassed as he ought to have been. "I could still catch an infection," he protested weakly. "Besides, until we get my spectacles, I'm as blind as I was before. The out-of-focus everything is almost more distracting—"

"Then cover your eyes," I growled. "Forrest wants you in one of the beds in the common area now, you don't need a private room anymore."

Another pause. Then Ransom spoke again.

"Ah don't think the good Physician would want us doin' out there what we been doin' in here."

"First off Ransom, shut up," I muttered, putting a hand to my brow and pressing as hard as I could, "second off, more information than I needed. And I say that both because I know from memories I will never be able to scrub from my mind exactly what it is you two were doing, and because it's obvious! How it is you've kept your relationship a secret so long, I cannot wrap my head around. You're miserable at it."

"Well, we only used t'go at it in a tent, in th' middle of the wilderness," Ransom, needlessly, reminded me. "And the fox and I didn' rut none when we was in town."

"Maybe go back to that for however little time we have left in this settlement," I said. "For my sanity, if not your own reputation."

"What do I care what a buncha' stuff-shirts from Amuresca think o' me?"

I slammed on the door again. "Dress, and get the hell out of there!" I demanded. "Puck can keep resting in the commons if he wants, but Ransom, you are meeting me outside, then reporting for duty! Understood?"

"Yes, sir," the coyote snidely replied, and I sighed angrily and stormed off.

Half an hour later, I was about ready to go back inside and separate the two men by force if need be, when I heard the distinct gait of the coyote, his paws crunching in the loose, dry earth outside the triage unit as he made his way towards me. The sky rumbled overhead, forewarning a rare storm during this 'dry season' here on the Dark Continent. It had rained on and off a few times over the last few days, but the storms were always brief and failed to nourish the earth in any real way.

Ransom lit a cigarette as he approached and blew the smoke out through his nostrils with a long sigh. "Goddamn," he muttered, "don't think ah've ever gone two days without a smoke since I was..." he paused, scrunching up his muzzle, "seven?"

I arched an eyebrow. "Spirits forbid."

"Right?" The coyote replied, either missing my sarcasm or deliberately ignoring it. "Awful cruel o' Forrest not t'let me light up when we was in a back room 'n all—"

"Ransom—"

"Ah mean, it ain't like Puck's not used to it or nothin'—"

"Ransom," I persisted.

He blew out another trail of smoke. "Y' reckon tobacco smoke kin give you an infection?"

"I don't know, but the risk probably outweighs your need to feed a bad habit," I growled out, then reached forward and grabbed him by the collar, tugging him down a few inches and surprising him.

"What'n the hell, cat—" he stammered.

"I just," I grated out, "came back from the Optician."

That got the coyote's attention, his ears tipping forward. "And?" he asked, expectantly.

"He said it was an uneven trade, but I think he knows we're abandoning ship soon, and he was willing to take coin." I sighed. "So... I sold it."

Ransom looked hesitantly happy for a moment, then his posture drooped with some regret. "Shivah," he murmured, "Ah'm sorry. I should've found a way t'do this myself. I know it was one of the last pieces o' him you had left."

I put out a hand, stopping him. "It was a pistol, Ransom. That's all. I don't need it to remember him, and I had no plans to use it. Besides," I found myself staring down at the ground, mostly so the coyote wouldn't notice I was blinking rapidly, "he would have wanted me to use it in the way that did the most good. I think this is probably the best possible way to re-purpose a weapon in a positive way. I like to think... he would have been proud of my decision."

The coyote gave a silent, sorrowful nod.

"So, does he need t' see the fox again?" He asked, at length.

I shook my head. "No, he said the one visit was enough. Besides, he said it's a fairly common prescription. More people have had this surgery than you think."

"It's a bloody travesty the tribes don't s'much as know about it," the coyote muttered. "Even Puck didn't. He said one'a the first things he's gonna have Forrest teach him once his eyes is fixed is how t'do this surgery."

I smiled softly. "He'll be able to help a lot of people, when he returns home."

"If," Ransom reminded me darkly, his eyes sweeping the skies. "We still gotta get outta this hell-hole." He spat what remained of his cigarette onto the ground and stomped it out, then fished about in his pocket for another. "So, how long 'til the damned things is done, then? I already gave him my part."

"I have them in my bag."

Ransom's eyes widened. "Why didn't you—"

"I thought maybe it might be best if you both at least got dressed, first."

"It's... bright... out here... ." A still somewhat sleepy voice mumbled from behind us. Shocked, I turned to see the fox warily inching his way out into the cloud-diffused daylight, blinking his dark brown eyes slowly and holding a hand up over them partially to shield them.

I still couldn't get over seeing his eyes like that. It took me a moment to gather myself. When I was able to think straight again, I reached down and tugged the fox's hood up.

"Not just for the light," I explained, "it's going to rain soon."

"I know," he said, dragging in a slow breath through his nose with a small smile, "I can smell it."

"Think yer nose's super-powers is gonna fade now 'at you can see?" Ransom asked, curiously.

The fox wrinkled his nose. "I don't see how that's possible. My sense of smell never really improved, I just paid a lot more attention and built a mental library of what everything smelled like. I don't see why that knowledge would leave me, now."

"What'n the hell's a 'library'?" the coyote muttered.

The fox rolled his eyes at me, as if I'd join in his amusement. I just stared at him blankly, and shrugged, "I'm with him."

Puck sighed. "I've gotten too used to being around intellectuals..."

"What's an—"

"I swear to— If you're about to say 'what's an intellectual', Ransom—"

"Well, I wouldn't'a said it like that exact. S'a long word."

"I think I got that one," I said with a frown, then arched my eyebrow at the coyote, "I'm fairly certain he's calling us stupid, Ransom."

"I am not!"

"Well," the coyote snorted, and marched purposefully up to the fox, holding out a hand to me. I fished around in my bag for what I knew he wanted, and handed them to him. He toyed with them for a moment before figuring out how they worked, then leaned down carefully over Puck. "Yer stupid friends brought you somethin'."

The fox seemed wary for a moment, until Ransom carefully placed the spectacles over the bridge of his nose. Puck blinked behind the lenses, looking at the both of us, agape. He was silent for so long, I began to worry.

"Please tell me they work," the coyote sighed.

"They do," the fox choked, giving a trembling smile. "How on earth did you afford these?"

Ransom's expression dropped some, and he replied, "Ah'm sorry, fox, but I had t' sell the rings. What little coin I had weren't near enough."

Puck actually laughed and leaned forward against the coyote's chest, nuzzling into his suspenders. "They didn't fit, anyway," he chuckled, swiping a few fingers underneath the lenses of his new spectacles to wipe away a tear or two. "Besides," he looked up at the coyote, "this is a far better engagement gift."

Ransom smiled back for a few moments, before he inclined his muzzle towards me. "It wasn't all me, fox."

Puck looked to me, and I forced a soft smile. "I sold Grant's pistol."

The fox's ears fell. "Shivah, you didn't—"

"Don't you start," I sighed. "It was just a thing, Puck. A weapon. If Grant was still here, you know for a fact he would have sold it himself if it meant you could see again."

Our conversation was interrupted by another low rumble of thunder. I'd been feeling the occasional cold pinprick on my fur since we'd stepped outside, but now they were coming faster.

"Storm's moving in," I said with a sigh. "You should get inside, Puck. Are those things safe to get wet?"

"They'd better be for what we paid for them," Ransom muttered.

"We need the rain," Puck said with a soft smile, pulling back his hood and closing his eyes, tipping his muzzle into the drizzling water. "The land is parched, and I haven't felt rain on my fur in so long."

Neither of us had the heart to interrupt the fox, as he stood in the lazy drizzle of rain and slowly swept his eyes across the street, the buildings, and the far more distant sights beyond... the mountain range that surrounded us, the clouds, the ancient trees that grew up around us like a green womb.

"This place is incredible," the fox said in quiet awe. "It reminds me of the forests of old, in the legends. When the world belonged to the Gods, and everything grew as tall as the sky."

I nodded slowly, really taking in the sight of the land surrounding Serwich, perhaps for the first time. I'd marveled, of course, at this place when we'd first arrived, but even then that awe had been dampened by the knowledge of the threats lurking in the rain-forests, tainted with fear. I'd never really just taken it in, in all its beauty.

"You two gonna be alright?" the coyote asked sardonically.

"I'm fine," the fox replied, still smiling. "Although, I think I might want to walk a little. I don't want to go back to bed just yet."

"It's rainin'," the coyote said with an arched eyebrow.

I took Puck's arm. "I'll accompany him," I promised. "You need to report to your post, or Johannes is going to make you work the night shift."

"Yeah, yeah," the coyote muttered, hefting his rifle up over his shoulder. "Y'all don't stay out here in this weather too long, y'hear? Especially you, fox. Yer still s'posed t'be laid-up. Ah get that y' want to gush about mountains or whatever, but just make it quick, a'ight?"

Puck nodded, but I don't know how much of the coyote's warning he actually heeded, because he was soon tugging me down the road, looking on the world like a child. As much as I knew Ransom was right, I couldn't bring myself to put a stop to the little fox's journey. I couldn't even imagine how much this must have all meant to him. Even though he'd had his sight back for a few days now, this was the first time he'd been able to really see in focus, and the first time he'd seen the world outside the small medical room in over a decade.

So I smiled despite myself, and just made sure to walk with him. He wasn't exactly as oriented to sight as most people, after so long without it, and he made simple mistakes often, like forgetting to look down at the ground he was walking on.

"I know you said 'burn it,'" I sighed at the fox, as he once again tripped and I stabilized him by the arm, "but maybe you ought to consider carrying your walking stick for a while longer."

"It's just," he attempted to explain, stubbornly, "this city. It's built Amurescan style. I'm not used to cobbled roads, or these raised platforms in front of buildings."

"They have to build it that way for the rainy season," I sighed. "Johannes explained it to me once. The streets flood. The wet season here is very wet. Speaking of, it's really coming down now, Puck. We should get inside."

The fox dipped his paw into a forming puddle, and giggled, of all things. I arched an eyebrow at him, confused. He looked up at me apologetically. "I'd... forgotten what ripples looked like," he explained. "Sorry. I don't know why I found it so funny."

I reached down to tug up his cloak hood, doing the same for myself. It wouldn't help much at this point, honestly, I was already quickly becoming soaked, and so was he. I was about to remind the fox that we needed to get inside, when I noticed he'd gone still and was staring down an alleyway towards a field behind the buildings that lined this street. I saw what he was looking at, and went cold.

"That's the city graveyard," I murmured. Hesitantly, I reached for his shoulder and squeezed, not sure exactly what was going through his mind, but hoping I could offer some comfort. It was only a few days ago that he'd been facing his own mortality, after all.

When I looked down into his face, though, it was only curiosity I saw. Curiosity, and the look I'd often equated to Puck thinking about something, working something out in his head. I tilted my head, and leaned down to query, "Puck?"

He was silent a further few moments, his gaze dropping to his feet, standing in the small puddle. He didn't reply to me at all at first, which worried me. Only tugged free of my hold and began walking down the alleyway, towards the graveyard. I followed because I was worried about him, increasingly so with his mystifying behavior.

"Puck!" I called out, when he'd gotten a fair distance ahead of me. I jogged to keep up, nearly running into his back when he stopped at the end of the narrow alley. He was on the edge of the vast graveyard, which took up nearly the entire back meadow behind the buildings on this side of the city, wedged up against the river. It was near to the triage unit for obvious reasons, so I'd unfortunately seen it many times.

Puck was staring at his feet, intently. Or, more specifically, I realized as I made my way to him, he was staring at what he was standing in. It took me a few moments to realize he hadn't been walking a random path to bring him to where he was. There was a small drainage ditch dug into the side of one of the buildings near the alleyway, so shallow it was barely noticeable.

I swept my gaze back towards where we'd been standing in the road. Puck had walked the path of the water to where he was standing now. The rain was coming down hard enough that a small, sparkling line was draining down towards the thick, grassy meadow of the graveyard, where it disappeared into the earth.

Puck's eyes were wide, and in an instant, as though he'd been struck by the distant lightning of the storm, he sucked in a breath and spoke, with certainty.

"Ground water."

I stared at him, merely confused by his words, but knowing something very profound was happening.

Puquanah turned to look up at me, gripping my sleeve. "I know how it's spreading!" he exclaimed.

"Ground water?" I repeated, sitting gently on the cot beside the fox as he buzzed beside me, pushing his new spectacles up a bit as they slipped down his nose in his excitement.

"Water that seeps through the ground," he attempted to explain. "Rain water," he gestured with one hand, in a trickling motion, "when it hits the earth, it drains down through the dirt. Some of it makes it deep underground, which is how wells draw up water. But a lot of it just moves along the surface, or close to the surface, and drains into nearby bodies of water. Like rivers."

I nodded. "Alright. So... it's coming from the ground somehow?"

"No," the fox sighed. "Look. We always knew there was a water link. It's no coincidence that so many towns along the rivers were being hit. You could say that's just more likely because there's so much trade along rivers, so many people who could potentially be spreading it, but the frequency was so great back home, I always assumed it had to be more than that. Rourke's men were traveling along that river, slaughtering and burning the bodies of infected people, which should have kept the contagion from spreading. Dead people can't travel, can't go to the river for water, can't spread their waste in the river."

"So then how?" I asked, baffled.

"The disease isn't being spread by the living," the fox said, the certainty in his voice burning with passion, "It's being spread by the dead. Graves, especially mass graves, full of infected people. I'm willing to bet you'd have to burn a body to ashes to completely destroy the illness inside it, and they were hardly cremating those people. I never saw them, but I'm fairly certain there was plenty of flesh left on those bodies, judging by what I smelled—"

I held out a hand, my stomach turning at the memories. "Puck," I said quietly, "please."

"Anyone infected who dies near the water," he said intensely, "whether by the hand of Rourke's men, a traveler, or a villager buried by their own people, is a source of the contagion. Rain water washing down through graves into a river would spread the disease like wildfire. And mass graves, like the sort Rourke's men were creating, would create enormous blooms of it. That's why so many villages were affected along our river, one after another." He paused for a moment, and then his expression darkened. "And that's why it hit Otter tribes and those around them so hard."

"Because they live on rivers?" I asked. "A lot of people live along rivers, in Carvecia. Most of the tribes are at least near one."

Puck shook his head. "No," he said softly, "because Otters always bury their dead near running water. It's tradition. They believe it's the path to the afterlife."

I looked down. "Rourke's people..."

Puck's gaze also fell. "Every burn pile we found was on the outskirts of town, near the river. I have no doubt he did so intentionally. The man might have been mad, but I think in his own mind, he was honestly trying to help those people. He wanted them to pass on in the way his people believed was best."

I shook my head, pushing a hand up through my increasingly frayed mane. "Connall's bloody plan," I said bitterly. "All this time, they were only making it worse."

"No one was taking the time to understand this disease," Puck said. "It's like a living thing. You have to understand how it lives and moves before you can hunt it, before you can find the best way to eradicate it. And that takes a lot of minds. A lot of information. They wanted an easy solution. But you can't batter down a plague with brute force."

"Can we beat it?" I asked. "Now that we know this?"

"I don't know that we'll ever beat it," Puck replied. "It will probably always exist in the world. But so long as we can convince the tribes and the settlements to stop burying people near sources of water, and to steer clear of wells near rivers where water carrying the illness could penetrate—"

"Like Serahaven," I said in sudden realization.

Puck nodded somberly. "It also entirely explains why Amuresca's outbreaks have been small and isolated." When I only tilted my head at his words, he explained, "This disease is new. It came from here–from the Dark Continent–so it hasn't been on other continents for very long. Amuresca is over-populated, and their settlements are old, especially along their rivers. They've killed all their fish, and ruined their water... no one uses the rivers there for anything other than transit and washing. They drain their waste into them. No one drinks from them anymore."

"That's disgusting," I muttered, wrinkling my nose.

"Even if an infected person got their waste into those rivers, they aren't a source of sustenance for their people anymore," Puck said. "And I'm willing to bet any graveyards they have along the rivers have either been buried by cities, or are too old and too crowded for any new bodies. They've unintentionally spared themselves an outbreak."

"The rivers are our lifeline, back home," I said softly.

"We've taken it for granted that our water is safe," Puck said. "Because it always has been. But the world is changing. New people are bringing new threats to us, and this isn't a threat most of our tribes were prepared for. It's no wonder it's been so devastating."

I slowly swept my eyes over the room, watching the many Otherwolves here, foreigners to this country just as surely as they had been to ours, not so long ago.

"This could happen again, couldn't it?" I asked quietly. "I mean, a different disease. Or something else, something worse."

"They've brought a lot of good as well, Shivah," Puck said gently. "But, yes. The world is vast. There are many incredible things out there, beyond the limits of our tribal lands. Things that can change our lives," he adjusted his glasses, meaningfully. I couldn't argue with him, when he was looking—really looking—up at me, for the first time in the two years I'd known him.

"For better or for worse," he said. "But the dam's burst, now. It's too late to go back. We just have to adapt."

"You have to get this information back home," I said suddenly, gripping his hand. "If this dies here, a lot of people die with it."

Puck nodded, his ears flattening seriously. "I know. And I need Forrest as well, to get through to the Colonists. We both need to make it back to Arbordale, or one of the larger cities back home."

"We have to get out of here alive first," I sighed, turning and intending to go for the pitcher of water resting on the bedside table, when something across the room caught my eye.

And I cursed under my breath. Because in all the chaos this morning, I'd forgotten I was supposed to be keeping a vigil.

I sprung up and rushed across the room, nearly knocking into and bowling over a nurse carrying a tray of breakfast for the patients. I didn't so much as take the time to apologize. I heard Puck calling out to me questioningly as I sprinted towards the cot, now in an isolated corner of the room. The man had the cup to his muzzle, and I was certain I was too late, but I doubled my pace despite it.

I reached the emaciated Otherwolf just as I saw him take his first swallow, and batted the cup out of his hand. The clay mug fell to the floor, bounced once, and spun, its contents spilling across the floorboards. The nurse beside the man looked up at me, horrified.

"What in God's name—" she began, but I cut her off viciously.

"Tell me," I growled out, "the last time he's eaten or drunk anything willingly!"

The nurse, some kind of tabby feline, flattened her ears down, seeming to realize my point. The emaciated amputee spat out a curse and weakly collapsed back onto his bed with a sob.

"Just let me pass on!" He cried, hoarsely. "This world is nothing but pain for me now!"

I heard Puck quietly padding up behind us. He knelt beside where the cup had fallen to the floor and picked it up gingerly, sniffing it for a few moments. When he looked up at me, his expression both confirmed my fears, and heightened them.

"Shivah," he said, gesturing to me. I knelt down beside him, as he turned the cup over in his paws.

"I trust your nose," I said implicitly. "Poison?"

"Not just poison," he said, his tone somewhat haunted. "Len'sal. A lethal dose, by the sheer strength of the scent. He would have passed on peacefully, at least, but—"

I sighed. "When will those damned berries stop haunting us?"

"Shivah," the fox said meaningfully, "they shouldn't be here."

"I think I caught him in time," I said. "He only took one swallow—"

"No, I mean, the berries used in this tonic," Puck pressed, "should not be here. They don't grow on this Continent. In fact, they don't even grow over most of Carvecia. They're specific to the region around your Valley, and further north.

My blood ran cold. Puck's expression, I knew, must have mirrored mine. Remembrance, fear, pain. I hadn't wanted to believe it. It had almost been more comforting to think I was mad. That I'd truly put it all behind me. That the ghosts that had haunted me, had nearly burnt me up inside, were truly gone. But if she was truly here, alive still, it wasn't over.

"When I went through my pack after I came back into the world of the living," Puck murmured, "most of my poisons were missing. Including almost all my Len'sal. The only dried berries left were the ones you'd found. I had a larger pouch of them. It was gone."

I stood slowly, my eyes sweeping the room. But a silver fox, I would have picked out in the current crowd, no matter how well-disguised. And I'd never forget those eyes.

"Shivah," Puck began, gripping at my sleeve in an attempt to stop me. He couldn't possibly. All I could see any more was red.

Leaving him, his heart slowing against my palm.

Spilling out on to crumbling moss, sinking into the earth.

Staining my hands, tinging the air with the scent of death.

That scent had sunk deep into the recesses of my mind. I thought I'd never be able to forget it. And I hadn't. Because here it was again, uninvited, forcing its way back into my every sense, taking me over.

I was helpless to this anger. I'd been a slave to it for years, and I thought I'd beaten it. But all I'd ever really done was put distance between myself and it. I wasn't nearly as strong as I like to imagine myself, when it tested me like this.

"Shivah, don't," Puck pleaded from beside me. His voice sounded muddy. Far away. I was already trying to pick up her scent on the air. I wasn't even certain I'd know it if I caught it. She'd always been so far out of my grasp. Like a specter haunting my life, but never quite entering it. All she did was hurt people in a halo around me.

I felt Puck's paw settle on my arm, and I flung it aside, turning an icy stare down at him. He tucked his tail behind him, looking frightened of me. Before he could say any more, I drove forward and gripped the emaciated canine by the collar of his dirty shirt, forcing his weak frame back up into a sitting position, so he'd have to face me.

"Where is she?" I demanded.

The man gave a wracking cough and weakly tried to pry my hand off his shirt with his one good arm. When he didn't reply past that, I shook him.

"What did you tell her?" I spat. "I know you've been communicating with her! What information did you trade for that poison? She wouldn't kill you unless you gave her something! What was it?"

"Nothing of value," he growled out, his voice hoarse and defeated.

"I'll determine that for myself when I catch her!" I snapped. "Where is she heading? Where does she meet them?"

"There's no point," he gasped, "None of this serves any point. She has nothing. They'll kill her anyway."

"Where is she going?" I demanded again, snarling. The nurse was frantically tugging at me from behind, trying to get me off the man, and I could hear Puck hesitantly pleading with me, but none of that mattered.

"You want to die, too?" the man asked in a rattling laugh. "Fine." I released him, and he slumped back down onto the bed. After he'd taken a moment to regain his breath, he continued. "The Brood mother. She's going to meet with the Brood mother."

"Who the hell is that?" I asked, frustrated.

"The one who truly leads them all," the canine stated. "The one who brought all the tribes together to fight us."

"They're lead by a woman?" I asked, uncertain I'd heard him right.

"There are chieftain males," the man sighed. "But, yes. The Cathazra are always led by mothers. Those with the most powerful clutches." He glared. "Our force would know that, if they'd ever bothered to learn about their people."

"You could have told them all you'd learned," I said accusingly. "You were with them. You lived with them. I'm sure you learned more than anyone else ever has."

"I'm afraid to tell Denholme," the man said in a tired wheeze. He looked up at me, and the fear in his eyes was so palpable, I began to understand for the first time what sort of a position this man was in. "I love my people. I don't want our men or our colonists, to die here. But these creatures don't deserve to be slain, either. Our people are an anathema to one another. Every time we meet, blood is spilled. They killed her," he sobbed, "they killed the one who was looking after me. Because she wanted to bring me back to my own people! That was her only sin!"

"Calm down," I stammered.

"Denholme will turn anything I tell him into a tactical advantage," the man insisted. "He'll use it to cripple them. To win this. That's what he does. He doesn't like to lose... No matter the cost."

"So you're selling out your own people instead?" I demanded.

"I haven't sold out either side!" the Otherwolf cried out, then coughed again when his voice cracked.

"Prove it to me," I said. "Tell me where the vixen is going. You know these people. You must know where she's gone to find this 'Brood mother.'"

The Otherwolf gave an exhausted whine, tipping his muzzle back. At length, he breathed out in a long sigh, closing his eyes. "The river. She'll be following the river."

It was still raining when I made it to the river and began following the banks upstream, into the mountains. Puck's final words to me rang hollowly in my ears, about the danger of going into the wilderness here alone, let alone when visibility was this poor. I'm certain if Ransom had been there, he would have tied me to a chair to keep me from this fool chase.

Every rational fiber of my body knew this was reckless to a near suicidal degree. But I knew I'd never again in my life come so close to catching this shadow that had nipped at our heels, pursued us and been pursued by us, for so long now. Her namesake was dead on. She was the greatest force of evil and pain in my life, and I'd never seen her except out of the corner of my eye, at the edge of my life. She was there every time I'd let down my guard, orchestrating the many tragedies we'd endured over the last two years. But I didn't even know her real name.

That ended today. No matter what I had to do to accomplish it. I'd tried so hard to come to terms with my anger for this woman and all she'd done, but if the mere mention of her could turn me inside-out like this, than I had to accept that it was, and would always be, unfinished business that would forever keep me from finding real peace. One way or another, I needed this chapter of my life to close.

The memory of what had transpired with Methoa'nuk had not left me, of course. I was determined I wouldn't kill the woman... Not until I'd absolutely gotten the closure I needed from her. Vengeance had done me no good in the past.

That being said, I wasn't certain if I was given the chance at a kill shot, that I'd be able to stop myself from taking it. Grant was gone because of this woman. Countless people had died at her hand, and she hadn't Xeli's excuse. As far as I knew, the vixen was perfectly rational, she was just cold. Evil. She was evil. Sometimes, it wasn't an overstatement to use the word. There was real evil in the world, and I'd never believe otherwise.

I wasn't going to let her slip through my fingers this time. Not again. If it meant killing her to stop her, I would.

My feet pounded into the red, muddy clay along the riverbanks, my paw-pads catching the occasional sharp edge of jagged slate and the other unforgiving mountain stones that collected along the river's edge, sending pangs of ache up through me that I was ignoring as surely as I was the building ache in my lungs. I'd lost track of how long I'd been running now, I knew only that the river was widening and becoming more tumultuous, and that I'd passed the wall nearly an hour ago, which meant I was far past the safe zones. I was moving into enemy territory, and the river itself was one of the most contested areas.

And I was moving in the open, because it was faster. I had to hope the Cathazra wouldn't be out in force today, due to the lack of sunlight. That was my only possible saving grace.

She'd gotten a good head start on me, I was certain. And I'd seen for myself in the past that she was fast. Possibly faster than me. I had one fact on my side, though, she didn't know I was chasing her.

That didn't mean I wasn't being vigilant, though. I knew a fox's hearing was nothing to snuff at. If she heard me coming upon her over the sound of the rain, she could easily make it to a hiding spot and I'd pass her without knowing, or worse yet, she'd have the perfect opportunity to take a shot at me.

Both of our bows would be wet. So this would come down to whose weapon was in better condition. I kept my bow dry nearly all the time, and waxed my string often. I had it stowed as much as I could beneath my cloak now, so when the time came, I'd have the best possible chance. But rain was always a problem. Always.

Something flitted past the edge of my vision, and I went still, backing into the reeds, scanning the treetops for whatever it had been. It couldn't be a drake, not so low and not in such dark weather. Besides, it had seemed smaller. Could I have caught up to her? Could she have taken to the trees?

It was two bright pin-pricks amongst the dark recesses of foliage that caught my gaze, and drew me towards the dense clump of leafy branches where he sat. Black, and small, and not a bird native to these lands. And those eyes. There was no mistaking those burning eyes. Like embers.

My breath came out in a halting gasp. "why?" Was what I eventually managed, at last.

The creature stared back at me impassively. Not speaking. He never spoke when I needed him to.

"Why?" I screamed up into the branches, heedless of any need for stealth in that moment. "Why are you still tormenting me? You've never helped me! You won't even leave my life, when I'm trying to let go!" I felt my voice catching in my throat, and swallowed back pain in my throat. "I tried... to help you," I said. "So that you could let go. So that we could let go together. I thought you'd gone. I thought I'd never see you again. Why do you always appear right when I'm at my weakest? When I'm hurting, when I'm uncertain what to do? All you ever do is push me towards the worst decisions! Do you just enjoy watching me burn up inside?"

Still, the spirit didn't answer. He simply stood in the branches, staring down at me with those burning eyes, standing out against the dark silhouette of his body.

"I thought I was done with you," I said, my voice shaking. "I thought I was done, with... with all of this. I want it to be over." I balled my fists, and then I screamed.

"I want you to go away! Leave, and never come back! I want peace!"

The spirit shifted suddenly, and began to take off. In a flash of black wings against the grey backdrop of the sky, he was gone, and the branches shifted against the absence of his weight.

Or perhaps they were moving in the breeze.

But in that moment, I caught sight of something else. A second pair of eyes, behind where the branches had once been. Catching the cloudy light of the obscured sun, flickering green for just an instant. I never would have seen them, had it not been for the shift in the foliage.

I undid the clasp for my cloak, pushing it off my shoulders, and pulling my bow, slowly. The glint in the eyes had not shifted yet, so I had to assume she thought she was still hidden. But that wouldn't last, once I leveled a shot.

I moved forwards slowly, pulling an arrow from my quiver and nocking it to my bow, but keeping my head turned towards my side of the river, so she'd think I didn't quite know where she was. The vision out of my peripheral was better at catching movement, and I knew she'd move as soon as she realized I'd detected her. That would be my only shot. She was too much behind cover, now.

Alarm bolted through my blood when I caught that flicker of movement out of the corner of my eye, and I twisted, pulling my body ramrod straight into a firing stance. Just as Ransom had shown me, over and over again, in the months we'd spent in the valley. Just as I'd always run over in my mind, when I thought of hunting down Methoa'nuk, the Raiders, the many people in my life who'd wronged me. I'd always feared I might panic, might act hastily.

But in this one moment, I was deathly calm. I was not the woman I'd once been. I was not weak. I was not helpless. I was prepared, and I was a hunter. And this time, she was my prey.

I waited for the right moment, and it came. She was dropping down through branches in the tree, making for the ground. And no matter how spry, no one was as dexterous while climbing as they were on foot. She was five feet from the ground when I saw my shot, between a gap in two thick branches.

I released my arrow, and it sung through the rain. I heard her cry out as it struck her, right where I'd intended, into the meat of her thigh.

I was taking off across the rocky shore almost before she'd hit the ground. I leapt through the shallows as far as I could, before I was forced to wade. I was lucky the river wasn't wider here, or forging it could have been impossible, not just difficult. By the time I made it to the opposite shoreline, I was soaked head to toe, and nocking another arrow to my bow was probably a futile gesture, but I did it anyway.

I could hear her moving, stumbling through the brush. I closed in on the sound, and soon I could hear it all. Uneven footsteps, staggered breaths belonging to a woman... and the unmistakable scent of a fox.

It felt as though I were at the end of a funnel, my vision and my life all closing in on this one moment. Everything around me seemed black save the trail ahead, leading to my prey. She was right there. She was weakened, she was on the run, for the first time since she'd begun haunting me.

And then I saw her. Really saw her. I broke through a thick mass of palms, and she was just... there, standing in the clearing ahead, as soaked as I was, my arrow still protruding from her thigh. Her cloak was torn from falling through the trees, I could smell her blood in the air, and she'd resorted to pulling a thin blade, to defend herself with.

I pulled back my arrow, and leveled it at her. At this close a range, no matter how fast she was I would not miss.

I was about to demand her surrender, when she shocked me by speaking first. But it was more the words than her voice that stunned me so.

"Why do you haunt me so?" She cried out, in a voice hoarse with exhaustion. "Why did it have to be you? Why is it always you? Have I not avenged you? Leave me be, spirit!"

CHAPTER 11

Full Circle

I stood frozen before her, my hand trembling where it gripped my arrow. Her words made no sense to me, yet somehow, they filled me with a dread I couldn't describe.

This wasn't the first time someone had called me a spirit. Methoa'nuk had once accused me of the same, when I'd cornered him.

"What do you mean?" I demanded, trying to keep my voice steady. "I am not a spirit. I'm flesh and blood. Stop trying to confuse me!"

"I should say the same to you," she snarled, and I saw a mirror of my own frustration and helplessness from not a few minutes earlier, in her every word and expression. I knew in that moment that she believed what she was saying, as surely as I had when I'd screamed at Crow across the river.

"I saw you die," she insisted. "I saw them bury you. And I avenged you! I made them all suffer for what they did to you. I evened the scales—and yet you dog me... You've followed me, haunted my dreams, haunted my waking life... Ever since that day. What more must I do to be free of you?"

"Wait," I stammered, lowering my bow simply because I couldn't hold it taut any longer. My body suddenly felt weak, all the outrage and anger leaving me in a torrent, replaced by a dark, sinking feeling.

"You slew my tribe," I hissed between my teeth, "and my husband's tribe because of me?"

"Because of what they did to you," she said, venom in her voice, although none of it directed at me. If anything, what I saw in her expression towards me was pity, and fear. "Because they still practiced that archaic tradition. But no longer. It died with them. And I made sure your husband suffered," she said with a menacing flash of teeth. "He and the cowards who tried to buy their survival by turning on their own. I let them live so that I could force them to endure the pain they inflicted on the women of your kind. They paid it all back in blood, those months we kept them."

"How did you even..." I was at a loss for words. It took me a full few moments to gather myself, before I could clarify my statement. "How—when—did you see them bury me?"

"We traded with the Anukshen for many years," the vixen said, matter-of-factly. "We work along the river, and your tribe traded along the river. Food for weapons, usually. Where do you think the men in your tribe got their metal blades?"

I felt nauseous. The elders of my tribe, and the warriors, like Methoa'nuk, had to know who the Raiders were and what they did. They were allowed to leave the village, they went to the same trading post Ransom and Puck did, and everyone there had seemed to know them. All this time, my people had been supplying them?

Methoa'nuk had not lied. My tribe truly had invited them in. I'd wanted all this time to believe that he'd been deceiving me. But it was all exactly as he'd said.

"We had an arrangement with them that benefited both of us, for years," the woman continued. "Your tribe was too isolated to become infected, and they were reliable traders. I dealt with that man who called himself your husband, for years, before knowing what kind of a man he truly was. It was his own fault that his evil became known to me. He met with us on the same outing he took to bury you. He showed us what he and his people had done to you. Intentionally. He looked on it as a mark of pride. He never saw eye to eye with Xeli, for having a woman amongst his 'warriors'. I suppose he meant to send me a message. And he did," she curled her lip. "He certainly did."

"You killed them all," I helplessly repeated, "because of me?"

I'd always feared it had all been my fault, somehow. I'd convinced myself by now that it wasn't. How dare she force this guilt on me again!

"Xeli couldn't abide the torture and execution of an innocent, healthy woman any more than I could," she said, her voice soft and compassionate in a way that made my skin crawl. "And you can't reason with ignorance. The only way to end archaic practices like the one you endured is to end the groups that perpetuate them. They call it 'honor killing,'" she snuffed. "Disgusting."

"Don't act high and mighty," I snarled. "You can't demonize an entire tribe for killing an innocent, when you've done the same countless times, yourself!"

"I never took any pleasure in putting innocents to the torch," she said, seeming hurt by my words. "It wasn't malicious. It was necessary."

"How many people amongst my tribes did you kill unnecessarily, then?" I demanded. "There were good people amongst even the Anukshen. Innocents. Young ones, and men and women who had no choice! Methoa'nuk was a monster, but you can't blame the people in my tribe who were frightened of him for taking part in the ritual! If they didn't, they were at risk of his rage, of the warriors singling them out for punishment, as well."

"They had a choice," she spat. "Everyone has a choice to reject a way of life, when they know it's wrong."

"If you can say that, you've never been weak," I said. "You've never known what it means to be truly helpless. Sometimes people just don't have the means, or the strength to leave everything they know behind."

"That is weak," she countered, coldly. "And no, I've never known what that's like. But it sounds like an excuse, not a reason."

She gave a sudden hitch of breath, and it took me a moment to realize she'd pulled the arrow out of her leg. Unlike her, I didn't barb my arrows to cause any unnecessary suffering, but it still had to have been tremendously painful to pull it out. And her expression had barely twitched.

Now that she was closer to me, I was able to get a better look at her. She was not a striking woman, in any way except appearing fearsome. She looked weathered and haggard, and probably older than she was. Her fur was graying in areas that weren't natural, even for a silver fox, she was thin as a rail and barely recognizable as female. Her voice was rough and her face was scarred, most noticeably along her cheek. This was a woman who'd lived a hard life, possibly harder than mine. But much of it had been her own doing, I had to keep reminding myself.

And yet despite all of this, she seemed terrified of me. She was trying very hard to keep her voice strong, hoping, I'm sure, that I would not notice she was shaking. But she was. She was weak, and exhausted, and desperate to get away from me.

It had never occurred to me that from her perspective, I really must have seemed like a relentless specter, stalking her across the countryside. I'd always attributed that to her; that she had been haunting me. But we'd been the ones who'd gone after her and her men, had been trailing them trying to find them. We'd had countless chances to give up, and we never had. Not even when it had cost us lives.

You could call it fate, as well. We'd both had parallel goals all this time that had kept us circling one another, inexorably drawn to one another like winds on the prairie, coming together in this final vortex of destruction. We mirrored one another, in the worst of ways. I could see so much of myself in her. But I couldn't understand her, or her reasoning.

"I am not a spirit," I said at length. "I'm flesh and blood, like you. I survived what Methoa'nuk did to me. I was pulled from the earth by two strangers, and nursed back to health." I lifted my chin. "If you'd really wanted to help me that day, you could have done what they did."

"You were dead," she insisted.

"Did you ever bother to check?" I asked simply.

"I know a dead body when I see one," she spat. "And no matter what trickery you attempt on me, you'll not fool me. You are not the weakling that man murdered, not any longer. You are changed."

"I am," I nodded. "But I'm real."

"The Great Thunder and the Lightning Twins are real," she replied. "But that doesn't mean we cannot hear his bellowing, or see the spirits of the sky split trees in twain. Spirits are alive, and I'm sure many believe they are flesh and blood. But I know what I've seen."

Her words struck a chord in me, reminding me of something the elders in my birth clan had once said. That a person could go their entire lives without speaking to or seeing a spirit, and to that person, they would always seem weak and quiet. But if that same person believed, they would begin to see them, would be able to hear their voices. The spirits were as real as we perceived them to be. Belief is what made them a stronger force in our lives.

To this woman, maybe I was a spirit.

"Fine, then," I said quietly. "You want me to stop hunting you? To leave you be?"

"You can kill me, if you wish," she said, defeated. "I don't care anymore. Only let me do this final task. Please."

I arched an eyebrow, staring her in the eyes. "What task?" I demanded.

"I have an arrangement with the Cathazra," she said, holding up a hand. "I came here because Xeli and I had heard, many years ago, that this is where the Fever came from, that the people here might know how to treat it. I never believed it was anything more than a myth," she admitted, a hint of pain flashing through her eyes, "But... before I lost Xeli, it was the last thing he asked of me. The last lead we had to follow. I nearly drowned getting here, I-I've... fought so hard to get to this point. I was captured and nearly eaten by those beasts when I first tried to contact them. It took me months to get any useful information out of that cripple. But I finally have something of value. Something I can trade, for the secrets to the Seer's Fever." She looked to me plaintively. "Xeli's death... all of those deaths... will not be in vain, if you'll only just let me do this. Please. It is all I have ever wanted. It is all he ever wanted."

My gaze softened only slightly. "You really cared for the otter, didn't you?"

"He was like a brother to me," she said, her voice cracking slightly on the last words. "A kindred spirit. You don't know what sort of man he was, before the disease really took a hold of him. What became of him was not his fault. It was the Fever. It is always the Fever. It destroys people's lives."

"Xeli was a murderer," I said quietly, "like you. Madness aside," and when I said that, I couldn't be sure if I was including her in that statement. "You killed hundreds of people. Innocent people. For no reason."

"It was for the greater good—"

"No, it wasn't," I cut her off, decisively. "It was for nothing. All for nothing. And this final task of yours..." I almost hesitated in my words, because I could see the pain and passion in her eyes, and I knew what it meant to be on a mission, and how terrible this would feel to hear. But at length, I said it anyway.

"This task of yours is pointless, as well," I said, flatly. I saw her ears fall, her tail go limp, and knew that on some level, she believed me. Perhaps because she viewed me as more than I was. A spirit, not just a person. Crow had often destroyed my resolve, when he'd told me I had failed. And that's what I was doing now, to her. But I had to. She needed to know.

Also, I needed to wrest the truth from her, for the sake of others who were peripherally involved in our clash.

"What did Finn—" I began, then cut myself off with a sigh. "What did the crippled man tell you? What is this information you think will be so valuable to the Cathazra?"

She was silent long enough that I knew she was considering keeping quiet entirely. I raised my bow again, just to let her know I was serious. I needed to know what the man had said, for the sake of his comrades, and the security of the colony.

"The basin," she said, finally. "Your men are planning a raid on the basin. One of their holy sites. As some form of distraction. The Cathazra expected there would be a diversionary raid to buy time for an evacuation, but they weren't sure where. It took me months to get it out of that man."

I blew out a soft breath and lowered my bow. I'd been worried, because in truth, the choice for the raid hadn't yet been determined, as far as I knew, but that was only as far as I knew. It was possible the Admiral had already chosen a location and I just didn't know it. Which meant I wouldn't know if she had the right information or not.

But this was most certainly wrong, and that meant Finn had lied to her.

"The basin," I said evenly, "is a graveyard." I saw the wind go out of her lungs as I spoke, her entire figure seeming to deflate. "We already investigated it as a potential attack site, and dismissed it just as quickly. It's three feet deep in water most everywhere, and holy or not, it's essentially just a cesspool. We can't burn it. We can't even really attack it, there's nothing to attack."

She was silent.

"He lied to you," I said, stonefaced. "He told you what you wanted to hear, because he wanted your poison. I don't think that man was ever a turncoat. He just has sympathy for the enemy."

"Shut up," she hissed bitterly, and raked her claws through her bedraggled mane.

"It doesn't matter," I said. "No matter what you got from the Cathazra, it's no longer necessary. And to be honest, I don't think they ever could have helped you. They're an entirely different people, physically. It's possible the Fever doesn't even affect them, and if it does, treatment would be different, wouldn't it?"

She looked at me, astonished. "How do you know all of this?" She asked, warily.

"Because I have a very smart friend," I said, trying to keep the bitterness from my tone. "And you nearly killed him. He's been studying the disease, too. Actually studying it, not just trying to wipe it out by killing everyone affected by it."

"The government tried—"

"Well they didn't try hard enough, then," I snapped. "You, and Connal, and all the men who were behind your plot, you all wanted a fast solution. And you only made things worse."

"We were trying to stop the spread!" she insisted. "You haven't seen what happens when this disease ravages an area! It was only just beginning, in the Valley."

"I'm sorry for what happened to Xeli's people," I said, quietly. "And likely yours, I can only imagine."

She gave a snarling smile. "Oh, the 'settlement' I came from survived our outbreak. We had a Physician in town who was able to treat many people."

"Then, why..." I stammered.

"My family couldn't afford him," she said with a clack of her teeth. "So they boarded us up. Locked us in our house, so we couldn't infect others. I only survived without catching it because my mother locked me in a room by myself. I had to break the window to get out, after they all died."

My muzzle twisted up. "Then how," I asked, horrified, "could you subject others— You were doing the exact same thing to all of those tribes you hit! You didn't give them a choice, except to die! If people in your town survived, you knew it could be treated! How could you do this all these years, knowing that?"

"Because my settlement survived," she said, coldly. "My family sacrificed themselves for the greater good. And I should have died with them, were it not for my mother. I couldn't make sense of why I survived, for the longest time. People in town all looked on me, with guilt, shame..." She scoffed. "It's so easy to feel mercy and pity after the fact, isn't it? But it's a lie. When it came down to it, and it was their survival or ours, they chose. The way I see it, it's worse to regret your decision when you've already committed the sin. Hypocritical. Weak. They should have just owned up to who they were. Sometimes the world needs people who can make hard choices like that. Someone has to be the villain. Someone has to sacrifice their soul, so that others can live happy lives."

"I'm sorry," I said quietly, "that you came to see the world this way. You went through something terrible, and I'm sure coming to see things this way made it easier, but it's not so. There's always a way—"

"No, there isn't," she stated, with cold determination. "Sometimes terrible things happen, and the only way to prevent them is to commit terrible things. That's the way the world is."

"You might be right," I admitted, which seemed to surprise her. "But... the problem is, we can't know if a solution will work until we've tried it. It's always worth trying to find a better way. You, and Connall, and even Xeli, jumped to the worst-case, without ever trying anything else first. And maybe in some cases, that would have been for the greater good. But this time, you were wrong."

"You can't know that," she retorted.

"I do know it," I said. "Because we found the solution."

"What?" her ears fell back.

"Puquanah," I said softly, "the fox you nearly killed. He and the Physician here determined how the disease spreads. It's been spreading through ground water. Through rain, washing through graves. Especially the mass graves, like the ones you and Xeli piled up all along the river's edge."

She said nothing, but I saw her eyes falling to the ground, following the rivulets of water washing from where we stood down towards the shoreline. Thunder crackled in the distance, lightning lit the waning sky for a moment, and that last bit of defiance left her eyes with it.

"Your efforts were only spreading it faster," I said. "I'm sorry." I wasn't sorry for her, but I truly was sorry for the people she'd killed unnecessarily. So I meant it.

Her stare was hollow when it came back to mine. I knew she believed me, whether or not she wanted to. The helplessness there, I'd seen—felt—so many times, myself. I'd felt it when I'd slain Methoa'nuk, and taking my revenge had not in any way healed the pain in my heart.

This is all a life like this wrought. Taking out my anger on the world had only carved me out inside. I'd come so close to becoming a hollow, burnt-out shell of a woman, chasing vengeance across the world. And now, here, I had living proof of what would become of me, if I'd let myself be consumed by it. For her it had been a disease. An enemy she couldn't ever truly conquer, no matter how many she killed.

For me, it had been despair, loss. I'd been trying for so long now to replace the pain with anger, because it felt like it was the only way I could live with it. But ignoring a wound didn't work when it was on your skin, let alone in your heart. All it did was allow it to fester.

I still hurt. Remembering Tale'nuk, remembering Grant, remembering my family, my tribes... Remembering all I'd lost still ached, still made me cry. Made me feel weak, and defeated. Powerless.

But denying all of that meant denying their lives had meaning, other than to turn me into an instrument of vengeance. This woman had taken that to the most literal level, justifying her family's deaths as necessary, to beat back the invisible enemy they'd fought. And she'd been subjecting that very same fate on so many others, using that same justification. I suppose it made it easier for her. It made everything that had happened to her make sense.

I couldn't kill her. She deserved to pay for her crimes, but I couldn't be that justice, or I knew, somehow, I'd never come back from it. This was the hardest possible circumstance I might ever face... I had to show mercy. Because it was hard. Because I had to learn how to show mercy. Those tendencies for anger, that need to 'balance the scales', as Shadow herself had said, were inside me as surely as they were inside her. And I'd never overcome it in the future if I didn't do so now. But I needed to know one last thing.

"Grant," I said the name softly, because I didn't want her to know how weak my voice had become. "Why did you kill him? Why did you involve us in all of that, if you were trying to escape me? Why did you shoot him," my throat felt dry, "and not me?"

Her eyes widened marginally. "The Marshall?" she asked. When I only nodded, she replied in a stoic, quiet tone, "You were never supposed to be there. None of that was ever supposed to happen. But my men got sick, and we couldn't control them. They stopped listening to Xeli and I. They never trusted Xeli like I did. When they abandoned us, I knew they'd spread it. They had to be eradicated."

"I know you're the one who slipped the note under our door," I said.

"That note wasn't meant for you," she said, sounding confused. "It was intended for the Marshall, and whatever men still followed him. I knew he was still in town. He was hard to miss. And Connall wouldn't hire him back, but we needed men to take on my Raiders. We were badly outnumbered. We hired two mercenaries in the area, but that wasn't enough. I told Connall... Just hire back the men he'd let go. They could do their job, kill the Raiders, and we'd start over again in a few months with a new group. But the pit bull was stubborn," she growled. "He wanted it all done quiet, so that when we began anew, we could still use the 'Rourke' name. I told him it would never work, and that the four of us alone couldn't take on the Raiders. I told your Marshall because I knew he held a grudge against my men, and I knew he'd take the bait. I knew he had followers, but... not you," she said, that edge of fear still in her voice.

"You didn't have to kill him!" I said, angrily. "We fell into your plot willingly, and we did the job you needed done! Why kill him?"

"I wouldn't have," she stated. "I had no grudge against that man. But he went into our camp, and fought with my men, hand-to-hand. He had an injury. I saw it."

I swallowed, remembering.

"I killed him because he was infected," she said, coldly. "That's all. It's my policy."

"Then you're a hypocrite," I replied, icily. "Because you were the one who infected your men. You got sick, and you survived. If you really believed what you preached, you would have ended your own life."

Her eyes fell to the ground. And after a few moments of silence, save the distant sounds of the storm and the chorus of raindrops falling all around us, I heard her say something I'd never anticipated.

"You're right." She looked back up at me, plaintively, "But, I felt I had more to do. I couldn't die, having failed."

"Grant had a lot more to do with his life, too," I said, swallowing heavily. "So did everyone you've ever killed."

"End my life, then," she said, resolutely. "I'm tired of running from you. And I can't live... knowing I failed."

"It hurts, doesn't it?" I murmured. I saw a stab of anger flash through her eyes. "Living with it, living with the knowledge that you failed, hurts a lot more than death. I failed to protect my son. I failed to protect the man you killed. And it hurts. Terribly. Every day."

"How can you live feeling so weak?" She asked, bitterly. "How can anyone?"

"Everyone's weak, in some way," I replied quietly, my thoughts drifting to my friends, most especially Ransom. "Even the strongest people you know."

"Don't give me rhetoric! How is it you've clung to the world, with such a frail spirit?" she snarled. "I have never been weak! I've never let myself become a victim. I have fought too long, and too hard, to fail. It must be you!" She stabbed a finger at me. "You are a cursed spirit! From the moment you came into my life, you've led me to make poor decisions. You've pushed me to the brink of destruction, haunted my every effort!"

"You made your own decisions," I said. "You always have. And I'll..." I felt the breath collect in my lungs, a strength I didn't know I had blossoming in my chest, "I'll forgive you for them. Because it isn't entirely your fault."

"I don't want your forgiveness," she growled.

"It isn't for you," I said, narrowing my eyes. "It's for me. I'll never be free of you if I can't."

"Enough," she said, her lip curling to reveal her yellowed fangs. "I don't believe you. I don't believe anything you've said."

"Yes, you do," I replied quietly.

"I have a mission!" she screeched, frantically. "A mission I am finally on the verge of accomplishing! If you want to stop me, you'll have to kill me!"

I pulled up my bow at the last moment, to remind her she was in my sights, but before I'd so much as pulled the arrow back, she tugged something—a knife, like one of the small ones the wolfhound carried—from beneath her cloak, and flung it at me. I just barely managed to roll out of the way, losing my arrow in the process.

By the time I came up, she was limping for the river. I cursed, grabbing for another arrow, the shafts gone slippery with rain water. I'd gotten one good shot at her before, but my bow was soaked now, visibility was getting worse, and she was heading for the water. If she got into the deeper currents, I might never catch her.

Time seemed to slow, each of my footfalls on the muddy earth feeling farther apart as I pursued her down towards the rushing waters. She was waist-deep by the time I made it past the treeline. The frail, ragged woman was wading into the deepest waters, nearly black in the waning light. She clung to a slippery, rocky outcropping for a moment, and I saw her turn to stare back at me, her green eyes catching a distant flicker of lightning.

In the tumultuous chase across this foreign forest, our minds both so intently-focused as they'd been, something keenly important and potentially fatal had slipped away from both of our thoughts. We were deep in enemy territory.

I saw the rock begin to shift before she did, and sucked in a gasp to scream at her.

Her hands clawed helplessly at the shifting, moss-covered surface as it began to slowly shift upwards. What had looked a moment ago to be an uneven, broken slab of slate revealed itself, patterns of scales emerging as it straightened its back and stood on two towering legs, a broad, thick tail sweeping out from behind it in the twisting currents.

I had never in my life seen a beast so enormous. It stood as tall as two men at the shoulder, its whole body covered in mottled green and grey scales that, until now, would have rendered it all but invisible in the river waters. I saw little of its face from here, save that it was reptilian, thick-jawed, and ringed with sharp teeth.

I understood now why the people here shot these creatures on sight. Why they'd killed the one that had tried to bring Finn back to their colony. The creature—this thing they called a 'Basilisk'—looked like a beast of legend.

I watched helplessly as the vixen shrieked and swung her arm into the creature, the tip of another of those small daggers flashing before she buried it into the beast's scaley hide. It gave only a burbling, low growl, and reached down almost casually, its massive clawed hand closing around the woman as she struggled against the currents.

My hands shaking, I raised my bow, trying desperately to nock an arrow to it. Before I could effectively level a shot though, her eyes caught mine. The beast was pulling her up from the water from the midsection, her arms pinned in its grasp, legs weakly struggling beneath.

She shook her head at me, slowly, and spoke. I could barely hear her over the river, and the rain.

"Run," she choked out, her voice constricted by pain, as the creature crushed her. She took a few halting breaths, and I knew she was crying. "Do what I couldn't," she pleaded in a final cry, before the beast dove beneath the water with her. And I ran.

It was a full two weeks before I could bring myself to report on what happened on the river. I'd told Ransom and Puck, of course, but only because I had to. Puck knew what I'd gone out to do that day.

The entire experience had left me numb, unsure how to feel. It wasn't like when I'd slain Methoa'nuk, though. It wasn't that hollow, helpless feeling.

I felt, at last, that I had some closure. But it was neither satisfying nor disappointing. It simply was. I couldn't bring myself to feel that the world had balanced out, even though it seemed like that was exactly what had happened. Nothing had truly been accomplished by the vixen's death. Much like her life's work, all her death had ultimately brought was more death. It didn't undo the wrong she'd done. It didn't undo the wrong that had been done to her.

It was just death. I'd seen enough people die over the last two years to last me a lifetime. So, no matter how much I dug around inside myself, I could take no solace from what had happened to her.

Ransom seemed to find it all amusing. So at least there was that. He'd certainly had a bone or two to pick with the woman. And even Puck had tried to console me by reminding me that she would have been executed if I'd returned her to Serwich justice. And not even for the crimes she'd committed in our country. Treason was a high crime here.

I was slowly beginning to come to terms with the fact that my life would be more than this. There would be no grand finale today, or tomorrow. There might not be for years. It had felt for so long now that my purpose, my very life story, began and ended with these two years of strife. In a way it did feel like it had all come full circle. Shadow—in the end, I'd never learned her true name—entered my life at the very moment I'd been poised to be reborn into the world. The day 'Shivah' had been born. And now, it felt as though that identity had died with her.

I couldn't follow a path so obviously devastating any longer. Shadow had shown me where it ended. It was a part of me, would always be a part of me, in the same way Crow was a part of me. I couldn't deny it, because I'd lived it. I'd felt it, often fiercely, for so long now. And in a very real way, she, and Crow, had kept me alive.

But I was ready to reclaim the life I'd had before. I just wasn't sure where, or what I'd do, and that left me feeling lost. Everyone else in my life seemed to have a very certain purpose. Mine, at this point, was simply to live.

But where I'd go or what I'd do, trying to decide had been agonizing. And I was running out of time. Something felt wrong about returning home. I didn't want to stay another day in Serwich if I could help it, but I also wasn't certain I was ready to return to the world I'd known, to the mountains and rivers of my childhood, and confront the pain I'd left behind. Not yet.

The voyage we'd taken, the time I'd spent in these foreign lands, had been terrifying and bewildering. The land, the conflicts, the people... It was all so distant from what I knew. But that distance had given me the first real peace I'd had in years. It wasn't peace in the sense that I'd been able to rest easy. Certainly not that. More that having to adapt, having to take in a world changed and strive to understand things so far beyond my understanding had been challenging, in a way I relished. It had distracted me from my pain. Forced me to focus on the present, instead of the past.

And I'd begun to see the world. Really see the world, which wasn't something most tribal peoples from my Valley could boast, let alone women.

I was coming to a decision, slowly, but it felt more and more certain each day. I wasn't sure how to tell my friends. But I knew eventually, I'd have to.

"I really wish you'd told me about this earlier," Johannes muttered, as we walked the docks towards our destination. The wolfhound had been in a poor mood all day, and I knew he would be even moreso once I asked him this favor, so I figured it was as good a time as any to heap on more news that would make him irate.

"But, I mean," I stammered, "it all worked out. For your people, at least."

"That depends on your standpoint," the wolfhound sighed. "Finnegan is still ill, and he's more determined than ever to end his life, now. I have pity for his situation, but I don't know how to help him. He's asked to remain in the city when we abandon it, and let come what may with the Cathazra. I don't have the heart to deny his final request. I know he must have his reasons, but I feel like we lost the man."

"But he never betrayed you," I said softly, putting a hand on the tall Otherwolf's arm.

He glanced down at me, his gaze softening slowly. "I suppose you're right," he said at length. "Luther's trust was well-placed, this time. I wanted to have the same trust in the man. I really did. I just..."

"People like you and I don't trust easily," I murmured.

"The world's disproven me too many times," the wolfhound agreed, his tone hard. "I can't look on people the way Luther does any more. Not even old friends."

"I think friends like ours need people like us, though," I said with a gentle squeeze of his bicep. "So don't bemoan our lost innocence too much. There's a place for cynics."

He gave me a mildly amused smile, before glancing sidelong at the ship we'd reached. Then all mirth fell away from his expression, and he gave a long, ragged sigh. "I can't believe I'm doing this," he repeated for about the fifth time in the last hour.

"You said you owed me your life," I pointed out, poking him in the chest. His ears fell back and he almost glared down at me. Almost. "So no backing out now! It's a pretty minor favor for a life-debt, I'd say."

"Allow me to disagree," he muttered. But he began making his way up the gang plank, to the Manoratha. I followed in step behind him.

As we made our way on to the massive warship, I took a moment to pause at the railing and look out over the bay, and the sweeping landscape beyond. It was just after dusk, the brief rain we'd had a few weeks ago had done little to quench the land, and the heat was steaming off the trees all along the steep mountain basin, making the stars quiver in the sky. Distantly, the great mountain was sending a steady stream of drifting smoke into the sky, speaking to the fires still burning within. But there had been no fiery explosions since we'd come here. No maelstrom of burning clouds and ash.

Nonsensically, I wondered if the mountain was mirroring me. I knew, of course, that that was ridiculous, and arrogant. To think the very land and the goings-on of my life were tied. But I couldn't help but feel a connection to the distant land mass. The mountains in my own Valley slumbered quietly, sleeping giants that would likely never wake again.

This mountain was a simmering cauldron still, poised to erupt and destroy everything, and everyone, in a radius around it. In my dreams, when I'd been at the height of my anger, Crow had been the same, burning from the inside out. He wanted to die in an explosion, the way his fabled star mate had, and he'd wanted me to do the same.

Or I had. I'd known that myth since I was a child. It was entirely possible, I'd begun to accept, that everything Crow had told me, everything I'd dreamed, every time he'd taunted me and every time he'd given me strength... it had all come from my own mind. Crow was my totem animal, after all. And I'd thought of the myth of the star, likely because the death of a loved one mirrored the struggles in my own life. He'd given me strength when I'd needed it, and taunted me with my failings when I'd most hated myself. Had I created him, entirely?

Shadow's perceptions of me had turned me into a spirit in her own mind. I was certain she'd died believing it still. It was a hard thing to accept. But if Shadow had seen a specter every time I'd appeared in her life, hunting her, than I had to accept that it was possible I'd seen a spirit in a series of birds, and happenstance. There were some instances that were hard to deny, but the mind can play tricks.

For all it felt disheartening to believe I hadn't actually had the attention of a spirit all this time, it also meant that all those times I'd summoned the strength to survive, to endure... That had been me. I had pulled myself from the earth. I had summoned the strength, of my own body, to come back from the brink of death. And that meant I was stronger than I'd ever thought possible. But then, who knew?

The fact was, spirits were mysterious, fleeting, and hard to understand, intentionally. They were not of our world. And Crow was, after all, a trickster. Maybe he wanted me to doubt my belief. Maybe he wanted to remain an uncertain force in my life. I would probably never know.

"Belief makes it so," I said quietly.

"Hm?" The wolfhound came to a stop ahead of me, turning to regard me.

"Nothing, I'm just..." I sighed. "Your demons. You've never even seen them, have you?"

The wolfhound shook his head. "Not all demons take forms."

"But you believe they exist? You have no doubt?"

"They've affected my life," the wolfhound said. "I cannot deny their existence."

"Mnh," I nodded, turning my eyes at last from the horizon.

I had not seen Crow since the river. Since I'd demanded he leave my life, forever. And I might never again. I realized over the last few weeks, I'd stopped looking for him. I wasn't sure if he'd left me because I'd bade him to, or if he'd left me because he'd never really been there, at all.

But I hoped, wherever he was, out in the world, or inside me still, he'd been able to let go, to find peace, at last. The way I had.

"Hey now, the cavalry's arrived," Ransom said unenthusiastically, as we made our way into Grayson's cabin. I stepped inside, the wolfhound having to stoop somewhat to follow me. And he couldn't have done so any more haltingly if he tried.

We were greeted secondly by a sudden eruption of raucous laughter. I'd been prepared for it, and reached out to grab the wolfhound's arm before he could beat a hasty retreat.

"No—no! You must be joking!" the Privateer rasped, between laughter so apparently gut-wrenching, he was bent double. "He's our priest?!"

"Not if I'm to be mocked for it!" the wolfhound snapped. "Now shut your damned muzzle before I leave! This isn't a favor for you, it's for her."

"And I really appreciate it," I said emphatically, reaching down and taking his hand, and giving him my best plaintive eyes. "So, please, don't—Grayson, shut up! Please don't leave. You came this far."

The wolf stumbled backwards into a chair, covering his muzzle with one paw and wiping his eyes with the other, as he continued to laugh uncontrollably. At least now he was muffling it, for the most part.

The wolfhound rolled his eyes and strode forward into the room, brushing past both Ransom and Puck, whom I only now noticed had made it here as well, he was just sort of tucked against the wall, looking shy and wanting no part of the disagreement between the two Captains.

Johannes made it to the Privateer and thrust out a paw. "Give me the damn book already," he commanded.

Grayson sniffed and swiped the back of a paw over his muzzle, before slowly pushing himself up and giving a few bubbles of continued laughter as he made his way over to his cluttered table. He rooted through one of the piles for a few moments before, at length, he held up a small, worn black book.

"Ah-ha! And here we have it, folks," he smirked good-naturedly as he turned around, dropping it into the wolf-hound's paw. The Otherwolf immediately opened it and leafed through it rather purposefully, like he knew exactly what page he needed. Grayson watched, still with that shit-eating grin on his face. "See, it's as I said," he said. "Mumbo-jumbo. But it's the only holy book I have. Still, it's no good to me if I can't read it."

"Where did you even get this?" the wolfhound muttered.

"You probably don't want me to answer that."

The wolfhound glared at him a moment, then licked his thumb and leafed a few more pages, until he got to the section he was apparently looking for. "Here," he said at length. "The rites are here. And it's in Old Amuraic, not 'mumbo-jumbo'. Have a little respect for your ancestors."

"They're only half my ancestors," the wolf pointed out.

"Mngh," the wolfhound grumbled, then sighed, looking past me to the two other men in the room. "Let me be clear," he sait at length. "I am not performing this ceremony. I'm simply translating. It's sheerly through a bloody loophole that this is even legal, and even that will be amended, eventually. I don't honestly know why this is so important to you. No one will honor it save men like," he glanced at Grayson, "him."

Puck was silent. He hadn't said a thing yet, and I could tell even with his darker fur that his ears were flushing.

Ransom, however, took a moment, but he eventually spoke up. "It matters cuz it matters to us," he said, with his usual bluntness. "An'the way I hear it, that's who it's s'posed t'matter to. So ain't that enough?"

Johannes was silent a few moments, then just nodded. "Alright, then. Stand... together. I don't care how. Let's make this fast." A chortle nearly broke up the moment, and the wolf-hound glared behind him, then before I could stop him, reached over and grabbed the wolf by the dreads, yanking him up so he was face-to-face with him.

Grayson actually whined in pain, batting at his shoulder. "Bloody—that hurts!"

"You listen to me, you son of a bitch," Johannes snarled. "I am doing this for her. The fact that I had any part in this does not leave this cabin."

"Alright, alright-ow!"

He pulled him closer at that, so hiz muzzle, and more importantly his canines, were inches from the wolf's face. "And if I ever," he growled, "find out that you've told Luther about this I will personally keelhaul you. Are we understood?"

"Lord, alright," the wolf muttered, then gave a simpering smirk. "Now would you stop makin' moon eyes at me? We're not the ones getting married, so far as I know."

Five minutes later, Puck had managed to stop the bleeding. I wanted to feel for the wolf, his nose had certainly seen better days, but really, he'd brought it on himself. And I got the feeling being punched in the face was a common occurrence for him, seeing as he was still in good spirits when the actual rites got underway.

For the most part, it went exactly as Johannes had said it would. He translated, and Grayson pretty much just parroted his words, until we'd gone through everything that was necessary. Ransom had absolutely refused to kiss Puck in front of two other men, and Puck had kissed him on the cheek while he'd been arguing.

And then I'd hugged the two of them, because I felt it was warranted. And Grayson had started crying, and tried to insist it was because of the busted nose. After further prodding, he'd insisted he'd only done it because people were supposed to cry at weddings, and no one else was.

If Johannes had rolled his eyes any harder, they would have fallen out of his head. I don't think I'd ever seen the wolfhound more uncomfortable. And that was saying something, because he was just a naturally uncomfortable-looking person.

When Grayson announced we should all break open a bottle of wine, Ransom seemed to remember Magpie was onboard the ship tonight, and insisted we go find him before we did any celebrating. And that's how we all ended up on the deck, drinking under the stars. Even Johannes stayed around, although I think it was more because he enjoyed my company than anyone else here. He didn't even drink.

It was a beautiful night, the air on deck amongst our small group was remarkably festive, and I should have known that something terrible was going to shatter the moment. At this point in my life, I really should have known.

It was Puck, fittingly enough, who had only just regained his eyesight, who saw it first. I felt the small fox tugging on my sleeve, and was glad for the interruption from one of Ransom's baudy drinking songs, which of course Grayson had now insisted on joining in on, even though he didn't know the words. The result was a cacophany the likes of which the world had never heard.

"Shivah," Puck said, and pointed out over the railing, towards the distant cliffs. "Look."

And I did. At first I barely noticed it, because it was such a distant light, and it was somewhat obscured by the fog drifting in from the harbor. It almost seemed a trick of the eye at first, like one of the lanterns nearby on deck was confusing my eyes. But this was definitely a light in the mountains, and it looked to be growing.

"Hnh," I hummed thoughtfully. "Well, it's been very dry. I don't know how it started, but, in weather like this, forest fires..."

I stopped dead, when my thoughts closed in on just where it was I was looking at. Those weren't just cliffs. Those were the cliffs to the east, the nesting grounds. I gasped, looking to Johannes, but his eyes were equally pinned on the horizon, and he looked just as shocked as I was.

"You didn't!" I demanded.

He opened his muzzle for a moment, stammering, before looking down at me. "I didn't. I swear to God," he uttered. "I don't know how—"

"Ransom!" I growled, and stormed for the man, grabbing the hapless coyote by the collar of his shirt and yanking him out of his song.

"What'n the hell!" he yelped, then I forced him to stare in the same direction I was. He went dead silent when he saw where we were all now looking.

For a long time, no one said anything. We all just stared, as the fires began to engulf the distant cliffs. Horror sunk into my bones, at the realization of what had to be transpiring there, so far away. It felt so distant, so unreachable. And I knew there was nothing I could do to stop it. I'd feared from the moment we'd found those grounds that this would happen. I'd forgotten that fear for a long time now, because I'd had assurances none of us were going to speak on what we'd found. We'd all agreed it was only reserved for the worst-case scenario, only when we'd exhausted all other options. But then, who had?

"I told the Admiral," a voice from behind us stated.

I knew from the second I'd heard him say it that it was Gabriel, but I didn't want to believe it. When I turned, he was standing behind our group, arms crossed over his chest loosely. His expression was cold.

"Why?" was all I could bring myself to ask.

"Because I knew you lot wouldn't," the rat replied, simply. "Do you think yer group was the only one who saw the nests? We ran into a few on our own way down."

It had honestly never even occurred to me.

"Shivah," the rat sighed softly, "for what it's worth, I'm sorry. I hate seeing that look on yer face, directed'at me. It was our job. There's a lotta innocent folk in this place'at were dependin' on us. The cliffs were the best option. Best chance we'll have to save a lotta lives. This's war, sweet'art. People are gonna die. That's just how it goes." His ears twitched and fell back for a moment, but the expression on his face never wavered. "You can hate me if y'want. But at least ye'll live."

I didn't know what to say to the rat. I was still caught somewhere between outrage and pure shock, but I also couldn't deny the man's logic, cold though it was. We hadn't found any other options nearly as likely to work, in all the time since we'd found the cliffs. If we'd pushed a little harder, worked a little harder, maybe we would have.

A distant noise made all of our ears twist. A chorus of church bells, ringing out through the night, echoing across the colony. One after another, like they were answering one another.

"That's the evacuation signal," the wolfhound said, his voice quiet but resolute. "I need to get to the Cerberus." He looked down to me, and our small group. "This is farewell, I'm afraid. It's been an honor serving with you all. Miss Shivah," he bowed. "You most especially. Please take care."

"To arms, then," Magpie said, then looked to Grayson, who still seemed shocked into silence. A rarity for him, to be sure. "Captain?"

"Right," Grayson said at length, his voice lacking any real strength. "To arms."

The wolf looked down at me, regretfully. He reached a hand out for mine, a remarkably gentle gesture for the Privateer. "I don't suppose I'll see you again, either," he said, forcing a small smile. "It's... been a hell of a time."

I didn't take his hand. Not yet. I only turned and made my way towards Puck and Ransom. He seemed hurt, but he'd be less so later, when I returned.

"Come on," I said, making my way for the gang plank. "We need to get to the evacuation vessels."

"I have to go to the triage unit first," Puck insisted.

"What?" Ransom snarled. "To hell with that! I don't care what you left there. We're not missin' our ride outta this shithole."

"I have to make sure Forrest gets to the ship as well," Puck said pointedly. "And if I know him, he'll stay until the last minute, making sure everyone gets out of there. I can't do what I need to do in Carvecia without him."

"Grnhhh!" Ransom gave a guttural growl of frustration, and unshouldered his rifle. "Fine, fox. But both of you stick close. Ain't gonna be safe in that colony much longer..."

The battle had not yet made it to Serwich by the time we made it to the triage unit, thankfully. The hospital was a complete disaster, though, families trying to get their injured and ailing loved ones out, belongings strewn through the streets everywhere as the colonists overflowed from their homes in a panic to escape. It was a warzone unto itself.

"The boats can hold everyone, can't they?" Ransom shouted over the din of voices, checking a man in the shoulder who nearly bowled into Puck in his rush to head for the docks. The coyote, luckily, had been able to cut us quite the path, walking with a loaded rifle.

"Some people volunteered to go with the fleet," Puck said. "Soldiers, navymen, or last-minute enlistments. So... should be?"

"Great," Ransom growled.

The hospital was even worse on the inside than it seemed from outside. And I soon saw why. There were men with fresh injuries here. Fresh enough that they must have just happened. And the wounds were gruesome. They looked like they must have been made by absolutely enormous weapons. Most of these men, I knew, would not survive.

The few nurses who'd remained to tend to the soldiers were frantically trying to patch them up well enough to get moving, but some of them were simply being left in their beds. In a better situation, we might have been able to save some of them, but for the most part, they were gone.

I recognized a few of them. Many of them were from the same scouting patrols I'd been a part of. And one of them was...

Puck gave a soft noise of shock, rushing forward towards a bed, where Forrest himself was tending to the critical patient. When Ransom caught sight of the scene, he cursed under his breath.

"Well I hope yer wolfhound can command a fleet," he muttered. "Because th' Admiral ain't survivin' that."

I moved up towards where the cattle dog was lying. Forrest had a needle between his teeth, and one hand pressed down over a massive wound that cut down from his shoulder, across his collarbone. I couldn't imagine what had made it, but judging by the sheer amount of blood seeping down into the mattress beneath him, he would probably be one of the casualties we left behind.

His chest was still rising and falling slowly, and he seemed aware enough to look as though he were in pain, though. So, maybe there was still a chance.

"These are the men from the cliff raid," I said quietly, "aren't they?"

"Yes," the Physician growled out from between his teeth, wiping a bloody hand across his muzzle. "Puquanah, keep the pressure up, would you? I can't see past the blood to knit the wound. I need to clean it, first."

"We don't have time," Puck warned. "We can stitch it later, once he's on board a ship."

"I can't move him until I stitch it," Forrest insisted. "He lost enough blood getting back here—"

"Then we'll bind his arm so his shoulder doesn't move," Puck said, determinedly. "And I have poultices that will help the blood clot, until he's ready to be stitched."

Forrest looked to him, uncertainly.

"Please trust me," Puck pleaded.

"Alright," the Physician said, at length. He grabbed for a shoulder bag near the Admiral's bed, which must have been what amounted to his possessions—or more likely, his tools.

"Let's get him ready to move. And then you all had better get me to that boat."

We arrived at the Cerberus first, where a group of the Admiral's men were ready to take the injured Otherwolf onboard his ship. The man was in terrible shape, and I wasn't sure he was going to survive. But Puck had been the one to temporarily bandage his wound, and if I were in the same position, I wouldn't trust anyone but Puck.

We made our way for the evacuation vessels next, amidst a seething throng of colonists. And I knew my time was running out. I had to tell them.

It was on the final pier, fifty feet from the trade vessel that would take my friends, Forrest, and so many others to safety that I stopped. A few more planks, and I'd be on my way home.

Puck and Ransom both noticed I'd stopped, and turned to regard me. Puck looked frightened already, like he somehow knew.

"Puck, Ransom," I took a breath, "I'm sorry—"

"Shivah, no," Puck said in a small voice.

"C'mon, cat," Ransom said in a no-nonsense tone. He reached for my shoulder, but I moved back, away from him.

"Shivah," the fox pleaded, and crushed himself against my side, wrapping his small arms around me. He buried his small muzzle into my cloak. "No, no, no..."

"Don't do this to us," the coyote grated out. "We came here together, we leave here together."

"You'll all be fine," I said, reaching down and cupping the trembling fox's ears gently, stroking his fur. "But the people here still fighting, the fleet... They're going to need help. I can't abandon them."

"So you're abandonin' us?!" Ransom demanded. "How long've we stood by you, Shivah? We're your damn family. I ain't leavin' family in a warzone!"

"I'm sorry," I said quietly. Puck looked up at me, sniffling. He wiped his eyes beneath his glasses, and I gave a soft smile, hugging him a little tighter. "You'll make it home," I said, certainly. "But I'm... I'm not ready to go home. And the more people stay here, the better chance your fleet has to escape. We need to fight them. We need to be the diversion. Remember? That's always been the plan."

"You weren't supposed t'be a part of it!" Ransom insisted, the coyote's composure dropping.

"I'll see you both again someday," I promised, knowing in that moment I'd made a commitment I could not break. "This is only goodbye for now. Just for now."

"There isn't enough time in the world for me to say goodbye to you," Puck cried softly against my chest. "Shivah..."

"Shivah," the coyote said. I looked up to him, and he stared me straight in the eyes. I felt in that moment as I had the first time I'd seen him. Like he was boring straight to the center of me. "This something you have to do?"

I swallowed, and nodded slowly. "It is."

"Alright," the man said, his voice breaking only partially on that last word. He reached forward, and grabbed the fox by the shoulder, tugging him away from me. "C'mon, Puck. We've gotta go."

"No..." the fox mumbled, looking back at me forlornly.

I couldn't take it any longer. I'd told myself I wouldn't make this harder on them than it had to be. But I couldn't let them walk away, couldn't part from them, so simply. They really were my family.

I moved forward and flung my arms around both men, pulling them into a tight embrace. Puck sobbed against my shoulder, and Ransom was stiff, at first, but eventually he relented. I felt his ears fall, and he nuzzled into my hair. The man dragged a breath through his nose, harshly, and growled against my ear.

"You come back home, y'hear? You ain't allowed to be as stupid as me. You jes... jes come back home, as soon as you can. We'll be waitin' for you."

"I promise," I swore, softly. "I'll come back home."

EPILOGUE

I'd thought that, considering how much time had passed, it would be considerably more difficult to find the clearing. But as soon as I made it into the woodlands where it had all happened, it was like a memory etched into my bones. I barely thought. I simply followed my paws, walking the trails we had so long ago.

The forest smelled the same. Every tree, every flower, every wind that swept down from the mountains carried with it a scent so intrinsically a part of me, I could not have forgotten them in a thousand lifetimes.

Some of the memories warmed me. Made me feel younger, newer to the world. But many of them were painful, of course. And this place, I'd known, would be the heart of that pain. I'd been bracing myself to return here for ten years.

It wasn't just that he was buried here. This place had become something of a marker for all the pain I'd endured in those times. I would never know where Tale'nuk was buried, if he'd been buried at all. I would never again be able to find the precipice in the mountains where we'd all once gathered, after we'd rescued Ransom from the clutches of his own dark memories. And I didn't feel I'd ever be able to re-visit my tribal grounds, to see what had become of the lands I'd grown up in. By now, they were probably settled.

But this place, I'd known would be the same. This place was deep in the woodlands, hidden away, of no importance to anyone save me, and the man who had died here.

"Are we here?" the young girl behind me asked, carefully stepping down past a ridge of large boulders into the clearing where I stood.

"Yes," I said with certainty, looking out over the small glen. It was early spring now, the trees were just beginning to unfurl their full leaves and the ground had erupted with green undergrowth. Amidst it all, spread out across the clearing, were small, red flowers. They hadn't been here long ago, although to be fair, it had still been late winter then.

I padded forward towards the small patch of ground. There was a tree nearby and a rock twenty or so paces away. I remembered exactly where we'd dug. I could never forget.

I stood there in silence for a long time. It wasn't that I felt I needed to be silent, I just... wasn't certain what to say, at first.

Thankfully, my companion was a far more talkative young woman.

"Is this where you buried my brother?" she asked me, with a paw on my arm. When I nodded, Anna's muzzle broke into a smile, and she stepped up to my side, readjusting the bundle in her arms.

"How've you been, brother?" she asked, of the earth. I smiled somewhat despite myself, at her always congenial demeanor.

"I've gotten a lot bigger," the rusty-colored husky continued, "as I guess... you can probably tell." I saw the first hint of sadness pass over her features, but she soldiered on. I envied her strength. "You haven't been home, so... I should catch you up. A lot's happened. Um... Well, most of the boys enlisted. They're all over the place now," she smiled again, "breaking hearts, and making trouble. They all grew up so handsome. Just like you. And Hannah—oh, Hannah met this wonderful man. I know you'd be suspicious, because he's from across the pond, but he's honestly the nicest guy. He's, um," she looked to me, blinking her bright blue eyes at me questioningly and lowering her voice, embarrassed. "What's it called again? You know, the blue-bloods?"

"Pedigree," I filled in for her. "He's a pedigree."

"Right," she smiled, and chuckled, "and rich, so, y'know... there's that. She's really happy. They live somewhere really cold, but she says it's beautiful there. She writes to me all the time. I'm glad she got out of Debriss."

She adjusted the bundle in her arms again, and I considered offering to take him from her. She'd been carrying him for much of the last hour.

"She had a few pups last winter," she said with a nervous twitch of her tail. "Her and her husband are going to be great parents. I, um," and at this she paused, "I also met someone. But... he was less fond of the idea of being a father."

I put a hand on her shoulder, comfortingly. And it seemed to assure her, so she continued on. "But, it's okay," she said, her nose dropping to nuzzle the tiny pup in her arms. "Your friend... Miss Alongsaa has been writing to us for years, now. I learned how to write just so I could read her letters about you. She told me so much about you I never knew. I hope you don't mind," she said quietly, "because... because I know you never married, or anything, but... but I'd like to call her my sister. That's okay, right?"

I squeezed her shoulder softly, and she sniffed, and smiled up at me. "She brought me here, to you, and she says she's going to help me take care of Roan. Out here, where... where the air is clean, and there are flowers, and trees, and... I left Debriss, a-and I'm never going back, Grant. I'm never going back." She squeezed her eyes shut for a moment, a tear streaking down the white fur of her cheek.

"We made it. We all made it out of the slums. Okay? I just... I wanted you to know that." She sniffed again, and held her pup close to her chest. "We wouldn't have made it, if it wasn't for you. So wherever you are, you can rest, and be happy."

She stood with me for awhile longer, before looking up to me and smiling. And then she slowly moved off, leaving me alone near the small patch of earth covered in that red carpet of flowers. It seemed especially vibrant here.

I'd barely spoken, and I knew I needed to. But all the words I'd prepared over the years were freezing up in my throat. I felt I could say nothing more profound than what Anna had already said.

Remembering, I swept a hand beneath my cloak and tugged the old locket I'd carried all these years up over my head. I don't think I'd removed it once in all this time.

I knelt and placed it on the ground, returning it to him, just as Anna had once asked me to do. She might have even forgotten it by now. But I hadn't.

"I..." my voice faded, and I closed my eyes for a moment, trying to decide what to say. "I... have to go," I said, at length. "Puck and Ransom are waiting for me, in Serahaven. They're homesteaders now. Hard to believe, huh?"

I managed to smile, really smile, as I thought of their letters. Puck had written to me often throughout the years, and difficult though it was to intercept letters while sailing around the world, we'd managed to stay in a few ports long enough that I'd kept up an occasional correspondence. If Puck's tales of the two mens' continued trials and tribulations were any indication, they still bickered like small children. But ten years was a long time, and apparently even Ransom had tired of the traveling life eventually. I was glad for them. They'd spent long enough traversing the countryside, fighting the Fever. They deserved some peace.

I was tired, as well. But I'd seen so much, it was hard to ever believe it had been a mistake to stay on the Manoratha. I'd seen places I'd never imagined, forged bonds of friendship and cameraderie with people so varied and strange, I'd never thought their like existed. And I'd lost many of them, as well.

Losing Grayson had been the final leg of my journey. I'd known, of course, that the wolf couldn't live forever. Not with his condition... Not with the life he lived. It hadn't come as a surprise when it inevitably happened, but it still hurt. And it felt empty, continuing to sail on the Manoratha without him.

At the very least, the crew was in good hands, with Magpie taking command. I wasn't worried for them. The rat had proven to be one of the toughest, most enduring companions I'd ever had.

That Anna had contacted me, telling me about her situation, had just been timely. I knew it was time to come home. Sometimes things work out exactly as they are meant to. Even

death and abandonment, when it brings two people together, could be the beginning of family, and love.

"I'll take care of her and her boy," I promised Grant, softly. "So don't worry." I gave a painful smile and leaned over the grave, smoothing out the chain of the locket into the mossy, flowery earth.

"I never really... found anyone, after you," I said, swallowing. "There were men, but... never anyone like you. I don't think I can replace what we had. And I don't think I want to." I smiled. "I have such amazing friends, I have such incredible memories, and so much more to do. It hurts to think I could have shared all of that with you."

I was silent for a long time after that, gathering myself slowly. The pain was as sharp inside me as it had been the day I'd lost him. But, I'd learned how to live with it. I remembered. And then I looked forward.

"But, I'll see you again someday," I said, getting to my feet. I lifted my head, and looked through the light filtering down through the leaves, to the blue sky above, and the mountains beyond. "Wherever your journey ended, mine will, too."

I swept my eyes back towards the earth, and felt the life beneath my pawpads, smelled it on the wind, heard it surrounding me. Everything—the whole world—was laid before me, reminding me that I was still here. That I still had living to do.

"Just not today, alright?" I said, and I breathed, the mountain air filling my lungs in a deep, peaceful sigh. "I've still more trail to walk."

ADDITIONAL ART

Lightning Source UK Ltd.
Milton Keynes UK
UKHW02f0655040518
322038UK00005B/263/P